About the author

Nick B. Ponter was born near Windsor, England in 1968. His interesting career started as a carpenter, then in the army and foreign service. He now works as a business English trainer in Germany. A school prize in English was an early indicator for his interest in writing fantasy. Nick gained a Bachelor in International Studies, influencing his story telling with a focus on modern contemporary issues. He loves travelling and lived in Asia for six years. He is inspired by outdoor activities and heavy metal. Most of his story was written in a tent at the River Weser and in the Alps.

CONNOR JACKSON AND THE MEMORY THIEVES

Nick B. Ponter

CONNOR JACKSON AND THE MEMORY THIEVES

Vanguard Press

Dedication

For the moles, who decimated my garden and gave me the inspiration for this book.

Acknowledgements

I thank everyone who has contributed towards this book. Andrea, for her improvements to my writing style; Monika, for checking the story; Ike, for the cover illustration; Jens for the photograph; and all family and friends for sharing the world of Connor Jackson. A campsite next to the River Weser provided my inspiration and space for writing.

Prologue

He stopped his jeep some distance from the forest, got out, opened the rear door, picked up a large block of roughly cut salt and walked slowly into the woods, taking each step carefully so as not to make any noise. At the clearing he placed the block of salt on top of a wooden post and fixed it firmly into position with a piece of wire. The hunter then retraced his steps and walked slowly out of the clearing back to the car to collect his equipment – a rucksack, a hunting rifle, his green jacket and a hat. On entering the woods again, he walked in the direction of the clearing but this time stopped at a wooden hunting perch, climbed up the ladder and made himself comfortable in the chair at the top, always taking care not to make any noise. He slowly brought his rifle up and rested it in a wooden support, pointed it in the direction of the clearing, looked through the telescope and adjusted the settings with a few small clicks of the dial. The white block of salt was now clearly in his sights, glistening in the light of the full moon. Now, all he had to do was wait for an unsuspecting deer to smell the salt and come over and lick it; being an easy target for him today and Sunday roast for tomorrow. Easy.

The hunter waited patiently in the silence of the night, maybe waiting as long as two hours, but this was normal practice for this type of work - ninety-nine percent waiting and one percent squeezing the trigger. The light of the moon, silence and the salt were his friends today. A rustling movement in the forest signalled that his one percent time had come. He slowly edged into position and adjusted his aim at the block of salt again. Ready.

"Come on now," he whispered to himself, breathing out ever so slowly and held his breath to steady his aim. Then there was silence again. "Where are you?"

All of a sudden there was a crash in the undergrowth directly below him and the startled hunter looked down to see what was causing the commotion. A deer had broken out of the trees, surprisingly making a lot of noise, as they are normally careful animals, and banged straight into the wooden legs of the hunting perch. The deer stopped, looked straight up at the mystified hunter, nodded in his direction, turned around and ran back into the woods. It was as though the deer wanted to thank him for something.

"Playing games with me are you," the hunter whispered to himself. "Well, we'll see who'll win," he said stroking his rifle and smacking his lips. He looked into his sights again and took aim at the block of salt.

"Blast. Where is this damn block?"

The hunter moved his rifle left, right, up and down, frantically attempting to aim at the block of salt. But there was no block. It was gone. He moved his head away from the rifle, looked at the clearing in disbelief and then scratched his head. He climbed down from his perch and walked quickly towards the post to find out what had happened, this time not taking too much care to be quiet. No point being secretive now he thought. To his sheer amazement the block was not there. Not on the post nor was it on the floor. How very strange he thought. Just disappeared into thin air.

***

It wasn't the only place which was dark and silent.

A muffled click could be heard in the distance and the black was suddenly interrupted by a thin slither of penetrating light, shattering the intense darkness. The silence was broken again by a very faint noise of approaching feet - soft, slow and purposefully placed. Then the noise stopped, as though whoever was making it was being extremely careful and cloaked in deep secrecy; this was followed by the sound of a creaking door and the inward rush of light.

The dark shape of a human, silhouetted against the white sheet of light, stood in the doorway displaying nervous actions. A quick look to the left and a sharp look to the right before entering the room, dimly lit from the corridor. The room had smooth walls made of what seemed to be dark brown earth and was only equipped with a simple wooden rickety table. Directly above the table was a metal plate in the wall.

The person moved slowly and apprehensively towards the table and looked around again to check that nobody was following. The old and wrinkled hands removed a key from the jacket pocket and shakily inserted it into a slot in the plate. With a squeal of metal hinges, the plate exposed a small dark opening. The only thing behind the metal plate was a small bottle of tablets hardly visible in the dull light. These old hands gently removed the bottle. It was made of transparent brown glass, had a red screw top and the words Eternity Project elegantly written on the label. The hands then unscrewed the top and tipped some tablets into the palm of one of the hands. The tablets were counted as they were put back in. "One, two, three, four, five." He stopped and gasped. "Where is the sixth? Stolen. I knew I couldn't trust him!" The man spoke with obvious fear in his voice.

Hastily locking the metal plate, he put the tablet bottle in his jacket pocket along with the key and carefully checked left and right before closing the door. Then darkness and silence returned.

The man walked back along a few well-lit tunnels, glancing nervously behind as though he was expecting to be followed. At a tunnel junction, he took a quick look behind again, before turning right and merging into the crowd walking past. A block of salt with wire hanging over it was being wheeled on a trolley in the opposite direction.

Chapter One
The Molehill

People might well call my style of decoration and furnishing rather retro and, I must admit, I cannot entirely disagree with this point of view. My parents left me this house in Trout Lane, Lower Molehampton, with all of the furnishings in it when they passed away. This occurred several years ago and I still hadn't changed a thing. And why should I? There is a saying that one should never change a running system, and I believe in it. My bedroom is sparsely furnished but it is practical and it has everything I need. I have plain, angular wardrobes, bedside tables and a clothes chest all made of the same plain light wood. The wallpaper is light green, decorated with white flowers. My curtains are a gaudy bright yellow with a kind of tree pattern on it. Plus, I have a carpet. A dark brown carpet. Why should I care what it looks like? When I sleep, I have my eyes closed. Yes, it is rather retro.

I am not sure what awoke me first on this particular morning. Was it the chirping of the busy morning birds or was it the first rays of the early morning June sun penetrating their way through my curtains? Whatever was first is irrelevant as my night's sleep was now coming to an end. I squinted, rolled over onto my stomach and pushed my head firmly into the pillow so that the sides folded up and covered my ears in an effort to block out the light and the chirping. To no avail — I was awake. Although I like summer, I can certainly do without the early morning wake up calls. So, I lifted my head out of the pillow and reached out for the clock from the bedside table, gently brushing against the glass of water. My large round alarm clock was merrily ticking away and had not yet gone off. I now realised how early it was - quarter past five. I am the type of person who cannot easily go back to sleep after waking up so I decided to give in and get up out of bed. Well, let's look on the bright side - I would now have more of my day and I certainly had enough to do, like most of us do with our busy lifestyles.

I pushed myself up out of bed with a groan, stuck my feet into my tartan slippers, stood up with another groan, stretched and slowly shuffled across to the window to open the curtains. On my way I passed by my washing basket, on the floor, which contained three single and different socks. Have you ever asked yourself why, sometimes, only one sock remains from a pair after washing, even though two were clearly put in the machine? The other sock is never seen again. Also, have you ever asked yourself why you often see items of clothing on the side of the street? Sometimes I see a single sock, a single shoe, a single glove. Why? I mean, who would throw away a shoe and just walk with one shoe? It doesn't make any sense. I looked at my basket again, shaking my head in irritation, then pushed the curtains slowly to the side so as not to be taken by surprise from the sun.

My bedroom window overlooked the garden and, like my house, I did not put too much effort into making it look nice. I had very little interest in nice flowers, letting the plants in my garden naturally take over, unlike my neighbour Mr Lawnsworthy. I'll tell you about him later. But I did at least keep it tidy. In June my garden was in full-bloom, accompanied by the twittering of birds and the early morning dew sparkling in the first rays of the sun. But something was different today and the dew wasn't the only thing sparkling in the sun! I wasn't yet sure, but I could sense something was out of place this morning. And there it was. Right in the middle of my lawn was a big mound. I rubbed my eyes, squinted and focused on the mound again. I don't know if I was imagining it but I had the feeling that there was something like a small angular pipe protruding out of the top of the mound, just like a submarine's periscope. It appeared to be slowly turning 360 degrees and suddenly reflected in the sunlight. It was hard to see exactly what it was from this distance, but something was definitely there. I decided to have a look and put on my dark red dressing gown.

I walked down my creaky, wooden staircase, into the kitchen and opened the door which led directly into the back yard. Right in the middle of the lawn was a huge mound of earth, dark brown, fresh and still steaming in the sun. "Damn moles," I cursed under my breath. I didn't really have anything against moles, not being the keenest gardener, but this was just too much. In the past I had never had too many molehills - just now and then. But this one. Well, this one was like the Taj Mahal of the mole world. It must have taken them the whole night to build it. Why me? Why my garden? I actually didn't know too much about moles - only what most people know. They are blind, dig tunnels and leave their annoying earth hills in our gardens. But I must admit I had never seen a mole in my entire life.

It was then that I saw it again. Something glinted in the sun at the top of the molehill, but this time I was closer. Was that a piece of white metal at the top? I quickened my pace towards the molehill. Just at that moment the object, which I had assumed was a type of periscope, turned directly towards me and stopped. So did I. Then the top of this huge molehill fell away and an object fell out, rolled down the side, leaving the top of the molehill open and exposed. The moles must have sensed that I was approaching and decided to dash for cover. But what was with these strange objects? With a sense of trepidation, I slowly walked the remaining metres across the lawn. Oh, my goodness, the molehill nearly came up as far as my knee — unbelievable. I heard molehills were good for aeration but my garden was just fine and didn't need any extra assistance from these moles. A closer look revealed an upside-down glass jar lying half way down the mound. "What on earth," I mumbled to myself. This was most strange. I stooped down and carefully picked it up. It was a small glass jar with a white metal lid, just like a jam jar. The glass was dirty, dusty and one-third of it was filled with a creamy white sort of liquid. There was a plaster stuck directly on the outside of the glass with a name written on it. Professor Wingnut. This really was most strange indeed. Where had this come from? Had somebody been snooping around in my garden last night? Maybe thieves? Surely not in our sleepy, serene village of Lower Molehampton. The last reported burglary was five years ago when unknown assailants broke into Mr Tinker's ironmonger store and stole his whole supply. In the same week, the glass jam jar factory in Lower Molehampton was also robbed of its entire supply of jam jars. It had the whole village in an uproar and Sergeant Dawson had never found out who the robbers were. I looked at the jar in my hand, then at the molehill and contemplated the connection between the two events. "Don't be silly, Connor," I said to myself. What have they got to do with each other — it must be a coincidence?

Nevertheless, this was not a normal morning in Trout Lane and a thorough inspection of my garden was needed to see if anything else was out of place or if there were any signs of intruders. I looked inside the molehill and could quite clearly see a large chamber and a metal object lying on the floor. I very carefully put my hand in and grasped the object. Upon further inspection, it appeared to be exactly what I thought I had seen. It was a mini periscope, no bigger than the size of the palm of my hand. It was not perfectly manufactured, but nonetheless, it seemed to serve its purpose. There was a small glass at the end of the elbow and a small window on the side at the bottom. It seemed to be made out of old scrap metal and taped together, certainly a home-made product.

I walked to the back of my garden and opened, with a loud creak, the rusty clasp and bolt lock on the door to my rickety shed, while still holding the glass jar in my hand, slowly peering inside and pushing the cobwebs out of my face. It was a typical garden shed — dark, damp and full of dirty tools, pots and sacks. My first impression was that there was nothing missing. Not that I had any particular order in my shed anyhow. But all appeared to be in the place I had last left it.

I was suddenly jolted out of my thoughts by the sound of my doorbell, which I could just hear through the open back door. Who would call on me at such an early hour? Maybe a neighbour needing help? It certainly wouldn't surprise me this morning. I stretched out and placed the glass jar and periscope on the closest shelf I could find, turned around and slammed the door shut, followed by the sound of falling tools. "Damn," I cursed the second time this morning. "I'll have to sort that mess out later!" I pushed the bolt back into place, quickly threw the clasp over it to lock it in position and started walking back towards the house. I don't know why, but as ordinary as the jar was, there was something about it, something important that could not yet be explained. So, I turned around and walked the few steps back into the shed, opened the door with another creak, stretched out my hand, grasped the jar, put it in my dressing gown pocket and walked briskly back to my house to see who was at my door.

I walked through my house, unlocked the front door and cautiously opened it, half hiding behind the door — I mean, I was still in my dark red dressing gown. The answer was easy though. Nobody was there. I took one step across the door step, looked to the left and then to the right. Nobody. The street was completely deserted and everything was quiet in Trout Lane this morning, just like every day of the week. Maybe it wasn't my doorbell after all.

Although it was still early, I decided to take a shower, get ready for work and begin my often-mundane daily routine. Walking up the stairs, I asked myself if I should tell my colleagues about what had happened this morning. No, better not. Knowing my colleagues, they would presumably believe I was imagining things. I took off my dressing gown and felt the weight of the jar in my pocket. "Can't leave it in there," I said to myself and put it in a safe place.

***

"Oh, just how divine," squawked Felicity Forsythe-Twyke. "Since when have you had this little darling," she added in her high-pitched voice. "What's its name?"

"This, Felicity, is Cromwell," replied Jemima Kingston. "I've only had him since last week. It was rather strange. The doorbell rang on Thursday last week and I found Cromwell just sitting on my

18

doorstep, looking up at me. Nobody else was there and also there was no note. Just a dog collar with the name Cromwell on it."

"Really?" Felicity Forsythe-Twyke replied slowly and somehow sheepishly, but didn't look surprised when she said it. She coughed, composed herself and carried on. "One just doesn't abandon a dog on one's doorstep. Surely someone from that rabble at Lower Molehampton," she added haughtily. "We, from Upper Molehampton, just wouldn't do anything like that. How could anyone? He is just so delightful. I love dogs. Our family has always had dogs. I'm sure you know it is a toy fox terrier," she said with the aloof authority of a school mistress. "In fact, I just love all animals."

"Have you got anything to do with this Felicity? You reacted as though you have a hand in it."

"Jemima! Shame on you to utter such a thing. Of course not."

"And anyway Felicity, it's a Chihuahua," retorted Jemima smugly.

"Oh, I knew that. You know they are very similar," Felicity Forsythe-Twyke now sounded a little defensive.

Jemima looked at her with delight. "And what's more. He's so cute I can carry him in my handbag, and even take him to work."

"Jemima dear. Why the devil would you want to take him to that dreadful, ghastly place? It is full of bland and boring civil servants."

"Darling, Felicity. I am the manager of this place. Believe me it is not at all dreadful and ghastly."

"Oh, so the rumours are true then? It's more than just a government office?"

"Felicity. I wish you would stop listening to rumours. All we do is routine office work. Nothing sinister as a lot of people imagine," Jemima said abruptly. "And how is your business going darling?" Jemima was eager to change this unpleasant subject rather quickly. "Animal lover you said?"

"Absolutely, you know. I love animals. This meat industry is good for my pocket and at least the animals have a purpose in their lives," Felicity added cruelly.

"And what purpose may that be exactly?" said Jemima urgently, wanting to know.

Felicity frowned and looked serious. "To make us happy of course. Summer barbeques followed by the fattening up for Christmas. Peak time, Jemima dear. People just want to eat meat. More and more of it these days and so they should. Eat and don't ask is my motto!"

Cromwell was having a bad day. He had been bathed, scrubbed and brushed for ages and he hated it. He was more than capable of cleaning himself. Then there was this stupid tartan coat Jemima Kingston forced him to wear. But the nail in the coffin was being carried in her handbag and shown off to whoever was, or was not, interested in dogs in Upper Molehampton. It was only a small village and not many people lived there but Cromwell had the feeling that he had been presented to all of them. All morning he had people patting him on his head and uttering silly dog comments.

"There, there. Oh, how sweet."

"Aww, look so cute."

"Fine, fine."

Cromwell could just see over the top of the handbag; plus, it wasn't particularly comfortable. He couldn't find himself a comfortable position between the house keys, lipstick, purse, smart phone, sweets and used tissues. This was a very bad day indeed.

But there was more to Cromwell than meets the eye. He knew that this life as a show-off dog would soon come to an end and he had to go through with this masquerade as his perfect cover. Nobody would ever suspect the sweet and cute Cromwell!

For Cromwell's plan to work he needed to make contact with someone and the opportunity was now. His problem was that even though he was sitting on Mrs Kingston's smartphone he was the centre of attention. He needed to wait until they were all distracted before he could use it and it didn't take long. Whilst Mrs Kingston was nattering to her friends in one of Upper Molehampton's many boutiques, Cromwell disappeared below the rim of her handbag and activated the phone. He had already watched her enter her password and memorised it. MI5 — how simple! The message he sent was short and simple.

"Number three Trout Lane, four a.m. tomorrow."

All of this took him less than a minute and went completely unnoticed. Yes, this would soon all be over because Cromwell was waiting for a visitor — the renowned Professor Wingnut. Things would soon be very different from here on, indeed.

He quickly poked his head above the rim of the handbag, once again being met by yet another pat on the head. Cromwell quietly snarled to himself!

***

"Come on Sid. Can't you go any faster?"

"Bill, really! I'm digging as fast as I can," replied a heavily panting Sid. "This earth is such hard work and there are loads of stones to move too. All you do is push that silly glass jar in front of you."

"I know its hard work but we have a deadline to meet and it's getting close. We've got to make the delivery at four a.m. and certainly before it gets light. It's too dangerous in the light, you know that, Sid."

"Yes, yes, I know. I also heard the instructions. How the heck can they expect us to dig the tunnel and take the jar with us in this short space of time? It's not normal. We usually have a team of six for such tunnelling work. And today I have to tunnel by myself because you are just pushing the jar," complained Sid.

"Come on, Sid. It's not as though you are doing all the work. Yes, I have to push this jar, which isn't light by the way, but I also have to dispose of the excavated earth behind us."

"Who gave us this mission anyway? All of this top-secret work really gets on my nerves. Everything is always top secret but this one is even more top secret than top secret!" exclaimed Sid.

"I have absolutely no idea. I have the same information as you, Sid. All I know is that it is a super tip-top secret mission and we have to deliver this jar at four a.m. sharp, which is not a long way off I would like to remind you again. I received a hand-written note this afternoon with an official authorisation code, just like you, ordering me to be in that room at a certain time. That's where we met. I know as little as you regarding where the glass jar with our delivery instructions came from. It was too dark in the room even when the lights were briefly switched on. Someone high up in the Council I suppose," retorted Bill.

Sid was now frantically digging the earth away, pushing the excavated earth under his belly and behind him. Directly behind Sid was that large glass jar, pretty much the same diameter as the tunnel with only a small clearance between the jar and the walls. Bill was pushing the heavy jar and also had to push the excavated earth behind him filling up the tunnel as they went. They were expert tunnel diggers and left little trace of their path. Bill also carried a metal periscope on his back as an essential piece of equipment needed for delivering goods to the surface. Both were equipped with head torches and Bill even had leather gloves with metal spikes to help him dig faster. It was actually normal work for moles to carry out delivery jobs. This job though was very different.

After another two long hours of digging, panting, sweating and groaning Sid suddenly stopped.

"Hey, Bill," he said quietly. "My direction finder has started blinking so we must be approaching the location. I will start tunnelling towards the surface now. We must be careful and very quiet."

"OK, Sid, careful now. Remember our instructions were explicit. Utmost silence and utmost secrecy. We are to make contact with the courier and only hand over the jar to him."

"Yes, I know. However, I am not so sure such a large molehill is quite so secret," Sid added sarcastically.

He carried on tunnelling and angled slightly upwards. Now he was much slower and very careful not to attract any attention on the surface. Another fifteen minutes had passed when Sid stopped again.

"We are here!"

"OK," replied Bill, also in a whisper. "I'll pass you the periscope as soon as you break the surface."

Sid very carefully dug the remaining section until he reached just below the surface. He now pushed the excavated earth ahead forming a mound above the surface and a chamber below, large enough for them to move around in. Normally their mounds were much smaller but this one was large owing to the space the jar needed.

"Let's take a look then," said Sid. "Pass me the periscope, will you?"

Sid pushed the periscope through the mound until it broke through the surface with some loose earth falling down onto his head. The periscope was a small pipe with an elbow at the top equipped with a piece of glass. At the bottom was a small window which Sid now peered through.

"Blast," he said quietly.

"What is it?" asked Bill.

"We've missed the delivery deadline. It's already getting light."

"Damn," muttered Bill. "Well, we're here now and better late than never. We know how important this delivery is so we'll just have to make the best out of it. Can you see the courier, Sid? Have a good look around."

Sid rotated the periscope 360 degrees a few times, thoroughly inspecting the garden they had just entered.

"Who are we looking for anyway? I don't even know who the courier is," asked Bill.

"I received separate instructions and all I know is that we should expect a dog to take the delivery. They even gave me a password for extra security. I've never had to do that before, Sid. I have to say 'Trout Lane' and the reply must be 'number three'. This is all so very strange indeed."

"Can you see anything out there, Sid?"

"Well, we are in a garden. I am looking at a red brick house and an old shed. A nice garden by the way. Very natural. I can also see the neighbour's garden. Wow, that one is just perfect. There is nothing out of place — not a leaf on the ground. Even every piece of grass appears to be cut exactly the same length. Bill, we'll have to remember to go back to this place to decorate it with some molehills," said Sid mischievously.

"But can you see the courier?"

"Nope. Hang on, I can hear something. There is movement coming from the house. Maybe the dog lives there," replied Sid.

"Yeah, of course. That must be it. Do you not think we should push the jar to the surface now so we are ready? I mean, we are already late and this has to be quick."

"Maybe we should. It is dangerous though, Bill. What if this is not the courier and we lose the jar?"

"I know, but I think we have to take that risk, Sid. Why don't we just push the jar further up the mound right to the top and then quickly push it out at the last moment?"

"OK, Bill. Let's do it."

Sid retracted the periscope and started pushing the jar into an upright position. The thick white liquid settled back to the bottom of the jar. The plaster on the side was covered in dirt. With collective effort they managed to get under the jar and push it straight up the mound. The metal lid was now poking out of the top of the mound.

"Hold it in position, Bill! I can't yet see who is coming. I'll have to use the periscope again."

"It's damn heavy, Sid. Hurry up!"

Bill braced his legs and with all his might held the jar in position above his head. Sid pushed the periscope through the mound a second time and started rotating it.

"I can't hold this for too long, Sid," stammered Bill. "Can you see where the noise is coming from?"

"It's definitely from the direction of the house. Wait, the door is opening. Drat! It's a person. He's walking straight towards us and he doesn't look very happy. Let's get out of here. Quickly now!"

Sid retracted the periscope too fast. The mound was higher than their normal ones and the sides were therefore weaker. With the jar and the periscope at the top it was just too much. Suddenly one side of the mound fell away with the jar following suit! Bill was standing there with his hands above his head holding an imaginary object when the early morning sun shone straight on his head. Sid and Bill nodded at each other and started digging their way back down. Digging for their lives!

***

This was a particularly elegant conference room, probably the type only used for very important meetings. The room was an elongated oval shape with no windows and two doors, one at each end of an also oval shaped table. The walls were covered in finely-crafted, dark-wooden panelling which smoothly followed the perfect oval shape of the room. This room had clearly been made by a master of his trade. It was devoid of any pictures and decoration. The table was built to the same high standard as the panelling — quite possibly by the same craftsman. It was perfectly polished, just like an ice rink with the grain majestically shining through the gleam and its legs were fat, solid and beautifully carved. This room had been built for one purpose — to show power. Judging by the old, dank smell it was not often opened. There was no ventilation and one could quite easily believe it was deep underground. The table was surrounded by twenty-two chairs, each one was exquisitely hand-crafted from the finest wood and upholstery. There were twenty-one red chairs. The chair at one of the heads of the table was royal blue. All of the chairs had very high backs. It was therefore impossible to see who was speaking from outside the circle. Neither was it possible to hear exactly what was being spoken. But with the voices sounding intense and panicky there was a real sense of uproar in the room.

Bang, bang, bang!

The three hammer blows on the table were slow, deliberate and powerful. The first blow brought immediate silence to the cacophony of voices. On the third blow there was total and utter silence in the room, not even the sound of breathing could be heard. It seemed like an eternity until the voice in the royal blue chair spoke.

"Members of the Council," boomed a male voice with mighty authority.

"Members of the Council. We have a mole amongst us," he abruptly declared.

As if ordered, the twenty-one members gasped in shock and amazement.

"Yes, Councillors, a mole and a crime of the dastardliest you can imagine." A pause then followed a serious gaze around the room. "Professor Wingnut has been stolen. The dreadful deed was committed just a few hours ago."

There was another deep gasp in the room. This one even deeper than the last.

"Councillors," the voice boomed again.

"We must act with all haste to find the professor. He cannot be too far and we have already despatched our police to track the culprits down and to retrieve the professor. They have a two-hour head start but my sources tell me that the scent has already been found. I therefore instruct all of you to put your emergency plans into action and follow my directions. Exercise all powers. The professor must be found. You all know he was stored in our warehouse and all members in this room have access to it. One of you sitting in front of me is responsible for this aggravated theft and I will find out who. I, as President, will stop at nothing to uncover you."

A final loud gasp turned into another cacophony of whispering.

"Council members!" roared the President. "Go with all urgency. Our security and our future now depend on you. And the success of this mission. Hunt, leave no stone unturned, no tunnel unexplored, no molehill unsearched. Go!"

Bang!

A final thudding blow of the hammer brought the meeting to an abrupt end. One of the two doors opened and the twenty-one Councillors could be heard scurrying out. The president remained, deep in thought about the consequences of losing Professor Wingnut. His dark thoughts were interrupted by a firm knock on the door.

"Enter!" roared the president.

A man in military fatigues entered the council chamber. "Mr President. I have news."

The president's high-backed chair swivelled around to face the man who had come in behind him. The only thing to be seen of the person in the royal blue chair was the top of a black bowler hat protruding above the top of the back rest. "It had better be good news, Colonel Pickle," replied the president seriously.

"We managed to pick up the tracks of the assailants following a newly-built tunnel. It exited in the garden of house number three Trout Lane in Lower Molehampton. I'm afraid there was no trace of the assailants nor any of the whereabouts of Professor Wingnut. I've instructed my police to watch the house."

"Colonel Pickle. Are you telling me that the Professor has not only been stolen but has been brought to the surface and is now lost?"

"Mr President. We're doing all we can," the Colonel added nervously.

"All you can is not enough!" the president shouted. "Have you got any idea of the importance of this matter? We need to know where the professor is."

"Well, we have noticed an increase in activity around number three and suspect that the professor could be held in the house."

"Could be? And what are you doing to find out where he is exactly Colonel?"

"I believe the best course of action is to lay in wait and see what happens. We want to catch the assailants red handed and get the professor back at the same time. I fear that if we go into number three we might lose both. So, patience is now the best course of action. We are certain that whoever stole the professor is not aware that we are also watching."

"You had better be correct in your beliefs, Colonel and I suggest you increase the surveillance on number three. Use cats, they're good. You have my permission to use all assets of the Special Operations programme. Get some humans into a house too, people nobody would suspect. They must not be noticed. Do it now and report back to me, Colonel."

"Yes, Mr President."

"Dismissed, Colonel."

Colonel Pickle spun around sharply and left the room leaving the President once again alone in his thoughts.

***

Cleopatra, a large brown and black Doberman Pinscher lay below the bushes in the perfectly kept garden next to number three. She witnessed the unusual events in the garden with shock. The dog had been waiting well before four a.m. to make sure nobody else endangered the mission. She saw the moles arrive late and the man from the house pick up the jar. When he put the jar in his shed, the Doberman decided urgent action was needed to regain the delivery. So she ran through the garden straight up to the front door of number three and rang the doorbell. She then speeded back to her position in the garden and watched the man return to the house. Cleopatra waited for the man to close the kitchen door and then headed towards the shed. She tried as hard as she could but the latch had dropped and the door was closed securely. There was no chance for her paws to open the shed and retrieve the glass jar. She would have to inform her boss and get somebody else to do it. She also needed to get to Cromwell with all haste and let him know what had happened to the professor. It was unavoidable but for the time it took Cleopatra to get to the other side of the river and inform Cromwell number three Trout Lane would have to be left unguarded. Speed was now of the essence and Cleopatra bound off towards the River Angler, hoping the ferry would be operating.

***

The newly-built tunnel was dark and damp. The end of the tunnel was boarded up but in the middle of the wood was a small metal grate. The mole slowly approached and knocked on the wooden board. From the other side of the board a voice simply said, "Fourteen."

The mole replied, "Twenty-one." This was the secret code for the day.

"Did you complete the mission, Colonel," asked the mystery voice behind the wooden board.

The mole nervously replied, "Yes, the glass jar was successfully stolen."

"Excellent. And was it safely delivered to Cromwell?"

"Err, not exactly. The two moles arrived in the correct location but were late. It was already light so they took a course of action which unfortunately didn't go according to plan."

"Explain! Was our agent not waiting in place to take the delivery?" shouted the voice.

"Well, it's like this," the mole started slowly. "The glass jar did reach the surface and exactly where it should have but a little later than the planned delivery time. It was already light. Unfortunately, just at this moment a man came into the garden and picked up the jar. Cleopatra was only a few metres away but powerless to stop it."

"So where is he now? Where is the professor, you imbecile?"

"According to Cleopatra he is in the garden shed of number three," the mole replied.

"Are you one hundred percent sure of this, Colonel?"

"Yes, most definitely. Cleopatra saw the man put the jar in the shed. She then had the clever idea of distracting him by ringing the doorbell. She then ran back into the garden to retrieve the professor but the man had already locked the shed door. When Cleopatra realised that she could not open the shed, she immediately informed Cromwell. We have in the meantime sent her back to guard the house."

"My goodness, Colonel. Go and get the professor then. Send someone else who can open the shed. This shouldn't be too difficult," the voice added with frustration.

"I'm afraid a human has to do it," the mole answered quickly. "Hands are needed for this job."

"A human? Well that will complicate matters. Our plan appeared to be so simple but now we have to involve others and jeopardise our mission. Colonel, I recommend you firstly increase the surveillance on number three. Use dogs, they're good. You also have my permission to use our sources in the Special Operations programme. Get some humans into a house, people nobody would suspect. They must not be noticed. We must not get caught. It is imperative for us to first get this glass jar before we make our next move," the mystery voice said.

"Yes, sir," replied the Colonel.

"And, Colonel Bacon."

"Yes, sir?"

"Do not muck it up this time. Make sure you choose somebody reliable and loyal. Report back to me when you have everything in place. I will inform Cromwell of the — hopefully — short delay."

"Ye..."

Before the Colonel could reply a wooden cover was firmly slammed into place, closing the metal grate from the other side. The tunnel appeared to be a dead end and the mystery voice was gone. Colonel Bacon turned around and scurried back up the tunnel wondering who he could choose for the stake out.

On the other side of the wooden board a smartphone was activated and a call was placed.

"Minister. What news?" Cromwell answered the phone rather impatiently.

The mystery minister informed Cromwell about what course of action had been decided.

Chapter Two
Number Three, Trout Lane

Trout Lane is at the top end of Lower Molehampton and sits on top of a hill offering a perfect view of the whole area and surrounding streets. From my bedroom window I have the view that I so love. A clear view of the River Angler slowly meandering down the lush, steep-sided valley. In fact, I have a crow's nest view of the whole valley. Not only can I see the river, but I have a clear view over Lower Molehampton itself with its jam jar glass factory, meat processing plant, campsite and football pitch on my side and Upper Molehampton with its castle ruin on the other side. I am sure that in its day the ruin would have imposed its control up and down river. I can hear the car ferry clanking its way across the river on a steel cable as the Molehamptons no longer have a bridge.

The Molehamptons are situated on a large, sweeping bend in the river. Upper Molehampton is on the outside bend, where the river is at its fastest, and over the years has carved out a steep side in the valley with a very narrow floor. Lower Molehampton is on the inside of the bend, where the river is at its slowest and has created a wide flood plain over the years. As a result, Upper Molehampton is squeezed into a narrow stretch along the river and spread out up the hill to the castle ruin. Lower Molehampton has the freedom of the flood plain and has, over the years, formed into a circular looking town.

Looking up the valley, away from the towns and ruin, I can see Mr Rye's old, stone farmhouse. It is on my side of the river and sits in the plain a few hundred metres from the river. At the same height as the farmhouse is a large, majestic willow tree bending over the river like an old school headmaster imposing his will on a student. On this particular day I could just make out a dog running around Mr Rye's fields, barking loudly. I always wondered what it was like to be a dog. I mean, they really didn't have much to do and spent most of the day dozing around. In a way I was quite jealous because dogs didn't have to go to work, go shopping, do the cleaning and many other things. In fact, everything was done for them.

Many years ago, Upper and Lower Molehampton were united, but fierce rivalry between the villages led to the two sides of the river going their own way. Visitors today cannot see the rivalry but for those living in the Molehamptons it has always just been simmering below the surface. It all stems from the way the two sides of the river developed over the years. According to local folklore, there was once an all-powerful and ruthless lord who lived in the castle and had total domination over the whole area. His family lived on the side which is now Upper Molehampton and the servants and workers, who tended his estate, lived on the other side of the river, what is now Lower Molehampton. The noble family fell from grace and the castle fell into ruin.

The mayoress of Upper Molehampton, Felicity Forsythe-Twyke, not well-known for her scruples, claims to be from the same stock as the noble family, through many distant relatives. Not only is she the mayoress but also the owner of the meat processing plant in Lower Molehampton. She supplies the whole region with meat and brokers no competition.

The two towns were once connected by a stone bridge but constant arguing and bickering between both sides over who should pay for the upkeep resulted in its slow decay. It was a very sad day when it was eventually closed and today the bridge itself has collapsed and only the stone ramparts on either side remain. That was the high point of the rivalry and today, thankfully, relations are much better. We still don't have a bridge though, but we do have a ferry, thanks to Mr Cross from Lower Molehampton. Not only does he offer useful access to both sides of the river but also makes a tidy profit as well. Today the towns live in relative harmony, but the history of the rivalry can still be seen. The townsfolk of Lower Molehampton think the people of Upper are arrogant and haughty and the townsfolk of Upper think the people of Lower are a common rabble. The two towns are different in many ways. Upper has its castle ruin, is very picturesque and attracts quite a lot of tourists with its hotels, nice cafes, posh boutiques and expensive shops. For a tourist, it may be nice but not practical for those living there who cross the river to buy the more reasonably priced goods on the other side. Upper also has a government building on the outskirts of the village offering employment to many people in the area, who simply call themselves civil servants. Nobody knows for sure what they do but it is rumoured to be a secret listening station. As it is a secret we of course do not know what they do, because if we did it would not be a secret. Upper also has an equestrian centre, a well-frequented location for the people on their side of the river. It is run by Mrs Farrow, a lady who has a very good relationship with the mayoress — they are as thick as thieves. Lower has most shops you would expect to service a town: a butcher, a baker, a supermarket and much more. The most popular is Mr Tinker's ironmongers store — he stocks absolutely everything and there is nothing he can't get for you. He is of course famous in the whole area for keeping pigeons, a past time he is absolutely passionate about. Lower is also quite rightly proud of its campsite which is frequented by people from far afield. It sits directly at the river, right next to the ferry and is famous in the region for its smoked fish — quite a delicacy — and relaxed attitude to campers. Cyclists, canoeists, caravans — yes, everyone likes to visit the wonderfully friendly campsite and enjoy the beautiful view of the river with a barbeque and open fire. The smell of wood smoke laced with fish often wafts its way into noses around the village. The people from Upper are fast to put the people from Lower down but are more than content to buy in its shops, frequent its pubs, especially the Anchor Inn, and get a good fish and chip takeaway. Mr Cross, the ferryman, is a very busy person indeed!

***

The Kennedy brothers are notoriously bad crooks. They live in Anglerton which is quite a large town and is also situated on the River Angler. The people from Upper and Lower Molehampton often use the bridge at Anglerton to cross the river when Mr Cross's ferry has stopped work for the day. It is a popular route for the people from Upper to return in the evening after collecting fish and chips from Lower.

Joe and Gavin Kennedy are petty crooks and I'm afraid to say not even very good at that. The only success stories they have are from being caught in the act by the police.

On this day, they were walking, stooped over so as not to be seen, along a hedgerow behind a house. Like normal, they did not have a real plan and just waited for an opportunity to arise. Their intention was to go into a garden and steal something of value. Some birds were circling above them high in the sky, following their every movement. It was hard not to see them for they were overweight and both wore red tracksuits. Not the best of camouflage next to a hedge.

The birds suddenly stopped circling and entered into a steep dive in the direction of the stooping brothers, looking like fighter jets about to attack their target. They flew unusually low over the brothers, dropped their load of white droppings and soared back up into the sky. The birds' droppings found their target with uncanny accuracy.

The brothers, unaware of the birds, started to climb over a small wooden fence to get into the back garden of a house. Whilst they were both straddling the fence, they heard a whooshing sound above their heads and looked up into the sky, losing balance in the process. It looked a strange sight — those two fat brothers sitting astride on top of the fence in their red tracksuits when the birds' droppings splatted right in the middle of their foreheads. The fence wasn't very robust and couldn't hold the weight of the wobbling brothers. They crashed down to the ground in a heap exactly at the same place that they were before and sat there in bemusement, just looking at each other.

Joe looked at Gavin and started laughing. "Ha ha. You've got bird poo on your forehead!"

Gavin looked back at Joe and also started laughing, "Ha ha. So do you!"

The brothers weren't the most intelligent of young men and they looked quite dopey to tell you the truth. So, it took them a while to understand what had just happened to them. They both started rubbing the bird droppings off with their hands, quite obviously very disgusted. But then all of a sudden they sat bolt upright and their eyes and faces lit up as though they were hit with a brilliant idea. Quite out of character they stood up with a jolt, looked at each other and both said at the same time, "Come on then. We've got a job to do. Let's get to Lower Molehampton. Quickly now." They proceeded back along the hedgerow to the road where they had come from. But this time they were not stooped or slovenly, but were instead upright and with a sense of purpose and urgency.

***

Living in Lower Molehampton, despite the awkward relationship with Upper, is actually quite nice. It is peaceful, well-kept and the people law-abiding. Nothing untoward ever happens in Lower Molehampton. OK, there were the glass jar thefts and the visits from the Kennedy brothers. But, all-in-all a peaceful and tranquil place to live. I say nothing untoward and this is, as you already know, of course not quite true. It is October already and I have pretty much forgotten about the strange molehill and the discovery of the glass jar back in June. It seems just a distant memory and I must admit I haven't thought about it too much since then. But that event marked the beginning of some strange happenings in Trout Lane.

My parents sadly passed away when I was thirty-four and left me the family house, which I have been living in, alone, since then. It is a detached house made of red bricks built in 1901 — a rather old house but still very solid and very well-built. It has of course been modernised but it still retains its one hundred years plus of charm. There is a small porch for me to keep my shoes and umbrella. The

35

bright red wooden front door has small milky windows so you can't look out and, more importantly, can't look in of course. When you enter the house, there is a long hallway with a door on the left, about half way along, leading into the living room with a large bay window looking out onto Trout Lane. All streets in our housing estate are named after animals. There's also a Hippopotamus Road and Giraffe Mews. In fact, Trout Lane is not really a lane but a cul-de-sac with five detached houses equally spaced around a small roundabout painted on the road. I live in number three, right at the end of the cul-de-sac.

My desk is right next to my bed and from my window I have a beautiful view of the whole area which also overlooks the street. The coloured autumn leaves on the trees are dancing in the crisp October sunlight and blustery wind. I can see my front garden, the neighbouring houses and back gardens directly to my right and left of numbers two and four. Of the other houses I can only see the front gardens. The Pike family live next to me in number two — Edward and Edith Pike and their child, Earl. The Pike's recently had a greenhouse built in their garden which had milky glass, so I had no idea what they were growing in there. To my right in number four is Mr Lawnsworthy. Mr Lawnsworthy lives up to his name. Really! He must be around seventy and I have known him since I was a child. Mr Lawnsworthy, as his name suggests, loves his lawn probably more than anything else in his life. He spends endless hours on his hands and knees crawling across every centimetre pulling out anything which does not resemble a blade of grass. With a spirit level and a pair of scissors he makes sure all of the grass is at exactly the same level. I always imagine that his grass represents hundreds of thousands of identical people who he has probably given names to. From spring to autumn, he cuts his lawn every three days unless the weather stands in his way. He is endlessly adding some sort of concoctions to his grass to ensure it is healthy and the richest, darkest green you can imagine. It does look nice, really nice, and if he enjoys it then that's just fine with me. Do you know that I've only ever spoken to him once in all of the years? And that was to ask him if he could look after the key to my house just in case there was an emergency. He hung it on a hook in his hallway and it's probably still there now. Since then just a nod of the head in polite recognition and that is it. Oh, and he also hates leaves and therefore autumn is the worst time of the year for him. Leaves are not allowed to fall anywhere in his property. For the few weeks in the year when the leaves fall, Mr Lawnsworthy is on permanent guard duty, armed with a metal stick with a sharp end and a bucket. He is always there — from the first moment I look out of my bedroom window to when I close my curtains before going to sleep. There he is, running around in his garden spiking any leaf which dares to enter his property. When it is dark, he even wears a powerful head torch to light up a few metres in front of him. It is quite funny to watch sometimes, especially on a windy day when he spikes some leaves, turns around to get some more and then turns around again and screams in anguish as more leaves appear again where he has just cleaned. Mr Lawnsworthy has never changed since my early childhood memories. He is still exactly the same — always wearing blue garden overalls and wellington boots and, apart from looking older, he hasn't changed a bit. It certainly keeps him fit because I have never seen him sick, or with a limp, or any sort of injury. No day would be the same without Mr Lawnsworthy of Number Four Trout Lane. Come to think of it, I have never even seen anyone visit him nor have I ever seen any family members or grandchildren.

The only child I have ever seen in his garden is Earl. And the only reason I know Earl is because he was the first person ever to come up to me in the street and introduce himself. The people in Trout Lane are not the most talkative bunch. They are reserved but polite and law-abiding people. You will not believe it but we never really introduce ourselves to each other. Just a quick nod of the head is sufficient. It was a Saturday and I had just left my house and walked along my small driveway to the pavement when suddenly, from behind a hedge, a small boy appeared on a bicycle. He screeched to a halt in front of me with his back wheel sliding in a cool braking stop.

"Hello," he said, looking up at me. "My name is Earl, I am seven years old and I live in number two. And who are you?"

I was completely startled, not just by his sudden appearance but his directness. We are very quiet in Trout Lane and not accustomed to such dramatic activities. I composed myself and with a short pause said, "Hello Earl, nice to meet you. My name is Mr Jackson from number three."

"That's a strange name!" Earl studied me, inspecting me with his large, round, inquisitive eyes.

"What do you mean?"

"Well, your name is Mr Jackson from number three and I've never heard of a name like that."

"No, my name is Mr Jackson and I live at number three!"

"Oh, well then that's OK for a name I suppose," said Earl.

"Hmm, thanks. Very kind of you Earl," I said now smiling at the young boy.

I don't know how long it lasted but it seemed like an eternity. Earl on his bicycle looking at me. And me, just standing there, neither of us saying a word, just staring at each other probably waiting for the other to say something.

Then Earl made the first move, "What do you do, Mr Jackson from number three?"

"What do you mean, Earl?"

"Well, I mean what do you do for a living?" he replied.

"Oh, OK. I'm a civil servant."

Earl's eyes inspected me again. "Wow, you're a servant! For who?"

"No, Earl, I'm not a servant for anyone in particular. I work for the government and people who work for the government are called civil servants."

"So, you serve people with tea and biscuits and things like that?"

"No, Earl." This was getting a little annoying now. I have never had any experience with children before, so I was not used to this line of questioning. "I work in an office and deal with paperwork. I'm not really a servant as you imagine. We are probably called servants because we work for the government and therefore the people."

"Oh," said Earl but I could see he wasn't convinced. "You do look, kind of ordinary, so I suppose that suits you."

I didn't quite tell the truth to Earl that day. Well, kind of the truth, because I really do work for the government and I really do deal with paperwork. The only problem is that I work in a special department and I am not allowed to say what I do; therefore, we are always told just to say that we are civil servants and work in a government office. I actually work in the government's information collection agency, which, as I am sure you can imagine, is rather secretive. This encounter with Earl was a little awkward because no one had ever questioned me about what I do before. Thankfully I could remember the training and came out with the standard answer. Can you imagine if I hadn't thought about it and just blurted out, "I work for the government and we collect information about people and many other things." Not a good answer! So no, I didn't lie to Earl but I didn't fully explain what I do. I was just careful with the truth I would say. I wasn't quite sure if I should have been insulted about 'looking ordinary' or should I have just taken it as a compliment. I suppose looking ordinary is a good cover for my job. To be honest I wouldn't describe myself as an outwardly exciting person. No, I am in a way quite ordinary. But I do possess a very analytical mind and hence am very good at analysing information and making the right decision. I think long and hard about things but more often than not I draw the correct conclusions and act accordingly. That, I suppose, is one of the reasons why I have the job in the agency and am very good at it. I just love collecting information and you never know when you might need it. I certainly wouldn't consider myself a spiritual person and certainly have no time for talking about things you cannot prove. No, I am a man of documents, photographs and recorded voices. Yes, these things are my physical world. Proven events that really happened.

Just as quick as he arrived he disappeared. He didn't say anything, just stood up on his pedals and cycled away as fast as he could. He then turned his head and shouted, "Nice to meet you, Mr Jackson from number three!"

Yes, Earl is the only person I have ever seen in Mr Lawnsworthy's garden. One day I was sitting at my desk doing some work when all of a sudden I saw a small boy on a bicycle ride across Mr Lawnsworthy's front garden. Not even leaves are allowed in his garden, let alone boys on bicycles. The tyres left marks on the grass and when Mr Lawnsworthy ran out of his front door he shouted something incomprehensible to the boy I now know as Earl and chased him down the street. Quite athletic for someone of his age! It was quite a sight, the small boy cycling as fast as he could and Mr Lawnsworthy running after him in a dressing gown and slippers. And it was a close race until Mr Lawnsworthy ran across the front garden of number five and tripped over a molehill. He flew in slow motion across the grass and his face landed right in the middle of another molehill. Earl fled to the safety of his own house while Mr Lawnsworthy brushed the grass from his dressing gown and spat out the mud. It would be unfair to judge Earl just because he rode his bicycle across Mr Lawnsworthy's front lawn. However, he did strike me as a mischievous young boy then, even though he was actually quite polite when he met me.

The people at number one, at the entrance to Trout Lane, moved in at the end of June this year. I saw my previous neighbours move out. They had lived there as long as I can remember, but I never saw the new neighbours move in. They sneaked in in the middle of the night. I heard a vehicle and I heard the sound of things being carried into the house. It only took them a few minutes. Certainly not a normal house move. Who moves in the middle of the night? First, I presumed that they arrived from somewhere far away and only dropped off some essentials with their main move to follow but it never did. Over the last few months I've heard activity from the house and seen their lights on. During the day there is no sign of anyone. I've never seen the people, but I know they are there!

Now to the last house, number five, which is also at the entrance to Trout Lane and directly opposite number one. Strangely enough, I haven't got much to say about number five either. That's because the exact same happened as with number one. Only one week later though. A quick move in the night. And again, I've not yet seen the new neighbours, but I can hear them. They are there!

The molehill in my garden and the discovery of the glass jar started a chain of strange events — the people moving out to be replaced by unknown people. But that's not all. I have also witnessed an unusual increase of animal activity in our street and I'm talking about domestic pets of course. Dogs and cats are naturally not out of place in any street and Lower Molehampton is certainly no exception. But the large number of dogs and cats over the last few weeks. And I'm not talking about seeing a cat in my garden or two every now and then. No, I'm talking about five stray dogs and five cats in the street. All at the same time but never on the same side of the street. But the real odd thing is that I have the impression that they are all watching my house. They are watching ME. Yes, I'm serious. Have you ever had the feeling that you are being watched? Well I have now. These dogs and cats are actually staking out my house — that I am sure about. But I have a problem, just like the discovery of the glass jar. I cannot talk to anyone about this — because who should believe me — especially not where I work. I'm afraid I have to keep these suspicions to myself — for the moment at least. The other strange event which has been happening over the last few weeks is the huge amount of new molehills. We live in the country, yes. And it is therefore normal to have molehills but all in Mr Lawnsworthy's garden? That is most certainly very odd. He was on permanent duty in his garden with a spade and various other devices. Seriously, I am not talking about ten molehills. I am talking of around one hundred. His garden looked like the crater of the moon. And all in the last few weeks — odd is all I can say. I felt so sorry for the old man.

Mr Lawnsworthy must be at his wits end to see his beloved lawn being slowly destroyed. He is fighting against them and has gadgets which make noises down the holes because supposedly moles don't like them and go away. Not in this case. He is also putting pellets into the holes on some evenings. I think these then create gas which is poisonous for moles — or so they say. I am sure it's not legal but nevertheless it hasn't stopped their digging. There must be a whole colony right under his garden. Apart from the large molehill I had in my garden some weeks ago there is now no more activity on my side of the fence. But there was more. At night time I can hear some sort of rattling and shaking noise, just like a door being shaken in its frame during a storm. But there is no storm. It sounds like the door of my garden shed but every time I take a look I can see nothing untoward. One day I even checked the door and inside the shed but everything seemed to be as it should, apart from the tools which had fallen over some weeks ago. Yes, I must tidy it up. I closed the door again and firmly secured the latch to make sure it was really shut. But the shaking noise at night carries on.

What I could not know was that my life in the serene Trout Lane was about to change.

Chapter Three
A Very Strange Evening

The sensation of being watched had intensified in the last couple of weeks and so did the frequency of visits by cats and dogs. I still couldn't tell anyone, because everyone would most likely think I was out of my mind. I therefore decided to take things in my own hands. As I worked in the government's information collection agency, I had professional listening equipment readily available to me. Of course, I wasn't allowed to use it for private purposes, but I was convinced that I was being watched, and it could be by a foreign spy agency. With the job I had it would certainly make sense. If it was only that I could inform my superiors, but how was I to explain the cats and dogs? I was in a quandary and decided to smuggle the equipment out secretly. I had to do it piece by piece and it took me several weeks. I set up my listening post in my bedroom and started to observe the street and monitor the radio frequencies using every spare moment of my time. After some weeks I began to doubt my mission because I found absolutely no evidence of being watched or proof any other strange activities were going on. Only once did I detect a faint signal, which I could not classify. I tried to trace the signal again but unfortunately, I was unsuccessful.

This evening, like most evenings now, I was sitting in my bedroom, headphones on, observing the street and listening. It wasn't really any different to any other night, but I had the advantage of the full moon lighting up the entire night sky. There was nothing going on in Trout Lane. But then what should be going on? It must have been around ten and Mr Lawnsworthy still had his living room light on. Earl was probably in bed. As to my other neighbours at numbers one and five — all I could see was the dim glow of the bedroom lights behind old, battered curtains. It was also a cold autumn evening with a very light breeze and I could hear the leaves rustling in the trees and also the sound of traffic from a nearby street. Nothing untoward was going on and everything in Lower Molehampton appeared to be in order — just as it should be.

When I heard a faint signal, I had been using my listening equipment for at least two hours and was thinking or turning in for the night. I had heard that signal before. And there it was again, but it was very faint. Untrained people wouldn't have recognised it but for me it was quite audible. I sat closer to my receiver and started fine tuning my dials and direction-finding equipment. The only other noise in the room was the click of the dials being slowly turned. And there it was again. I could then make out some sort of voices but couldn't understand what they were saying. But yes, this was definitely some sort of communication. Maybe this was it. The breakthrough I had been waiting for. Evidence that I was being watched and something to report to my superiors. But it was difficult to stay tuned in on the communication so I adjusted my receiver again to get a clearer signal. When at last I managed to locate it, the realisation dawned on me that it was possibly not coming from a human source. The signal was local and very close by. But it was certainly coming from below the ground. This was not the tangible evidence I needed to report to my superiors. How exactly could I tell my superiors that I was being spied on from below the surface? And also, by cats and dogs — I don't think so! I then did something. I really can't explain what made me do it, other than out of frustration. I pressed a button, paused, swallowed hard and spoke into my headset microphone,

"Hello. Who's there?"

The voices stopped immediately and then there was only silence. You could have heard a pin drop in the room. Every beat of my heart could be heard booming through the night. I obviously had just made an error of judgement. Oh well, so much for my hair brained plan! I sat there for a while longer waiting for the signal to appear again but there was nothing. I felt uneasy about the situation, so I saved the tracking information on a small memory stick and decided to hide it. I don't know why — just call it instinct. I held the memory stick in my hand, looking around the room for a hiding place.

***

Two men were in a room devoid of any sort of decoration. Just a desk, two chairs and a small rectangular rug on the floor. On the desk a radio and headset. The room had a rich smell of curry and spices about it. One of the men were sitting on the floor in the corner holding prayer beads in his hand whilst looking devoutly at the floor; his face deep in concentration. He was dressed in an immaculately clean and well-pressed white robe, had a long, jet-black beard with dark and menacing eyes. The other man, of similar appearance to his colleague, was on a chair about one metre from the window. The window was partially closed by curtains to make sure nobody from the outside could see the powerful camera and microphone. The man was totally focused on the house — the target house — well-lit by the street lights and today's full moon.

Their radio crackled into life.

"Hello Golf one. This is Foxtrot eight. Over."

The man on the floor jolted up from his sitting position, sprung towards the radio and put the headphones on.

"Assalamu Alaykum wa Rahmatullahi wa Barakatu. This is Golf one. Send. Over."

"Golf one — Move on the asset now. Implement Plan H. Over."

"Foxtrot eight. Confirm. Inshallah."

"Golf one. This is Foxtrot eight. Out."

***

In another house two overweight men in dirty red tracksuits looked like they had not washed in an age. An old battered couch, a fridge and a desk with a radio were the only items in the stuffy room. It smelled of sweat and stale air. One of the men had his hand in a big bag of crisps and stuffed handfuls of them into his mouth with loud crunching noises, with most of the crisps landing on his fat belly. The other man sat by the window slurping from a drinks can, his face deep in concentration looking at the house . Protected from view, with old, dirty lace curtains, were his tools — a large camera on a tripod and listening equipment. The target house was well-lit by the street lights and today's full moon.

Their radio burst into action.

"Hello Victor three, hello Victor three. This is Mike one. Come in. Come in. Over."

The man dropped the bag of crisps on the floor with a scowl of discontent, waddled over to the radio and donned the headphones.

"What."

"Your target is moving. Move, move, move. Over."

"Moving now."

***

There was a loud crack and the sound of breaking glass. I was still standing in my room, with an uneasy feeling in my stomach, thinking of a place to hide the memory stick. The noise was in my house and came from downstairs. I froze on the spot. Someone was walking around downstairs. Silence… and then the creaking of my wooden stairs. Yes, someone was coming up, very slowly though, trying not to make any noise. Burglars! My heart started to race and the palms of my hands became sweaty, my mouth was dry. I had never been in a situation like this before and I really didn't know what to do. The door out of my bedroom led straight to the stairs — exactly where someone was coming from. "OK, I really should move now," I thought. Not wanting to make a noise and give my position away to the intruders, I slowly lifted up my foot and placed it a short distance away from me, just like in slow motion. But the silence was broken by the loud creaking of the wooden boards when my foot eventually touched the floor again. I panicked and ran towards the window, as that was the only way to escape from this room. With a loud creaking noise, I prised my window open and put one leg outside. But the bedroom door burst open and then I saw them. Two tall men silhouetted in the light from the hallway– jet-black beards and wearing long white robes. Like something from a film but obviously real. Why here? In my street, in my house and in my bedroom?

They were quick and professional. Before I was able to move they dragged me away from the window and back into the room. The window was slammed shut and the curtains closed. They said nothing. One of the men pinned me to the floor in a powerful vice-like grip. The other went across to my radio.

Then there was a second loud crash in my house. I now had a faint glimmer of hope that help was on its way. Maybe Mr Lawnsworthy had seen or heard the commotion and called the police. The two men froze, stayed silent and looked at each other in disbelief. This was obviously not part of their plan. Again, without saying a word, they nodded. I wanted to shout but before I could utter a word my head was violently yanked back and a piece of material was stuffed in my mouth. Like a sack of potatoes, one of them threw me over his shoulder. The other one gave up looking at my radio and moved rapidly to the door. A quick look and another nod. Then they both charged down the stairs with me dangling over one of the men's shoulder. With a loud crash the kitchen door suddenly flew off its hinges and there in the doorway were two more men. Overweight men dressed in dirty red tracksuits who also looked at each other in confusion. So, here we were, two men dressed in tracksuits blocking the doorway; two men in white robes at the bottom of the stairs and me, hanging over the shoulder of a complete stranger. Without anyone saying a word, the four intruders all charged in the same direction at the same time towards the front door, which was still intact.

What did they want? I wasn't a rich person and I certainly had no expensive possessions.

"Grab him!"

It was at this moment that I realised for sure that it was me they wanted, and when I mean they, I mean both sets of uninvited guests.

But why would they want me? Could it really be that this was a direct result of the radio communication a few minutes before? How could all of these people react so quickly? It couldn't be. And then it dawned on me that I still had the memory stick firmly clenched in my hand. I wanted to shout for help but I had a piece of material stuffed in my mouth. I was helpless. What on earth was happening?

All four men charged the front door at the same time and then there was a huge tussle with everyone pushing, grabbing, punching and shoving. I felt hands all over me pulling me in different directions. Grunts from grown men fighting over their prize. One of them managed to open the front door and we all spilled out ending up in a heap of five people lying on the porch!

The vice-like grip on me relaxed and I managed to roll off the heap of men as I had fortunately ended up on top. Quickly looking up, I realised there was a glimmer of hope to escape, so I took my chance and ran across my front garden towards the house next door. The men looked up, looked at each other and charged after me. I didn't think about it at the time because I was only thinking of saving myself, but looking back it was probably quite a sight. Me, running across the garden in tartan slippers, a dressing gown and a piece of cloth in my mouth chased by four men in robes and tracksuits. All four of them were now together in one group, struggling to catch up. I kept on glancing behind as they were making ground on me. Needless to say that running in slippers is difficult but running in long robes or being overweight is also not so easy! It must have looked like a comedy sketch.

There was a real tussle going on now in the race across the gardens — first left and then right, over small fences, around bushes and through Mr Lawnsworthy's immaculate front garden, trampling on his flower beds along the way. One of the men in tracksuits put out his foot and tripped up one of the men in robes, who went flying into a small hedge, much to the glee of the man in the tracksuit. In his delight, he forgot to look in front of him, running straight into a fish pond and landing with a gigantic splash. Two down! The two remaining men were running neck and neck, gaining on me quickly. Pushing, pulling and punching each other as they were trying to be the first to me. The one in the tracksuit then moved violently to his right knocking the other robe guy completely off balance and directly into a bush. Only one remaining! I looked over my shoulder and saw him running as fast as he could possibly manage — still gaining on me. It didn't take long until I felt the trampling of his heavy feet behind me, heard his panting, smelled his bad breath and thought it was all over when his sweaty hand grabbed my shoulder. Then out of nowhere and perfectly on cue some molehills sprouted up right in front of me. I was too desperate to think why and just weaved frantically between them. But the tracksuit guy didn't see them and tripped over landing in a heap directly behind me. Yes! I was in the clear.

I stood there for a few seconds surveying the scene — four men lay strewn around the damaged front gardens and my front door was wide open. I was now standing in front of Mr Lawnsworthy's house and saw his bedroom light go on. At last, he had heard the affray and would hopefully call Sergeant Dawson. But before I had the chance to do anything I heard the squealing of car tyres and realised the action wasn't quite over yet. I still had the memory stick in my hand and really needed to do something with it. In a knee-jerk reaction I stuck it into one of the new molehills at my feet and stamped it flat. I was sure it was the stick they were after so better not have it on me.

I decided the best thing to do now was simply run and headed for the exit of Trout Lane. Just at that moment a van screeched into the road and slid to a halt right in front of me. The side door opened and two men in white robes were in the back. I turned around and before I knew it the two robed intruders from my house pushed me towards the van, picked me up and threw me in. The doors were closed and the van screeched off without a word being uttered. I had just been kidnapped!

It seemed like an age, but it might have only been a few minutes, when the two men sitting on me stood up. They were rather heavy and it wasn't the most comfortable experience. However, my brief comfort was soon to end as they picked up some rope and bound my hands together, then my feet and to finish it off tied me to a metal ring on the floor of the van. I was going nowhere. Sitting on the floor of the van with my hands and legs bound together was terrifying and there was nothing I could do. Even more terrifying was the fact that I had absolutely no idea where I was, where we were going or what they wanted from me. There were no seats in the van, so we were all on the floor — one man to my left, another to my right and the other two directly in front of me who didn't utter a word, staring at me the whole time. Long black beards and dark glaring eyes. Spies? I still had the cloth in my mouth until, probably out of fear, I started to gag on it and they removed it. After a while I made an effort to find out what was going on.

"What do you want from me? What have I done?"

No reply.

"Where are we going?"

Again, no reply. I gave up and realised they wouldn't talk to me. So I just sat there contemplating my dire situation. I became cold as the shock wore off and I started shaking, slowly realising what had actually happened. I could make absolutely no sense of it.

Then I felt the change from a normal road to that of loose stones. The stones then gave way to a rough and bumpy country track until, eventually, I heard and felt the van drive over a cattle grid. Some minutes later the van stopped. The driver turned the engine off and got out. There was a tap on the side which prompted the man to the left to put a hood over my head. Then the van door slid open and I heard my captors getting out. I was untied from the side of the van and dragged to the door before being lifted out of the van by two men.

We all received kidnap training for our jobs, which had not really helped so far, but some things were slowly coming back. Do not utter a word or make any sudden movement seemed the best course of action at this stage — I wasn't capable of moving anyhow. I was numb with fear and completely incapable of any form of resistance.

Footsteps sounded like we were on a stone floor. A door was opened and a few moments later I sat on a hard, cold floor. The stones were icy and cold and I started to shiver uncontrollably — it was about the only movement I could make and it was completely involuntary. Someone removed my hood and then unbound my hands and legs. Again, all in complete silence. After my eyesight adjusted, I recognised that I was in a damp, stone-walled room, like an old country farm house. One of the bearded men threw some clothes on the floor next to me and left the room. He didn't say a word.

I remembered that in a hostage situation you shouldn't offer any form of resistance and do everything you are told to do. As this was the only course of action I knew, I decided it would be best to follow it. Although I was still shivering badly, I managed to take off my dressing gown and put on the clothes. A pair of jeans, thick woollen socks, a T-shirt, a thick sweater and a pair of boots. The strange thing was that all of the clothes fitted me perfectly, even the trousers. I have short legs and I always need to have the trousers taken up when I buy a new pair. But these fitted perfectly. Even the shoes. How in God's name could they know so much about me beforehand? Even the exact size of my clothes. They must have been observing me for ages. I had so many questions swirling around in my head in the meantime. And what about the tracksuits? Who on earth were they? In fact, why was I being followed at all and especially by two sets of people? Surely listening to their communication couldn't have been so important. Or come to think of it — maybe the glass jar? But who would be interested in an old and dirty glass jar. Come to think of it — where did I put it?

The windows were boarded up, the door was locked from the outside and my only companion was the light of a paraffin lamp in the corner of my cell and a wooden stool. Again, an age went by and then I slowly started to smell food being prepared — a very strong smell and rich in spices. Like Indian food in a restaurant and it would make sense because my captors certainly looked like they came from that part of the world. Maybe from the sub-continent. Maybe India, Pakistan, Bangladesh or even Sri Lanka. I couldn't tell exactly where from and that was the least of my concerns.

Maybe he was one of the four who kidnapped me or maybe he was another person — they all looked the same to me. A man with a jet-black beard and white robes brought a plate, put it on the floor next to the stool and left again, locking the door behind him. The plate was filled with a piece of flat bread with burnt black patches, a chicken thigh covered in sauce and some sort of runny, yellow vegetables. The smell was strong. So strong that owing to my fear and lack of appetite it made me feel quite nauseous. "Eat when you have the opportunity," I thought. But eating was the last thing on my mind. However, common sense is important and I remembered something else from my training. Keep your energy levels up and understand that you never know when you will eat your next meal. I decided that this was the best thing to do and started to eat some of the food very slowly. I really had to force myself to eat. About an hour ago I would have probably vomited out of fear at the sight of food. But now, and a few mouthfuls later, my stomach had settled down a little and it even tasted quite good. It took me a while but I managed to finish everything on the plate and even used the bread to mop up the yellow vegetables and sauce. It was certainly good to have some warm food in my stomach to ward off the cold. As soon as I put the plate down a man came in, handed me a plastic cup of water, took my empty plate and left the room again. No word.

It must have been around seven a.m. when the first rays started poking through the wooden planks covering the window. I had been up all night but strangely didn't feel tired owing to all of the excitement and fear. Rain was smashing against the building and the wind was blowing a gale. Yesterday's good weather seemed to be over. I heard the sound of a vehicle approaching through the din of the wind. It came to a halt followed by the sound of footsteps on the gravel. Then I heard a few people speaking very quietly outside my cell. The door opened and a man with a jet-black beard entered the room. He was taller than the others and was dressed in a grey robe.

"Assalamu Alaykum."

I coughed slightly and didn't really know what to say. All I could utter was, "Hello!"

"So you're Connor Jackson. I must now apologise for what happened to you last night. For the kidnapping. But things didn't quite work out as planned and the other visitors at your house were completely unexpected."

"Unexpected! What do you mean they were unexpected? You were all unexpected. You stormed into my house, kidnapped me in the middle of the night and now I'm in the middle of nowhere being kept against my will."

He sat down cross legged on the floor and looked at me long and hard. "It was for your own good, Connor. I can truly understand your fear now and you probably think we are terrorists. And why not? Men with long black beards dressed in robes. Yes, your traditional looking terrorist. You may be happy to hear that we are not in fact terrorists and we are here to help you. We are here to protect you."

"Protect me! Help me! How can you explain your actions as any sort of help? If you want to help me just drive me home, repair my house and apologise to my neighbours for destroying their gardens. Quite simple if you want to help. I have another definition of that word," I said strutting around the room.

"I'm afraid life is not as simple as that, Connor. You will not be returning to your house. Not today, not tomorrow, not next week. Never!"

"What do you mean I won't be returning to my house?" I said with a look of sheer panic on my face.

"Quite simple, Connor. You are about to embark on a journey and you won't return here."

"I'm sorry, I really don't understand," I stuttered.

"Connor. You found something that is very dangerous and you must be protected. The other men are not as nice as we are. We now need to hide you from them so your discovery remains with us and not with them. All we now need to do is recover it before we give you a new identity. However, their reach is long and we fear that they might know where we are. So, we have to move you to a safer place and very far from here."

"What do you mean I found something dangerous? I only listened to voices on my radio. Nothing else."

My question went unanswered.

"We've been monitoring you for some time, Connor and when you heard the communication last night we realised we had to act immediately, which unfortunately started this chain reaction. The other side was also monitoring you and reacted at the same time. We didn't expect that. We were rather hoping we would have time to search your house and take what we were looking for."

"What are you looking for and who exactly are you?"

"All in good time, Connor. The others now know that we have you and they are looking for the same thing. They also wanted to search your house. Now they will presume that we know where it is."

"Know where what is? Could you please start answering my questions? What are you looking for? Who are you? Who are the others?"

The man sighed and added, "I completely understand all of your questions but I'm afraid this is too complex and there is no time to discuss or explain now. All you need to know is that you are now in our care and we will protect you. It is imperative to get you far away and to a safe place."

"Please answer this question," I added. "How did you react so quickly last night? I mean, you were on to me in minutes and the others appeared very shortly after, too."

"We were in number one, Connor. We didn't know then but we now know that the others were in house number five right opposite us."

"So, you've been watching my every movement and observing me?"

"Yes, Connor. And so have the others. You have something of great value. We want it and so do they. You will have to tell us everything but not now. Now, we need to get you to a safe place."

The man stood up to indicate the end of the conversation.

"Enough for now, Connor. We have problems to deal with. The others will want to search your house and so do we. Unfortunately, one of your neighbours called the police last night and they have now sealed off your house. It will be very difficult for humans to get inside to do the search. So, we have no choice but to use animals, I mean special forces. We leave in five minutes."

With that he spun around and left the room.

Use animals? Special forces? This was getting stranger by the minute and my previous levels of nervousness had now returned. I stood there with my mouth open.

Two of the men came into my room and motioned for me to sit on the stool, which I did without the slightest hint of protest. They held me in position with vice like grips of their strong hands. I was completely at their mercy. Then one of them uttered the first words since yesterday evening.

"Don't worry, Mr Jackson. This won't hurt. You are about to go on a journey and to a very safe place."

I saw a glint of shiny metal and then felt the sharp prick of an injection piercing my skin. Before I could even think of replying everything began to slow down — first my thoughts, then my vision and lastly the intense drowsiness. I entered into a world of dreams from which I occasionally stirred, periodically making out blurred images before falling back into a deep darkness again. It was as though I was in a dream that I was powerless to escape from.

Chapter Four
A Wet and Windy Day

It was a wet and windy day with swirling dark clouds buffeting around in the turbulent sky. The strong gusts of wind were enough to dislodge the few remaining golden leaves on the late autumn trees, which fell into the river below. At this particular spot on the river the water had eroded some overhanging willow trees so that all of the roots were exposed, forming a natural shelter for the river bank wildlife. It was exactly here that the ducks found their shelter and their ideal feeding ground. The river was rich in plants and insects, just the right type of food for these dabbling ducks to fatten themselves in preparation for the oncoming winter. Some of the ducks were swimming in the water and every now and then dunking their heads down into the river to feed on whatever happened to be passing by. They looked funny with their beaks submerged below the water and their rear ends jutting up towards the sky as though they had crash landed in the river. One particular duck, with a beautiful green head and a bright yellow beak, was resting just below the roots of the willow after feeding. Now feeling full, lazy and slow after the wonderful meal of river insects, the duck decided to venture out of the shelter and take a short swim in the river. It was always a good idea to have some exercise after such a nice meal. It was late afternoon and the day's light was slowly disappearing.

***

The wet, windy and cold weather didn't bother this dark chocolate coloured Labrador retriever. He lay in wait right next to the river as his excellent sense of smell had picked up the scent of the ducks from as far away as Mr Rye's farm house. He was hungry because his owner strictly controlled his diet, so he did not get too fat. He was also frustrated because he was trained to just fetch the shot-down birds and bring the tasty prey back to his master — that was his job as a retriever after all. However, on this particular day he was especially hungry and his master was away — delivering fresh vegetables to a hotel in Upper Molehampton. The Labrador had worked most of the day, hunting with his master and the afternoon was now drawing to a close. And who would notice a missing duck? He carefully crept forward towards the old willow next to the river. Silent. There were a number of ducks in the river, obviously unaware of the danger. He was almost within striking distance and didn't want to lose this chance. Although he was excellent in the water, he didn't want to attack too soon and give the ducks the advantage to react to the noise of him splashing into the water. No, he had to wait for the right chance. He crept forward, one paw at a time, belly low on the ground, not making a noise, until he was in the first roots of the willow, only one pounce from the river. But today was his lucky day! Just below him a lone duck, with a green head and a bright yellow beak, paddled out right below him from the shelter of the roots cut away by the river. The duck was fat and slow, probably full after a nice meal, and completely oblivious to the dog's presence. Perfect. He stood up and slowly moved along the roots, crouched, waited and then pounced. He caught the duck in one swift movement without entering the water, only just getting his paws wet, and then turned and ran away with his prey firmly grasped in his jaws. The duck was still alive and trying frantically to escape the clutches of the dog's jaws — but to no avail. The Labrador decided to run back to the farm, only a few hundred metres away, to devour the duck away from preying eyes. He approached a narrow, wet, leaf-covered road.

***

She constantly looked across at the smart phone in eager anticipation of a message. The music was booming out of the pickup so loud that the plastic fittings in the car door were shaking from the noise. Boom, boom, boom. The woman was moving her head in rhythm with the music. Her left hand was on the steering wheel, a cigarette in her right hand and her smart phone on the passenger seat alongside a bag of fish and chips from the takeaway in Lower Molehampton. The phone blinked and vibrated so she put the cigarette in her mouth, stretched out her right hand and grabbed the phone. She typed a reply with her nifty fingers, held the steering wheel with her left hand, clamped the cigarette in her mouth and glanced at the road every now and then. The road was narrow but she knew it very well. She often went to Lower Molehampton to get fish and chips as it was the best in the area — in fact the only place. It was now late afternoon and she forgot that Mr Cross's ferry had stopped for the day. So, she had no choice but to drive quickly along the other side of the river to Anglerton, over the bridge and then back down the other side of the river to Upper Molehampton. She just hoped that the fish and chips would still be hot when she got home. The song finished with a loud crescendo, she nodded her head in time with the finale, stabbed the send button on her phone, took a deep draw on her cigarette and looked back towards the road just in time to see a brown dog with some sort of bird dangling out of its mouth, right in the middle of the road. Her eyes opened widely in the dimming afternoon light. The dog looked towards the pickup with its eyes also wide open. The bird turned its head towards the pickup and also opened its eyes widely. The woman then did what she was taught never to do and that was to brake hard when you see an animal on the road. She saw the animal but didn't see the white van careering along the road in the opposite direction. The brakes screeched, the tyres slipped on the wet leaves as the pickup started to slide across to the opposite side of the road in the direction of the old willow. Then everything happened very quickly. The pickup hit the dog and its prey. The jet black bearded driver of the white van slammed on his brakes hoping to avoid the pickup but lost control of his and spun, also heading in the direction of the tree. Then both vehicles, with the dog and its prey stuck to the front of the pickup, careered towards the willow. The van went to the right of the tree, the pickup to the left, and then straight into the river with a big splash. All of them submerged below the surface, followed by the escape of hundreds of exploding bubbles on the surface before the river returned to its normal appearance. There was nothing left on the road to indicate that something had happened, after all there was no contact with the vehicles and no debris left behind. Just the wet leaves of a typical autumn road.

There was no trace and no evidence that the vehicles and occupants had ever been there.

***

Being kidnapped was a horrifying experience but at least my hosts treated me well. After all, they were supposedly my protectors. Well, they kept tying me up, putting a hood on my head and moving me around all day from location to location, but at least they did not threaten me.

The drugs they injected me with usually wore off quite quickly. When I slowly came out of my drugged state again, I found myself in yet another cold, damp room with the only natural light coming from a thin crack in a boarded-up window. Through the crack I saw that I was in the countryside very close to a small farm with an old crooked willow tree right next to it. I wasn't yet fully awake, and it was also getting a little dark in the disappearing light of the evening, but I thought that this farm looked rather familiar. The willow formed a straight line with other trees, so I suspected they followed a stream or a river. It was stormy, wet and the gusty wind carried the sound of a dog barking in the distance and the smell of a log fire, possibly from the farmhouse.

I had nearly regained all of my senses when the door flew open. One of my captors burst in and without saying anything, put a sack over my head, pulled me roughly out of the room, pushed me outside into the cold wind and threw me onto the cold metal floor of the van. This time I was not drugged and not tied up and I had a feeling that this was a very rushed exit. Maybe something had gone wrong. Maybe the others had found us. The van was moving down a rough track in a hurry and bumped up and down quite severely. Then it left the bumpy track for a smooth road, but the journey was certainly not smooth. I was thrown around the back as the driver really put the van through its paces. We were careering along a windy country road at quite some speed when all of a sudden there was a squeal of brakes. I was flung forward and hit the metal wall separating me from the driver's cabin. I knew we were in trouble when I felt the van getting out of control, skidding and swerving all over the place with me bouncing off the walls of the inside of the van. It was hard to work out what exactly was happening, but I had the feeling that we were now careering down a slope and then, with an almighty smash, hit water. I still had my hood on but knew I was right as I was dunked in cold, fast rising water. The van hit something — possibly the bottom of wherever we were. The darkness returned again as I was flung against a hard surface.

Chapter Five
The Box

I turned over and stretched myself with a relaxing groaning noise. I obviously wasn't fully awake but felt myself coming around slowly. I opened one eye, snapped it shut again and yawned loudly like a content cat. But wait! I opened one eye again. Even though I really liked to sleep in a dark room I never had it this dark. It was still pitch black in my room when I opened both eyes and I couldn't remember my bed being so hard. I was obviously still asleep and this was just a dream. Yes, a dream — the last I could remember was being flown around the back of a van and the sensation of being wet. I moved around a little and then pinched myself but actually this did not seem to be a dream. So, why was it so dark in my bedroom that I couldn't see my hand in front of my face? And why was I fully clothed? I slapped my face lightly to make sure I wasn't dreaming.

Had I gone blind in the night? The best thing to do was to find the light switch, so I decided to get up. I gingerly put my legs over the edge of the bed and expected to place my feet on the floor when I realised I was already on the floor. I was not in a bed. Maybe I had fallen out of bed in the night and then rolled underneath. That would explain the darkness but when I put my hands up anticipating to touch the underside of my bed there was nothing, no bed, just air above me. I wanted to stand up but my head smacked against something hard and I fell back down again. I tried again but realised that it was not possible to fully stand up. Below me was a hard surface, above me was a hard surface, also to the left and to the right. I was locked up with no light. Panic now set in. What on earth was going on? But then I remembered the kidnapping. For my protection they said, but this certainly didn't feel very much like protection if you ask me! Hang on, maybe the others had caught me and… Connor, calm down, there must be a rational explanation for this. I turned over on my knees, put my hands on the floor in front of me and started crawling very slowly. Two paces were all I managed to move until I found the wall. I then moved around the edge of the wall expecting to find a light switch or the door. Nothing! All I managed to work out was that I was in a long wooden box with no entrance and no exit. It was completely bare. Oh my gosh, I was going to suffocate.

Then I heard a noise, a kind of scuffing and scratching. Then nothing. I held my breath and listened intently for the noise. This time it was more audible when I heard someone scratching again on the outside of the wooden box. The noise got louder and louder as though someone was trying to break in from the outside. Phew, at last I was going to get out of wherever I was.

"Help. Help. I'm in here!" I shouted as loud as I could.

"Won't be a moment." The reply came swiftly. I'll be with you in just a mo!"

"Where am I?" I asked.

"I'll explain in a jiffy."

"Why am I in a box? It feels like I am in a wooden box."

"You are in a wooden box. But don`t worry. I'll be right with you."

The voice on the other side did not belong to any of the kidnappers and this conversation was so odd that I didn't react immediately to what he said. I woke up in a pitch black room which wasn't a room in the end but a wooden box. And now this guy who was trying to get in from the other side sounded like this was an everyday situation. Of course it's quite normal to wake up in a pitch black box: that explains everything. Yes, yes. Quite normal indeed.

"I am in a box!" I screeched in panic.

A hatch or a door on the side was wrenched open, accompanied by a large creaking noise as some sparks of light raced through the darkness. I squinted and put my hand up to shield my eyes from the light shining through the hole in the box.

"Come on now. Out you come," I heard the voice say in a hurry.

Where the hell am I? What's going on here? I didn't care because under no circumstances did I want to stay any longer in that box, so I squeezed out of the jagged hole into what appeared to be a freshly dug earth tunnel. My head nearly reached the top of the tunnel when I stood up to my full height. I peered down the tunnel and saw that it was dimly lit with small light bulbs suspended from a cable. Everything smelt of damp earth, just like the smell in the garden when digging a hole into the soil.

"Well, that worked well," the voice now said from behind me.

I slowly turned around and found myself facing a brown, furry mole. He was armed with digging tools and a head torch, wore brown overalls and looked at me with a big grin on his dirty face.

"Welcome to the arrivals," he proudly exclaimed. "My name is Sid."

My mouth opened and I barely managed to stammer. "And, and, my, name, name is Connor, Connor Jack... son."

The mole was exactly my size... and it was talking! I collapsed on the ground in a heap and darkness enveloped me again. This was just too much. I don't know how long I was out for but I was woken up by someone gently pushing me.

"Connor. Connor. You really must wake up so we can get moving. It's not good to hang around here for too long. I have deadlines to meet you know."

"Who are you? Am I drunk or is this a dream?" I was just staring at the mole. "Where am I?"

"No, Connor, this is not a dream. My name is Sid, just in case you have forgotten. You are in transition by the way, but don't worry I'm your guide for today. Everything is OK!"

Sid held out his clawed hand to help me up. Up to this moment I had still been hoping for everything to be just a bad dream and that the lights would be put on fully and I would come around to my senses. But there were no lights. There was no bedroom. I felt the warmth of his hand and realised I wasn't dreaming at all. This was obviously real.

"Arrivals to what? Heathrow Airport? Humans usually don't travel in boxes and now you want to be my guide for today. Guiding me where exactly? And what do you mean, transition?" I was now really desperate and shouting at Sid. "You are a mole. Why can you talk?"

"Please calm down, Connor. You are correct on all counts, apart from being at Heathrow Airport, wherever that is. And of course we can speak. How else do you expect moles to communicate? You humans are just so arrogant at times!"

"Err, sorry Sid. I didn't mean to offend you. You must understand that this is an extremely frightening situation for me. I was, where was I? Oh yes, I remember, I was in the back of a van which seemed to have had an accident. And then…? No I can't remember what happened next. I woke up in this box and now I'm standing in a tunnel talking to a mole who just happens to be the same size as me. This is certainly not an everyday experience," I carried on. "And for your information Heathrow Airport is near London."

"London? Never heard of it. Is it a suburb of Lower Molehampton?"

"No. Not really," I said wondering what this was about.

"But don't worry, Connor. Most people react like you," chuckled Sid.

"Aha, don't worry." I slowly moved around to survey where I was. The tunnel was just a little bigger than I was and apparently freshly dug with nothing to support it and a lot of loose earth on the floor. I put my head through the opening of the wooden box again to have a good look at it. It was a large box, very large. "Crikey, this was built for at least twenty people!"

"No, Connor, it's part of the arrivals process. All living beings, dogs, cats, cows and so on, have different sizes. After death they filter down into these boxes and are transformed in the process because it would be impossible for us moles to dig tunnels for full-size humans. And what about horses? Just impossible. Look, Connor

I don't expect you to understand everything at the moment and I'm sure you've got a few questions but we really must get moving now. I have to fulfil my daily quotas or I will be in big trouble."

"Did you just say after death?" I pinched myself to make sure I was alive and could certainly feel the sensation. "And I definitely have more than just a few questions," I added sarcastically. "We are not going anywhere until you start explaining."

"You're the fifth arrival today. I really hate this job because I am the one who has to break the news about being in transition, or even dead. Always! It's really not a very nice job and I have to go to counselling to help me with the stress. I used to be a tunnel digger before, which was much more exciting, but after one mission went terribly wrong a few weeks ago I was demoted to collecting the new arrivals," Sid added rather sadly. "I belong to the box release crew now. Connor, it's a very busy day today and I have a schedule to keep to. I really don't have the time to explain everything to you but what I can tell you is that humans call it death and we call it being in transition. Nobody can really die, Connor, not fully anyhow."

I just stood there with my mouth open, staring at the talking mole.

"Do you know something, Connor? You look rather familiar. I'm sure I've seen you somewhere before but I just can't place it. Strange!"

"And how would you recognise me? I live in a house in Lower Molehampton and not in a tunnel. Yes, in a house. In Trout Lane to be precise," I said with a very sad tone to my voice.

Sid's eyes opened wide, "Did you just say Trout Lane? Number three Trout Lane by chance?"

I decided to ignore what he said because how should he know my house. And anyhow, I could hear, talk, smell and I had the sensation of feeling. I obviously wasn't dead. And what's more I could see myself and I knew who I was. Yes, I was Connor Jackson and I was alive and kicking. Still, this was not a normal day and the only choice I had was to follow the mole to wherever he was guiding me.

"Come on, Connor. Let's get a move on to our transport. We've got to get to the arrivals terminal and have you processed and everything explained to you by those whose job it is to do so."

Sid scuttled very quickly down the tunnel and I had to jog to keep up in the soft earth. After what seemed to be about one hundred metres the roughly dug tunnel joined a much larger tunnel which was much more professionally built with smooth walls, hard floor, wooden supports and permanent lighting. Sid turned left and scurried for a few more minutes before coming to a stop at a crossroads of tunnels. The intersecting tunnel was completely dark again and there was a sign on the wall, which read 'Level 5, Line 4, Station 871'.

"OK, Connor. We've now arrived at the station and just have to wait for our transport shuttle to take us to the arrivals terminal."

I remained silent and just stared into the blackness of the tunnel.

First there was a rattling noise followed by a whooshing sound which announced our transport shuttle. It sounded just like a train arriving in an underground station. The noise was getting louder as the shuttle approached and in the distance I could now make out some lights which were erratically zipping down the tunnel as the shuttle was obviously moving at great speed. I stared in awe at a transparent plastic tube sliding to a dusty stop in front of us, like an aeroplane sliding along on its undercarriage. The tube had red plastic caps screwed to both ends which looked exactly like the plastic tubes we used at work for our pneumatic postal system in the building. I remembered that a few of them went missing a while ago. The cap at the front had a large round hole cut into it and a dirty, dust covered mole with a flying cap and goggles sitting in a seat behind it. The mole wiped the dirt from his goggles and shouted, "This is line four to the Arrivals Hall. Come on, jump in, we haven't got all day you know!"

Sid moved forward and opened a hinged door upwards, allowing access to three rows of two seats. I sat in the seat right next to him in the first row, as he beckoned me to do. The driver turned around, looked at me and said, "Come on, shut the door. It doesn't shut by itself does it now."

"Sorry," I mumbled, and pulled down a handle at the top of the door.

The door closed and the driver turned around again and said, "Gentlemen, remember the health and safety rules down here. Put your seat belt on and also wear the helmet under your seat. Sid, you know the rules so make sure your newbie does what he's told. I don't want any injuries today. Only yesterday we had an injury because a chicken refused to wear the helmet and cut his head on the ceiling. Unbelievable how much time I wasted on the injury report for the authorities; I've really got better things to do. I was lucky to get away with just a reprimand."

Sid showed me how to put on my safety belt. Well, actually I wouldn't call it a safety belt, it was more like a piece of garden rope. Neither would I call the seat a seat, as it seemed to be cut out of a flower pot. And the helmet, well, if you ask me it looked like the metal top of a bottle. In fact, as I looked around everything seemed to be made of trash from my human world — hmmm, strange!

"Hold on, Connor, this is going to be a bumpy ride!"

The driver adjusted his goggles then pressed a button in the cockpit. I was just wondering how this strange contraption worked when a transparent hose above my head, which went from the cockpit to the back of the tube, started shaking and fizzing. I turned around and saw a spark coming out at the end of a cable igniting some sort of fluid in a container. Then the transport tube started shaking wildly with a puff and an explosion as the fluid ignited fully. The driver released a lever and the tube lurched forwards into the darkness getting faster and faster, bouncing off the top, the bottom and the side of the tunnel. I was holding on to my seat with all of my strength as the tube shot down the tunnel at breakneck speed, careering off the round walls. It felt like being in a food mixer and my stomach was churning as my nails dug into my seat and the safety belt tore into my sides. I had absolutely no idea how far we had travelled, or how long and I was very happy that I used this bottle top helmet as my head was heavily smashed against the top of the tube.

"Hold on, landing in a few mins!" shouted the driver above the din of the noise.

He then flicked a switch and the noise at the back suddenly stopped, slowing the tube down immediately. As the tube became steadier in the tunnel the shaking was now not so bad and I saw some light ahead of me. When the driver pulled a lever towards himself, he had to use all of his strength. He was groaning and even left his seat through the effort. The lever was obviously the brake and I could hear something digging into the ground below me when the tube skewed left and right and came to an abrupt halt at a station similar to the one we departed from. We were now at the Station four hundred and eighty-four.

I thought my day had been extremely strange so far, but it was just about to get even stranger. From the tunnel, to my left, a brown dog accompanied by a mole appeared. Both were exactly the same size as me! The mole greeted the driver with a nod of his head, got in the tube and motioned the dog to follow. They sat down next to Sid and me and fastened their seat belts.

"Hello, do you understand what's going on here?" The dog was talking.

"Erm, I was told we are in transition but I don't really know what that means. Or we could be dead! No idea." I looked at the dog with large eyes and apparent disbelief.

"Yes, I think we are actually dead. I was run over by a pickup when I was just crossing the road only a short while after I had successfully caught a duck, so it would appear that we are in fact dead," he slowly replied with a very deep voice, as though he thought carefully about every word he said. "Very sad indeed. I was on my way home and really looking forward to my tasty meal. My name's Ludwig by the way. Nice to meet you."

"Oh, nice to meet you too, Ludwig. I'm Connor. So you do know what's going on now? I mean, are we really dead? But then why can I speak? And you can also speak. Amazing. A dog that can talk!"

"Of course I can talk. I have always been able to talk with all other animals, something you obviously can't do. It's only humans who we can't communicate with. We understand what you are saying but you are incapable of understanding us because humans can only communicate with each other — quite backward if you ask me. In fact, you are the first human who has ever understood what I am saying. Now why is that?" Ludwig asked.

Sid looked at both of us and said, "Don't worry, all of your questions will be answered shortly."

The driver went through the same safety talk and then we were off again, hurtling down the dark tunnels. The only light was the dim beams coming from the front of our tube. At the next stop two more passengers entered our transport. This time a mole accompanied by a duck with a green head and a bright yellow beak.

"You!"

"You!" Ludwig shouted back in surprise.

"You dopy dog! It's because of you that I am here," the duck screamed. "I'm truly scared now. This is not normal and this place is scary. I'm sitting together with a dog, with my mortal enemy. What is happening to me? Have you shrunk or have I grown?"

Ludwig tried to make himself invisible whilst the duck just stared at him in anger.

"Do you two know each other?" I asked the duck.

"Ask him!" replied the duck as Ludwig shrank further into his seat.

"What's your name?"

"My name is Basil and I really shouldn't be here. I need to get back to my river. My family will starve if I don't find them food. Do you know how to get out of here?"

"I'm sorry, Basil. My name's Connor and I am as confused and scared as you are."

The tube careered along at breakneck speed again for what seemed to be an age, numerous other tunnels joined from the left and the right, forming one giant tunnel, enough to fit at least five tubes side by side. It was knocked and bumped left to right as it met other tubes jostling for the first position. Ahead I could begin to see lights and lots of different creatures sitting in the other tubes. A cat, a deer, a cow, sheep, foxes, squirrels, a hedgehog and even a frog. And people too.

I stared in awe at this amazing sight as we all stepped out into a gigantic cavern with tunnels entering from all sides, like the hub of a bicycle wheel with hundreds of spokes. The cavern was huge, so huge that is was like standing in a cathedral looking up at the far away ceiling. That's why there are so many molehills. They naturally need somewhere to put all of the excavated earth!

Every few seconds more tubes came flying into what I would now call a huge railway station. The noise level was nearly unbearable when the tubes stopped with the squealing of brakes and a big thud into the earth, kicking up a big cloud of dust, followed by the screeching of instructions to alight the tubes. I turned around slowly until I had completed a circle trying to take in the most awesome and confusing site ever to meet my eyes. Hundreds of animals, all the same size, swarming around, looking confused and disoriented. What on earth is this place? Is this what death feels like?

"Come on now all of you," shouted Sid. "We must stay together!"

All of a sudden lots of umbrellas popped up in different colours, mostly blue or red with numbers. "Come along with me now! You just need to follow this umbrella."

Sid opened a red umbrella with the number five on it and scurried off with all of us anxiously following him through the crowds. A sheep bumped into me frantically trying not to lose its umbrella. "Oh sorry," it said and was then pushed or pulled in another direction.

Then a chicken pushed me. "Out of my way, human. Not so special now are you!" I also saw a man in long white robes and a jet-black beard. We briefly looked at each other with recognition in our eyes as we passed, frantically trying to keep up with our designated umbrella.

The mole bumped, knocked and pushed his way through the crowd. It took my best to keep up with him, followed by the dog and the duck. It wasn't easy because he looked the same as all of the other moles so I tried to keep my eyes fixed on the red number five umbrella. When I lost sight of it for a moment, I stopped to scan the crowd to find our umbrella again. A colourfully dressed woman was not paying any attention at all to where she was going. She was just staring into her smartphone and stabbing away at it. "No damn connection," she said brushing past me.

"Connor, come on, we're in a rush," I heard Sid's voice through the racket.

Ah, there he was and off we were again. Eventually, we reached the wall of the cavern. Below a red sign with the number five on the wall was a smaller tunnel. This was where Sid led us.

"Phew, made it. Not far to go now. We're off to your arrivals briefing and instructions for the rest of the day!" Sid was panting from the exertion. "Follow me!"

Before I followed him into the tunnel, I turned around to have another look at these spectacular scenes. I had never seen so many people, animals, beings, call them what you like, together in one place, standing shoulder to shoulder. Not too far away to my right, some moles were herding a lot of animals directly towards a conveyor belt. Mostly cows, sheep, chickens and pigs. Above the conveyor belt I saw a sign — The Factory.

"Come on, Connor, must go now," Sid shouted out to me. "Just be happy that you are not heading for that conveyor belt," he added very seriously.

"Why? Where does it go, Sid?" I asked.

"Oh, don't worry yourself with that. It will all be explained soon. Come along now."

We followed Sid along the tunnel, passing by two other moles who were pushing a trolley with a block of salt on it and numerous doors with signs above them along the way. 'Lost Property', 'Counselling', 'Job Interviews', 'Massage', 'Dog Hair Stylist' and many others until we eventually reached a sign which read 'Arrivals Briefing'.

"In you come now." Sid opened the door and closed it behind us after briefly wishing us well and saying goodbye for the time being. He didn't follow and we were alone in some sort of briefing room with rows of seats facing a small stage. Well, I say seats — they were really blocks of scrap wood to sit on, but served their purpose at least. The stage was made from an old wooden wine crate.

Everything down here seemed to be made of items from the human world, either from scrap or items that were stolen, just like in the transport shuttle. Over the next few minutes the door opened a few times and various groups came in until all of the seats in the auditorium were taken, maybe around fifty in total. I sat next to Basil with Ludwig behind me, trying to keep out of Basil's way and beady gaze!

The colourfully dressed woman came in with the last group and sat down on the spare seat to my left, still staring into a smartphone. "Damn thing doesn't work. Why can you never get a connection when you really need one?" She said stabbing at the keys on her phone without even looking up.

Eventually she turned around and saw me. "Aaah, at last a human," she said. "I can't believe what's happening here. Can all of this be true? Am I really, well, am I actually dead?"

"Well yes, it seems to be. We are apparently all dead, or in transition as they call it here, although I must say that I always imagined death to be different — kind of the end if you know what I mean, so I am as flabbergasted as you. I'm Connor by the way."

"I'm Vanessa. Vanessa Forsythe-Twyke. How did you get here? What happened to you?"

"I'm not sure. All I can remember is that I was kidnapped, thrown into the back of a van, went for a swim and now I'm here."

"Oh, how awfully exciting," Vanessa replied. "I had just gone to get some fish and chips but was running a little late. Mr Cross's ferry had stopped running for the day so I had no choice but to drive over the bridge in Anglerton. I was driving down the country road, in a bit of a rush I must admit, when a stupid dog with a duck in its mouth ran straight out in front of me. I tried to brake but I lost control of my car when I hit the dog, just missed a willow tree and ended up in the river. Come to think of it, I think I saw the headlights of a van coming the other way."

Basil the duck and Ludwig the dog just stared at Vanessa.

"So it was you who spoiled my dinner," Ludwig said in his customary slow fashion.

"And it was you who caught me in your greedy teeth in the first place." Basil span around and looked at Ludwig menacingly.

"OK, calm down children. I'm sure there will soon be a decent explanation for all of this!"

"Forsythe-Twyke. I know that name. Your mother is the mayoress of Upper Molehampton and also the owner of the Food Factory in Lower Molehampton, isn't she?" I instantly recognized this typical haughty Upper attitude.

***

The prefab building was old but was kept in immaculate condition. The pathway from the road was made of shingle with white-washed stones marking the edges, and the beautifully tended garden was easily a contender for the best garden in the village competition. Sergeant Dawson, the Police Station's occupant, was famous for keeping his area clean and tidy and also the whole area of Lower Molehampton. He boasted about having the lowest crime rate in the whole county, with the last reported crime five years ago, when in one night not only had Mr Tinkers shop but the jam jar factory had been broken into and the whole supply of glass jars reported stolen. This case embarrassed the Sergeant a lot because it remained unsolved with the file still sitting right in the centre of his desk. Who else but the Kennedy brothers were the main suspects of the crime. They were from the next largest town, Anglerton, and they were always the prime suspects for any wrongdoing in the region, but this time there was nothing to implicate the brothers in the crime. In fact, this file was the one and only file relating to any sort of unsolved crime on his desk. That was until yesterday.

Sergeant Dawson was rudely awakened at home late yesterday evening by Mr Lawnsworthy reporting the strangest of events. He claimed that there was a great commotion coming from the house next door, number three Trout Lane. And that there were strangers with black beards and long white robes running around in the street. Had Mr Lawnsworthy been drinking? Quite stroppily, he retorted that he had not been drinking and demanded that the Sergeant came with all haste. Eventually Sergeant Dawson jumped straight out of bed and squeezed his rather rotund body into his uniform, ran down the stairs and jumped into the village police car. It took him a while to find the switch for the sirens as he had never been called out for an emergency before, and he only just managed to get the sirens going when he was a few hundred metres from Trout Lane. A white van came screeching out of the Lane in the opposite direction as he drove around the corner. The driver had a black beard, just like Mr Lawnsworthy had described on the phone. The Sergeant stopped the police car in front of a wildly waving Mr Lawnsworthy, prised his rather large body out of the small car, and stared at number three. The front door was wide open and the front garden a right mess. He gazed around the street and found all of the gardens had been trampled on, plants squashed, bushes destroyed and that there were lots of molehills, especially in Mr Lawnsworthy's garden.

"I see you have a problem with moles, Mr Lawnsworthy!" Sergeant Dawson had never been confronted with such a crime scene before. He was the only policeman in Lower Molehampton and quite out of his depth. Mr Lawnsworthy was so outraged that he started shouting at him until he had no breath left and poor Sergeant Dawson, quite out of his depth, made a call to the nearest police station for support.

When the team of policemen from Anglerton arrived half an hour later, they proceeded to cordon off the street and in particular number three. The house was searched thoroughly but the only notable items of interest were the electronic listening devices in the bedroom which were deemed suspicious and duly entered in the report. There were no obvious signs of robbery with most possessions you might expect to be stolen still in the house. The only thing really missing was the occupant himself and so the policemen assumed that Mr Jackson had possibly been kidnapped. It was strange indeed.

Sergeant Dawson had felt rather surplus to requirements and gone back to bed after the house had been sealed off and an Anglerton police car stationed outside number three Trout Lane. When he got up the next morning, he went to work as normal. Two files were now on his desk: the unsolved robbery from five years ago and the recent disappearance of Mr Jackson. The phone rang when he was sitting there pondering about the evening before, slowly munching on his toast.

"Mrs Forsythe-Twyke, please calm down. I can't understand anything you are saying." Felicity Forsythe-Twyke was frantically screaming into the phone but he could not work out much apart from the word 'daughter'.

It became clear to Sergeant Dawson that a second person had gone missing last night. This time from Upper Molehampton. Mrs Forsythe-Twyke should have called her village policeman but since he was on holiday he had his phone redirected to the police station in Lower Molehampton. The Sergeant wrote down all of the facts and promised to investigate the matter. He knew exactly what to do as it was common knowledge that Vanessa Forsythe-Twyke often crossed the river in the evening to get fish and chips from Lower Molehampton, much to her mother's displeasure. When he left his police station, he first cycled to the fish and chip shop where Mrs Batter remembered 'the stuck-up spoilt brat from across the river' quite clearly. And Mr Cross, the ferryman, confirmed the Sergeant's suspicion. 'The snooty girl from Upper Molehampton had crossed the river to Lower Molehampton late last night but missed the last ferry back home. Sergeant Dawson then decided to follow the route she would have driven to cross the bridge in Anglerton but found nothing out of the ordinary. The old willow tree guarding the river was not going to give up its secret today.

Sergeant Dawson now had three files on his desk, and two missing people. He had unsuccessfully tried to comfort Mrs Forsythe-Twyke, sat down with a loud thud into his office chair and dropped a slice of toast on his desk. When the phone rang for the second time on that day, Sergeant Dawson looked at it long and hard, hoping nothing else had happened. He was wrong. A very sad Mr Rye reported that his dog Ludwig had gone missing from his farmhouse. Normally a missing dog would have been top priority in Lower Molehampton but with two missing people there was not much the Sergeant could do. He expressed his sorrow and promised to keep an eye out for the retriever.

When the phone rang again, Sergeant Dawson picked it up with a sense of dread. What now he thought to himself? He already had four files on his desk: two missing people, one missing dog and the unsolved robbery.

"Sergeant, this is Detective Inspector Samantha James from Anglerton. We might have a lead."

"Oh, go on please, Detective Inspector," replied Sergeant Dawson with great relief and dropped another slice of toast on his desk.

"We found the Kennedy brothers returning to their house at Trout Lane this morning. They were completely covered in mud and we believe that they were involved in the incident last night. They claimed to have no recollection of the past few days at all when we questioned them. Very strange indeed but of course we don't believe them. We won't give up until they tell us the truth."

"It would be a very positive lead if we could link them to Mr Jackson's disappearance and found out what happened to the man. And what about Vanessa Forsythe-Twyke. Do you think they could also be involved in her disappearance?"

"It's still early days, Sergeant, but I agree it's just too much of a coincidence. The events could be connected but we have nothing to go on yet."

"By the way, Detective Inspector, Mr Rye, a local farmer, has just reported his dog missing."

"Look, Sergeant, I know it's sad but we really do not have the resources to start looking for a dog," replied Detective Inspector James rather sharply.

"I know, Detective Inspector, but I just thought two missing people and a missing dog all in a few hours. Rather suspicious if you ask me and any information might prove useful."

"I'm not asking, Sergeant Dawson."

Sergeant Dawson stared glumly at the receiver after the Detective Inspector had hung up rudely and then at the four files on his desk. He picked up his slice of toast but before he could take a bite his phone rang again. This time Sergeant Dawson did not grab for it but let it ring. Whoever it was would give up he thought but the phone rang and rang and rang until he finally decided to answer and find out what file was going to land on his desk next. It transpired that the local hunter wanted to report a block of salt being stolen from the woods. What a day!

Chapter Six
Arrivals

"Quiet please, everyone." A rather stern, overweight and authoritative looking female mole, dressed in a tweed skirt and white blouse, entered the room through the stage door and waddled up on to the stage. Her voice boomed through the room again, "Your arrivals briefing will now commence."

"Welcome back to the Inbound Processing Centre… again," she said with a wry smile.

The mole coughed slightly for more attention but as soon as she said 'again' there was a loud murmuring in the room. I turned around to Vanessa. "Again. I've never been here in my life."

"Me neither," replied Vanessa. "It's all new to me."

"Yes, welcome back to the Inbound Processing Centre, commonly known as the IPC — that's what we call it for short," she thundered. "You are all wondering why I welcomed you to the IPC again and that is because you've all been here many times before but obviously have no recollection of it. As you have no idea what is happening to you I will now proceed with the briefing so please be quiet and listen up!

"I know you haven't had time to digest what has happened to you and will have lots of questions, but please bear with me for the moment and I will explain everything to you. Questions can only be asked at the designated times during this standard briefing. The next group is due to arrive shortly, so it's imperative to finish on time.

"My name is Miss Strictland and I am Head of Arrivals for the Red Five Zone. In my former life as a human I was the headmistress of a boarding school and because of these skills I am ideally suited to be the head of Red Five, which is the training school at the IPC," she explained.

"Briefing item number one — where are you? You are in the world of moles and to be more specific in the IPC. Our job is to collect all arrivals from the surface and bring them here for processing during the transition phase. Or send them directly to the Factory," she added slowly and seriously.

At the mention of the word 'factory' the audience started muttering nervously again.

"Silence," she boomed out. "Briefing item number two — the three spheres of life. You are now all in transition, which some of you might call death, but that isn't technically correct. Death has different meanings for different beings but for us here it is quite simple. From the perspective of your physical body on the surface of the earth, you are indeed dead and no longer exist in that form. Sphere one, that's how we call your physical body down here. It's made of flesh, muscles, organs, tissue and so on. And sphere one is now left behind to decompose. What remains is your original factory setting comprising of your processor and memory and this is the stage you are in now, which is the reason why you are all the same size and can all communicate with each other. I'm sorry to inform you but your former life is over."

"You see, I told you we are dead," I whispered to Vanessa. "But I must admit I never believed in any life after death theories until today. Most strange. I can't remember ever having been here before."

Miss Strictland glared at me and carried on.

"Sphere two is your memory. It can never be destroyed and lasts an eternity. You will have noticed that your memories and functions are intact, but only for the moment. One of the IPC's most important jobs is to separate your memory from your processor — sphere three. Your processor is the sphere which is reprogrammed for the relevant being you will be assigned to. This does not necessarily happen immediately and some of you could remain in transition down here a while longer in the reverted last saved processor setting. This explains why some of you are still wearing clothes —

just in a smaller size now — and you still have your physical properties to see, touch and hear each other."

"May I ask a something, Miss Strictland?" A horse put its front right leg in the air to indicate that he or she would like to ask a question.

"Please do not interrupt," she retorted.

"So, to put it in a nutshell, you are indeed dead as in the physical sense, but your memories and processors are still intact just as they were a few hours ago. You may now ask questions!"

The horse stood up and asked, "I was shot this morning because I was deemed to be old and too expensive to keep. I can't see any bullet holes or damage. Why is that?"

"You have reverted to your factory settings and appear as the last saved processor property before death," she answered gruffly. "Why do I always have to repeat myself? Don't waste my time."

"How did you die, Miss Strictland?" asked a cat.

"Oh me, I was pushed out of a fifth-floor classroom window by some boisterous kids whilst they were playing some sort of game. Awful accident I seem to recall," she replied.

"What a surprise!" whispered Vanessa to me. "Accident. Really?"

"Briefing item number three — the role of moles," the former Head Mistress carried on firmly but added even more seriousness to her voice. "It is our responsibility to administer and run this world below the ground. Administer and run, so what does that mean? Well, basically new beings need to be reassigned to vacant positions and we are responsible for separating their memories from their processors so they can be reprogrammed for these other assignments. At the same time, we must make sure that their memories aren't lost after processing but stored down here for an eternity, and for that we need lots of space. Also personnel, planning and logistics. Tunnels need to be dug, warehouses built to store the memories, we need food down here and doctors, shops and much more. Moreover, all of the excavated earth has to be deposited on the surface. I'm sure you've all seen the molehills on the surface, haven't you? Unknown to creatures on the surface we pretty much have a parallel world down here and it all needs to be managed. That's what we do. The moles manage and provide political direction for all of you. Everyone is equal down here and you will want for nothing. Just do, say and think what you are instructed and you will get on just fine."

"That sounds somehow like a threat if you ask me," I whispered to Vanessa.

Miss Strickland stared at blank faces looking at her. "I can see you all understand that. Good!"

"I have a question," said Ludwig, standing up.

"Sure to be a stupid one," whispered Basil, just loud enough for us all to hear.

"What is a processor?"

"How did you know how to bark? How did you naturally know how to interact with other dogs?"

"I don't know, Miss Strictland. I could just do it," replied Ludwig. "I'm a dog so of course I can bark."

"Exactly. You knew how to bark when you were born because you were assigned a processor with the appropriate features. And this processor was programmed for a dog by moles. But not only that. We have a very advanced system here. A dog is not just a dog. Each breed of dog is processed with its own features. A Labrador, for example, is programmed to be gentle when holding things in its mouth. You were born knowing how to be a retriever just like a human is born with the capability of talking and writing, a chicken can lay an egg and a cat instinctively knows how to catch a mouse."

"See, I'm a gentle creature, so it wasn't so bad after all!" Ludwig patted Basil on the head.

"If it wasn't for you, I'd still be swimming around on my river with my family," blurted out Basil. "But no, you had to catch me. And then you didn't even eat me — no! You got us killed by a car. Do you know how disgraceful that is for a duck? I just hope nobody else knows up there!"

Miss Strictland coughed and looked at everyone disapprovingly. There was immediate silence.

I stood up. "Who decides what processor is assigned to what being?"

"The moles of course. We manage everything," replied Miss Strictland.

"Yes, but how can you produce enough processors. I mean the population of animals and humans is continuously growing."

"That is not true. The surface population cannot exceed the number of processors we have — it's not possible. You might believe that, but it is certainly not the case. We have a certain allocation of processors, I think it is one million and this is fixed. Sometimes there are more of one being and less of another. That is all based on the allocation. We also have a reserve stock of processors for peak seasons. Turkeys and ducks for the human Christmas time for example," explained Miss Strictland.

Vanessa and Basil stood up at the same time to ask a question.

"You first," said Miss Strictland, pointing to Basil.

"What is the connection between ducks and Christmas? I don't understand."

"That's easy. Humans eat ducks, and especially so at their festive season of Christmas."

"You would eat me?" It obviously never occurred to Basil that humans could also be his mortal enemies the same way as dogs. He moved further away from me when he sat down and looked at me with a question in his face that needed an immediate answer.

"Oh no, surely not," I said embarrassed by the question.

"Well I would," Vanessa said sharply. "And now my turn, Miss Strictland. What is the allocation?"

"The allocation is the number of processors for certain beings we are instructed to programme for reassignment. We receive this from a higher authority?"

"But…" Vanessa started but was abruptly cut off.

"Enough. No more questions on this subject. Any other questions?" she shouted.

"You mentioned one million processors. But there are far more creatures in the world than one million," I stated.

"So you are the clever one?" said Miss Strictland looking at me. "But unfortunately you are quite wrong. Our world consists of Upper Molehampton, Lower Molehampton and Anglerton only. One million processors are clearly enough."

"But what about London?"

"There is no place called London. It doesn't exist," Miss Strictland retorted, obviously feeling uncomfortable.

"Yes, it does. I was there only last month. And so does New York, Berlin and Paris to name but a few."

Miss Strictland just looked at me with menacing eyes and simply said, "No, no and no again."

"What on earth is she going on about?" I whispered to Vanessa feeling rather confused.

"No idea but I suggest you keep quiet for the moment. I think you've upset her."

"What is Lower Molehampton?" Ludwig asked us quietly.

"Lower Molehampton is where the rabble live," said Vanessa sarcastically.

"Briefing item number four — what happens from here." Now Miss Strictland was in her routine again. "There is a lot of work to be done running this place down here. Therefore, we may well need some of you for a longer period of time and offer numerous jobs at the IPC. For example, we have clerical positions, jobs in the supply chain, as chefs, drivers or tunnellers available. You may apply for a position or be selected directly by us — our standards are high and we do not accept everyone." Miss Strictland looked at Basil and raised her eyebrows in a look of displeasure.

"She's got your cards marked," I whispered jokingly to Basil.

"Don't worry, I've got her cards marked too," he said with a mischievous grin.

"You will be split into two groups from here. Group one is assigned to the Factory and group two is for debriefing. During debriefing you will be questioned about your experiences from your recent assignment and based on that we will then decide what to do with you. If we have no further need for you, your processors will be reprogrammed and you will be sent back on another assignment," she explained. "I'm now going to read out a list of names so please identify yourself when you hear your name and stand up."

"Excuse me, Miss Strictland," I nervously shouted out. "I have one more question. May I?"

"If you must. But make it quick," she curtly responded.

"When I am reassigned, will I keep my name and memory?"

"My, you really don't understand this. Of course not. Your memory will be separated from your processor and then the processor reprogrammed. Only a factory default processor remains which is then reprogrammed for the necessary being, for example you could be reprogrammed as a hedgehog and will have no recollection of your former life. I have already explained this. However, it doesn't always work one hundred percent correctly and some processors are not fully wiped which means that some memory may be kept in the next assignment. This is why some humans believe in reincarnation or in a déjà vu. However, we have refined our technology and it doesn't really happen anymore. Understand now?"

Vanessa and I looked at each other with sadness in our eyes. "Sounds pretty much like death if you ask me."

Miss Strictland held out her clipboard and read out the names; only a few of us remained seated including myself, Vanessa, Basil and Ludwig. We were all alarmed and fearing the worst when suddenly the door next to the stage opened and five moles came in. They were all armed with batons and wore riot protection equipment. "OK, would all of you standing please make your way to the door and follow the moles to your next station," ordered Miss Strictland. "Quiet now please!"

Even though some animals tried to ask questions, they dutifully did what they were told and shuffled out of the auditorium. Only a cow tried to protest insistently but was grabbed roughly by two moles and forcefully dragged away, kicking and shouting obscenities.

I didn't know yet if this was good or bad. Miss Strictland returned to the stage and stared at us slowly and sternly. My sense of fear was high and rising. When I looked around, I estimated that there were about fifteen remaining. "OK, you are the lucky ones. The others have just been taken to the Factory for onward processing. You have been selected for reassignment or a job and will now be taken away for kitting out and shown your accommodation. Expect to stay with us for a while."

"Miss Strictland," Vanessa said.

"Yes, my dear," replied Miss Strictland, surprisingly kindly.

"What does the Factory actually mean? Where are they going?"

"Oh, that's an easy question to answer. You see, our duty is to supply the Factory and keep up with the demand and these animals have been designated for the food chain." She said with a large grin. "Remember, Christmas is not too far away and the human demand for meat is very high. We must work much faster down here now and reassign them immediately! So, we actually bypass the debriefing at this time of the year. It's not worth it anyhow as many of these animals will return to us in a few weeks. Generally, once you are in the food chain you remain in the food chain. We simply turn them around and send them back. It's a rather fast-moving business so we even installed a conveyor belt recently to speed up the process. Does that answer your question dear?"

Vanessa gulped. "Err, yes, I believe it does. But how do you know how many animals are needed?"

"We receive instructions and execute the orders. Supply and demand I believe my dear."

The door next to the stage opened again and a mole entered the room. Miss Strictland introduced him as our mentor for the next phase. Vanessa, Ludwig, Basil and I were still together, as though fate deemed it this way, along with the remaining animals. There was a hedgehog, a pheasant, two cats, two hamsters, a cow, a horse, two pigs and a large black and brown Doberman Pinscher. The dog in particular raised my interest. It wasn't the athletic appearance; it was more its behaviour. I have had the feeling of being watched over the previous weeks in Trout Lane and there it was again. Every time I glanced at the dog it quickly moved its head away in a different direction confirming my suspicion. This dog was watching me. We all walked out of the room on Miss Strictland's command to await our fates. When I turned around, I saw the door through which we had entered the room some time ago open again. A new intake was now arriving for their briefing.

***

Our mentor was called Fraser. He was dressed in immaculately pressed blue overalls with razor sharp creases on the arms and trousers with shoes which shined like mirrors.

"Fall in behind me you lot," he barked very militarily to us. "We've got lots of admin to do."

We all sprang into action, helped of course after watching the other animals being assigned to the food chain. It certainly was a good motivation when the choice was a warming winter casserole or following Fraser, who started marching off down a well-lit tunnel signposted for the 'Kitting Department'. Two rabbits pushing a trolley with a block of salt walked passed us in the opposite direction.

We were now in a very professionally built area — the tunnel surface had been smoothly plastered and painted white. The lighting was accurately attached to the ceiling with plastic channels hiding the cables and there were proper signs hanging on small chains indicating where to go. This all seemed very permanent and was just like being in an underground system in a city. Despite the professional building work and built in ventilation shafts for air, there was no fresh air, far from it. The whole place smelt dank and earthy.

"OK all of you. My name is Fraser and as Miss Strictland has already told you I'm your mentor and guide during your time at the IPC. I'm open to questions at all times so just fire away," he now said kindly.

"I've got many questions," Basil shouted out from the back of the line as he struggled to keep up with the pace.

"Fire away then," Fraser shouted back.

"What's your background, Fraser?"

"Well, in my previous life I was assigned as a human and had a long military career before joining the IPC. There was a position free as a mentor, which I was perfectly suited for due to my work experience and reassigned as a military mole. And I love this assignment and have never looked back," he said proudly with his chest pushed out as far as he could. "Being reassigned as a mole from another life form also means that you get to keep your memory. It is the pinnacle of anyone's life and it is an honour to be chosen."

"What did Miss Strictland mean about separating memory and processor? It's been a very long day and I really have difficulties understanding this concept!" I said.

"I know there are lots of things you want to know and that is indeed one of the most commonly asked questions. All I can say for now is you will find out about that first thing in the morning before we start the debriefing phase. It's far too complicated to go into detail now and would only lead to even more questions, some of which I can't answer myself. What's important now is for you to get your kit and accommodation and something to eat. You must all be famished after such a long day. Don't worry all of you. All in good time," said Fraser, in a warm fatherly manner.

"Fraser, something else is puzzling me!" I said with a concerned look on my face.

"Of course, ask away!"

"Miss Strictland mentioned one million living beings in the world. But one million is far too low. In reality there are billions and everyone knows that."

"That's a typical human mistake and to be frank I asked the same when I arrived. But Miss Strictland is correct — there are no more than one million living beings and that is it. I'm afraid humans have some rather strange understandings of the world," Fraser answered with a slightly sad look on his face as though he knew he was telling a lie.

"But if you still have your memory then surely you know London?" I asked.

"Nope, never heard of it. Come along now," he shouted trying to get away from the question.

"Hmmm, that can't be right," whispered Vanessa in my ear.

"I agree but I am sure we will find out."

"Now, this is a confusing place for new arrivals because all of the tunnels look very similar and it's very important that we stay together and that you remember where you are. You are free to move around but you must stay in Red Five Zone and on no account are you to leave Level four unless you want to end up on the end of a fork! OK, we're nearly there now," said Fraser, rounding a bend in the tunnel. "Just file in here and go to the counter and tell them your name," ordered Fraser.

'Kit Issue and Returns.' The sign on the door ahead of us was simply titled. I was at the front and so I went in first as instructed. Behind a long wooden counter was a huge storeroom with rows upon rows of shelving and large racks going back into the darkness as far as I could see. A fat mole with round glasses and a name badge on his brown overalls waddled up to the counter. "Name?"

"Connor, Connor Jackson," I stuttered nervously.

"Connor, Connor Jackson," repeated the mole, writing on a note pad at the same time.

"No, just Connor Jackson."

"Right Connor, my name's Mr Rawlinson. Let's get you what you need."

"OK boys, give me a male human training kit." Judging by the sound, definitely more than one mole was scurrying around removing equipment from the shelves and throwing it into what sounded like containers, then moles appeared from all of the aisles simultaneously sliding empty food cans towards the counter with different sorts of equipment. Then the others came in and I heard the moles shouting out for a duck training kit, a dog training kit and finally a female human kit.

"OK. Let's go through to make sure it's all here and you can sign for it, " commanded Mr Rawlinson as he started emptying the containers onto the counter.

"Connor, go and get yourself a kit bag and shopping trolley from over there to put all of your equipment in."

Against the wall were rows of small shopping trolleys, exactly the type you find in a toy shop and right next to the trolleys was a big basket with a sign 'Kit Bags', with lots of individual socks. Was this the answer to my missing socks at home? Can't be. Then again, just like in the tube and in the briefing room everything down here was from the surface. But how would the moles get my socks?

Mr Rawlinson was still busy with my equipment. First a shovel and then a pillow landed on the counter which he ticked on the list. "One shovel, human type," he said. "One pillow, human," he added. He carried on and issued me a blanket, bed sheets, goggles, a note pad, a pen, red overalls, a miner's helmet, a plate, some cutlery, a watch, ten coins and finally a map of the tunnel system.

"OK that's it. Sign here," he indicated with a pen.

We were all issued with the same equipment but in different versions, human, duck, dog and also for the other animals in our group. I signed and squeezed my equipment in the sock I picked out of the basket. A sad looking mole was standing right at the end of the counter where a sign said 'Kit Returns'. He was handing in his equipment and I was sure it was Sid, the friendly mole who released me from that box some hours ago. I wasn't really sure as all of the moles looked the same to me, but then he looked across and nodded.

"Next group please," Mr Rawlinson commanded the next group waiting nervously outside.

"Let's go to your rooms now." We all set off again behind Fraser but this time pushing our shopping trolleys in front of us along the smooth surface of the tunnel floor. But this time the journey was confusing as we took a lot of turns. The tunnels were all immaculately clean, rather sterile and extremely well-built. All walls were white, the only decoration were signs and every now and then some posters with political messages like 'Equality is the key in line'. Another one declared 'Moles guarantee equality'. We passed by lots of different rooms — hospital, library, human restaurant and also one for cats, foxes, chickens, ducks, dogs and many more. There was something here for absolutely everyone. The different animals were wearing either blue or red overalls, some carrying shovels and some notepads and pens. I looked around in awe at this strange place I had ended up in. I never imagined death to be like this.

A quick glance behind me and there it was again. The large black and brown Doberman Pincher was right behind me, following my every step, its beady eyes fixed on me like glaring car head lights. Why was this dog showing so much interest in me?

The accommodation area was a massive warren of interlocking tunnels with room numbers.

"Here we are," gasped Fraser a little out of breath after the long march. "All of your rooms are next to each other. It's been a very long and stressful day for you so you should try to get some rest now. We will meet for breakfast at seven tomorrow morning. Please wear your red overalls. And after breakfast I will take you through the programme and explain the debriefing before you go in."

"May we walk around," I asked Fraser.

"Yes, sure but just don't go too far, remember not to leave Red Five Zone and to stay at Level four. Use the map I gave you as it's a trifle confusing down here for newcomers. Well, you're not really a newcomer! You've been here thousands of times before but you just don't know about it," he said with a grin on his face.

"I was issued with ten coins," said Vanessa. "Why do we need money?"

"Us moles make sure you are all well-catered for. You will see that there are things to buy down here to make your lives nicer. You don't earn any money but every week you are given a ration of coins and everyone gets the same. We believe in a happy, and above all equal environment."

Room forty-seven thousand, eight hundred and sixty-seven. Before entering my room, I took a quick glance to my left and right. The dog was in the room directly to my right, confirming my suspicion, and Vanessa to my left. The room was small and round with smooth white walls — just like everything else down here. The only light was from a dim light bulb in the centre of the room. The bed was basic and made from a wooden box which looked strangely like one of those boxes you would find fruit in at a supermarket and a plastic cupboard I would expect to find in a doll's house was

standing against the wall. Another sock was on my bed —
presumably my sleeping bag. "I sure hope it has been washed," I
whispered under my breath. How on earth did they get all of these
things down here?

I took off the clothes I had been wearing since the kidnapping
and put on my red overalls. This was the first moment I had, for a
while, to reflect on everything that had recently happened to me.
The molehill, the discovery of the communication under my house
and the kidnapping. And now this. I was surrounded by animals all
the same size as me and we were all supposed to be dead. I have
never really thought about it much. But this wasn't how I expected
death to be — I could feel, smell, touch and think — I had all of my
senses. I slowly unpacked my equipment and sat on the wooden bed
and rubbed my eyes trying to convince myself this was all real.

"Hello, Connor. I hope I'm not disturbing you," said Vanessa
while knocking on the door and poking her head in.

This was the first time I had chance to really look closely at
Vanessa since we had bumped into each other in the arrivals hall
earlier this day. I hadn't really paid much attention to anything until
now due to the circumstances but now started laughing for the first
time in a while. She was wearing a velvet green knee-length skirt, a
thick yellow self-knitted woollen jumper, bright red stockings and
dirty wellington boots. There was a lot of bad news in the last hours
but now I really couldn't help myself.

"What's so funny," she asked. "I can't think of any reason for
amusement down here at the moment!"

"It's just, well..." I chuckled. "Your combination of clothes is
rather, how shall I put it, colourful!"

"I'm a Forsythe-Twyke," she said looking sternly towards me
down her nose. "I am different and prefer to show how unique I am.
Oh, my mother hates it by the way. She would much prefer that I
dressed like all of the other posh people in Upper, but there is a lot
she doesn't like about me," adding quietly. "And these overalls are
so ghastly," she continued. "This just isn't me, wearing the same
clothes just like everybody else. Almost like in prison. And I'm not
the same as anyone here. I'm from Upper Molehampton I would like

to add, and we are certainly different than the others. Not at all equal," she said rather haughtily.

"I am sorry Vanessa. I'm from Lower Molehampton, one of 'the others' from across the river!" I purposefully put a lot of emphasis into 'the others'.

"Well, Connor, I suppose it's not your fault, is it?"

"I fear, Vanessa, that coming from Upper Molehampton doesn't count for much down here."

"Yes, I think you might just be correct on that point. I never thought I would say that to someone from Lower Molehampton," she said rather tearily.

I had heard a lot about the snobbish attitude from the people living in Upper Molehampton, even though I never really had any close contact with any of them. Vanessa was actually the first one I have ever spoken to at any length. A petite young woman who seemed fragile on the inside, trying to hide behind her exterior defence of colours and her haughty attitude, was standing in front of me. Coming from Upper Molehampton she was probably brought up with this attitude. It wasn't even her fault and I actually started feeling a little sorry for her. "You know, Vanessa, if you could make up your mind and change into these ghastly overalls we could have a walk around to get to know our bearings and see what there is without you ending up on a fork. I need to get out of this confined place," I said to her with a caring voice.

"Don't say a thing," she said when she returned wearing her red overalls.

We were looking at our maps which only covered an area simply called Red Five Zone — Level four. It was extremely confusing as it consisted mainly of numbers rather that names, like I was used to on the surface. No nice names like Trout Lane. Also, we had difficulties finding out our location because the whole map was a maze of thousands of tunnels. Eventually I found a tunnel named forty-seven and a half thousand to forty-seven thousand nine hundred and ninety-nine and judged that we had to be in that tunnel due to my room number being forty-seven thousand eight hundred and sixty-seven. I looked right and as far as I could see we were standing in a long, straight tunnel with what seemed like hundreds of doors on both sides. I turned around to look in the other direction and exactly at that moment the dog came out of my adjoining room, looked at me menacingly and sat down right outside its room.

The dog's presence and its apparent interest in me was beginning to get a little annoying so I decided to introduce myself and break the ice. "Hello, my name is Connor Jackson. Nice to meet you," I said formally but the dog just kept on staring at me.

"Well, erm, maybe you can't speak my language. What's your name?"

The dog got up slowly. "I know who you are and of course I can speak your language. In fact, we all can. My name is Cleopatra!" Her voice was growling and with that short burst of communication, she sat back down again, licked her mouth a few times and continued glaring at me.

Before I could say another word both Ludwig and Basil burst out of their rooms and into the tunnel. They looked at us and simply said in unison: "We are coming with you!" All four of us looked at our maps and went off down the tunnel to see what awaited us and guess what, passed two rabbits pushing a trolley with a block of salt on it. Strange. Why all the salt and where was it coming from?

***

The President and the Colonel met once again in the Ministers' grand conference room. As usual the President was finely dressed, wearing a black pin-striped suit, a light pink shirt and a black bowler hat. When he entered the room, he was using a downturned umbrella as a walking stick with the click-clack of the umbrella's metal tip reverberating around the room.

"Colonel Pickle. Do you have the Professor?"

"Actually, not quite, Mr President, but nearly," said the Colonel.

"What do you mean by not quite? As you've called this meeting I presumed you have something of importance to report. Either you do, or you don't," boomed the President.

"Hmm, he is within our grasp but there was an unexpected problem. Our stake out team watching the target house was obviously not the only team at the place. It also transpired that the man at number three had been intercepting our signals and tried to communicate with us which forced us into action much earlier than planned. We managed to take the man captive but it all turned rather messy and became a little too public when the other team also tried to kidnap the target."

"Yes, but do you have the Professor?" asked the President again.

"No, but we are sure that Mr Jackson, that is the man at number three, knows the whereabouts of the Professor," replied the Colonel confidently.

"Well, Colonel, as you have Mr Jackson under your protection why don't you just simply ask him?"

"That is not so simple anymore, Mr President," responded the Colonel slowly. "The thing is. The thing is…"

"Oh, spit it out, Colonel."

"There was an accident whilst we were moving safe houses. I'm afraid Mr Jackson and the van ended up in a river and he is now down here in the Arrivals. He is in transition."

"Are you telling me that Mr Jackson is down here with us and the Professor is somewhere unknown up there? Great. It couldn't get worse, could it, Colonel?"

"I'm afraid that is the situation at the moment, Mr President. But Mr Jackson is due for debriefing tomorrow, so we will very soon find out the whereabouts of Professor Wingnut and close this case."

"Colonel. I trust you are correct this time. Mr Jackson cannot know anything about the Professor and I want him watched every minute. Day and night. Do you understand me?" ordered the President.

"Yes sir. I already have it in hand. Our Special Operations team has been active from the moment the Professor was reported stolen and Cleopatra, our very loyal and robust asset, has been watching him ever since. Unfortunately, we also expect the thieves to know where he is. They will most likely try to get to him as well, but Cleopatra will report any contact anyone makes with Mr Jackson.

We might be able to kill two birds with one stone," said Colonel Pickle confidently.

"Very good, Colonel. But do we actually know anything about the other team at number three. Who are these people and who are they working for?"

"No, Sir. During the operation someone obviously called the police. When we heard the siren, we had to get out of there very quickly and did not have the opportunity to capture the other people. Nor did we have time to search the house, that would have been far too dangerous."

"That is unfortunate. But at least you were able to capture Mr Jackson and get him to safety. I now presume we will get him to tell us where the jar with the Professor is and then we can focus on smoking out our thieving mole and his conspirators."

"You are quite correct, Sir."

"But we should also make another effort and search the house. It would save us a lot of time and I am sure the other side are also not being idle, whoever they are. Can we not get a human in there?" asked the President.

"I thought of that, but the police have sealed off the house and put a guard outside. We tried to infiltrate one of our agents, but it was hard for the birds to find their targets. I mean the birds on our side of course. It is a rather confusing situation because there are a lot of birds and nobody knows who is on what side. There is bird poo everywhere and the policemen spend most of the time in their car."

"I understand. But, Colonel, one last thing. At the moment we have no control of the activities on the surface. The system is obviously open to abuse and whoever the traitor is must be a minister because they also have access to the Special Operations assets. I never thought anyone down here would cross us. We must wake up to the danger that someone is attempting a coup and our lax system plays right into their hands. It is of utmost importance to implement a system of double checks with a few selected ministers authorised only."

"Yes, sir."

"This situation must not be allowed to happen again. Time is of the essence now, Colonel, and we have pressing matters to solve. Keep the house watched and report back to me as soon as the debriefing is over. And, Colonel, be careful in the debriefing. Mr Jackson cannot suspect anything. We must get to the Professor first. Before the mole does."

***

The stranger and the Colonel once again met in the dark and damp tunnel.

"Colonel Bacon, I truly hope you have something positive to report. Do you have the Professor?"

"Errrm, no, but we are close, very close. We suspect that he is in number three's shed," said the Colonel uneasily.

"Still in the shed of number three? He's been there for far too long. Are you telling me that nobody has been able to retrieve him?" retorted the mystery voice angrily. "What about the humans we sent into action?"

"The humans did not turn out to be as expected. I'm afraid they were not quite up to the task."

"Well, Colonel. What happened and what is happening?"

"The Kennedy brothers from Anglerton had been watching number three for some time and our dogs were also very active and tried to get into the shed on a number of occasions. Unfortunately, they were continuously disturbed by annoying stray cats who woke up the whole neighbourhood with their loud meowing. Presumably the other side also trying to get to the Professor. The problem is that we do not know for sure if these cats are real or special ops. All rather confusing I must say."

"Don't waste my time with your lame excuses. Tell me something real, Colonel. I'm listening."

"It appeared that the man at number three had some sort of listening equipment and overheard some of our traffic. We had to make an immediate decision when he then tried to get in contact with us. However, when the Kennedy brothers turned up to get a hold of the man they found their target being kidnapped by a team of men in white robes and black beards."

"Yes, and now? Do I need to prize every answer out of you?"

"I am sorry, but it is all rather confusing I must say. The Kennedy brothers were just too slow I'm afraid. After a brief and, unfortunately a rather public tussle, the target was taken away in a van by the other men. When the police turned up, the Kennedy brothers had to scarper and were not able to lay chase."

"So, Colonel, you actually have no good news to report, just bad news," shouted the stranger through the grate. "And what about the Kennedy brothers? What if they are captured by the police?"

"We have already dealt with the Kennedy brothers. They were deactivated and know nothing about what happened. But just after Connor Jackson was kidnapped, they thought enough commotion had been made and it wouldn't make a difference. So they went into the shed to look for the glass jar."

"So we now have the jar, Colonel?"

"Well, no. They didn't have much time before the police entered the garden. The shed was a bit of a mess and I'm afraid they couldn't find the jar in a hurry. I can understand if the situation sounds bad but…"

"Bad! Bad! It's not bad, Colonel. It's a disaster. And can we rule out that the Professor might be somewhere else?"

"No we actually cannot. But it's not all bad. We now know who the target is and most importantly where he is. His name is Connor Jackson and he is currently in the Arrivals — a bit of a long story and you don't need to know all of it. The important thing is — he is here, and he is due for debriefing tomorrow."

"How in God's name did you find that out, Colonel?"

"Cleopatra, our asset in the Special Operations team, has reported back in. She witnessed the whole event at number three and then managed to pick up Mr Jackson's trace, followed him to a farmhouse and then down here."

"Hmmm, it sounds a little less than absolutely disastrous now. So, we know that Mr Jackson is down here. We also know that Mr Jackson might have the Professor or at least knows his whereabouts," said the stranger menacingly. "Do we have anyone loyal in the debriefing team? I am sure the others will also be aware that Mr Jackson is here, and they will also know that someone else is looking but they don't know who we are. We must keep our identities secret, Colonel."

"Yes, sir. We most certainly do. We have a loyal scribe and she has been assigned to Mr Jackson's debriefing tomorrow. She will be able to report back to us and we will just have to be quicker," responded the Colonel.

"Yes, we must. The others will not be idle. Both sides know of the others' intentions and we are both looking in the same place and watching the same person. It must be difficult to tell who is on our side on the surface."

"You are quite correct, Sir. It is a confusing situation."

"We should send a team into number three, Colonel Bacon? Some humans, we must be quick about it though?"

"I have thought of that but unfortunately the police have sealed off the house and are watching it. I have tried to infiltrate the police team but not had any success so far. Our birds are trying to land their poo on one of the policemen but unfortunately, they have retreated into their car which is already absolutely splattered. The other side are obviously also trying to get someone into the house."

"Colonel."

"Yes sir?"

"If we get caught, we will all be sent to the Factory."

Chapter Seven
The Pub

Close together and in a straight line, we started walking down the tunnel, followed not too discreetly at a distance by Cleopatra. At a T-junction we thoroughly studied our maps again and decided to turn left into a tunnel which apparently led into what looked like the centre of the area and into larger tunnels. We just kept walking through another tunnel where everything looked the same, apart from the fact that I recognised some of the rooms which we must have walked past when Fraser took us to our accommodation. The next junction came out into an even larger tunnel, much larger than the ones we had been walking. Just like in other areas, this tunnel was very professionally built with smooth concrete walls, clean paint, cables, lighting, pipes and signs. But it was still different to the others. Not only because it was bigger, but the air smelt slightly fresher too. There was a constant draft and I felt this fresh air finding its way to us through some vents in the ceiling. Not much though. It was still damp and musky down here. Also, this tunnel was painted a very light blue, and obviously important enough to be indicated on the map, it presumably meant some sort of main tunnel. The map also indicated that this tunnel met with a red tunnel not too far away. And just like Oxford Street in London this red tunnel went straight across the whole centre of the map. Many more creatures were going through the tunnel, most of them going in this direction. So we decided it was best to simply follow the crowd — a man, followed by a woman, followed by a dog and finally a duck. It must have looked a strange sight indeed as we fell in behind some sheep.

"I've heard that there is a new supply of gas for us tonight and music. Going to be a great night and I'm sure it will be packed. Let's get moving so we don't have to queue."

"A great night with gas and music?" Vanessa looked confused.

Vanessa, Ludwig, Basil and I stood in the middle of the junction and gazed in amazement at the scene around us. We had come out on what really looked like a main thoroughfare of the mole world. Just as my map indicated, the tunnel we had entered was painted a light red and it was huge. A busy shopping street with the hustle and bustle you might expect from Oxford Street in London, just without the buses and the day light. There were flashing lights, billboards, posters, glamorous decorations with flowers and even outside cafes on Mole Boulevard. Yes, this time there was a street sign with a name on it — not just a number. A professionally made street sign made of metal, produced by the sign making shop on Mole Boulevard. Across the street a digital billboard was flashing political messages like — 'Equality in Life Provided by Moles' or 'Superiority is a Myth'. The moles really seemed to have everything under control here.

The tunnel was cram packed with lots of different animals and humans, carrying shopping bags, takeaways and coffee to go. Buildings were cut into the tunnels, meticulously mirroring life on the surface with traditional looking shop fronts. In sheer amazement we walked passed a chemist, a supermarket, a cow grooming boutique, a sheep shearing service, a Chinese takeaway and a massage parlour. Something for everybody seemed to be down here and Miss Strictland was not wrong when she stated that this was a parallel world. But she was also wrong as it was not all the same down here. There was no real fresh air as it cannot simply be produced, so the dank and earthy smell was everywhere and at times overpowering. So were the noises of all of the different creatures mingling and talking with each other. Just imagine talking cows — completely unrealistic.

But just imagine there was a parallel world directly below your feet and you never knew about it. This visual sensation of us all being the same size was one of the most surreal experiences. I still had my sense of smell, taste, sight and hearing and they were all working perfectly well as far as I was concerned. But seeing so many things that were the same or very similar to the surface was extremely difficult to comprehend. I therefore added another sense — the sense of amazement.

"Look, over there," I said pointing to a wooden sign above the shop. "There's a shop called Mr Tinker's. Unbelievable! Just like the one in Lower Molehampton."

"This must just be a coincidence, Connor," retorted Vanessa. "How could it look the same? It's a ghastly shop with disgusting pigeons crapping their loads all over the village. Well, at least down here he cannot keep these horrible birds, can he?"

"I must have a look inside!" I was so excited and headed off for the store instantly with the others following after me, Vanessa rather reluctantly.

The doorbell rang to alert the shop keeper of our presence as we entered through a red wooden door with a glass panel and windows either side of the door with old wooden frames. This shop was a replica of Mr Tinker's store in Lower Molehampton with an identical sign; even the paint was the same colour. Just the goods on offer were different and everything was on a smaller scale.

"My goodness," he exclaimed. "Connor Jackson?"

A man wearing a brown knee-length workman's coat came out from the back of the store and stood behind his counter. This was clearly too much. My mouth dropped open and I just stared at him.

"Well, are you?" asked the man again.

"Yes, I suppose I am. I am Connor Jackson. Most certainly." I said stammering back.

"You know this man, Connor?" asked Vanessa, frowning.

"Yes, yes, I do, Vanessa, and you might know him too. This is Mr Tinker. Mr Tinker Senior from Lower Molehampton. But he died some years ago and so his son took over his shop."

"No, Connor, I don't know any Mr Tinker. I do not go shopping in Lower Molehampton. And why should I? We have wonderful boutiques on our side of the river but maybe our caretaker would know him," she said, again sounding very snobbish but I wasn't really paying any attention to her.

"Connor, you are correct. I am Mr Tinker Senior and I passed away a few years ago. Good lord, I've known you since you were a small child. Fortunately for me they were looking for someone of my skills so they kept me in my current form to work down here. I was allowed to keep my memory which is very nice and the reason I do remember you, Connor. What happened to you anyhow? You are still so young and already down here — shame."

"It's a long story, Mr Tinker, and I am not quite sure where to begin. This is our first day and we only arrived a few hours ago, at least I think it was a few hours ago," I replied. "We've just started taking a look around and are amazed about everything down here. And to find your shop of course."

"Aah, first day it is for you? I remember my first day," he said very sadly. "Well, I am sure you will find out all about life down here in the next few days and thank goodness you didn't end up in the Factory. It's awful at the moment — so many good animals are being sent to the Factory, far more than before. It's a rather worrying trend and we are all scared stiff of making a mistake. I can't understand why the people up there need to eat meat in such quantities. If I were you, I would apply for a good job. And make sure to keep your nose clean and out of trouble," said Mr Tinker kindly.

"Yes, I think I will do that," I answered.

"So, are you going to introduce me to your companions, Connor?"

"There's no need for that. I am more than capable of introducing myself. My name is Vanessa Forsythe-Twyke and I am from Upper Molehampton. I don't believe we've met but nevertheless, nice to meet you," she said with an air of authority.

"A Forsythe-Twyke? Haven't met one of your lot for years. Well, there's no castle down here for you, young lady," he said sarcastically.

"Don't worry about me, Mr Tinker. I can look after myself, just like my family has always been able to do."

"So if you can look after yourself, why is there a dog outside my shop guarding you?"

"I have nothing to do with that dog," said Vanessa, sharply.

Like a dutiful guard dog, Cleopatra was sitting right outside the shop with her back towards the window, watching over the street. There was a strange silence as we were all looking awkwardly at Cleopatra and two rabbits pushing a block of salt past the shop.

"Well, if nobody is going to introduce me then I will do it myself. My name is Basil and I was about to have a nice after lunch swim on my river minding my own business. But before I knew it, this brute of a stupid dog jumped out and grabbed me when I had just come out from my nice home right under the willow tree," said Basil, frowning at Ludwig.

"Look, sorry Basil. But dogs eat meat and you looked just so nice and tasty. Don't take it personally. I'm sure you also eat other animals. Come on tell me which ones?" Ludwig eagerly wanted to know.

"Well, yes I do actually," admitted Basil. "A nicely balanced diet of insects, snails, worms, small fish, and sometimes, their eggs. I mainly eat grass, weeds and roots though. But there is a difference, Ludwig. We eat what we catch. Immediately, and not like you. You caught me but then… you kept me in your jaw and I was still alive I would like to add. That was rather painful. And you didn't pay any attention when you crossed the road and had both of us hit by this woman here, taking us with her into the river," said Basil, now attaching the blame to Vanessa.

"Look you two. We didn't come here to talk about the ethics of life. We wanted to take a look around this area and grab a bite. And I am really thirsty," said Vanessa, curtly.

"I can recommend a nice pub if you want to relax a bit and take stock of things. The beer is great!"

"Now that's the best idea I've heard today, Mr Tinker," said Vanessa, breaking into a rare smile. "I would prefer a cocktail though. Where is that pub anyway?"

"Just go left out of the shop and there's a pub on the right after about a five minutes' walk called the Tunnellers' Arms," explained Mr Tinker.

"But we don't have that much money, Mr Tinker," I said alarmingly. "We've just been issued with a few coins and I am sure it won't get us far."

"Oh, don't you worry Connor. Essential items like beer are free down here. The moles cater for our every need."

"For everyone?" I asked.

"Yes, of course. The moles like to keep everyone happy and we are all equal in our world."

"What's money?" asked Ludwig, innocently.

"What's beer?" asked Basil, just as innocently.

"Yeah, what's beer?" copied Ludwig.

"Come on, let's go," said Vanessa, completely ignoring Ludwig's and Basil's questions.

"No, not yet," I said. "I have a question. You mentioned 'in our world' and everyone so far has spoken of the world as only Upper Molehampton, Lower Molehampton and Anglerton. Surely a lot of former humans down here would know the world is more than that. I've been to London."

"London? Never heard of it, Connor. I don't understand what you mean and I suggest you don't ask too many questions. It could be dangerous down here," he added sternly.

"It was nice seeing you again, Mr Tinker. It's been a long time." I didn't say anymore and decided it was best to go for now.

"Yes, Connor. Please do come back in the next few days and certainly before any reassignment. At least you know me — for the moment at least."

Signalled by the doorbell, the four of us exited Mr Tinker's store and turned left with a dutiful Cleopatra following us down the tunnel. We passed by various shops including a bookshop, a bakery, a supermarket and lots of shops trading their wares to all of the different animals; but the extent of the operations down here became fully evident when we passed by a small wooden hatch with a sign saying 'pumping station' attached to it. I couldn't resist the temptation and my interest got the better of me. Behind the hatch I found a sump with a fully operational yellow and black waste disposal pump. It was a real-size pump and therefore a little larger than me. I was literally standing in a parallel world and as far as I was concerned was definitely not dead, but not really alive either. Absolutely amazing.

"Oh look, a dog salon." Ludwig stopped outside and looked through the window where dogs were sitting on chairs being beautifully groomed by humans. "How wonderful," he said excitedly. "I must visit here in the next couple of days and maybe I will meet the she-dog of my dreams."

"Hmmm. Dogs seem to be rather well looked after by humans I see. Why do you eat ducks?"

"Because you taste nice and that is your purpose in life," replied Vanessa, rudely to Basil.

Our first impression of the Tunnellers' Arms was a huge roar of happy, beer drinking voices coming from behind the closed door. From the noise I was somehow expecting to enter a wild west saloon and to then be met by silence. On the contrary. When we pushed the door open and slowly stepped into the pub, nobody battered an eyelid and the crescendo of noise carried on. Nothing surprised me anymore but what awaited us inside the pub was impressive.

In this strange world below the ground there was a pub, not only for humans, but also for all of the animals. It looked like a traditional pub you might see in any English village with a roaring fire in a brick fireplace, a long wooden bar, lots of small round tables, leather arm chairs and even a pool table. Typical pictures depicting angling scenes and fish adorned the walls, along with farming tools hanging from the ceiling and white walls with black wooden beams were hiding the tunnel wall behind it, just like in a rustic country pub. The pub was extremely crowded with humans and farm animals drinking and discussing intensively together to create an awful din. Every table was taken and animals were even standing two thick at the bar, surprisingly not forming into their own group but mixing amongst each other. The only thing we all had in common was that we wore overalls in many different colours.

"Come on, Vanessa. Let's go and get a drink and show these two what beer is all about." I had to practically shout to her to be heard as we manoeuvred between the tables and chairs until we got to the crowd at the bar.

"Let me do this, Connor," shouted Vanessa back above the din. And with that she was off forcefully squeezing herself between a cow and a deer to get some drinks.

I looked around to survey the scene. Next to the fire place a woman was talking very intensively with a fox and gave me a brief nod of her head. At the table to my right two sheep, a horse and a cow were having fun playing cards. Most of the animals were in small groups of two or four but to my left a rabbit was standing alone quietly enjoying its beer, which, by the way, it could hold quite securely in its hairy front paws. Some pigs stood together at the bar looking glaringly in my direction as though I had done something wrong. And in a corner, two humans sat at a table staring at their smartphones in obvious disappointment.

"What are they doing? I've seen lots of humans down here staring into these things." Basil asked me with a confused look on his face.

"Oh those things. Those are smartphones, Basil. Humans use them for communication."

"Communication! With who?"

"Well, with other humans of course. We can also use them to write messages to each other, look at pictures or find information. Which is why they are called smart," I replied.

"Doesn't sound smart to me if you need something to help you communicate. Can't you simply talk to each other? But then again communication has never been a strong part of humans' characteristics."

Before I had found a suitable answer, a loud cough made me turn around to see Vanessa balancing four beers in her hands. The beer wasn't in glasses as I might have expected, but instead in thimbles. Of course thimbles are normally designed to cover the tip of a human finger but down here they were the perfect size of a good glass for beer. Oh well, at least they have a better use of thimbles down here than I do, I thought to myself, and took one beer from her. Ludwig and Basil just looked at the thimbles then at us as if asking what they should do with them.

"Well, Connor, Mr Tinker was correct. Beer doesn't cost anything down here. Fantastic!" said Vanessa, joyfully. "But where the heck do they get all of these thimbles from?"

"I have been asking myself exactly the same question since our arrival. Where do they get all this stuff from? They surely can't make everything down here. I'm certain we will find out in the next few days. Anyhow, do you know what the beer is called?"

"No idea but I saw some pipes going through the ceiling. That's where the beer came from."

"It's from the Angler Inn," said the rabbit next to us. "Sorry to butt in but I overheard your conversation. I presume you are new here. My name is Dusty by the way."

"I'm Connor. This is Basil, this is Ludwig and this is…"

"And I'm Vanessa. So you say it's from the Angler Inn. How does that work?" she asked, interrupting me.

"A long time ago some tunnels were dug into the cellar of the pub directly above us. It's called the Angler Inn. Basically the beer is siphoned from the pipes in the pub and fed down here directly to us. Great, isn't it? I had never drunk beer until I came down here. Just like these two probably," he said looking at Basil and Ludwig.

"The Angler Inn?" I asked.

"Yes, very nice of them to share their beer I must say," added Dusty.

"There is an Angler Inn in Lower Molehampton. Surely It can't be that one?" I asked.

"Oh, I have no idea. Places on the surface mean nothing to me. But let's not wait for the beer to dry! Cheers and down the hatch," exclaimed Dusty, with a smack of his thimble against mine obviously copying the others in the pub.

"Yes, cheers Dusty," and I too took a swig of my beer.

Ludwig and Basil looked at their beers and followed our lead. It was easy for Ludwig to lap the beer out of the thimble and even Basil managed the challenge just fine, judging by the noise he made with his long beak. Whilst Vanessa on the other hand just sipped her beer and stood there disapprovingly looking at Basil and Ludwig, both of them finished their drinks in a matter of seconds!

"The beer does taste awfully familiar," I said. "I bet it's from my local. Do you recognise the taste Vanessa?"

"Do I look like someone who would go to your local," she frowned. "In Upper Molehampton I go to a wine bar. But the barkeeper told me they only have beer when I asked for a cocktail and he told me this was a pub and not a wine bar. Oh well, it's all there is so better than nothing I suppose."

A table nearby became free and Dusty motioned to us to sit down with him. "Aaah, that's better after a hard day's work," he said.

"Dusty, I've been wondering why these overalls come in different colours. Ours are red, yours are blue and there are other colours, too. Does that mean anything?" asked Ludwig. He had been rather quiet since he saw the dogs' salon, but the beer seemed to have an effect on him.

"Yeah, sure does Ludwig. Red is for the new intake and you will remain in red overalls until the end of the transition process. It's just much easier to see who is who."

"I understood that first we are debriefed and then we are put back to the so called factory settings and reassigned without memory. If that's so, why are you in blue?" asked Ludwig again.

"My goodness, didn't you listen to Miss Strictland," said Basil, sarcastically.

Dusty carried on. "Yes, it's a little complicated on your first day I must admit. The moles run the administration and the management for the training and allocation of animals as well, but for that they need people to work for them. They can't do it all themselves! I work for them in the memory warehouse, a job particularly suited to rabbits because we can jump high in the racks. Quite simple really. If you work for the moles, you get a blue overall. But don't worry, it will all be explained to you in more detail. Just remember that the world is totally controlled by the moles. They decide on the allocations, who is to be sent back, in what form, what we eat and most importantly, what we need to know. Just do as they say, don't ask questions and you'll be fine."

"So, I could get a job down here, just like Mr Tinker?" said Ludwig, excitedly.

"Yes, that's right, Ludwig. My advice is to play your cards right and tell them as much as you can in the debriefing. They might find something useful in you, some skills they can use. Think of it like a job interview."

"It would have to be an extremely basic job for a dopey dog?" added Basil, teasingly but Ludwig was obviously very serious about everything he said.

"Oh very funny. I am just very scared of losing my memory," he replied.

I glanced towards the pigs again. They were still staring intently at me. "Dusty. Those pigs over there. Why do you think they are gazing at me? They look angry but I don't even know them."

"That is a problem we have down here indeed. Pigs and some other animals too, don't really like humans because they keep them in poor conditions and give them bad feed just to fatten them up. Basically they are treated as if they were simple products. And when they get slaughtered you put pictures on trucks and adverts showing how happy they are. That's why they don't like humans!"

I nodded in slow agreement and was just about to comment when it suddenly became very quiet in the pub. Not completely silent but most of the animals stopped talking and looked towards the door where Cleopatra was standing in the entrance, searching the pub with a beady eye until her gaze landed on me. Again. She passed our table and then headed towards the four card players. All she needed to do was look at them and they vacated the table. The barkeeper scurried across as fast as he could with a beer. Cleopatra took a seat and sat alone, constantly looking at me.

"Who is that?" whispered Vanessa. "She's been following us around since we've arrived."

"That is Cleopatra," said Dusty with a sense of dread. "She… is one of the others."

"So you mean from Lower Molehampton," said Vanessa, sarcastically.

"She belongs to a special group and comes here often. I should warn you not to mess with her."

"Well, she came in today with our arrivals group and is accommodated in the room next to me. Her eyes have been on me the whole time and she follows us everywhere."

"Really? That's very interesting and very scary too," said Dusty, with concern. "There must be something about you Connor. Do you have something special that she needs? Or do you know something she could be interested in? She wouldn't follow you without orders!"

"I can't think of anything, Dusty. And what special group are you talking about?"

"It's only a rumour and nobody knows for sure. It is believed that there is a special group who return to the surface on certain missions. But you should be careful about talking about this subject — you don't want to be sent to the Factory. In fact, it's best that you forget what I just told you!"

"Who would need something from somebody from Lower Molehampton?" added Vanessa, smirking.

"So the beer is working, Vanessa?" I smiled back. "Why not tell Cleopatra that you are from Upper Molehampton? I am sure she would be much more interested in you then!"

"Do you two fancy another beer? I've finished mine already," asked Dusty.

"Oh yes!" shouted Ludwig and Basil in glee at the same time.

Dusty jumped up and bounced across to the bar, his big ears flapping along the way.

"Nice chap, isn't he," I exclaimed.

"Chap? He's a rabbit, Connor!" said Vanessa.

"Yes, I know but as everyone is equal down here I can call him a chap. I hope we can meet up again before we are reassigned. He works for the moles and I am sure he's got lots of useful contacts."

"Do you also eat rabbits?" asked Basil.

"Yes," said Vanessa, looking menacingly at Basil. "Very nice in a stew — adds a lot of flavour."

Dusty bounced back with some beers but this time a little slower so as not to spill anything, put the thimbles on the table and sat down again. We sat together for a while just chatting about life. Dusty was generally very interested about life on top of the earth and very eager to return in some form, sadly accepting the fact that his memory would be deleted if he was reassigned. He asked me lots of questions and I presumed that it was interesting for rabbits to learn more about the life of a human. But strangely, he also wanted to know about what I kept in my house and where. Maybe just innocent questions, but in view of what had recently happened it made me a little suspicious. However, for the moment he was content working for the moles and he promised to tell me more about his job when we met again.

Then Basil interrupted the silence. "Dusty. Do you know that those two would eat you?" he blurted out and then looked squarely at Vanessa and I.

"Yes, I am aware that humans eat rabbits but I feel quite safe down here. So long as I do a good job for the moles, I believe I have nothing to worry about."

"We don't eat everything with fur and feathers, Basil," I said.

"Yes, Connor is right. We remove the fur and feathers before," said Vanessa, laughing her head off.

We all sat in silence for a while slowly drinking our beers and taking in our surroundings. The thimbles brought back a childhood memory. I remembered my father collecting thimbles, not a few but hundreds of them. I was young at the time but I still didn't forget boxes of them being delivered to our house and I always wondered what they were for. In fact, I couldn't even remember seeing them in the house after my parents' deaths. What did my father do with all of those thimbles?

"Come on you guys. The pub's closing soon so we should get a move on," said Dusty.

"What time does it actually shut?" asked Vanessa.

"Well, I've heard it's when the Anchor Inn closes and turns off the pump for the beer. I am not sure but it sounds like a good reason. However, the beer stays in the pipes a while longer so we can stay open until the pipes are empty."

"Well, in that case it must be around eleven p.m."

Time didn't seem to be important down here. I had no idea how late it was as we were below the ground and there was no sunlight down here, but according to Dusty it was already night time.

"That sounds about right, Connor. Come on, let's go. I'll walk with you some of the way," said Dusty.

Cleopatra was still sitting at the table next to us. She hadn't moved the whole time but when we got up and walked by her towards the door her head turned and followed in our direction. Just as we were leaving the pub I saw her get up and follow us. We turned left and walked back the same way we had come some while ago. The shops were now shut and the tunnels fairly empty.

"So how can we arrange to meet up again, Dusty?" I asked.

"Oh, I come here every evening after work so you should find me easily."

"OK but I have a little problem, Dusty. How will I know it's you and not another rabbit? I really can't tell you apart from. Sorry to say but all rabbits look the same to me. So do cows and horses and all the other animals by the way."

"Yes, I also wondered that," added Vanessa. "To me nearly all of the animals look the same, especially on the end of a fork!"

"Yes, a typical human weakness which most of us animals do not have. I can see the difference between the two of you and I can guarantee you that rabbits also do not all look the same. But I understand that humans generally have difficulty differentiating between animals. Look. There's another rabbit over there. Now she is much different to me. Can you see?"

"Well I can't see any difference. Both of you are furry with large floppy ears," said Vanessa, curtly.

"I can see you are going to need some training in this area," replied Dusty.

Cleopatra followed us down the tunnel at her usual discreet distance of course, but then stopped outside a door. From behind the door we heard the deep, rhythmic beat of extremely loud music which reverberated in the tunnel around us. In front of the door stood two moles in black overalls with security written on the back. The door opened to allow a donkey to leave and the full force of the music suddenly escaped onto the street like an explosion. We had a brief glimpse into the room and saw hundreds of animals dancing in the haze of disco smoke and the flashing lights rhythmically punching the air with their limbs. They were all laughing and having a great time. The door shut again and the loud music disappeared with it. Boom, boom, boom.

"What in God's name was that?" asked Vanessa.

"Oh, that's one of the nightclubs. There's a rave evening today," said Dusty, very matter-of-factly.

"A rave evening?"

"Yes, with music and smoke. It's actually quite funny. Humans generally don't like moles in their gardens and often use gas to kill them. What they don't know though is, that the poisonous gas they use is really laughing gas to us lot down here. And the music, well, that's similar. Humans have developed devices to scare moles away. So they play music through our tunnels which they think we don't like. The funny thing is that the moles, and the rest of us, love this music. Great, isn't it?" said Dusty, with a huge grin. "Lately, somebody up there is trying to fight us very hard. We've never had so many good parties in just a few weeks. If only they knew," he said chuckling.

I instantly thought of Mr Lawnsworthy directly above us fighting against the pesky molehills with his poisonous gas and noise making devices. He used them all the time. If only he knew! We walked back to the intersection near Mr Tinker's shop and parted our ways when, and yes you have guessed correctly, two rabbits pushing a trolley with a block of salt passed by. We walked back to our rooms the same way we came with Cleopatra never far behind us.

"OK, I'm tired now. See you all at seven a.m." said Vanessa who went straight in and slammed the door.

"Well, I suppose that's good night then!" added Basil.

The remaining three followed suit and we all went to bed.

***

Cleopatra remained on guard for a while longer but instead of going to her room she went back down the tunnel and met the Colonel in one of the secret Special Operations rooms.

"Cleopatra. Your loyalty is well-appreciated and has been noted. You will be rewarded for your work. Now, tell me. What have you to report?" the Colonel asked with keen interest.

"Connor has befriended three other beings who all arrived together. A human named Vanessa, a dog named Ludwig and a duck called Basil. Apart from that they are all acting as you would expect someone is acting who has just found out that they are dead, or in transition at least. They are all a little overcome with their experiences today."

"Have you noticed anyone watching or trying to make contact?" enquired the Colonel.

"There have been two contacts. One with Mr Tinker in his shop but I don't think we need to follow that up. It was Connor Jackson and his friends who went into the shop, apparently unplanned, so the contact did not come from Mr Tinker. The other was in the Tunnellers' Arms. A rabbit called Dusty, who works in the memory warehouse by the way, made direct contact with them. It's too early to say if it was deliberate or just by chance. I suggest we put a watch on the rabbit. Let's see who he might report to," reported Cleopatra with efficiency.

"I agree, Cleopatra. Well done and keep me informed of any other developments. Tomorrow will be Mr Jackson's debriefing and we, and the other side, will both be trying to find out what he has to say. We both want the same thing. The question is who will be quickest. And Cleopatra?"

114

"Yes, Colonel."

"Trust nobody. We have no idea who is on whose side," said the Colonel secretively.

Chapter Eight
Debriefing

"Here you go, Connor, another beer for you," said Vanessa, passing me a thimble, the beer sloshing out and dripping on to the carpet.

"Why, thank you, Vanessa, and just so practical drinking out of these thimbles. Isn't it just amazing where everything comes from, don't you think."

"Yes, Connor, I completely agree with you," said a voice coming from behind me just as Vanessa was about to reply. The man's voice was unmistakably recognisable. I stood up like a shot and span around to confirm my suspicion, my heart racing at full throttle. It was my father. I clenched my thimble so tightly that it shattered in my hand, so great was my surprise, the beer flowing down my hand and on to the floor. I was naturally so shocked at the sight of my father that I remained rooted to the spot like a statue.

"Aren't you going to say anything, son?" uttered my father, in a monotone voice lacking and sort of emotion. The tears welled up in my eyes as I struggled with the situation and to form a response. I wanted to speak but the words just wouldn't come out of my mouth. Unlike myself, my father appeared completely expressionless and spoke to me as though he saw me last only yesterday. My legs were like jelly and I just slumped down into the closest chair.

"I heard you were here and thought I would come and welcome you," he said flatly.

With great effort, I managed to stammer a reply. "Yes, apparently I died in an accident and have started a new life down here. This is not what I expected death to be like."

"It sure isn't, son."

Everything around me now appeared like a cloudy, slow motion scene. I gingerly stood up and surveyed the pub. Behind my father I saw my boss, Mrs Kingston, who was standing at the bar talking to Mrs Forsythe-Twyke. Sergeant Dawson was now speaking to Vanessa and eagerly writing in his notebook.

"Why are all of these people now down here in the pub? Surely they haven't all died as well?" I asked myself. Most confusing indeed. I turned around to speak to my father only to find him gone, but then saw him disappearing through the door of the gents' toilets. I followed him and opened the door to find him sitting on the couch in our living room. I turned around and opened the door again to find myself looking at our hallway, not the pub. I really started panicking now as my mind couldn't take in what was happening. Father. Pub. Home. What unexplainable things are going on here? I was now a stranger in the events going on around me, completely unnoticed by my father who had only greeted me a few minutes ago.

My father was clearly agitated and sat like a coiled spring on the couch, nervously looking at his watch. "Must be here any time now," he muttered to himself.

The doorbell rang, and my father sprang up and ran towards the door, barging past my mother who nearly got there first. Very out of character for my father who was normally so polite and actually quite a placid person. He ripped the door open as though he was excited about receiving a present from whoever might be there. It was in fact a man in brown overalls carrying a box.

"Here you go, Mr Jackson. The first delivery of thimbles and jam jars as requested. I think you will find all is in order."

My father grinned and snatched the box out of the man's hands like an excited child receiving a birthday present. "Oh, that is just wonderful. Wonderful indeed!"

I was an invisible observer to these strange events but still noticed how out of character this was for my father, who had never been the one to show much in the way of emotion when he was alive. How could anyone be so excited about thimbles and jam jars? But then jam jars were the subject of the village following the recent break in at the factory. The whole village was in absolute uproar about it.

"When will I get the next delivery of doll's house furniture?"

"You should get it next Thursday. Is that OK, Mr Jackson?"

"Yes, that should fit in with the plan. Thank you, Mr," my father paused, obviously thinking of his name.

"Rawlinson. My name is Mr Rawlinson."

My father then ran with the box back into the living room and sat like an excited child unpacking lots of different thimbles from the box.

"Perfect, just perfect," with a huge grin on his face. "The President will be most impressed!"

"The President? What are you talking about, Dad?" I said. But my father couldn't hear or see me.

My eyes flashed open as I heard Vanessa screaming obscenities at the top of her voice and the sound of a crowing rooster spitting out of the vents in my room. Where was I? Below the ground or at home? I was in my bed and extremely confused, so I slapped myself to find my way back to reality. It now dawned on me that I must have been dreaming and my father wasn't here after all. A light glow was coming through some of the small holes in the walls, slowly becoming brighter as though somebody was operating a dimmer switch. I covered my eyes for protection from the light and wondered how the moles could control everything down here. The rooster was now crowing louder, the light got brighter, and Vanessa was screaming at maximum volume. The night was definitely over and so obviously was my dream. There was no chance of going back to sleep with seven blasts of a horn exploding into my room, so I got up, refreshed my face with some water coming out of a pipe in the corner of my room and slipped into my red overalls. An old yoghurt pot served as a lavatory. So, this was seven a.m. down here. Cleopatra was already waiting in the tunnel with the same menacing glare. Politeness was maybe the best course of action, so I greeted her very friendly, "Good morning, Cleopatra!"

She replied with just a simple snarl.

"Good morning everyone," said Ludwig cheerfully.

"Good! What's good about being dead?" replied Basil. "And where is our lovely duck eater this morning?"

"She can't be still be asleep after all of this furore and screaming." I knocked on Vanessa's door.

"Leave me alone," she screamed from the other side. "I need my sleep!"

"Vanessa, I really think you should come out straight away. You are not in Upper Molehampton anymore. Just remember the Factory," I whispered as loudly as I possibly could at the door.

"Don't say anything. I'm not a morning person," she screamed and when the door opened an extremely moody and angry looking Vanessa stomped out.

"Oh really?" I muttered under my breath. "How could one guess that?"

It was good timing because Fraser came strutting down the tunnel like a drill sergeant. "Good morning, everyone," he shouted. "Everyone in a line. Quickly now." Fraser opened his clipboard and checked all of us against his names. "All present, that's good. Come on, let's be lively, there's lots to do. But first, follow me to breakfast and then I will explain what is happening today." And with that he turned around and marched off at a good pace down the tunnel with the rest of us following.

Fraser stopped in front of a big double glass door with a dimly-lit sign — 'Common Canteen'. "This is one of our canteens. Go in and choose whatever you like — you will find there's something here for everyone. Back here at the eight a.m. alarm call."

"Are there no bistros? I'm not used to eating in a common canteen and I'm certainly not everyone." said Vanessa, angrily. "Is there nothing else for me, Mr Fraser?"

For the first time Fraser now looked angry. "A nice bistro? I don't think so. There is one on Mole Boulevard but it only opens after work. I suggest, Miss Forsythe-Twyke, that you accept that you are exactly the same as everyone else down here. Now get in there and eat something or go hungry!"

Vanessa didn't notice that Fraser turned around and walked off. Instead, she was trying to avoid his angry gaze by looking down on the floor as she followed us through the door.

Inside the canteen we were met by a wall of noise. Plates clattering, the chinking of cutlery and the sound of hundreds of chattering voices. Around the edges were many different feeding stations with signs above them — dogs, horses, cows, ducks and also a sign for humans across the other side of the room. We stood there in awe looking at this large room and the frenzy of activity.

"Come on. Out of the way," said a fox wearing blue overalls pushing past. "First day probably," he tutted.

"Over there, Vanessa. That's where we need to go," I said pointing to our station.

What awaited us was a pleasant surprise. On our way to our serving station we had to dance around many fast-moving animals with their trays full of food. We also collected a tray and then patiently waited in the queue for a choice of a full English breakfast with bacon, sausages, beans and eggs and a large assortment of different types of bread, cheeses and jams. "What an amazing choice," I said to Vanessa. "The moles really do cater for everything."

"It's too early for me," she grunted back.

"Well, as we don't know what is going to happen today I suggest you get something to eat, Vanessa."

We got to the serving counter rather quickly and a human behind the counter shouted in a thick Scottish accent, "What will it be then?"

"Errm, two sausages, bacon, beans and a fried egg please," I shouted back, trying to be heard above the hubbub. I only now realised how famished I was and the smell of the food made the gnawing feeling in my stomach even stronger.

"One sausage only," shouted back the human and slapped the food unceremoniously on my plate. At the drinks station two squirrels were standing on a ladder next to a huge coffee pot, much larger than me and obviously from the human world. "A coffee please," I shouted. The squirrel at the top took a plastic cup, dunked it into the coffee pot, handed it to the squirrel below who then passed it to me. Vanessa followed suit with a plate of bread and some jam. She had obviously changed her mind.

In the centre of the hall there was row upon row of tables and hundreds of different creatures tucking into their breakfasts. Someone was shouting my name. Ludwig and Basil were already sitting at a table quite close to us, beckoning for us to join them. "So what have you got Ludwig?" I asked inquisitively. Ludwig looked at me with great content and indicated to the floor. "I, Connor, have a nice juicy bone. Truly amazing."

"Then I hope you do a better job with the bone than you did with me." Basil couldn't stop teasing.

"Oh not that again," replied Ludwig. "Can't you stop it now?"

"And remember, whilst you are enjoying your bone, another animal has given up its life for you, so you can have a nice meal. I hope you think of that," added Basil.

Ludwig just starred at Basil but elected not to answer.

"What did you get, Basil?" said Vanessa, her first real words of the day.

"I have got some lovely river plants and insects. Yummy."

"Hmm, not sure I would find that yummy but as long as you are happy," responded Vanessa, kindly and then changed tone. "If I knew what you eat, I wouldn't eat ducks. I eventually eat what you eat. Imagine that."

"You know I am a duck and not just something that you can eat, don't you?" retorted Basil angrily.

"Never thought about it, Basil. You normally come wrapped in plastic and don't look like a duck."

Basil rolled his eyes and simply said, "I give up!"

Then we all sat there silently eating our breakfasts, lost in our own thoughts and probably thinking about what was coming next. I looked at all of our eating utensils and realised that they were children's toys, probably from a doll's house set. How on earth did they manage to get all of these things down here I thought to myself, and not for the first time?

"I have no idea what I am going to say in the debriefing." The eerie silence was broken by Ludwig.

"Me neither," added Basil. "What can I offer the moles so I can stay alive a while longer?"

"I have a lot to offer. Surely they will keep me," added Vanessa, with a superior look on her face.

"I was up all night thinking about it and might have something but not sure if it will work," I said trying to sound positive.

"Go on, what is it?" asked Ludwig, impatiently. "I'm all ears."

But then the eight a.m. alarm sounded and everyone in the canteen stood up to return their trays and headed for the door. "I'll tell you in a mo," I said standing up. We all took our trays quickly to the collection point and walked to the entrance where Fraser was already impatiently waiting for us.

"Come on, everyone, get along now. Lot's to do. Follow me and be sharp about it," he barked at us.

We ran down a few more tunnels trying to keep up with Fraser, past lots of different offices and signs until we finally arrived at the debriefing area. "Wait here. I will go and register you." Fraser marched off straight towards a mole in a big open-plan office equipped only with individual tables and handed over a sheet of paper. The mole went through the sheet thoroughly, looking at the names and then indicated to someone. Fraser pointed in our direction and I had the uncanny feeling that he was singling me out.

"OK everyone. This is what happens from here. In the debriefing phase you will be questioned about your recent life. Be honest and tell them everything you can remember and answer questions thoroughly. None of you have been allocated to the Factory so you can relax, for the moment at least. Our debriefing teams want to find out what useful skills you may possess and if you are fortunate, you might be invited to apply for a job and stay in transition. This way you will not end up in the Food Factory or in a jar. Just think of that."

"In a jar?" asked Vanessa.

"Yes. A jar. All of the memories are stored jars. They have to be kept somewhere!"

"And where do they get the jars from," I asked suspiciously.

"From the surface. There is the glass jar factory and also a shop where we find them," said Fraser.

"Find? You mean steal!" I said because I remembered very well that just some time ago the glass jam-jar factory in in Lower Molehampton had been robbed of its entire supplies.

"No. I said find."

"Will we be terminated immediately if we are not fortunate to find a job?" asked Vanessa.

"Not always immediately. You will stay down here for a while and be allocated menial jobs until the time comes for reassignment. Then your memory is finally extracted and you will be reprogrammed and reassigned. Miss Strictland told you about that yesterday. Depending on the allocation system you may well be reassigned as a cat, for example," explained Fraser.

"Who decides what life form we might have afterwards," asked Basil.

"I really don't know. These decisions are made well above me. It's best not to ask too many questions because you don't want to end up at the Factory. Just stay quiet and do what you are told."

"Ok, everyone, go and sit over there and wait until you are called for your debriefing. Good luck, everyone!" added Fraser added. "I have to go and get another intake now."

"Will we see you again?" asked Ludwig.

"Yes, I will be back after the debriefings to help you in your next roles, whether it'll be temporary work or more permanent. Don't worry about that now. We'll sort it all out later," Fraser added kindly.

Fraser left and Vanessa, Ludwig, Basil and I sat there looking glumly at the floor.

"Huddle around, everyone," I said with my finger against my lips. "I want to tell you what I have been thinking about, but we have to be very quiet."

"Go on then," said Vanessa, with visible interest.

"Listen. I haven't told anyone yet but there might be a reason why I am down here. I thought about the whole thing long and hard last night." Then I went on to explain all of the strange activities since I found the molehill and the glass jar some weeks ago, including the attack on my house and the subsequent kidnapping.

"What a strange story," whispered Vanessa.

"For some reason somebody, or some people, believe I have something of value or know something. I just have no idea what it is but I have a suspicion. Come closer, everyone, I don't want to say this loudly," looking with mistrust at Cleopatra, who was not sitting far away.

The friends huddled together and I explained my idea. Vanessa, Ludwig and Basil all nodded their agreement. "It's very important to do exactly as I say for this plan to work. It might be our chance to stay down here a little longer and give me the possibility to come up with a more concrete plan."

"Mr Jackson. Connor Jackson!" shouted out a voice, interrupting our conversation.

"Yes," I answered.

"Follow me. You're on first."

Somehow this didn't surprise me. I followed a mole towards an open door and turned around to see the others looking at me rather nervously. There was no sign of Cleopatra now. The mole beckoned me to enter the room where I found a mole sitting behind a desk with another mole in the corner holding a notebook and pen. The mole behind the desk was wearing a tweed jacket, a checked shirt with a green tie decorated with some university style emblems. He nodded to an empty chair and I dutifully sat down. The mole in the corner was wearing a white blouse and a tartan skirt.

"Good morning, Mr Jackson," said the mole, politely. "My name is Mr Charles Donaldson and this is Miss Marjorie Shorthand who will take notes of the debriefing. Have you been told why you are here Mr Jackson?"

"Well, I believe I am dead, or in transition as you call it down here, and if I understand correctly, I will now be debriefed before my processor is reprogrammed, or I will find a job. Is that correct, Mr Donaldson?"

"Yes, very good, Mr Jackson. Every person who comes here is debriefed first before we work out what your next career move is.

More about that later. First of all, we just want you to describe some of your memories to us from your previous assignment. In your own time now, Mr Jackson."

"I have a question first."

"Go on."

"Why are we debriefed if our memories are stored anyhow?"

"Yes, good question. If we extract your memory immediately then we can't offer you any employment. Therefore, we try to find out if you have any special experiences or particular skills that might be useful to us. Now please go on Mr Jackson. Tell us about your earliest memory to begin with. Just relax and sit back."

After the incidents of the last weeks I knew that something fishy was going on, so I decided to open up and see if this interview would shed any light on recent events. I sat back, closed my eyes, concentrated on my earliest memory and started.

***

I'm not exactly sure how old I was but I must have been very young. I say that because I can clearly remember sitting in a swing in our garden and it was one of those with wooden sides and a back to stop me falling out. My father was sitting in front of me, probably only about one metre away, rocking back and forwards in a chair, engrossed in a book. He was obviously more interested in his book than his fatherly duties because he had some sort of stick which he was using to prod me with. In fact, it was quite rhythmic because he was prodding me in the same cycle as the rocking motion on his chair, so I could swing without my father leaving the lines of the book. Forwards and prod, backwards then forwards and prod again. All I can really remember was swinging contently in the garden and taking in all of the lovely impressions of this warm summer day.

The sounds of this day are still very vivid for me. The buzzing noise of the bees working furiously in the clover of the lawn. The rustling leaves of our cherry tree in the light breeze and the clicking sound of crickets in the undergrowth. The smells still linger in my nose today — the freshly cut grass, the scent of the flowers and the smell of a hot, dry summer's day. All these years later I certainly do remember all these smells and sounds and every time I smell, for example freshly cut grass, it reminds me of this time.

In my upward swinging movements, I turned my head directly towards the clear blue sky and observed the birds, which were circling high above us as though they were watching us. I saw something very small fall from the sky. It was so small that I couldn't really make out what it was but then some bird-dropping splatted directly on the paving stones between me and my father. My father didn't even flinch or move from his book. In the next seconds more of these bird-droppings landed with large splat sounds all around us on the paving stones. When I look back at this experience, it seems very strange how many of these droppings landed so very close to us I must say. And then I could see it coming, this one particular white bomb. It dropped with an uncanny accuracy directly towards my father like a missile seeking its target. I warned him with two words from my extremely limited vocabulary, "Bird Poo!" And when my father finally paid some attention to me and looked up from his book the white slimy lump splatted right in the middle of his bald head and then, after a long pause, he smiled, looked up and said, "All OK, Roger."

I still giggle today when I think about it and it was probably my father's strange reaction that made me keep this memory imprinted somewhere in my head. I mean, if a bird shat on your head would you look up and say; "All OK, Roger?" Well, I certainly wouldn't! So over the years I often mentioned this event with my parents as it was always a humorous talking point. Even though my mother told me one day that my father changed a lot after this event. He suddenly gave up his job at the bank and started collecting second hand items and things people threw away and didn't need any more. After some time, he became the manager of the scrap company in Lower Molehampton. And then of course there were the deliveries of thimbles to our house, none of which I ever saw again. And come to think of it, I can also remember him collecting sets of plates, cutlery, cups and so on from doll's houses.

***

"OK, Mr Jackson, that is most certainly very interesting. Please go on," said Mr Donaldson with keen interest. Miss Shorthand was busy writing in the corner.

I then went on to talk about my school years, my first job and the death of my parents. I described my house and Trout Lane in quite some detail and also spoke about my job and the people I worked with. All the while Mr Donaldson listened intently, he never interrupted me and gave me as much time as I wanted. But this changed with a knock on the door.

"Excuse me, Mr Jackson," he said, stood up and went to the door. I couldn't see who he was talking to, but I clearly heard Mr Donaldson say, "What did they just tell you? Are you sure? I suggest you stop the interviews and wait for me to finish here." He then came back in and sat down again.

"Mr Jackson," he said, looking at me very seriously. "Thank you very much for your detailed memories but we now need to press on and look at the final experiences of your life. Now, could you please tell us everything you know from your last weeks and months? And I mean everything — don't skip any detail!"

I was now very sure I had some sort of information that they wanted so decided it was best to find out what exactly it was that they wanted. I told them everything about the molehill, the mysterious jar with a name on it, the feeling of being watched, the kidnapping and the accident. Both Mr Donaldson and Miss Shorthand did not react to anything I said during the whole debriefing. But this changed the moment I mentioned the glass jar and Professor Wingnut. They sat up straight and looked at me, but Miss Shorthand returned immediately to her notes, her reaction unnoticed by Mr Donaldson.

"As I said at the beginning, Mr Jackson, the aim of this interview is to ascertain if you have any knowledge or skills that might be useful to us and I believe you do. You have told us a lot of interesting facts."

"Oh, I am glad," I answered trying to feign ignorance. I would not have been watched and kidnapped for no reason at all! "May I know what interests you in particular?"

"Yes, Mr Jackson, you may know. It is highly likely that you are in the possession of an object sought after by us and possibly others. Something extremely valuable."

"Well, don't keep me in suspense. What exactly is it you are looking for?" I asked directly.

"Well, let me come straight to the point, Mr Jackson. What did you do with the glass jar you found in your garden?" he said, looking at me in great anticipation to my answer.

It was obvious that I had something of great importance which meant that I was also of great importance. I was now thinking on the spot and knew this was my opportunity to play this out to win time for myself and my friends. It would have been very foolish to let them know the location. As a matter of fact, I could remember what I had done with it but I could sense Mr Donaldson's nervousness and also see Miss Shorthand twitching irritably. I had to play for time.

"Oh that," I said with false surprise. "I'm awfully sorry, Mr Donaldson but that was weeks ago and I honestly can't remember what I did with it. I mean it was just a normal glass jar — nothing special to me," I said making this up as I went along. "After all of the excitement over the last weeks, I have absolutely no idea where I put it. But I know it is in the shed, no wait, somewhere in the house I believe. I haven't touched or seen it since," I answered confidently.

"Come on now, Mr Jackson. Surely you must remember what you did with it," said Mr Donaldson with growing impatience. "Spit it out. Where is it? It is not every day that you find a glass jar in the middle of your garden. Come on, think harder!"

"Mr Donaldson. Have you ever put something somewhere and said to yourself that you will get it later and then completely forget where you put it?" I asked him.

"Well, yes, sometimes this has surely happened," he stuttered in reply.

"And exactly that has happened to me," I said with a serious look on my face. "I think I need some help in remembering."

"What can we do for you, Mr Jackson? To help you remember?"

I didn't care if he knew that I was playing for time. I had nothing to lose! "A cup of tea and some cheese on toast would help, thank you. It is very tasty. Do you like it?" I said with an innocent smile.

"A cup of tea and cheese on toast?" repeated Mr Donaldson.

"Yes please and thank you for the kind offer. I cannot think with an empty stomach." I was a trained analyst and I knew that I had the upper hand, and I knew that Mr Donaldson knew it too. I was very experienced in handling information and understood how to act in my favour in a situation like this. So, I was deliberately pushing the boat out to give the others time too in their interviews.

"OK, Miss Shorthand, let's take a break now. Would you be so kind and organise what Mr Jackson has requested? Thank you."

"Yes of course, sir," responded Miss Shorthand, speaking for the first time.

I don't know how long I waited and I rather enjoyed some time by myself and the peace of the room. But I felt rather smug as the last days had been hectic and the noise in this strange underground world was rather unbearable at times. Now that I knew it was the glass jar with the Professor they wanted, I was holding the key to my extended stay down here in my hands. When the door opened again after what felt like an age, Mr Donaldson and Miss Shorthand returned. She was carrying a plate with piping hot cheese on toast and a cup of steaming tea. One of my favourite dishes.

"Here, Mr Jackson, this is what you asked for. Enjoy your food now and then please tell us what you can remember," ordered Mr Donaldson rather sternly.

"Yes of course. Please give me the chance to eat and then to think about it." I sat back and ate as slowly as I could, pausing every now and then to take a slurp of my tea. Mr Donaldson became increasingly agitated and kept on looking at his watch, staring at me the whole time.

"I am sorry to take up so much of your time but I suffer from indigestion and my doctor told me to eat slowly. Do you suffer from indigestion, Mr Donaldson?"

"Look, Mr Jackson. We must press on. You know we can send you to the Factory if you are uncooperative," he said trying to threaten me.

"Really, but you want Professor Wingnut in his glass jar and I might be the only person who knows where he is. So you have to keep me alive to get him back for you, don't you? So please, Mr Donaldson, be so kind and answer my question. Do you suffer from indigestion?"

Mr Donaldson looked at me rather grimly. But I could see in his eyes that he knew he couldn't win so he finally gave in and replied with a sigh, "No. No, I do not."

"Well, lucky you. You can't imagine what it's like," I answered.

I finished my cheese on toast and my tea then placed the empty plate and cup on Mr Donaldson's desk. "Thank you very much. Greatly appreciated. OK, so where were we?"

"The glass jar, Mr Jackson. Please try to remember where you put it?"

"Oh of course. The glass jar. Yes. Now let me think." I sat back, closed my eyes and thought of my next strategy.

After a while Mr Donaldson coughed. "Can you remember now?"

"Well, I think I might. But can I ask you another question first?"

"Go on," said Mr Donaldson, slowly getting annoyed.

"How did you get this job?"

"Me? Well, when I was debriefed, some qualities and skills were noticed and I was offered a job."

"What were you before?" I asked.

"I was a psychiatrist."

"So you were a human, like me."

"Yes, I was a human, just like you, Mr Jackson. That was my former life," he replied a little sadly.

"When you say, offered a job. Were you reprogrammed? What happened to your memory?"

"I'm afraid that's confidential information, Mr Jackson, and I can't talk about it."

"Hmm, that's a shame because the whereabouts of the glass jar is also confidential and I can't talk about it either," I replied with a confident smile. "But maybe we can come to some sort of agreement. What do you say? And there's more. I recorded communication of someone whilst being watching and saved it on a memory stick. Maybe it was the other side?" Miss Shorthand twitched but this also went unnoticed by Mr Donaldson. "The information I have could well reveal who these people are. I am able to tell you where it is, Mr Donaldson, but all information has a price. The question is, are you willing to pay for it? And are you important enough to make such decisions, or do you need to speak to your superiors?"

Mr Donaldson stood up, threw down his pen and stormed out, "Interview over." Miss Shorthand followed him and I was alone in the room once more, not sure if I had overstepped the mark. I had to wait for what felt like an age, contemplating what would happen next when the door opened again.

"Mr Jackson, please follow me. There is someone who wants to meet you and I suggest you show him some respect, more than you did to me, and maybe leave out the cheese on toast trick this time!"

I smiled at Mr Donaldson and simply replied, "Thank you, that's more like it!"

We left the room and went into the area where I had left the others earlier on. There was no sign of them, Fraser, or the rest of the group. I just hoped that my friends explained in their debriefing what I told them to say and that they were OK. I knew I had ridden my luck so far but maybe I could push it a little further to keep my friends alive so that we would be reunited again.

"Mr Jackson. Come on, follow me. We really can't keep him waiting."

Mr Donaldson led me to a station for transport modules, like the one I arrived on yesterday, then he bid me farewell and told me to wait. In the now almost usual routine we had briskly walked down lots of similar looking tunnels and passed various offices with signs and numbers. This place down here was so confusing that I wondered how everyone knew their way around. I didn't have to wait long for the shuttle transport which arrived with a whooshing noise and came to a dusty, thumping landing right in front of me. The driver beckoned me to jump in and join him. He was alone and I readily complied with his instructions, opened the door, sat in the seat directly behind him and put on my safety belt and helmet. The driver ignited the fluid and we careered through the tunnel. This time though we did not stop at any station but rushed through at the usual breakneck speed. I just managed to get a glimpse of moles with headlamps and shovels digging feverously away at what appeared to be new tunnel work.

"Hold tight now," shouted the driver. "Might be a bit scary."

Looking over the driver's shoulder I could just make out the end of the tunnel in the weak lights of the shuttle's headlights. The driver did not brake, nor slow down, just kept careering towards the wall with me holding on to the seat in front of me in sheer fright, expecting us to hit the end of the tunnel. Then he killed the lights. The shuttle shuddered and went into a steep fall in pitch-blackness. The seatbelt was cutting into my stomach and I had the feeling we were in freefall with the transport module spinning uncontrollably downwards, but I couldn't see anything, not even the back of the chair I was pushing against. Unlike me, the driver seemed to be enjoying himself. "Woohoo, sorry for this but I have my orders. Just hold on tightly now, Mr Connor," he shouted with glee in his voice.

The steep fall ended and we levelled out carrying on in a straight tunnel for a while. Eventually, in the distance, I made out just a pin prick of light and before I knew it we rushed into a well-lit opening. We landed with a violent brake and a customary thud in the sand, with a cloud of dust all around us.

"Thank you for travelling with us today, Mr Jackson and glad to be of service," said the driver politely. Then he ignited the fuel again and careered off back into the darkness.

I stood alone, patiently waiting at a station which was devoid of any signs, numbers or seats. In fact, there was nothing. Just a dark tunnel. A mole in military fatigues came out of the darkness, he didn't say anything, instead he just beckoned me with his finger to follow him. A torch lit up our way through the dark but then he stopped and pushed open a door to a well-lit tunnel. Just like in the dark tunnel there were no signs or names on the doors. This was obviously a completely different part of this strange underground world, an area much different to the Arrivals. Almost secretive.

***

Ludwig was led into his debriefing room and went through the same procedure as Connor.

"Well, you certainly possess certain skills that we might need in the future, Ludwig. You are very loyal I can see. However, there is not a vacancy for your skills just at this moment so I have but to assign you for reprogramming," said the interviewer without any emotion.

"Wait. I can add one more thing to my skill set apart from my loyalty," added Ludwig, very slowly.

"It probably won't get you a job. But what is it then?"

"I have information regarding the whereabouts of Professor Wingnut," said Ludwig in what appeared to be a rehearsed sentence.

The interviewer's pen dropped onto the table with a loud clatter.

***

"You don't really have many useful skills, do you??"

"Now hold on there. I am a duck and have many useful talents," retorted Basil angrily. "I am an expert in the nature and different types of river food. Also, I can swim for hours and collect plants and insects on the river. I bet you can't do that."

"No you are right. I can't and neither do we need anyone like you down here. Why would an expert in river food be interesting down here? Try again next time you come back, whenever that may be. This time you are being assigned for reprogramming. You may now go."

Basil remained seated and just looked at the interviewer.

133

"The interview is over!" said the interviewer, gruffly.

"Not yet! I bet you don't know the whereabouts of Professor Wingnut. But I do," said Basil, cheekily.

He knew he had a hit when he saw the expression on his interviewer's face.

***

"Well, Vanessa Forsythe-Twyke, please proceed."

"Look Mr errrm, sorry, I've forgotten your name," said Vanessa with her air of arrogance.

"My name is Mr Windemere," he said with annoyance.

"Well, Mr Windemere. I have no desire to tell you about my life or to sell myself. Forsythe-Twyke's don't sell themselves and we certainly don't work for anyone. We have people to work for us."

"Then reprogramming it is. Interview over," said Mr Windemere with a glint of glee in his eyes.

"Don't be so fast, Mr Windy, sorry, forgot your name again. If you want information about Professor Wingnut, I suggest you do not reprogram me. I know where the Professor is. Now off you go and speak to someone important. We haven't got all day you know!"

The interviewer just sat there with his jaw dropped.

***

We stopped outside an office, where another mole in military fatigues standing guard opened the door and beckoned me to enter. "Please sit down, Mr Jackson," he commanded. I sat alone for a while, which I was now getting used to, but the waiting I must admit was making me a little nervous. The room was, like everything in this part of the mole system, without any decorative items — just a very basic table and two chairs. There wasn't even the tick-tock of a clock to keep me company.

"Mr Jackson. Pleasure to meet you at last. My name is Colonel Pickle." He was not dressed in a camouflaged uniform like the other mole but wore a very smart brown uniform, shirt and tie instead. He

134

also had a big, thick, black and bushy moustache which dropped down the sides of his mouth and carried a leather horse whip.

I stood up and went to shake his hand but there was no outstretched hand coming in my direction.

"Hello, Colonel. I don't think I need to introduce myself as I have the feeling that you already know a lot about me."

"That is true, Mr Jackson. I should apologise to you for being down here in this situation, but I won't," he said seriously. "Let's get down to business and cut the crap. You have a glass jar, which we want, and you know it is extremely valuable to us. But we understand you are not prepared to simply tell us where it is. Believe me, Mr Jackson, that would be the easiest option."

"You are correct, Colonel, and I also know you can easily put me in a jar and read my memory. But what would you do if my memory didn't tell you where the jar is? At the moment I can't remember exactly where I put it. I'm sure I will be able to get you to the glass jar if you offer me a suitable job and keep me down here. We just have to work out how. Or would you prefer your enemies get to it first?" I said with a certain amount of anticipation.

"You drive a hard bargain, Mr Jackson." Then there was a long pause, a very long, hard stare and I knew I had hit a nerve when he surprisingly said, "OK, I think I can make a deal with you. You certainly have dealt a good hand, but be careful, Mr Jackson, this is now a very dangerous game indeed."

The Colonel went on to explain what Dusty had hinted about in the bar yesterday evening

"There is a Special Operations department which is responsible for certain, what shall I call them, special missions on the surface. The people we choose for these missions are selected because of their special skills. Skills needed to complete certain tasks. Or they possess information critical to the successful outcome of a mission. I emphasise that WE choose who we need and not the other way around. You possess knowledge, Mr Jackson, and that knowledge we need. You know the rough location of the jar and the memory stick. As to your skills, well we shall have to see about that. Maybe you will be of further use to us or maybe not. That, Mr Jackson, is for you to prove."

"So what about my memory, Colonel?"

"Those chosen for their missions keep their memories and are not reprogrammed like the others. But you must go through a different training to ensure that you have the abilities for your mission. I won't say anymore on that for now but you will have to undertake this rigorous training before we can send you back."

"Are you saying that I would keep my memory and that Connor Jackson would kind of still be alive?"

"Yes, I am. But you will not go back as Mr Jackson in your previous human form — that life is finished and you have to accept that. You can only go back in another form but more on that later. Let me make it perfectly clear to you — I have only agreed to this so that we can get the Professor back into safe hands and the memory stick to root out the thieves. A win-win situation so to say."

"OK, Colonel, understood. But I do have one more request."

"Mr Jackson," said Colonel Pickle, slowly.

"I agree to your terms and I understand what you told me but I want to choose my companions for this mission. Vanessa, Ludwig and Basil. We arrived together and I left them behind in the debriefing area. I will need them to help me get your jar back. Oh, and one more thing — I need to be in charge of my own mission."

"That is a difficult request, Mr Jackson. Tell me why I should agree to this?"

"Easy, Colonel. Because I cannot go back in the human form of Connor Jackson, it will be difficult to get to the glass jar. But Vanessa, Ludwig and Basil all come from my area and I will most certainly need their local knowledge to fulfil this task and to ensure that this mission is a full success. After all you do want to retrieve the glass jar and the memory stick with minimal publicity. Or do you want the Professor to fall into the wrong hands? I don't, do you!"

"OK, Mr Jackson, I agree to this, reluctantly, but only for this mission. Only to get the glass jar. After that my side of the bargain is over and so is the agreement for your friends."

"Thank you, Colonel. You won't be disappointed."

"For your sake, and especially that of your friends, I hope not," added the Colonel, dangerously.

***

The mole in military fatigues opened the door and Vanessa, Ludwig and Basil all entered the room.

"Wow, how did you all get here so quickly?"

"Well, we all did what you said. After we told our interviewers that we knew the location of Professor Wingnut the interrogations were stopped immediately and we were all transferred down here for further questioning — that's what they told us anyhow. The information must be extremely important to them and we certainly will not be sent for reprogramming — not for the moment at least. It seems as if your plan worked, Connor and all we now need to do is find the mystery jar," said Ludwig with visible delight.

"Yes we sure do. Our interviews were stopped after we all refused to reveal the location of the glass jar, just like you told us to. We asked to be reunited with you and here we are! We were led away down here and endured a terrifying shuttle journey," said Vanessa. "Good plan, Connor. What now? Where is the jar anyhow?"

"One slight hitch in my plan."

"Go on, Connor," said Vanessa, in her normal abrupt fashion.

"I can't remember where it is. Honestly. I can remember putting it in a safe place but it is so safe I can't even remember myself. I do know it is in the house though."

"OK, well that shouldn't be too difficult to find. We just have to turn the place upside down until we find it. I mean you will," said Vanessa, cheerfully.

Chapter Nine
Red Five

"Welcome. I am Colonel Pickle. I am in charge of the Special Operations Department."

After being reunited, we were transported back to Red Five and instructed to go to our accommodation and await further instructions. We sat together and chatted about what had happened to us and a little bit about our very different lives which obviously made us all very sad as we had difficulty accepting our current situation. The role of moles and their total domination over all the life forms was completely against our held beliefs and it was such an incredible story that nobody would ever believe it. Then again, if it was true that on leaving here all memories were wiped, how could the story ever be told. But there was a glimmer of hope that all was not yet over, and we had to hold onto this at all costs. It was clear that acceptance into the Special Operations Department seemed to be our only opportunity to stay alive, in a strange sense that is, and maybe return to the surface. But simply finding the glass jar wasn't enough. We had to come up with a plan.

Eventually, after some hours of sitting around nervously waiting for things to happen, a mole escorted us to the training school, thankfully this time without any hair-raising shuttle journeys.

"You being here is rather unorthodox but the situation we find ourselves in is indeed unorthodox, so I will briefly explain what is going to happen before handing you over to one of our trainers, who will then guide you through the Special Operations training process," explained the Colonel in a quite military fashion.

He took a long pause and eyed us all very carefully. We had agreed that we needed to ask as many questions as possible and gather as much information so that we could learn how things worked down here, and hopefully come up with a plan. And we needed to think quickly.

"You must remember that not a word of Professor Wingnut must be mentioned to anyone. All of this is and must remain top secret. Do you understand?" He said bringing his whip down on the lectern in front of him with a loud crack, which made us immediately sit straight up in our chairs.

"Yes, Colonel!" we all shouted together.

"Good. So what happens from here? Let me explain about our job and life in this part of the world. Red Five is the area where everyone lives and works in our system. Those who have been debriefed and not selected for a job wait down here until they are called forward for reprogramming and a new assignment. Whilst waiting they are on tunnelling duties which is an essential task for the upkeep of our world. We cannot survive without new tunnels," he explained in short, simple sentences.

"Do we also have to do tunnelling duties, Colonel Pickle?" asked Basil.

"Yes, it is compulsory. Everyone who is new and either in training or awaiting reprogramming has to do it. That's why you were issued with tunnelling equipment on arrival and you will use it. That includes all of you," he continued, looking sternly at Vanessa. "Everyone who has been selected for Special Operations also lives here and must take part in daily life as part of their cover."

"And what about me?" asked Vanessa haughtily.

"And what about you, Miss Forsythe-Twyke?" responded the Colonel.

"It is not befitting to my level in society to do menial jobs like tunnelling, Colonel."

"Level in society? There is no level in society down here, young lady. You are all equal and must all do the same work. Believe me, you are not anywhere close to special," said the Colonel, harshly. "The only levels we know down here are the different levels of the tunnels."

"Now let me carry on. The agents in Special Ops are not known to the others and their roles remain a complete secret. Therefore, you must appear like all of the others and it is essential for you to integrate into the society here by taking on a job. You will undergo training in your jobs and also training in the world of Special Operations which is secretive of course. It will be carried out in the area you were all transported to yesterday," he carried on spitting out his words like a machine gun.

"I noticed that some people have different coloured overalls. Why is that, Colonel Pickle?" I asked reminding myself that we needed as much information as possible to slow the process down.

"The colour of the overalls denote your position. There are different levels of administration and management. All new arrivals wear red. Depending on what job you might be given this could change but until you have passed your training in a job you will remain in red."

"Why then do some people wear normal clothes," I asked again. "Mr Tinker for example."

"Remember, like you, everyone in arrivals is dead, on the surface I mean, and for most it is a very traumatic experience. Therefore, we try to make the living environment as normal as possible and some, like Mr Tinker, are permitted to wear their normal clothes for social reasons. You may have noticed this morning that the chefs in the canteens all wore white aprons and chef's hats. That is part of our strategy to make people feel at home and deal better with the shock."

"How long will we keep our memories?" asked Basil, as I nodded to him to keep it up.

"You will keep your memories as long as you work down here or are on special ops. During that time your memory stays with your body, just like now. Some people have been down here for very long and were allowed to keep their memories from their life on the surface and also the ones of their life down here. But if you are sent for reprogramming, then we will keep your memories. But don't worry, we look after them ever so well."

"What do you do with all of the memories?" added Basil.

"Well, memories cannot die, it is a physical impossibility. And a good job too. That is why we administer them after they have been extracted. We have been storing the memories of all surface animals since we were entrusted with this grand task from higher authority. But now one of these memories has been stolen. Professor Wingnut's glass jar was stolen and we need it back. That is the reason we are talking here now."

"And I thought you just said that you looked after them ever so well! And who exactly is Professor Wingnut?" enquired Ludwig.

Slightly taken aback, he carried on. "I can't say too much now but I can say that Professor Wingnut was one of the leading scientists in the field of Memming and Morphing. And this memory in the wrong hands can be very dangerous. In fact, it could destroy our world entirely."

"What is Memming and Morphing, Colonel Pickle?"

"Mr Jackson, so many questions today. You are a very inquisitive bunch. Memming is the technical process of extracting memories and during the process of Morphing, living beings are infiltrated with their memories intact, into another being. But this will be an essential part of your training. You will hear everything you need to know about this in the coming days."

"Cool. So I could be morphed into a human and discipline dozy dogs," said Basil, cheekily.

"Theoretically yes," replied the Colonel.

"Look, we must crack on now. Let me introduce you to Colonel Bacon. He is in charge of your day-to-day training and will start the process of the important job applications for you. I will see you again when you return to the Special Operations Department."

Colonel Bacon took Colonel Pickle's place at the lectern through a side door, where he had presumably been listening. Even though he was wearing the same uniform, his missing moustache didn't make him look as serious as Colonel Pickle. He coughed and said, "Welcome to my Red Five Training School. I have heard a lot about you and understand you have something special to offer. I am here to help you through your training process and get you fit for your mission."

However, as though he had been ordered to, his smile was not genuine and my gut feeling told me that he could not be trusted.

"Before we get going on the job application process, are there any questions?"

"Yes, Colonel Bacon," said Vanessa. "We have heard from Colonel Pickle about Red Five. I presume there are other areas, for example Red Four."

"Well yes, my dear Miss Forsythe-Twyke. There are of course other levels but as you might guess I can't say too much about them; however, I will tell you this. Red five is the working area you find yourselves in and you will stay here the whole time. There are other levels of course but these belong to the higher-level politics. You might remember from your arrivals briefing that processors are reprogrammed according to quota received from higher authority. It is exactly these type of functions which are performed at the other levels and there is a strict separation between these and our level. I myself have never been to another level — I don't have the necessary clearance," explained Colonel Bacon, very kindly. "Does that answer your question, my dear?"

"Yes, I suppose it does. Thank you, Colonel."

"Right, if there are no further questions let us get cracking. Firstly, we will go to the job centre so you can apply for a suitable job, then you will do your tunnelling duties. Tomorrow you will begin your new jobs for the next seven days. At the end of the seven days, and only when I am sure that you have integrated into life down here, you will begin your training at Special Operations, and not before. It is very important that you settle into a routine as quickly as possible so that nobody suspects you of being part of this secret programme. However, that aside, we have a certain amount of pressure to train you and send you out as quickly as possible owing to the special urgency with the Professor."

"One final point," he said speaking slowly and softly but still looking at us with his false smile. "Please note that I am your friend and feel free to come to me anytime if you need any help or have any questions. I can understand this is a distressing time for you."

"Sounds a bit smarmy if you ask me," whispered Vanessa in my ear.

"Yeah, I know what you mean. My intuition also tells me not to trust him," I whispered back.

The Colonel then turned serious again and shouted out, "Fraser!"

"Yes sir," replied Fraser meekly when he entered the room through the same door that Colonel Pickle had left and Colonel Bacon had entered a few minutes ago.

"Take this group to the job centre and help them find suitable work. Then assign them to their daily tunnelling duties," barked the Colonel.

***

At his usual pace, Fraser led us down a few tunnels, some lefts and rights, before arriving at a large intersection with a café on one side and a large office with a Job Centre sign hanging above the other. "Right, everyone. In here you will find several notice boards split up into different career paths. The job adverts give you a brief description of the job and the skills required. If you have difficulty choosing, the administrator will help you find something according to your skills."

"I have never applied for a job before," whispered Vanessa to me.

"I can believe that," I replied, and it really didn't surprise me.

Fraser opened the door and followed us in, firmly closing the door behind him. The walls were covered with notice boards, each with signs above them indicating the type of jobs available. On the left a serious looking female mole smartly dressed in a white blouse, a blue silk scarf and spectacles resting on the end of her nose was sitting at a single desk. The first sign I saw was 'Drivers'.

"Right, all of you, I suggest you start looking for jobs that may interest you. And of course are suitable for you. I will be waiting for you in the café right opposite. Good luck everyone!"

"OK, well, let's go and see what I can find for myself," I said so Fraser could hear as he left the Job Centre but then turned around perusing the room before indicating to the others to come closer. "Don't just look for a job that you like but have in mind what we need to achieve." I said with a very hushed voice. "Remember we need to collect as much information as possible and also useful contacts."

Then I spent some time browsing through the different job sections just to see what kind of jobs were on offer. One vacancy on the 'Drivers' board was for a transport shuttle driver.

Job Title	Transport Shuttle Driver
Life Form	Moles Desirable
Experience	Tobogganing in previous life
Skills	Reckless
Job Number	6874

Not so interesting for me I thought but probably good fun. No, I needed to find something which kept me alive for as long as possible. Something important. So I browsed further until I came across the 'Warehousing' notice board where a very interesting advert aroused my interest. That was it!

Job Title	Memory Warehouse Analyst
Life Form	Human Desirable
Experience	Analysing information and database management
Skills	Analytical
Job Number	2945

Just perfect I thought. This job was made for me considering my work experience as a civil servant and I walked straight towards the female mole sitting behind her desk with the spectacles still resting on the end of her nose and a 'You're speaking to Dawn' name badge pinned to her white blouse.

"Hello, I would like to apply for job 2945," I said.

"Do you have a ticket?" she replied politely.

"Ticket?" I asked.

"Yes. You have to pull a ticket and then wait to be called forward. The ticket machine is over there," she said pointing to a machine on the wall. "You can take a seat next to it and wait for the next free administrator to call you."

I looked at the machine, the empty seats and at her being the only administrator. "But there's nobody waiting here," I said.

With an air of civil service authority, she said, "Rules are rules. Now kindly pull a ticket or nothing happens here," and she looked down again at her desk to carry on with her work.

"Damn stupid rules just like in our local council office. No need to copy everything from the surface!"

The ticket machine just like everything down here was made of discarded items from above. It was a simple plastic dispenser with those type of index labels you might put on a document to remember a page. I pulled the next available ticket and I only had just sat down on an empty tin can with a small wooden board on top when Dawn called up my number. "Number twenty-seven please!"

"Please take a seat. How can I be of assistance?" she said seriously and full of importance when I handed her my ticket. There was even a small light glowing above her desk.

"I would like to apply for job 2945," I repeated. "I believe I am perfectly suited for it."

"Now let me have a look." She opened a box and rummaged through what appeared to be her filing system. "Here we are, job 2945. You are applying for the position of Memory Warehouse Analyst."

"Yes, that is correct," I answered politely.

"OK, you are, or were, a human so we are off to a good start. Now please tell me about your previous experiences and skills! Why do you think you are perfectly suited for this position?"

It did not take long for her to make a decision. She wrote down some details on a slip of paper and handed it to me. "Mr Jackson. I can see you are clearly qualified for this job and I have pleasure in offering you the position with immediate effect. Please take a transport shuttle on line six to station three hundred and twenty-seven and here you will find the Memory Warehouse. You need to report to Mr Stockwell at half past eight tomorrow morning. Thank you," she said, indicating that the interview was over and looking back down at the papers on her desk.

The others had obviously worked out what to do as well and were all sitting on the tin can seats next to the ticket machine. I walked over, very curious to find out what jobs they were interested in.

"Well, what did you get Connor," asked Basil.

"I have got a very useful job as a memory warehouse analyst. I think you might all agree."

Then the little light above the desk started glowing again. "Number twenty-eight please!"

"Oh, that's me then," said Basil and waddled off. "Wish me luck, everyone," he added.

"What are you applying for, Ludwig?" I asked.

"There's a vacancy for a storeman. I am sure I would have access to lots of things which could make our lives comfortable. It sounds quite interesting and I am good at retrieving things!"

"And you, Vanessa?"

"Look, Connor. This is a stupid exercise. I have never applied for a job in my life and I can't find anything that suits me. I'm afraid I will have to tell her about my numerous skills, especially in how to run the staff in a household, and see what she has. There must be a high-level job for someone of my status."

"I wouldn't be too sure of that," I added ironically. "I'm off now to join Fraser in the café. See you later."

***

I sat alone with Fraser for a while and it was a good opportunity to ask him questions about life below the surface and what he did down here — that was until he was called off to find out what tunnelling work had to be done for the day. He didn't tell me anything interesting though, or divulge anything he wasn't allowed to say, just towed the party line. It appeared Fraser was only responsible for the everyday work routine and had nothing to do with the special ops programme. He claimed not to know anything about it but I didn't really believe him. In fact, who could one believe down here?

I was becoming increasingly sceptical about the power wielded by the moles. What a vile idea to extract memories and store them for others to access. Memories are personal, something which belongs solely to the person who experienced them. For me this was just theft and I was determined to find out more about what they did with all of these memories. There were a lot of theories and questions running around in my head. I mean, how could other animals be converted into moles and keep their memories. Fraser's very simple answer was that moles were also born and died like others, but those others with extra special skills could undergo a special conversion programme to become a mole which was apparently something special and thought of as the highest one could ever achieve in the circle of life. More often than not, humans were converted owing to their technical advanced stage and achievements on the surface or their military skills. This is what happened to Fraser. Now, one of my theories about the Professor was that somebody was maybe trying to escape with valuable technology to break the power of the moles. So, maybe there was a good reason for it but who were the good ones and who were the bad ones? Were there any bad ones at all? My job in the memory warehouse was the perfect place to start answering these questions. Maybe I would even find out who stole the Professor. You never know!

"Connor. What are you thinking about?" said Ludwig in his slow, drawn out voice.

"Connor!" said Ludwig a little louder as he could see I was deeply lost in my own thoughts.

"Erm, hello Ludwig. What is it?"

"I only wanted to know what you were thinking about?" asked Ludwig again. "It must be very important."

"Oh, Ludwig. Just thinking about life down here and trying to make some sort of sense about it. Rather difficult though. Did you get the job you wanted?"

"Sure did. I am now officially a storeman. Great isn't it?" replied Ludwig, with visible delight.

"Well, that's certainly a good job and a very good source of equipment. You will have to keep those big ears of yours open and learn as much as you can. What's available in the store. Where does it come from? Can things be borrowed without anybody noticing? Anything you can glean would be good." I explained slowly.

"And look who we have now," said Ludwig as Basil waddled through the door.

"And what job have you got, Basil?" I asked.

Basil looked proud as punch and stood up as straight as he could and announced, "I am one of the Food Sourcing Administrators."

"And what exactly does that entail?" asked a confused looking Ludwig.

"I am not yet one hundred percent sure but I understand that I am responsible for preparing lists of food required down here and where it can be found or sourced from. My specialist area is river food. Perfect, isn't it?"

"Like flora and fauna or something like that?"

"No, more like fish I think. I'm sure I read something about there being a luxury fish restaurant down here. A restaurant only for the high and mighty moles I believe."

"Well, I can see you are extremely happy but I am not yet sure how that will help us. Let us see where you can be useful." I said.

At last Vanessa stormed into the café and sat down with a loud thud in a chair.

"I presume you didn't get what you wished for?" asked Basil.

"Oh well done, brains. Of course not. The stupid woman just wouldn't even listen to me. There were no managerial or executive jobs available and as I didn't apply for anything she did it for me.

How can she do that? She doesn't even know me. I'm a Forsythe-Twyke and we only do executive jobs."

"So, what did she give you?" I asked.

She mumbled something incoherent under her breath, which none of us could understand.

"Nope, didn't get that. Say it again, Vanessa?" I asked with a wry grin. Probably the first time I had grinned in a while. I now suspected something interesting was coming!

"She gave me a job at an observation post," she said glumly. "Fancy that. Such a menial task for a Forsythe-Twyke. Unbelievable! A damn observation job instead of a managerial position. Ghastly, just ghastly."

"And exactly what do you have to observe?" a puzzled Ludwig asked.

"Some sort of activities on the surface from a molehill as observation post. In case you ever wondered if a molehill had any purpose, then now you know."

"And what exactly are you supposed to observe?"

"What was it? Hmm, house number three I seem to remember she told me."

"And the road?" I asked with increasing interest.

"I think the woman said Trout Lane. Yes, that's what she said. Number three Trout Lane. I have to report somewhere tomorrow to find out what exactly I am supposed to look out for."

"Did you say number three Trout Lane?"

"That's what I said. Yes." Replied Vanessa gruffly.

"But that's my house," I said excitedly. "Or, it was my house until a few days ago."

"The day is just getting worse. Do you mean to say I have to observe Lower Molehampton? That as well! The thought of observing Lower Molehampton for someone like me is just awful. I will never live this humiliation down."

"But, Vanessa. That is very interesting. Very interesting indeed."

"Interesting? What could possibly be interesting about observing Lower Molehampton?"

"Stop behaving like a child throwing a tantrum. Think about our plan," I replied angrily. "Have you not understood what we are trying to achieve, Vanessa? I am trying to find a way of keeping us all alive and this job could be of vital importance of that I am sure. Don't you understand?"

"Yeah, you need to work with us on this, Vanessa," Basil chirped in. "This is not all about you."

"OK, crew. Let's go." Fraser was back and ready for action. "There's your daily tunnelling work to be done. We have to go back to your accommodation first to get your equipment and then go to the new area where work needs to be done," he ordered.

"And where exactly do we have to tunnel?" asked Vanessa.

"Let me have a look on my map."

Fraser opened the map he was carrying and showed it to us. His map was not like a normal map you or I would expect. A normal map shows the ground from an aerial view but this map was a cross-section. The surface showed some houses and below the ground were hundreds of criss-crossing tunnels with projected molehills plotted on the surface.

"Fraser. It doesn't really tell me anything. It is a cross-section. Where is that on the surface?"

"Oh, that's not so important Connor. We just have to dig. But wait. The tunnel planner has a legend in the corner. Oh yes, here we are. Hmm, this is obviously a new tunnelling project for Trout Lane in Lower Molehampton."

"Are you meaning to say that all molehills are planned?" asked Vanessa.

"But of course. You surely don't believe we just tunnel for the sake of it, do you? We don't do random down here. Random digging would be absurd and a complete waste of time. No, there is a planning committee and every day new plans are distributed and work delegated. Every single molehill has a purpose you know and apparently Trout Lane is a high priority job. It is not for us to ask why, just for us to dig."

"What a surprise," I added sarcastically.

There could only be one reason why they were interested in watching my house and that was to see if anyone tried to break in and get the jar. Whoever they might be.

***

The way to our allocated tunnelling area was newly dug, poorly lit and the driver extremely reckless.

"Don't worry ladies and gentlemen!" he shouted at one point. "First day in the job today. I was allocated this job after I applied and am so happy that I can offer the moles something. As a human I was very successful at tobogganing and because of that I was invited to be converted into a mole. And here I am. Great fun isn't it?"

"Did you represent your country in tobogganing?" asked Vanessa.

"I sure did. I represented the Molehamptons."

"But the Molehamptons is not a country," replied Vanessa.

"Of course it is," the mole said seriously.

Vanessa and I just looked at each other and frowned as the mole, now whooping with delight, steered the transport shuttle with no regard to our safety or comfort along the tunnel. We clung on with sheer fright as the shuttle was going up towards the surface at breakneck speed through steep tunnels, crashing off the walls and bouncing on the floor. At long last and with a hard thud we arrived in what resembled a new building area. We were glad to get out of the shuttle after a hair-rising journey and tried to compose ourselves whilst we were waiting for Fraser to give us further instructions, but he simply explained that he had his own work today and left us in the capable hands of our supervisor.

"So what have they sent me today?" a dog asked approaching us. "I can't believe it. How useless. Two humans, a duck and a retriever. Great. What should I do with you lot?" Said the dog with annoyance. "I am a terrier and we are expert diggers. You lot have obviously no experience in digging, apart from the retriever that is, at least somebody with useful skills. My name is Sapper, a very common name for tunnelling experts down here by the way."

151

"We might be able to help in some way," said a huffy looking Basil.

"Help! What the hell should I do with a duck? Apart from eat it of course," said Sapper with a growl. "Retriever. What's your name?"

"Ludwig is my name."

"Well, Ludwig. You are in charge. Follow me. All of you, put your head torches on and take care where you are walking. The tunnel has not been shored up yet."

Sapper led us through a dark, damp, freshly dug tunnel until we reached the end, where the tunnelling work had stopped. This tunnel was much narrower than most we had so far seen and we had to stoop slightly as our heads just touched the roof. The only light in this dark environment was that from our head torches. He took out his digging plan and a piece of rope and explained what we had to do. "You are to dig in a straight line in exactly the same direction this tunnel is now. No turns and no curves, and use the rope to measure your progress. At the end of the rope you are to start digging up in a vertical direction until you break the surface. Understood?"

"Yes," said Ludwig, obviously proud he was in charge. "What should we do with the earth we dig out?"

"My goodness. Why do they send me workers with no experience?" replied an annoyed Sapper. "Right. I suggest you do the tunnelling. Retrievers are fast. The two humans are useless at tunnelling as their hands are just not made for this job. They can use the buckets over there," he said pointing to a pile of equipment in a small cutting on the side of the tunnel. "And load the excavated earth on a shuttle to be taken away back to the station where we just met. Another team will deposit the earth on the surface close by. We are just below the surface already now so when you start tunnelling upwards you need to push the excavated earth onto the surface and form a hill. That's why we have molehills should you have ever asked yourselves. Report back to me when you are finished."

"So what should I do?" asked Basil. "I would like to be of use in this work."

"You can hold the rope in your beak," said Ludwig. "And ensure that we dig in a straight line."

Sapper turned around and disappeared back down the dark tunnel as we started our first tunnelling job with Ludwig digging furiously as Vanessa and I worked extremely hard to keep up with him. It was back breaking work to shovel the earth into the buckets and carry them back to the station. We were not used to that much physical activity and I envied Basil who clearly had the easiest job holding the rope in his beak, every now indicating to Ludwig he was going a little off course. I am not sure how long it took and how many buckets we removed, but at long last Ludwig reached the end of the rope and Basil proudly exclaimed that he could now start tunnelling upwards. He looked relatively clean whereas the rest of us were covered in earth. I mopped the sweat from my brow and glanced at Vanessa who, for the first time since I had met her, wasn't complaining. With only the whites of our eyes and her teeth glinting in the light of my head torch she almost looked like she was enjoying the work. It was probably a very new experience for her.

"OK, everyone. Let's go up now nice and carefully. I don't know exactly how far there is to go so I will go slowly and push the earth ahead of me," said Ludwig.

After some more scraping and pushing, Ludwig returned down the short section of the tunnel and looked at Basil.

"I've got a job for you!"

"And what is that?"

"You will see. Stand at the bottom and push your beak towards the top of the molehill. Connor and Vanessa will lift you up."

"Right, Basil. Now open your beak. You have a big mouth so you should be able to make a decent sized opening!" said Ludwig teasingly.

Basil angrily looked down at Ludwig but when Basil's beak broke the surface, a rush of fresh air shot down from above and the light of night sky shone down the tunnel. The smell of fresh air was fantastic and we all stood there breathing in deeply through our noses.

"OK, come back down now," ordered Ludwig again. "Now, Connor, stand on my back and see if you can look out of the top of the hill."

I slowly stuck my head out of the top of the molehill so my eyes were level with the top and couldn't believe what I saw. I was looking directly at my house — number three Trout Lane! I really don't know why I was so careful as we were invisible to those on the surface — that's at least what we had been told. Looking at my house not only made me sad but fed me with a strong desire to conjure up a plan to get us out of here. I didn't know quite how yet but I was sure I would come up with something.

I had a feeling that my job would prove to be rather useful.

Chapter Ten
Memories

My second night hadn't been any better than my first, and just like the night before, it was over with the call of the rooster blaring out of the sound system, but this time thankfully not accompanied by Vanessa's hysterical screams. Before I fell into a restless sleep I decided that, when or if I came up with a plan, it was probably best to keep all of my thoughts to myself. I did not want to risk unintentionally sharing information with anyone from the world of moles. So I had to be very selective or maybe even give them wrong information. I somehow needed to find out who I could trust. Who was good and who was bad. If this was at all possible because it seemed that even the moles couldn't work that one out amongst themselves. What if they were just using me to smoke out the Professor's thieves and they were the good ones? Maybe it was even best not to share too many thoughts with my three friends. For their own good.

It didn't matter how often I told myself that all of this was just a dream because I simply couldn't leave it, and right now I had to get up and go to work. As expected, Cleopatra was already waiting for us when we met in the tunnel to go to breakfast. Incidentally, this was the first time I had seen her since going into the debriefing yesterday. She looked her normal aggressive self but followed us much closer today and her panting breath sent chills down my back at every step. She was obviously trying to hear what we were saying so I whispered to the others to be careful and from now on not to trust anyone.

It was amazing that after just two days down here we all seemed to have settled into some kind of routine, basic as it was, and maybe even accepted our lot. We bid each other farewell after breakfast as we departed on our own ways for the day and promised to meet in the pub after work to share our first working day experiences and anything else which might prove useful.

'Take the transport shuttle on line six to station three hundred and twenty-seven. Report to Mr Stockwell in the Memory Warehouse at half past eight.' I took out the slip of paper from the pocket of my red overalls which Dawn had given me yesterday. It was now eight a.m. and I presumed thirty minutes should be plenty of time to get there. Thankfully I managed to work out where I was quite quickly. The map was similar to the one yesterday — with a cross-section showing the layout of tunnels and levels below the ground on one side and on the other side an aerial view of Level five. Just like on a London Underground map, I had to first identify my line using the legend on the side of the map showing all lines in different colours, and the one I was looking for was yellow. Now all I had to do was find the closest station.

"Can I help you?" growled a deep voice from behind.

"Maybe. I'm just looking to see where I am and where I have to go," I replied still looking at my map before slowly turning around to see who offered me their help. Cleopatra was standing so close behind me that I felt her warm breath on my face. I was usually not scared of dogs but here we were both exactly the same size and looking at each other squarely in the face, only a few centimetres apart.

"Where do you have to go?" growled Cleopatra at me again.

"Erm, line six to station three hundred and twenty-seven," stammering my answer back to her. "I'm just looking for the closest station but the map is rather confusing. I'm new here but, well, you know that better than anyone, Miss Cleopatra."

"Cleopatra will do and you can follow me. I have to go in that direction anyhow, so you can just come along," said Cleopatra and started walking without saying another word.

"Here you are, Mr Jackson. Line six station two hundred and ninety-nine. The shuttle will be here shortly."

It had only been a short walk and just a few moments later the rattling and whoosh of an approaching shuttle shot out of the tunnel, followed shortly after by the customary thud and cloud of dust as it arrived at the station. Cleopatra growled loudly as there was only one seat free between a cat and a cow, and this was more than enough for them to immediately unbuckle and leave the shuttle and the station as quickly as they could. "Thank you," gnarled Cleopatra as they went past her. All other animals in the shuttle remained fearfully silent as Cleopatra got in and sat down, directly to my left, her fur brushing against my arm as she buckled in.

"What station will it be first," shouted the driver.

"Station three hundred and twenty-six," ordered Cleopatra. "Then three hundred and twenty-seven for Mr Jackson." No other passenger was keen to volunteer any information on where they wanted to go and the driver also didn't bother asking.

***

I tried not to look at Cleopatra. However, out of the corner of my eye I could see her glaring at me the whole bumpy journey and when the shuttle stopped at station three hundred and twenty-six for Cleopatra to alight she put her wet snout right against my nose, saliva drooling from her jaws kindly wishing me a pleasant day before leaving her seat. That was enough excitement for me for the day and it was still early in the morning when I arrived at station three hundred and twenty-seven with an ashen face just some minutes later.

***

"Mr Jackson," shouted a voice but I couldn't see anyone at the station.

"Yes, it is me," shouting back and looking around when a mole appeared from around the corner of the station entrance.

157

"Ahh, Mr Jackson. A pleasure to meet you and perfectly on time. I like punctuality. We like punctuality down here you know. My name is Mr Stockwell."

"Nice to meet you, Mr Stockwell."

"Follow me please and the warehouse is just around this corner. Be there in a jiffy. Are you OK? You look a little, how shall I say it, pale."

"Am I OK? Well I just had an encounter with a scary dog, Mr Stockwell, which probably accounts for my pale face. Also, I might just have died or maybe not. So please excuse me if I am not my normal self."

"Of course, a new arrival. How insensitive of me but do not worry, Mr Jackson, you will be well taken care of down here. We have your best interests at heart," said the mole, scurrying along the tunnel.

"And here we are, Mr Jackson — the warehouse," Mr Stockwell exclaimed proudly and with a grunt of effort, he opened a heavy round door made of cast iron. As I went through the opening I took a close look at it and noticed that 'Property of Anglerton County Council' was embossed on it like on the small covers you might see on a pavement to access gas or water. Crafty moles I thought. They seemed to steal everything. Well, at least they kept the Anglerton police station busy!

We entered a dark room and Mr Stockwell simply said, "Let there be light, courtesy of Lower Molehampton electricity company," and with a loud click he pulled down a lever and the room lit up. What I now saw was more unexpected than anything else I had ever seen in my life and yet another sight down here more amazing than the last. We stood in a huge cavern, much larger than the arrivals railway station on my first day, which was only two days ago really but already seemed an age. There were five aisles leading into the distance with rows upon rows of storage racks as far as the eye could see, stacked full with glass jars. Each aisle had storage racks with shelves on both the left and the right, with diagonal ramps built to access each level. Each storage rack had about ten levels with lots of neat rows of glass jars on each shelf, stacked a few deep so it was not possible to see how far they went back. There must have been hundreds upon thousands of them in this aisle alone. Amazing!

"Well, what do you think, Mr Jackson?"

"I am flabbergasted. This is huge. Does each jar really contain a memory from a living being? There must be hundreds of thousands of them," I said in sheer wonder.

"I think hundreds of thousands is an underestimate. Over a million I would imagine, Mr Jackson, and added to daily I hasten to add. We are constantly expanding the warehouse and have to deposit the excavated earth on the surface. We are really quite tight for space at the moment as we need to make space for all of the memories from the Molehamptons and Anglerton. There are just so many of them and so much work to administer it all. Hence, why you are now here."

Before I could say or ask anything he just carried on.

"This is your work place for now and I have heard you bring skills well needed down here. Not many people are experienced analysts you know. I really look forward to working with you and I am sure learning from you too. I am so delighted that you are now down here to help us."

"More delighted than I am. I really had other plans with my life and this is not part of it. Sorry to disappoint you."

A rabbit suddenly came out of a side room from the right and quickly bounced up several ramps with a glass jar in its front paws and some sort of clipboard strapped to its back. The thuds of its paws landing on the metal could only faintly be heard as it was moving very carefully so as not to disturb the glass jars in the metal storage or to drop the glass it was holding. At level four the rabbit stopped in front of a free storage place and cautiously placed the glass jar on the shelf. He then filled something in with the pen that was attached to his clipboard. Probably the name and location of the memory.

"We preferably employ rabbits down here, Mr Jackson. They are perfectly equipped for warehouse work — quick, strong and extremely nimble. Come now, follow me. I will take you to your office and show you what you have to do."

We stepped into an open plan office with at least fifty moles feverously working on documents stacked high around them on their desks. The rabbit bounced back down and silently returned to the room it had just come from, and none of the moles dared to look up as we walked through. They all remained one hundred per cent focused on their tasks, almost as if they were afraid of being accused of slacking.

"This is our storage admin pool. These moles work very hard to record all necessary information relating to the jars. Names, dates, profession, storage location and so on. It is extremely important to record everything accurately, so we can find the memories if we need them. But our manual system is rather time consuming. That's why we need somebody like you to help us."

"Why would you need the memories again, Mr Stockwell?" I asked.

"Well, we sometimes have to retrieve the memories for further interrogation," he replied.

"What do you mean? Further interrogation? You can interrogate a jar?"

"Oh, Mr Jackson. You are new here and don't yet understand what we can do. Of course, we can interrogate the memories in case we need more information from them. We have a special sophisticated technology which allows us to speak to the memory and get the truthful answer — memories cannot lie. It's an amazing system you know. I will show it to you later today."

"That sounds extremely interesting and high tech," I replied, trying to sound impressed when in reality the whole idea made me want to wretch.

"So, here you are, Mr Jackson. Your office."

Apart from a table and a chair the office was completely empty. No filing cabinet, no papers, nothing.

"But there's nothing here, Mr Stockwell."

"Yes, quite correct, Mr Jackson. But don't worry about it. The position of Memory Warehouse Analyst is new, and it is your task to create your own job and responsibilities, with me to supervise of course. Let me explain what we want to achieve. At the moment we just store everything and don't really do anything with it. Also, sometimes, we need further information and then have to interrogate memories, but as you can imagine, it is very difficult to link our records to this abundance of information because we have never had anyone who could analyse information. Basically, your job, Mr Jackson, is to create a system whereby we can analyse all of the information we have in the world and link it to the memory jars for simple retrieval. Simple. Any questions?"

"You want me to analyse all of the information contained in the memories in the whole warehouse? For the whole world?" I asked in obvious disbelief. "But that would take an eternity!"

"Exactly, Mr Jackson, and now that you are down here you do have that eternity. Plenty of time, so please don't fret about it. To help you settle in let me introduce you to one of our senior warehouse workers. He will show you around and explain to you where everything is."

Mr Stockwell stuck his head out of the door and shouted, "Dusty!"

"Connor, nice to see you again. Have you got a job here with us?"

"You know each other?"

"Yeah, of course. We met in the pub last night," said Dusty with great delight.

"My word. It didn't take you long to settle in, Mr Jackson. I can do without the introductions then. Dusty, please show Mr Jackson around. He needs to know where the records are kept, how he can find things. Take a good look through the warehouse. I have things to do so I will see you both later. Mr Jackson, I like an open-door policy so please feel free to come and ask if you need anything."

"Come on, Connor — I'll show you the warehouse first. In fact, I am sure there is a glass jar to store in the Memory Inbound Department. Let's collect one, so you can see the whole process. Follow me."

The round door made of some scrap wood was simply signed 'Memory Inbound'. Dusty pushed it open and it closed directly behind us with a thud. The room was completely empty but painted a brilliant, sterile white. The only thing to see was a door in the opposite wall with a small red light above it. When the light started flashing, Dusty opened the door revealing a single glass jar on a wheeled board with a sheet of paper on top. A rather glum looking rabbit pushed the jar over to Dusty without saying a word and left through an non-transparent plastic curtain, so we couldn't see what was on the other side. Dusty manoeuvred the jar into the centre of the white room. It was approximately the same size as we were.

"What on earth is happening here?" I asked.

"The memories are being extracted on the other side of the room. I believe you might already have heard about the Memming process. The memory is extracted and then preserved in a special fluid in a glass jar. The sheet of paper has all the details of who the memory belonged to."

"And what about the poor creature on the other side?"

"Oh, they don't really know anything about it. It is quite painless I have heard. They just sit in the room and are sprayed with a special chemical to start the Memming process. I have never been in there, and I don't want to, but apparently there is an extraction system which then sucks out the memory and injects it straight into a jar with the special fluid."

"That sounds ghastly. What about the creature after this process?"

"Oh, don't worry. They feel nothing and as soon as their memory is extracted they have no recollection of even entering the room. The memory is stored in the glass jar and all that remains of the creature is an empty shell containing its processor. This is taken to another warehouse where it is stored until it is needed again. If the processor is assigned as a rabbit for example, it is then reprogrammed for that function on the surface."

"This is absolutely awful. Nobody has the right to do something like this," I said angrily.

"It might sound bad, Connor, but maybe you have forgotten that you are in fact already dead. Just let the moles deal with it, Connor, — it's their job. Speak to Mr Stockwell if you want to talk about it — he did say he had an open-door policy. I'm just a rabbit and I am very happy to have a job and I am not in a jar or on a dinner plate, you know."

"Hmmm, Dusty. I'll have to think about that. Anyway, what happens now?" I asked.

"We will take the jar and the documentation to the admin pool for record keeping. Then we have to wait until they tell us where to store the memory, so it can be found again."

Dusty pushed the glass jar through the swing door and all the way back to the admin pool. Isabelle, a female mole, took the very outdated paperwork consisting of two sheets with carbon paper for copying in the middle. She wrote down the storage location aisle five, column twenty, level four, place twenty-five and then attached one sheet to the clipboard on Dusty's back and put the other in a huge pile of paperwork on her desk.

"Come on, Connor. Follow me carefully please. We must not shake the jars in the storage system."

Dusty bounced off towards the warehouse, pushing the glass jar in front of him. Now I understood why rabbits were chosen to work in the warehouse. Their ability to bounce forward was the perfect motion for this kind of job, quick and smooth at the same time. I had to run to keep up.

"Slow down, Dusty," I shouted. "I can't keep up with you!"

I followed Dusty to aisle five, then along the aisle to column twenty and finally up a metal ramp from right to left all the way up the levels until we finally reached level four where a platform led us along until we found the empty slot at place twenty-five. Dusty placed the jar neatly on the shelf in between all the other thousands of jars with the name facing outwards. The name on this jar was 'Bill'.

"Bill. Is that it? What type of useless information is that? We don't even know what creature he was — nothing," I said.

"Ah Connor, look at the sheet on the clipboard. It has much more information," he said swinging it around to the front of him for me to see. "We are not that bad."

Name	Bill
Species	Mole
Position	Tunnel Digger
ID Number	Mole247934
Date of Memming	7th October 2019
Location	Aisle five, Column twenty, Level four, Place twenty-five

"No surname?" I asked.

"No. That is very human to have a surname I believe," replied Dusty.

"Maybe but it really is quite practical," I explained.

"You humans are funny. Look, Connor, animals possess more skills than you humans could ever dream of when it comes to differentiating between things. Our sense of smell and hearing for example is much more finely tuned than yours. Believe me, we don't need surnames to know who we are."

"If you say so. It's still practical," I insisted.

Dusty ticked a box on the sheet, signed it and swung the clipboard onto his back. And then he was off again, light-footedly bouncing back down the ramps with me in tow to hand back the paperwork to Isabelle. Then the peace of the admin pool was shattered with the ringing of a bell; when suddenly rabbits popped out of the side rooms and it became very busy around the warehouse with all of them bouncing along the aisles pushing glass jars to their locations at the same time.

"What on earth is going on now?" I asked.

"Coffee break is over now, Connor and everyone is going back to work. It's normally this busy."

"Coffee break! I've heard it all now."

"Union rules, Connor," said Dusty with a smile.

"OK, Dusty. It's my turn to decide what to do. If I am to oversee the setting up of a new system, I need to look at the filing. Can you show me how it is done?"

"I think it's best to ask one of the admin pool," replied Dusty.

I spent the next hour with Isabelle in a vast archive of paperwork. The records I must admit were meticulously organised in a paper filing system which cross-referenced in many directions, allowing to search by name, by species, by ID number, by position and even by date of arrival or Memming.

"This appears to be excellent, Isabelle. I am not sure you really need me."

"Yes we do. Mr Stockwell wants and also needs more information. We only have the basic information here. You may remember from your debriefing that somebody took notes about your memories. These notes for example are just filed with the records but not analysed. It is these notes from all debriefings which need analysing. That's why we need you!"

"Let's test the system then. Can you find the records for my old mathematics teacher, Patrick Donnelly, please?" I asked. "Let me think. He must have passed away in 2002, if that helps. He has a surname which should make finding the record easier!"

Isabelle had to hunt though a pile of records but it didn't take her long to come back with the requested information about the exact location of my former mathematics teacher.

"Now, Dusty, would you be so kind and get the jar?"

"Of course. This is the best part of the job. Have a look!"

I followed Dusty out of the office to another area of the warehouse and was amazed about his agility to bounce up the ramps. It didn't take him long to get to the jar. He took it out of the storage, pushed it to the end of the platform and around the corner to the top of the ramp. With a howl of delight, he jumped on the back of the trolley and hurtled down the ramps. The trolley perfectly followed the contours of a curved barrier at the bottom of every ramp down to the next ramp. It did not take long until Dusty had to use his hind legs as perfect brakes and he screeched to a halt right in front of me.

"Here you go, Connor. Mr Patrick Donnelly at your service."

"And Dusty, where was your normal careful manner just now? Was that ride not a bit reckless?"

"This is the old racking system, Connor, much better and stronger than the new ones. Unfortunately, the Purchasing Department sourced a much cheaper racking system and with this one we have to be very careful not to shake it around too much. The old systems are much more fun!"

"Thank you for that, Dusty. So far so good. Let's try with another name. How about Margaret Thatcher, a former British Prime Minister from the 1980s. I have some questions for her."

When Isabelle returned after almost an hour, she quite sadly informed me that nobody with this name was recorded in the system. And she gave me the same negative response again after I enquired about Winston Churchill — another British Prime Minister from the 1940s.

"Impossible I said. How can you not have them? OK, let's try another one. How about Mr Charles Twyford? He ran the local football team but sadly passed away last year."

"Shall I go and get the jar, Connor," asked Dusty when Isabelle came back with his record.

"No, there's no need for that. Thanks. So you have Mr Donnelly and Mr Twyford but not Margaret Thatcher and Winston Churchill. I thought you administered the whole world."

"We do," they both answered simultaneously.

I spent the next few hours looking through various records, documents, different paperwork and kept Mr Donnelly's jar next to my desk, trying to think of how to start analysing all of the information recorded on different forms. There was a wealth of more often than not really mundane information written down from different debriefings. Coco, a cat, often witnessed glass jars being stolen from the jam jar glass factory in Lower Molehampton sometime in the 1990s. And another record read, that Sam, a dog, reported a mass attack of birds on his master, all trying to land their payload of bird poo on top of him. He ran and ran but eventually he was hit. He lived in Anglerton. Linda, a mouse, reported various break-ins at the toy shop in Upper Molehampton. On one occasion she reported some of the dishes and cutlery being stolen from the doll's houses. On another occasion she reported some furniture being stolen. All in small quantities and never enough to be noticed.

"What do these records say?" I asked myself. I really wasn't sure how any of it could be useful. But I decided to search for the record of the deceased toy shop owner from Upper Molehampton to see if there was any further information on that. It didn't take long. Mr Player often reported small items missing. He never suspected theft and just thought his workers had misplaced them. It was never enough at one time to cause a fuss. But come to think of it, over the years it must have been a lot.

It was certainly interesting to see what was actually recorded and there was one obvious fact. All reports were from Lower Molehampton, Upper Molehampton and Anglerton. Strange. As if the world only really consisted of these places, as everyone kept on telling me. This would now kind of explain why Margaret Thatcher's and Winston Churchill's memories were not stored here. It did beg the question where they were stored if not here. I knew this all to be wrong but why did everyone else believe in it, even people like Mr Tinker who must know for certain that there was more to the world than the Molehamptons and Anglerton. This was just like the theory that the world was flat, and you would fall off the edge if you sailed too far. Ludicrous. Modern brainwashing, I thought. The moles seemed to have even more power than I originally thought. How scary!

"Dusty, the door to the left of the warehouse where you got Mr Donnelly. What is behind it?"

"Oh that. That's another warehouse. Come on, I'll take you there."

With a leap and a bound Dusty bounced off towards the warehouse and again I had to run to keep up. The room was large but smaller than the one before and only had empty glass jars stacked precariously on top of each other. Hundreds of them.

"This, Connor, is our glass jar store." explained Dusty, proudly. "We have a very high level of inventory at the moment but as you can imagine we always need lots of new ones."

"Where do you get them from?" I asked suspiciously as I remembered the report I had read just about an hour ago from the cat, who witnessed glass jars being stolen from a factory in Lower Molehampton.

"Oh, I don't know that, Connor. Like everything down here it is best not to ask. All we do when we need more is to complete a material acquisition form and submit it to the Logistics Collection Agency. One tip from me, Connor. Don't ask questions down here and just do as you are told. You will stay here longer and not in a jar — believe me," said Dusty, and I was certain there was now fear in his eyes.

"Come on, Connor. I'm going to show you a secret of mine." He bounced off towards the back of the room and had a quick look around to make sure that we were alone. He then pushed some glass jars out of the way and revealed a wooden board which covered a small hole in the wall.

"Come here, Connor. Look through this hole."

I stooped down and peered through the small hole, only large enough for me to cover with one eye. I saw another warehouse also with a racking system but couldn't really make out what kind of items were stored on the shelves as they were quite far away.

"What is it for, Dusty?" I whispered.

"It's the processor warehouse, Connor. This is where all of the processors are stored after the Memming process and kept here until they are needed. If a dog is required for example, then any processor from this storage can be reprogrammed for its future use as a dog and sent back out again. The warehouse used to be quite full but these days it is nearly empty. I have never seen it so empty before."

"Why is that, Dusty?" I asked.

"I am not sure, but rumour has it that the demand for meat by the humans on the surface is apparently very high. And it is getting more and more difficult to keep up with the global market for meat, so a lot of these processors had to be allocated to the Factory from the reserve stock. We should go though, this is dangerous. If we are caught, we also might end up in the Factory. And, Connor?"

"Yes, Dusty."

"You can never tell anyone about this spy hole. I found it some months ago accidentally whilst tidying up. Only you and I know about it."

"Of course, Dusty. I won't say anything. My lips are sealed."

***

"Mr Jackson, please come in. How is your first day? Could you make any sense of our records?"

"Yes, a good and interesting first day, thank you. I can see that your team are most efficient and the record keeping meticulously organised. I managed to find nearly everything I asked for but only for records from Lower Molehampton, Upper Molehampton and Anglerton. Is that correct?"

I had decided to visit Mr Stockwell because I wanted further information and I was extremely interested to see how he would react to certain questions. Also, I wanted to find out, how it was possible to speak to memories, Mr Donnelly's memory in particular.

"Yes," replied Mr Stockwell with a rather reluctant look on his face. "That is correct."

"I do have one more question, Mr Stockwell. In my opinion, memories belong to their owners and not anyone else. Why do you have to take them? For what purpose?"

"Surely it doesn't matter what happens with those memories. You do know by now that everyone down here in our warehouse is already dead when they arrive, Mr Jackson. And you didn't actually believe that when you die your memory just disappears, did you? Just imagine what a great loss that would be if all of the memories and the experiences with them were just gone. Can you imagine that?"

"But storing and using memories does not sound exactly very ethical to me."

"But we don't only store memories, as you would have been told, we administer the processors. This way we make sure that every living being on the planet has the correctly programmed system to complete their role in life. Without this, the creatures would have no idea what to do. Have you never asked yourself why dogs, for example do things instinctively from birth without being taught? Quite easy, Mr Jackson — because we programme them to do so. We programme each dog breed, so they are unique and can carry out their tasks. Retrievers for example are programmed to retrieve, and we make sure they do. And did you actually know that humans used to be able to talk to animals? Well, they could in the past but it was phased out a long time ago. It could easily be reprogrammed again but someone decided it is not to be."

"So, you are saying the moles totally administer every creature in the Molehamptons and Anglerton?"

"Yes, Mr Jackson. You've got it at last and we do a wonderful job. Anything else I can help you with?"

"For my research I would like to see how you interrogate memories. I was able to obtain the memory of Mr Donnelly, my former mathematics teacher. I remember that you mentioned a special room earlier and I was wondering if you would show me how an interrogation is conducted."

"Of course, Mr Jackson. I was waiting for you to ask me this question. This is really the most interesting part of our work down here. Come on now, please follow me."

Mr Stockwell wheeled Mr Donnelly's memory down a tunnel, past the Memory Inbound Department until we reached an office signed Memory Interrogation. He opened the door and switched the light on. It was a round room with chairs forming a circle around a single round table in the centre of the room. Some sort of electrical device with a lens hung directly above the table.

"Where did you get all of this equipment from?"

"I have no idea, Mr Jackson. It was here when I arrived, but I am sure it was sourced from the world above. Somebody who knew how to use this equipment would have come up with the idea.

Probably somebody from the Research and Development Department. But best not to ask questions."

"Let me show you how easy an interrogation is, Mr Jackson," he said as he lifted the jar from the trolley and heaved it onto the table. "Just pop the glass jar on the dot in the centre of the table and you will see it is perfectly aligned with the lens. Now sit down and press this button."

The room immediately became pitch black and a blue light started radiating around the jar from the lens above the table. It became brighter and brighter until the room was fully lit in a dull blue light. Then all of a sudden, a miniature version of Mr Donnelly appeared in the jar.

"There we go. Finished. You may now speak to Mr Donnelly. I will leave the room to give you some privacy. When you are finished, just press the button again and have the glass jar returned to the admin pool. It is important that a record is kept of what information is taken, when, by whom and that the jar is returned to the correct storage place."

I was now alone with Mr Donnelly's memory and wasn't quite sure how to begin.

"Hello, Mr Donnelly," was a good start.

"Who's there?" replied a voice which I clearly recognised as Mr Donnelly's.

"It's Connor Jackson. Can you remember me from school? You taught me."

"Of course, I remember you. Well, what a pleasant surprise. Tell me, Connor, what is the date?"

"It's the seventh of October 2019, Mr Donnelly."

"That mean's I've been down here for thirteen years and you are the first person I have spoken to since then. What happened to you, Connor?"

I only explained about the accident and the river but didn't mention anything about Professor Wingnut and the other strange activities. I didn't want anyone else interviewing Mr Donnelly and finding out about things I had told him. I was sure my activities were being monitored.

"Sorry to hear about it. So what career did you have?"

"I was an analyst for the Government's Information Collection Agency, which is the reason why I was chosen for a job here."

"Did you need mathematics for your previous job?"

"Not really, it was more about analysing information rather than statistics," I replied.

"That's good because you were never good at mathematics, Connor," said Mr Donnelly, laughing.

"You are correct there. So, tell me Mr Donnelly, what was the Memming process like?"

"What's that, Connor?"

"It's the name of the process where your memory is extracted and put into the glass jar," I replied.

"Oh that, didn't know it had a name. I can't really remember anything about it. I was told to go into a room, sit down and that's the last I can remember. The next thing I can remember is you waking me up a few minutes ago."

"Did you have a job down here, Mr Donnelly?"

"Yes, Connor. I was part of a programming process for a special project. A very interesting project and my experience in mathematics got me the job. I worked in a very skilled team researching new technology for a process we called Morphing. One day, just after we finalised our machine, we were all led off and the next thing I can remember is going into that room and then talking to you. Shame, it was really interesting. Ground breaking technology and such an experience to work with the renowned Professor Wingnut."

"Who did you just say, Mr Donnelly?"

"Professor Wingnut. Do you know him? Is he still working down here?"

"Know him?" I replied very hesitantly. "No, I don't know him but I have heard of him from someone but can't seem to remember why." I paused not really knowing what else to say. "Look, Mr Donnelly, I've got to go now and it was really nice talking to you, even though the circumstances and surroundings are not what we both planned but I promise to visit you again in the next days. I have the feeling you can help me a lot in my new job and it would also be nice just to catch up on old times again. Thanks for your time. I mean…"

"It was a pleasure, Connor and believe me, time is something I have loads of. Oh yes, if you are interested in my work, you should also speak to Ms Hullington. A delightful colleague."

I said goodbye to Mr Donnelly and pressed the button. The blue light stopped radiating and became dimmer and Mr Donnelly's figure slowly disappeared back into the milky fluid it came from. Then the room went black and the light was switched on again.

***

Vanessa arrived first, got a table for all of us and was already enjoying her second beer when the rest of us turned up. We spent the whole of the evening talking about our experiences at the first day of work. I told them about my strange encounter with Cleopatra in the morning and then some basic information about the Memory Warehouse. I wanted to be careful not to explain too much at this stage to my friends as I didn't know if they could keep it to themselves.

Ludwig had an interesting first day and as a retriever was usefully employed to get things in the store. He was able to tell me how the store system worked, how the inventory was kept up to date and how everyone down here could request items from the store. His most interesting story was about how he retrieved fish from the cold store, apparently for a dinner of the mole political elite which he had to deliver to a very remote place of the tunnel system. He said it was a very important looking place where military and police made sure that only those with authorisation were allowed to proceed further — so only moles of course. Ludwig delivered the fish as ordered and he presumed it was to the restaurant Basil had mentioned the day before. He also explained about some of the things he had to store away during the day including five blocks of salt, which were always brought in on trolleys by rabbits, two toy chairs and strangely thirty single socks. As it was Ludwig's first day,

173

he could not yet say who needed these items and why but said he would pay special attention to this and report back.

Basil had a productive day and he also had some important things to report to us. Apparently, there was a special group trained in clandestine operations to bring from the surface what is needed back down below. The Logistics Collection Agency. In his office everybody was responsible for different areas of food sourcing, and his area was river life. They all received requirements of food from the cafeterias and restaurants needed for the daily life below the surface. Basil's job was to tell the Logistics guys about the best places to get the food from the river who then went out and got it.

While Basil was telling us about his day, I remembered Mr Player's toy shop and all the missing toy furniture and then the jam jars. And socks! Come to think of it, nearly everything down here had been stolen. Scavenging was how they called it down here, but actually I would rather call it stealing.

Basil and Ludwig had both provided me with information which I was sure would come in useful when planning our escape. Yes, escape was what I had in mind. We had to get out of this awful place, even if it was only on special operations. I now had quite a clear picture of how the system of getting supplies worked down here and that's not bad considering the short time I was here. It was part of Ludwig's job to report how much fish was in stock and how much was required and Basil's job was to report the best place to catch fresh fish in the river. This was exactly what had happened for the exclusive dinner for the moles. So much about equality of life down here.

Vanessa was not overly impressed about working at an observation post and had not much to report on. However, she wasn't restricted to one molehill and therefore moved between molehills of number three Trout Lane and observed, changing her position depending on what she wanted to see. Yes, an abundance of molehills equipped with a camouflaged viewing periscope like the one I had found.

Apart from two policemen on guard duty outside my house, a flock of birds was permanently circling above their car as though they were watching every movement of the policemen. Every now and then when the policemen only attempted to get out of their car, the birds suddenly broke their formation and dove towards the car dropping their loads on the way, only for the policemen to retreat back into their car as quickly as they could. I assumed that the car must have been covered in hundreds of bird droppings, and even though it was quite a strange scenario when you come to think of it, it now began to make sense to me. In the house opposite Vanessa saw an old man in blue overalls frantically pounding down molehills with a spade in a wild frenzy, but unfortunately for the old man, he just couldn't keep up with the amount of molehills constantly appearing! She also saw a young boy on a bicycle with, probably, his mother stopping outside number three and looking towards the house for quite a while. Apart from that there was not really anything else to report but she wrote down everything she observed, regardless of the triviality, on report cards and gave them to her supervisor. What happened with this information I didn't yet know but it appeared to me that she had partly realised the reality of life down here and I was quite sure Vanessa's job would prove useful in the near future.

***

The approach of the President could clearly be heard in the distance. The familiar click-clack of his metal tipped umbrella was getting closer as he walked down the tunnel and to the conference room.

"Colonel. What progress? Are you any closer to identifying the culprits? Who are those damn, crafty moles who stole the Professor? I want answers. Do you know the location of the Professor?"

"Mr President. We are a little closer on all points. Mr Jackson has admitted to having the glass jar with the Professor somewhere in his house but could not remember exactly where. He also informed us that he recorded communications from what we believe could be the culprits. Mr Jackson is prepared to help us return the Professor and hand over the memory stick containing the transmission just as long as he can enter our Special Operations Department and carry out the mission himself."

"This is a high-risk course of action, Colonel. Don't you agree?"

"Mr President, I had no choice but to make this deal. We cannot put him through Memming and then interrogate his memory because he doesn't remember where he put the Professor. We need him to get back into his house. But there's more, Mr President."

"Go on, Colonel."

"Mr Jackson only agreed if some of his friends, also new arrivals who he met on the first day, are also part of his team. I had to agree to this demand as well."

"Colonel, this is very dangerous. Are you having them watched?"

"Yes. You already know about Cleopatra. And Mr Jackson has a job at the memory warehouse. So, Mr Stockwell will know exactly what he is doing all of the time and report back to us."

"When do you intend to carry out the mission, Colonel?"

"Not before two weeks. They must all settle into their jobs first and then undergo the special operations training."

"Have we infiltrated the policemen guarding Mr Jackson's house yet? It would be very important to have our ears and eyes on the ground."

"No, not yet. We have a permanent flock circling above their car but were unable to hit the targets. Our observation team reported that the policemen now stay in their car to avoid being splat on."

***

The smartphone rang, deep in a tunnel. It was answered by a mole. "Yes."

"Minister. Update please. When will I get the Professor?"

"Good news, Mr Cromwell. We are on to it, but certain stones have been put in our way. From our source in the debriefing we know that Mr Jackson admitted to having the glass jar and also a recording of our transmissions, but he refused to tell the whereabouts. Instead he used this information to get into the Special

Operations Department to go back and recover the wanted items. And not only that, he was clever enough to have three new arrivals joining him on this mission. We are observing the house closely but so are the others. Cleopatra is proving to be most useful and loyal, but we have to be very careful not to blow our cover. The others are most definitely waiting for us to show our cards, but we are quite confident that they do not know who we are." The minister sounded very nervous and not at all confident with his report.

"This does not sound like good news to me, Minister."

"Well, Colonel Bacon is in charge of their day-to-day training. So please don't worry, we will ensure that they do precisely what we need them to do."

"Have we infiltrated anyone else yet? But please, Minister, don't be foolish enough and use the Kennedy brothers again. We need someone with more skills and a better cover too. It is essential for us to get someone in the house before Mr Jackson and his friends do."

"Yes, I am aware of that but no, not yet. We have our eyes on someone though who also lives in Trout Lane, right next to Mr Jackson's house. In number four in fact."

"Don't make any rash decisions before speaking to me. Remember, I want Professor Wingnut, and I want him quick and without failure," said Cromwell and then ended the call.

***

"What was that, Felicity? Did you hear that voice?" said Jemima Kingston, faintly irritated.

"My dear Jemima, I didn't hear a thing. I think you're imagining voices. Look, I'm the one under stress, my dear, not you! And please don't stress me out more than I already am."

"Imagining voices? I know what I heard, and it came from inside my handbag. Surely you must have heard it too," said Jemima angrily.

"Your handbag does not talk and neither does your sweet little Cromwell here," said Felicity, patting his head. "Look, isn't he just so innocent?" said Felicity sarcastically.

177

"I was not suggesting my handbag could talk, or my dog. But I heard voices. Of that I am sure."

"Sergeant Dawson, did you hear anything?" asked Felicity Forsythe-Twyke.

"No ma'am, not a thing. All quiet and peaceful here — just like things should be," replied the Sergeant.

"Sergeant Dawson!" Felicity Forsythe-Twyke was now screaming. "Everything is far from being peaceful and quiet. My daughter is missing and you have done nothing to find her. If you would stop having tea and biscuits all the time, you might actually find time for some police work."

"Now Mrs Forsythe-Twyke, that's a little unfair. We…"

"Have done nothing. I know Sergeant. I hope next time I see you, you will be able to tell me something." Felicity Forsythe-Twyke was still shouting but then turned around to leave when her attention was drawn to Sergeant Dawson's feet. "Why are you wearing a sock on only one foot?" She asked very suspiciously.

"Oh that," came a slow reply from an obviously very embarrassed Sergeant Dawson. "Well, last night I laid my socks out on my trousers to put on this morning but this morning there was only one. And I was down to my last pair as the rest are in the wash. So, this morning I was in quite a rush and thought one is better than none!"

"Come with me, Jemima." Felicity was not shouting any more but it was obvious she was outraged when she barged past the poor Mr Rye and the local hunter who were just coming through the door.

"What did you think you heard anyway, Jemima?" asked Felicity as soon as she was outside.

"I am not sure but I was quite certain I heard someone saying the name Professor Wingnut and something about wanting him quick and without failure. Most strange, I have to admit."

Chapter Eleven
Scavenging

"Oh, please be so kind and give my kind regards to Mr Donnelly when you speak to him next. Such a kind man," she said. "Please do that, Mr Jackson."

"Of course, I will, Ms Hullington. Mr Donnelly told me something about the work he had been doing on the Morphing project but unfortunately, he was decommissioned before he was able to finish it and he told me I should speak to you to find out more about the project," I said.

"Yes, such a sad state of affairs but we were used to this. Just as soon as anyone developed something interesting or important someone else took over. Mr Donnelly was one of the key researchers in the Morphing project but was withdrawn just before the end. These moles are paranoid about someone having too much information. They decommissioned the person who finished the Morphing project too. He ended up in a glass jar as well. So, you should be very careful you know."

"Thank you for your advice, Ms Hullington and I will most certainly take care. But can you tell me more about the project? You worked with Mr Donnelly before you were decommissioned. Mr Donnelly said it was ground-breaking technology."

"It was indeed very interesting, Mr Jackson. Something completely new and revolutionary. Mr Donnelly was responsible for the Morphing machine and I was part of a team researching the technology of memories going back as themselves. It was extremely difficult and obviously very secretive. I only ever worked with two other people on the project."

"Are you telling me that you were working on a technology to send memories back as themselves — in other words getting your life back as it was?" I asked in amazement.

"Yes, just that, Mr Jackson. Of course, I never finished the project and as you can clearly see I was decommissioned and now must also live in a glass jar. In fact, I have no idea if the project was ever finished or what happened to any of my colleagues."

"What can you tell me about your colleagues?" Ms Hullington seemed to be one of the good ones and she was evidently prepared to talk. And I was determined to get as much information and as many names as possible to help me achieve my goal of getting out of here.

"There was Professor Wingnut. He was delightful and the brains behind everything. I do hope he is being well looked after down here. He had misgivings about the project, but he was forced to do it by another colleague. A shady character and I didn't like him at all. His only task was to make sure that the Professor followed his orders and he never contributed anything to the research himself," said Ms Hullington with great sadness. "He was some sort of political correctness officer."

"Can you remember his name?"

"Why yes. How could I ever forget him? A ghastly young creature. The last thing I can remember was the smirk on his face before I was led away. Cromwell. Yes. That was his name. Mr Cromwell."

***

The first week in our jobs passed quickly and we all began settling into the way of life and daily routine below the ground, just like everyone else. I say settling in but what I really mean was getting used to our surroundings. We were understandably all still in shock, which is not surprising considering everything that had happened, and spent most evenings talking about our past lives with the desire

180

to go back to the surface. I had a slight advantage over the others because they did not know what I knew, and I had no intention to share the information I had gleaned from Ms Hullington yet, just to be cautious. But it made me very optimistic and I spent most of my time wisely using every opportunity to collect information which could be beneficial to get us out of this place. I interviewed numerous memories but not only those I thought would be helpful to us but also completely random memories so as not to arouse anybody's suspicion. Meanwhile, I made Mr Stockwell and Dusty believe that my work was purely to organise myself and that I would start analysing memory information very soon. I also wanted to use the opportunity to speak to my parents. I mean, why should I pass up on the opportunity. However, when I made a search for them, there was quite strangely absolutely no record of them. It was of course very disappointing and somehow I knew they were being hidden for a reason. That will have to come at another time though.

Basil and Ludwig were as industrious as ever. While Basil managed to obtain very useful information about the logistics chain, Ludwig brought back lists of what was in the warehouse and how we could get things out without anybody noticing. Although his information was not particularly interesting at this moment, it was obvious that Ludwig was very meticulous. He missed nothing, made notes of absolutely everything and eventually he would unearth something very valuable. Now, I was just collecting information which could be useful to hatch a plan.

"That's the end of the first week," I said to myself, sitting back in my chair in the pub. I had used the week to start collecting information but there was so much information stored in the memories that I was somehow overwhelmed and did not know exactly what to do with it all. Mr Stockwell pretended to leave me alone — he just wasn't very good at it. I knew he was checking up on me and I let him believe he was successful in doing so by leaving notes on my desks for him to report back to whoever he needed to. Of course, the notes would lead to a confusing dead-end. As a trained analyst it wasn't much of a challenge for me to camouflage from prying eyes what I was really doing.

The moles seemed to consider themselves as all powerful and thought they had total control over everyone, but I found they were not as clever as they thought. I had already collected some extremely important information about Professor Wingnut's special projects from different sources and was looking for particular information to build up my plan, but I needed to be careful because it was impossible to know who to trust and who was on which side. In fact, it wasn't even possible to see who was good or bad. For my plan to work I needed equipment. Electrical devices like the ones I used in my previous job. Knowledge seemed to equate to power and I wanted to be the one who controlled the information. It was time to turn the tables, but how could I get my hands on this equipment?

***

I took a swig of my beer and had a look around the room for Cleopatra. I hadn't seen her for a while but as if on cue she came in and sat down at the table next to us and as normal, the animals sitting there vacated their places immediately as she growled at them.

"Good evening, Cleopatra," I said with a new air of confidence. "Nice day wasn't it!"

I didn't get the expected growl in response but the bared teeth treatment instead. I just smiled back and raised my glass to her. "Cheers."

"Don't antagonise her, Connor." whispered Ludwig in my ear, so Cleopatra couldn't hear him. "She looks dangerous and I don't trust her. You should always be careful of a Doberman Pinscher — they are great guard dogs and defend their turf fearlessly. Not like me — I am more of a really hard worker and a very loyal friend to have." Ludwig gave me a deep look with his faithful brown eyes.

"Don't worry, Ludwig. I just want to tease her a little." I wasn't quite sure what it was yet, but behind her dangerous appearance I could see something else. There was more to her than meets the eye.

"Good evening, Vanessa. Late today I see — you are normally here waiting for us," I said.

"Oh, just be quiet would you, Connor." Vanessa looked gloomy and responded angrily as she slumped down into the chair holding her beer in one hand. "How can you sound so positive in this awful place?"

"What's up? You look very annoyed. More than you normally are. Has something happened today?"

"And you are not annoyed or angry down here? How can you cope with this place?"

Ludwig and I looked at each other and nodded our heads. We didn't really know what to say so we just looked at Vanessa who seemed very dejected and sat cradling her beer and staring at the floor.

But then she broke the silence. "I was promoted to supervisor today."

"Now hang on, Vanessa. Why can you be so sad about that? Is that not the perfect job for someone of your standing!" Ludwig was trying to buck her up a little. "Perfect for a Forsythe-Twyke!"

Vanessa had not been content to be an ordinary observer and now managed to become a supervisor for the whole of Trout Lane rather quickly. A task which would most likely be useful, though that also did not seem to make her happy. However, her move to supervisor could not be credited to her hard work as she liked to make out, I thought. My initial idea was that she probably convinced somebody that a Forsythe-Twyke was without fail the best choice for a managerial position.

"Well, normally yes but it was the circumstances which concern me. There was a great commotion from the tunnel below me when I was standing on my ladder observing your house. I went down and found policemen and some sort of administrator rounding up a group of people from a list and taking them away. Most of them under loud protest."

"Why? Did they do something wrong?" I asked.

"That is the whole point. Apparently, the human consumption of meat is so high now that the moles changed the quota system and I was told that this was the Food Factory Gang. More of us must be put into the Factory to meet the demand and they now walk around with a list and press-gang animals into the Factory. I can tell you, the ones of us remaining were really frightened!"

"And what about the list. Do you know who is on the list?"

"No, but we all suspect that if you aren't good at your job or ask too many questions you end up on that list. The supervisor for Trout Lane for example questioned his superior about the waste of resources for one house and not long later he was rounded up. Also, some of the tunnellers on the project did not meet their targets and they were carted off too," explained Vanessa. "I think, that was because the old man who lives next to your house has become quite successful in destroying molehills and tunnels and has turned the Trout Lane project into a bit of a battle up there."

"I can vouch for that," said Basil who had just arrived and heard what Vanessa had said. "The Food Factory Gang also came to our area and took some of the team away. My colleague, Lucy the looter, that's what she was known as, was taken away today. She was responsible for identifying good sources for food, such as eggs or insects, but I heard that some of her information was wrong and the Logistics Collection team often came back empty handed."

"That's terrible. Incredible how much power these moles have." I whispered. It made me angry. And even more determined to act fast to find a way to end this nightmare for good.

"What's more, Connor, the animals they take away are not replaced. Which means that we have to do the same work but with fewer people." said Vanessa, and I could sense that she was not only frightened by this incident but also had become feisty. She seemed to care.

"Well, we shouldn't be so surprised about that should we. Humans have been doing this for years, but we wrap it nicely in names like 'restructuring' or 'streamlining'," I added sarcastically. "Only recently my department at work, in the real world I mean, was restructured and two people were made redundant. Government cuts we were told. But we all ended up having to split their workloads and achieve exactly the same in the same time."

"Yes, Connor, I know. But being made redundant is different to ending up on the end of a fork. If I ever end back up there on the surface as a human, I am never going to eat meat again. Ever. That I can tell you. You might end up eating one of us. Think of that!" Vanessa's voice was trembling.

Basil spoke for the first time this evening. "My, you have changed your tune, Vanessa. Only a few days ago you would have eaten me and Dusty as well. Remember?"

"Well, this place is beginning to open my eyes to other things in life."

"And because of that we all need to be extremely careful. It is perfectly obvious that the moles wield a lot of power. They seem to have their own view of the world and how it works and it's best that we politely agree and do what we are told to do. And that we never say anything which could put us in danger. Remember, we are only still here because of the glass jar and I cannot guarantee what will happen to us as soon as we have found it. But one thing I am sure of is that I haven't made us any friends getting this far. So please give me your trust and I will come up with a plan, but I need more information, and more importantly — more time. The moles have everyone believing that the world consists only of the Molehamptons and Anglerton and I am determined to prove them wrong."

"But it does," replied Ludwig and Basil with puzzlement at the same time.

Vanessa and I looked at each other and raised our eye brows. "Yes, of course it does!" we confirmed.

"Oh, Connor. I forgot to mention. You told me to report anything interesting. Well, today I saw the old man pick up something shiny from a molehill in front of his house."

"Something shiny. How large was it?"

"I'm not sure but it fitted in the palm of his hand."

"And what did he do with it?" I was wondering if Mr Lawnsworthy had found the memory stick I buried in a molehill on the night I was kidnapped from my house. If the moles knew about this, we could lose part of our bargaining power and so I was very glad that it was Vanessa who saw it and would certainly be clever enough not to share this information with anybody but me.

"He pocketed it in his gardening overalls and then hung them up in his shed."

Before we could carry on our conversation our attention was drawn to a lot of noise at the bar. We walked across the room and managed to push ourselves to the front where someone was putting up a poster advertising a football game. I read it out aloud with great interest. Of course, the County Cup competition and what a draw it was. Upper against Lower. If only I could watch it, I thought.

Saturday, 3pm
AFC Upper Molehampton vs FC Lower Molehampton
First round, First Leg of the World Cup
Apply at the Entertainment Office for Limited Viewing Hills

"What is it Connor?" asked Ludwig.

"It's an advert for a football match, Ludwig. And not just any football match. Upper and Lower are playing against each other in the first round of the County Cup. World Cup down here. What a game that will be and such rivalry."

Ludwig looked very puzzled at me. "What the heck are you talking about?"

"Football Ludwig. Football."

"And what is football, Connor?"

"Well, it's THE sport. Two teams of eleven players each play against each other kicking a ball across a big field. They can't use their hands — apart from the goal keeper that is — and they have to kick the ball into a goal to score. Whichever team scores the most goals wins the game. That is what we call football!"

"It doesn't sound that exciting to me, Connor. Why is there so much interest?"

"Not exciting? Come on, Ludwig. The cup is the biggest sporting event of the year and for the biggest rivals Upper and Lower to be drawn against each other creates so much passion you can't believe it."

"Oh well, if you say so but I'm not sure I can. Will you watch it?" asked Ludwig.

I didn't answer and just stared into space with open eyes. World Cup? Limited space!

"Wake up, Connor! I've just asked you a question."

"I have an idea and yes of course I will watch it and so will you and everyone else," I said with a broad grin on my face and I felt happy for the first time in a while. "Let's go and tell the others."

***

"A good first week!" boomed Colonel Bacon at us. "I had good reports about you lot. Well done."

"The next part of your training plan is to introduce you into the world of special operations, but we have to begin with the Logistics Collection Agency. That is the official name of our team and I am sure you have already heard of them. You will be trained as a scavenger — that's what we call them here."

Colonel Bacon was wearing his military fatigues as usual but spoke to us very kindly this time. We were in the same room in which Colonel Pickle had introduced him just a week ago after the debriefing and Colonel Bacon had explained to us everything about the Red Five Training School.

"Have you ever asked yourselves where all of the furniture comes from? The fuel for the transport shuttles, the transport shuttles themselves of course, the lighting, food, beer, salt for our food, socks for sleeping bags and so on. The list is endless and when you need something you simply have to complete an acquisition form and submit your request to the Logistics Collection Agency, but you might have already found that out. Well, once approved, you will have noticed that the items you asked for mysteriously appear? And you will also have noticed that nearly everything down here comes from the human world on the surface. That will be your job."

"You mean stealing?" asked Vanessa.

"Stealing? No, my dear. Not stealing. We call it acquisitioning," replied the Colonel. He was evidently very proud of his Special Operations team and made no secret out of it.

187

"As a mole I cannot say I am a great friend of humans, but their bodies are perfectly equipped to make things. Thanks to our excellent programming skills of course. And you will be trained to go back to the surface and collect these things for us."

Perfect! Exactly what I wanted. I had been contemplating about finding a way to get back to the surface and now this opportunity came up much more easily than I could have imagined.

"So, we will go back to the surface as we are? What happens if someone recognises me? Everyone thinks I'm dead." I asked excitedly.

"No, Mr Jackson, it doesn't work like that. Remember you are here in spirit form only and left your physical shell behind on the surface, which I am sorry to remind you has now decomposed. When you return for scavenging missions, you will have to go in your current size, only at night time and you will be completely invisible to all on the surface. Only you can see each other."

"But if we are invisible, then why do we only go at night time? Surely it doesn't matter?" asked Basil.

"You are invisible, correct, but not the items you will acquire. Just imagine an object moving by itself. That would be rather suspicious, don't you think?"

"I suppose so," replied Basil.

"What will we go and get?" asked Ludwig with anticipation.

"The Logistics Collection Agency will tell you what they need. Fraser is on his way and will take you to another area where everything will be fully explained to you, and you will be given your first mission."

"When are we going on these missions?" asked Vanessa.

"As I already said, only at night time. During the day you work in your normal jobs and at night you report to the Logistics Collection Agency for your missions."

"And what about my sleep, Colonel? You can't expect us to work twenty-four seven!" There she was again. The Vanessa we all knew.

"Yes, we can," replied the Colonel, menacingly. "And the quicker you complete your missions the quicker you can go to bed.

You have all just come from the pub I understand. Well, the beer comes from somewhere. So does the furniture and the glasses you drink out of. It doesn't just turn up like magic, my dear. We depend on people like you to volunteer for these missions to keep up our comfortable lifestyle down here." Colonel Bacon then changed back to his customary false smile. "Any other questions or anyone else unhappy with the way the Special Operations work down here?"

***

"This certainly sounds exciting," said Basil as they followed Fraser down a tunnel.

"Exciting? It's more than that," I replied. "This is our chance to go back to the surface. OK, not exactly as the real forms but at least we are out of here for a short period and can breathe fresh air again."

"Maybe I can go and see my master, Mr Rye," expressed Ludwig with hope.

"Look children. Stop getting too excited. We are invisible; the size of a mole and we can only go at night time. Don't get your hopes up too much," added Vanessa, seriously.

"You are such a killjoy, Vanessa," said Basil, angrily. "Why do you always have to be so serious?"

"No, she's not a killjoy," I whispered in Vanessa's defence. "She is just being realistic. Remember, if we want to stay down here for a longer time, we must take this whole thing very seriously and not give anything away. And when I say down here, I don't mean in a jar. Let's just do as we are told and learn as much as we can. I keep on saying that we need to play for time if we want to win this game, and I mean it."

"Yeah, I suppose you are both right," said Ludwig.

Fraser led us to the same train station from where we all went to the Special Operations Department after our debriefing. I still remembered this hair-raising journey down there and it seemed the same was about to happen again. Even though I wasn't religious at all, I sent a quick prayer just in case.

189

Fraser had a lurking undertone in his voice. "I will leave you here. The next shuttle will take you to the Logistics Collection Agency. You are to report to this station every evening at the time given and you are not to talk about it. For your own good. Do you understand the importance of this?"

Say nothing and just do as you are told. We all nodded silently, fully understanding the consequences of non-compliance with his instructions. I was hiding my smile from Fraser knowing what had to be done, and it certainly wasn't what the moles expected. The shuttle arrived with an unusual delay but then whisked us off to our destination where we were met by an unknown mole on the platform. Just as soon as our shuttle left the station again with a loud explosion of fuel, another shuttle bounced straight in with a thud. Cleopatra appeared out of the cloud of dust, shook herself off and followed us into the briefing with her beady eyes boring into my back. She was always on duty.

***

"Silence please everyone. How can anyone be heard in this din?" The mole at the front of the room bellowed into the crowd. "Now, let's get going with delegating tonight's scavenging tasks."

We had a quick newcomers' briefing about scavenging a few minutes beforehand. Actually, it wasn't a real briefing as we didn't learn anything new. The information was quite basic and mostly a repetition of what Colonel Bacon had already explained to us. All we were expected to do was to get a list of the equipment to be collected, find the tunnel to the surface and get the goods. And we were of course expected to execute our missions with the utmost care in order not to be detected.

"Cabling! We need twenty metres of cabling for some new tunnel projects. Location is from the housing area under construction in Upper Molehampton. There are apparently a few cable drums on the site. Any volunteers?"

"OK, next job. Four litres of lamp kerosene from the DIY store in Anglerton. Needed for transport shuttle fuel. Volunteers please?"

"What have we got on this acquisition form? Aaah, mole poison pellets required for the next rave. I can't say I approve but it's not my decision. From the garden shed in Trout Lane. You know which house I mean."

The room began to empty as, team by team, the volunteers left on their missions. Food, drinks, furniture, office supplies. You name it! Everything you can imagine that was needed to operate an underground world was sourced by the moles' Logistics Operations from above the surface.

"Mr Jackson and crew. Here we go. Something interesting for you. Here is your list and it is for a hairbrush, a can of hair spray, a bag of hair clips and a pair of scissors. Location is the hairdresser in Lower Molehampton. Collect your sacks from the pile over there. Good Luck on your first mission."

The mole was pointing at a trolley full of socks. Single socks. Used socks. I thought back to my washing basket and remembered all of my single socks. Had the mystery now been explained?

I smiled to myself and collected some socks for us and took my 'crew' to one side to go through our instructions on the acquisition form. "Listen, everyone. We need to go to tunnel exit Blue seventy-one which is the closest to the hairdresser in Lower Molehampton. Vanessa, do you know the place? I know where it is but have never been there." I should have known better but I thought I'll give it a try.

"Connor, do you really think I frequent hairdressers in Lower Molchampton? Have you seen how the women there look like? No. Of course not. Our coiffeur in Upper is the one I go to," replied Vanessa in her normal tone we had all gotten used to.

"Oh yes. Silly me! What was I thinking?"

"Who needs this stuff anyway?"

I looked at the signature at the bottom of the form. "Oh, it's for the dog salon."

"Dog salon? Dog salon! I've heard it all now," retorted Vanessa loudly.

"And why shouldn't we have a salon for pampering treatment?" piped up Ludwig.

"Well, look at you, Ludwig. You are a dog and you don't need a stylist," said Vanessa, bluntly.

"Believe me we do. And by the look of your hair you could do with a stylist too," said Ludwig. He obviously enjoyed how easy it was to tease Vanessa.

"OK. Back to business," I commanded with authority. "I know where the salon is, but we have to find out where exactly Blue seventy-one takes us out. Let's get going."

***

Blue seventy-one was a long and bumpy shuttle journey away but we eventually found our point of exit. A mole was already waiting in a small chamber at the bottom to push the earth away from the summit and put a ladder in place for us to exit. I led the way and was the first to poke my head out of the top of the molehill. The rush of fresh air was delightful. For the first time in a while, I was back on the surface breathing in real air and not the forced, musky air below the surface. It was a completely new experience though. From the size of a mole the village had a very different perspective. I had often wondered what is was like for a cat looking up to a human and I think I was beginning to understand. Lower Molehampton was now large and overpowering, not small and quaint.

"So, this was what everything looks like when you are small," I whispered to myself.

The weather wasn't good. It was wet and windy and clouds covered the light of the full moon, but that was to our favour as not many people would walk around on the streets in a night like this.

"Come on everyone. Follow me. We don't need to take care about being seen so let's take the most direct route. We just need to take care not to be hit by a car or trodden on by someone," I said.

"But what about the socks?" asked Vanessa.

"What about them?" I replied.

"Well, they are not invisible so what happens if anyone sees them moving?"

"Good point. But let's come across that bridge when it happens. Anyway, why should someone be interested in an individual sock? There are always things like socks and shoes lying around anyhow," I said.

"Yeah, I suppose so," said Vanessa, looking puzzled. "I've often wondered that myself too."

We exited in the village green, just opposite the Anchor Inn. The lights were on and I heard loud voices, music and laughing coming from within its welcoming walls. We scampered across the grass, which now came up to my knees, across the road and then came to the pavement, our first obstacle. We heaved ourselves onto the pavement, then past the Inn and into the small high street of the village. The hairdresser was only a few hundred metres away on the left and the road was empty of activity at this time of the night. According to the church clock, it had just gone nine-thirty.

"Stop. I can hear someone coming," I whispered an alarm to everyone. "Stand against the shop and throw your socks against the wall over there." We then all remained completely motionless.

"Come on now, Maxwell, calm down, there's nothing here. We've got to go home now, and the weather is awful," said the man curtly to his dog.

But the dog had picked up a scent and I was sure it was ours. I recognised the man. It was Mr Mason, the trainer from the local football club, who had taken over from Mr Twyford following his sad and unexpected death last year. Mr Mason and his German shepherd came straight towards us.

They got closer and closer and then the full size of the dog became obvious. He was huge and Mr Mason even larger. The next thing I knew was the wet snout sniffing right in front of my face. It felt like looking up to the top of a truck. Then Maxwell turned his rear towards the wall, cocked his right leg over Basil and shook his head with his slobber spaying over Vanessa. We all kept perfectly still and rooted with fear to the spot. Thankfully Mr Mason did not notice that his dogs slobber was suspended above the ground as though hanging on an unseen object. The dog was still busy smelling very intensively. Maybe it was our socks, but thankfully his Master was keen to move along.

"Maxwell. Come on. You can't pee everywhere. I want to go home. Come along now," said Mr Mason and pulled Maxwell forcefully along and they slowly disappeared around the corner.

I let out a long sigh of relief when they were out of sight.

"That dog just peed all over me. I stink," said Basil, angrily.

Ludwig went to Basil and sniffed him. "Oh, it's OK Basil. To me you smell particularly good now!"

"And me? What about me? I'm covered in this horrible dog slobber." Vanessa wiped away the slimy substance with the arm of her woollen jumper. "Disgusting."

"Let's go everyone. Basil — we'll spray you with something nice in the hairdressers," I said.

The final approach to the hairdressers was uneventful and we were now standing outside, looking up at the large glass door. "Now. How to get in?" I spoke aloud to myself. "Ludwig and Basil, can you please go to the back and check if there is a way in. Vanessa and I will take a look here."

"There's a strange, small flap in the lower part of the door at the back. Not sure what purpose it has but we can easily get in," Basil reported a few minutes later. "It's just our size!"

We all went to the back of the hairdresser to see what they had found. Basil was quite correct and the cat flap was easily pushed open to get in. The main room was illuminated by the street lights, so we started looking around. It was exactly what you would expect a hairdressing salon to look like — comfortable chairs, decorative mirrors, sinks and shelves full of articles for beauty treatments.

"We need a hairbrush, a can of hair spray, a bag of hair clips and a pair of scissors. Vanessa, could you please help me find these things?" I asked.

"Stop! Not yet. It stinks in here and we all know who and why," she said looking down her nose at Basil in revulsion. "The first thing we need is some spray to make the awful stench go away."

Vanessa looked up at a sink and spied some spray cans on a shelf directly above it. "OK Basil — follow me." She proved to be extremely agile when she jumped onto the chair's footrest and then pulled herself up on to the chair itself. She looked down at Basil who remained still.

"Come on, Basil," said Vanessa, impatiently. "I don't know about you, but I definitely want to go to bed sometime tonight."

"And how should I do that? I don't have arms to climb up this strange contraption," he sounded frustrated.

"May I remind you that you have wings. You are a bird and you can indeed fly. Flap, flap Basil."

Basil's beak looked like it was forming a grin as he started to move his wings and landed directly next to Vanessa with two noisy flaps. The smell of dog pee became more intense as he flapped around.

"There, there. Not so difficult was it." Vanessa was holding her nose with her fingers. "First I will wipe myself down." She took a small paper towel from the bottom shelf, wet it on a sink and wiped the disgusting dog slobber off her jumper before attending to Basil.

"Now, Basil. Stand there and when I start spraying just turn around in a full circle."

Vanessa pulled herself up onto one of the chair's armrests, balanced across and steadied herself with a great leap, landing directly in the sink. She then scrambled up the side, pulled herself up to the shelf and gracefully swung her legs onto the surface. But she needed to apply force to the spray can's nozzle and had to clamber onto another shelf above the spray can. Her climbing skills were amazing and from the proud expression on her face as she looked down on us we could tell that she was more than aware of that.

"Basil. Over to you now. On three, I want you to flutter your wings and see if you can hover in front of the can. Come on, you can do it," shouted Vanessa from the shelf. "One, two, three, go!"

With great precision, Vanessa jumped on top of the spray can and had to use her full weight to press the nozzle. At the same time Basil flapped his wings in front of the shelf. With a great hiss of escaping vapour, the nozzle dispensed a flowery smell covering

Basil in the process, who started coughing, and then landed on the floor with a thud.

"There we go. Job done. I don't think much of the quality of this spray, but it is better than the awful stench. We have much better products in Upper Molehampton but what should you expect as this is not even a proper beauty salon." She didn't get tired of telling us how much better Upper Molehampton was, but we just didn't have the time to react to that now. We had a mission to complete.

"Right, stay where you are, everyone. I think I can find everything we need up here." She could also be very practical and started pushing items around and off the shelf directly onto the chair below. A hairbrush, a can of hair spray, a bag of hair clips and a pair of scissors all landed in quick succession. She then light-footedly jumped down from the shelf, back into the sink and directly in one motion onto the chair. Vanessa handed everything down and we shoved it into the socks and were ready to start our journey back through the cat flap. Basil used his beak to pull one sock behind him, Ludwig was able to carry one in his snout and Vanessa and I had ours slung over our shoulders. These articles were large and heavy, but the real challenge was not to be seen with the bulging socks moving around outside. The journey back to our molehill would undoubtedly be more difficult.

***

Wind and buffeting rain didn't make his evening any better. He looked miserable and was miserable as he sat down on the bench. Sergeant Dawson walked, not particularly in a straight line, from the Anchor Inn in Lower Molehampton and decided to take a rest on his way home in the village green, which was actually very close to the pub. His week had been bad, really bad. From a well-respected local policeman to an utter, incompetent fool in one week was no mean feat and he had managed it with flying colours. His career and reputation were in ruins and more importantly his quiet life was over. He sat down with a slightly sozzled expression on his face and just stared at the ground.

Maybe the wind had blown the litter right in front of his feet — the weather had been very bad lately. Sergeant Dawson looked up at the wind moving the branches and then fixed his gaze back to the ground, but there was nothing. From the corner of his eye he saw that the rubbish had moved from the left of the bench to the right. A sock. No four socks. He counted them carefully and slowly again and tried to focus on what he was looking at. The socks were open and filled with things which looked like a hair brush and a pair of scissors. Why? He was confused. He was in fact not one hundred percent sober, but he was sure that these objects were moving. Sergeant Dawson may not have been the quickest of cats, but he knew when something was out of place.

"Stop it!" he said out loud to himself, or anyone else who might be listening. "I might have had a few drinks, but I can see you very clearly."

"Stop!"

He looked sharply to the left and gazed in that direction for a moment and then quickly turned his head back to the right and to look where the socks were now. They were gone! He stood up and walked to the last place he saw them, stooped over and inspected the ground. There they were.

"Stand still," he shouted again and staggered towards the socks. "Stop moving!"

He looked up at the trees and then back down at the ground. They had moved again. Up. Down. Up. They moved each time he didn't look. Not much but enough for him to notice. They were now in a line about ten metres in front of him.

"Stand still! Who are you?" Sergeant Dawson was now screaming at the socks.

"Been drinking, Sergeant?" came a voice from behind the bushes.

"Err, what," replied the Sergeant.

"Been drinking I asked? You are making too much noise. It's after closing time and especially you should know better than shouting around in the middle of the night!"

"Who's there?" asked Sergeant Dawson squinting towards the street light.

"It's me. Mr Rye."

"What are you doing here?"

"Looking for my dog. Remember? My loyal Ludwig went missing about a week ago. Never seen him since. Very strange I must say."

"Sorry about that but we really don't have the resources now. With Mr Jackson and the Forsythe-Twyke girl disappearing. You can't imagine how much pressure I am getting from her mother."

"Yes, I can as a matter of fact. But what are you doing here, Sergeant? And who are you talking to?"

"To the pair of scissors and to the hair brush. They are moving over there."

"Been a hard week I know!" Mr Rye looked at Sergeant Dawson pitifully.

"You could say that. But they are moving."

"Who is moving," Mr Rye asked suspiciously.

"The scissors, the brush and the socks of course."

"OK. I really should take you home and let your wife take care of you," said Mr Rye softly.

"You don't believe me. Look yourself!" insisted Sergeant Dawson and pointed to the ground.

"Look at what?"

"Well, the socks. Over there."

"But there's nothing to see!"

Sergeant Dawson's head darted towards the ground, to the left and then to the right. "Where are you?" His voice was panic-fuelled now. "Come on. Where are you?" He stumbled across to the bench, slumped down with a disenchanted face and stared at the ground with his head in his hands.

***

The mole had to move out of the way quickly as a man clutching a sock fell through the hole onto the floor of the small chamber. Then a pair of scissors landed tip down in the ground right next to that person followed by a duck with a sock. Then a dog and a woman also landed in a heap next to each other. All of them apart from the dog burst out laughing as earth was still crumbling on top of them.

"Wow, that was close," said Basil. "I thought we were not going to make it."

"Yep. That was a close shave," said Vanessa, laughing her head off. "I thought Sergeant Dawson was going to cry. He was so confused. Brilliant!"

"I thought he was going to stand on me," I said sitting back, holding my sides in laughter.

"He nearly did, Connor. He was stumbling around frantically looking for the things and nearly stood on you," said Vanessa with tears streaming down her cheeks.

"It's not funny," shouted Ludwig. He looked very sad. "It's really not funny."

There was a sudden silence and everyone looked towards Ludwig.

"What's up, Ludwig?"

"It might have been funny for you, but it certainly wasn't for me. The other man was my master. He was so sad and still looking for me and I couldn't do anything. I so wanted to shout out and say that I was there but I didn't want to give us all away."

Ludwig settled on the floor with his tail between his legs and his ears flapped down.

We all looked at each other in ashamed silence. Basil was the first to speak.

"Sorry, Ludwig. We really didn't know."

"Yeah, Ludwig. If we knew that was your master, we could have done something," added Vanessa.

"Done what?" said Ludwig. "We're all dead. Haven't you noticed? You are all acting as though nothing has happened."

"We didn't mean to offend you, Ludwig," I said. "I am really sorry."

"Look at yourselves — only interested in your own things. What about my master? I was right next to him and he was hurting so much. Maybe death is not all its made out to be. We are all OK and found another life — for the moment anyhow. We know that death is not really as bad as we imagined it to be and it is certainly not the end. But what about those who we left behind? Maybe they suffer more than we do?"

"You are correct, Ludwig. Yes, we had good fun this evening, but we should think about everyone we left behind. But we are neither really dead nor alive and this is just a transition phase. When our mission is over, we might end up like everyone else — our memory in a glass jar and our processors reprogrammed. That is being dead and we are not there yet." I was trying to calm Ludwig down.

"Ludwig's right though. What about everyone we've left behind? We are only thinking about ourselves. Come on, let's deliver this stuff and go to bed," said Basil thoughtfully.

"Stop everyone!" I said quietly. "Listen to me. I have a plan to get us out of here and keep us all alive, but I need you to trust me and do exactly as I say. I don't want to say any more about it for the moment. Ludwig, I can't promise but I will do my best to reunite you with your master. OK?"

Ludwig stood up and said, "Just tell me what you want me to do and I'll do it. Come on, everyone. Let's go." He almost looked cheerful again as he dragged his socks down the tunnel.

***

The next day was a normal working day and time for the first phase of my plan to be put into action. After spending some time in my office, I decided to make my move and left my office. I went directly to the Entertainment Department and knocked firmly on their door.

"Enter!"

I opened the door and found a mole sitting behind a desk looking straight at me.

"Here for the football match I presume? Well, you're too late. All of the viewing hills have been taken."

200

"Well, I am here for the first round of the County Cup football match but I wasn't going to ask about a viewing hill." I said.

"County Cup. What's that?" asked the mole.

"It's the football competition. Different teams from the county play in the cup against each other."

"But it's the Word Cup, isn't it? And there are only three teams playing," said the mole a little confused.

"Oh, of course don't worry," I said kindly. "I have put some thought into it and a plan to televise the game in the pub. I wonder if you would be interested," I continued with confidence.

The mole sat up straight with apparent curiosity. "What's your plan?"

"It's difficult and a little laborious but if it comes off we can all watch the game on the big screen down here. All we have to do is acquire some items from my old work place like cameras, smartphones and various electrical devices. Don't worry about how to set it up. I'm a bit of an expert in this field and I know how to do all of that. I just need to go back there and I need you to sign the acquisition form for me. Surely the moles down here would love it!"

"It certainly sounds adventurous. You have my approval and I suggest you complete an acquisition form and then we will see if the powers here approve it too. If yes, then your plan may just work.

***

It was only some nights later that my task was actually authorised and delegated to 'my crew' to collect the items I needed. Until then we had busied ourselves collecting items for the good and benefit of everyone. On our second mission we went into a local supermarket on a mass raid with other scavengers to collect an assortment of food. On the third it was animal food from Angleton's pet shop and on the fourth night we collected building materials from a construction site near Trout Lane. During these missions I studied the moles and their procedures, and my plan turned into something more concrete. I knew exactly what I needed to do and how I could make it work.

Great. The first part of my plan proved to be easy. I got the authority for a scavenging mission to my old work place even though the acquisition form I submitted for my electrical equipment was more than vague. I had managed to convince the Entertainment Department that I knew what to get and that I would have to decide exactly what equipment to take on site. They had signed the form without further questions. Now it was up to me to brief the others about the first part of my plan.

"Listen to me, everyone. Our next scavenging mission is to my old workplace to collect items for televising the football match at the weekend. This will not be as easy as the other jobs. It is a top security Government site and there are guards about at night time. And it will be much harder to get in. You must do exactly as I say and remember — stealth is the key to our mission."

"Is this part of your plan to reunite me with my master, Connor?" Ludwig was wildly wagging his tail.

"I would prefer not to say too much at the moment but, Ludwig, yes it is part of the plan. But secrecy is very important if this is to work which means I can only tell you part of the plan. It is for your own good too, so all I ask is for you to trust me. Please."

"If you think that's best, Connor. I really hope you know what you're doing," added Vanessa.

"I can't say my plan is without risk, but we have nothing to lose, have we? If it doesn't work, then we will all end up as a long-lost memory in a glass jar. If it works — well just maybe we can stay alive down here in some sort of role until we can find a definite way out."

"But, Ludwig, I would like to ask you for your help now. I need you to get some items from the store and keep them in a safe place until I need them. Secretly, of course. Can you do that?" I asked.

"Ah, yes of course. Just tell me what you need, and I'll sort it," replied Ludwig, beaming with pride after being asked to contribute something important to our mission.

"I need four tunnelling overalls, shovels and a large bucket too — just the equipment a tunnelling crew normally uses."

"Consider it done, Connor."

We had to endure a very long and bumpy ride through various tunnels to get to our exit point. The Government building was on the outskirts of Upper Molehampton and probably one of the furthest points away in the tunnel system, or at least near the end of the mole world! We exited the shuttle at the end of the line with a wooden board containing a metal grate in the middle blocking any further journey. The shuttle driver was also our tunneller. He quickly dug a narrow tunnel, skilfully pushing the earth upwards and created a fresh exit for us on the surface. This was now the second part of my plan.

"Off you go," said the mole. "I couldn't get a ticket for the football match, so I really hope your mission is successful. Everyone is already talking about it. We all love the World Cup but have never seen it live before. Only some lucky ones from the vantage position of their molehills."

"And I thought my plan was a secret," I said with sense of delight in my voice.

"I'm a Lower Molehampton fan by the way. Which team do you support?" The mole was now looking at Basil.

"I have no idea what you're talking about. I only support my family. Well, I did until…" Basil said with a grim look at Ludwig.

"Well, I will wait here in the shuttle and try and get some sleep. Just knock on the side to wake me up when you come back."

I took the lead and climbed up the ladder until my head poked out of the molehill which was on a small patch of grass next to the car park at the back of the building. It was all clear. There was no sign of security staff around, so I quickly gave the order. We all climbed out and ran to the edge of the building carrying our socks and my blue bag.

"Why are you carrying this blue bag with you?" Vanessa was completely out of breath from that short run across the car park. She obviously was a good gymnast but not such an arduous sprinter.

"Oh that. It's nothing really," I replied.

"It's not nothing because I can see you are guarding that blue bag," she said becoming angry.

"Yes, you're right, clever clogs, I need it to carry back my goods in. I am going to use it to protect some items inside the socks, so they don't rattle against each other. We are about to collect very sensitive equipment you remember," I explained. "We've got lots to do. Let's go."

I had only ever used the main entrance when I worked here, and I knew that the building was highly secured for obvious reasons. The windows could therefore not be opened. Not from the inside and certainly not from the outside. Fresh air was provided by an air duct system with vents in each room. And this vent system I assumed was probably our best way to get in. I was hoping that the air duct system was on the roof and tasked Basil to fly up. It proved to be an advantage to have a duck in the team. With a flap of his powerful wings, he was up in the air and disappeared out of sight when he reached the top of the roof. After just a few moments he came back with the good news.

The rest of our team had to use the fire escape ladder on the outside of the building. We made sure that there was no security, crossed the car park to the other side of the building and started climbing up exhaustingly steep human-sized rungs. We arrived at the top, panting like steam trains.

Basil had been waiting for us for quite some time. "Took your time, didn't you?" he quipped.

"Wings are an advantage here, Basil, but not always, remember that." I had to suck for air before I could say anything. "OK everyone, on to the next part. We have to squeeze through the grate and just drop down through the duct system. I think it has smooth corners, so we shouldn't get hurt."

"How do we know when to stop, Connor?" Ludwig seemed to be a little concerned about sliding blindly down through the unknown duct system.

"I believe when we reach the bottom! Look, I'll go first and the rest follow at sensible intervals."

I climbed up to the duct and squeezed through the bars until I stood at the top. "Wish me luck and see you soon." I jumped into the darkness and started sliding down the dim pipe. It felt like being on a slide in a water park. Left, right, right left and down at the same time with nothing to hold on to. Hilarious. I was thrown around all over the place and could hear howls of delight from behind me. Ludwig was obviously enjoying the racy journey down and most certainly had no concept of a sensible interval. Eventually I hit the last bend and found the bottom. As expected, Ludwig landed straight on top of me with a bang, closely followed by Basil and Vanessa, all of us forming a heap on the floor.

"Wow. That was fantastic." Ludwig was wagging his tail at a furious rate.

"I am not sure I could agree with you there. I found it horrifying" Vanessa was visibly shaken. She was quite a delicate person and probably bruised after being bounced around inside the duct.

"I'm sure my wings are destroyed," cried Basil and started flapping to see if there was anything broken. "Lucky me. But this means of transport is most unsuitable for flying creatures!"

We exited the duct system through another grate into a room and bypassed the long way down to the floor climbing down the shelves of a filing cabinet, turning on the light as we passed the switch.

"I don't recognise this room so I am not sure exactly where we are in the building. I have to get my bearings first and then find everything we need."

"And what should we do?" asked Vanessa.

"Just stay here everyone and relax. I need to locate my old office. That might be a while."

"Relax. Oh, that sounds good. I'm quite good at relaxing."

"We know!" said Basil, Ludwig and I in unison.

"Basil. Change of plan. You are going to have to come with me and open the doors," I said as I realised straight away that being so small certainly had disadvantages.

"So, you do have your uses!" said Vanessa teasing Basil.

Basil powerfully flew up to the door, pressed the handle down with his beak and landed on the floor again. The door opened just enough for Basil and I to poke our heads out into the corridor. We looked left, then right and we were off. The door closed behind us with a quiet click.

***

"They've been gone almost two hours already." Vanessa was bored and complained pointing at a clock on the wall. "Surely, they must come back soon. I've had enough relaxing time for now."

"I'm rather enjoying this mission. I miss relaxing for hours and hours," replied Ludwig with a deep yawn. "Why do you always have the urge to do something?"

"Quiet, Ludwig. I can hear something," whispered Vanessa anxiously. "I think someone is coming."

"Well, we don't need to hide, do we Vanessa? We're invisible. Quite cool really."

"No, Ludwig. I suppose not but nevertheless it is a very strange experience. Don't you think? Let's at least hide the socks," she said as the footsteps came closer and then stopped directly outside the door. "Oh no. We've left the light on!"

The handle was slowly pressed down, and a security guard expressed his displeasure with a tut and a shake of his head. He gave the room a thorough inspection as Basil and I slipped in through his legs unseen when he shut the door and switched off the light smothering us in darkness.

"I hope the light didn't give us away," said Vanessa.
"No, it didn't, Vanessa," I said from the doorway. "People often leave the lights on in their offices and he patrols all offices anyhow. It is nothing unusual."

"What took you so long?" Vanessa sounded annoyed.

"I had to collect a lot of stuff from different places but now I am finished. The only problem is that it is too much, and too large and heavy for just Basil and I to carry. We will all have to go and get it."

206

I led them along a few corridors and up a flight of stairs to an office where I had left the door ajar.

"Is this your office, Connor?"

"Yes, Vanessa. Was my office I should now say."

"So, where are the goodies, Connor?" asked Vanessa, like a child waiting for its Christmas presents.

I pointed towards a transparent plastic tube with red caps on both ends. "In the sock inside the tube. But I'm afraid it's jam-packed and rather heavy."

"My! That looks just like one of the transport shuttles," exclaimed Ludwig with real surprise.

"It sure does but that is not the original purpose of these tubes. It appears that they are being collected from this place and converted into shuttles. Quite ingenious really," I said.

"Did you travel in these, Connor?"

"Ludwig. Really! How do you expect humans to fit into them in their real size? They are being used for transport purposes, yes, but for documents, not people. The whole building is connected by a system of pipes and the tubes are sent from office to office with air pressure. Quite convenient, actually. And it is exactly how we are going to get out of here. Basil and I have already got a plan."

"Travel in these? Are you serious, Connor?" Protested Vanessa. "It's getting worse by the hour — first the duct and now you expect me to climb into this piece of plastic. Have you gone insane?"

"You've been travelling in them below the ground for the last couple of days, so why not here? It is far less bumpy. Anyhow, how do you propose getting out with all that stuff? Up the air duct to the roof?"

"You might have a point there, Connor. So, what's your plan now?" asked Vanessa, reluctantly.

"Don't worry, Vanessa. All we need to do is lift this tube onto the chair and onto the desk and then push it into the pneumatic post opening in the wall right over there. We all get in, except Basil. He presses the buttons to send it directly to an office in the basement after we have sealed the cap from the inside. We've already been down there and found a ventilation pipe to get us out of the building."

"Are you sure this is going to work?" Vanessa was afraid.

"It works for documents and it will work for us! Really Vanessa, don't worry. Trust me please."

It was hard work for us to heave the tube onto the desk, which was unfortunately not directly against the wall, so we were forced to use a folder to bridge the gap to the flap and roll the tube across in a collective effort. With all of the goods tightly stuffed at the back of the tube it was a very tight fit indeed as we all squeezed in. Ludwig got in first and was crammed against a sock with Vanessa lying on top of him and I had to crouch to fit in at the front to pull the cap into place.

"What the dickens have you got in here, Connor?" Ludwig asked as he was uncomfortably pressed against my collection of equipment. "Are you sure you need all of that stuff?"

"Oh, don't worry about that, Ludwig. Let that be my concern and please don't damage anything."

"Oh no," screamed Vanessa out loudly. "I've just realised that we left the spare socks in the room we were in first."

I wasn't worried that anybody would ever suspect a sock had some sort of an evil role and gave the thumbs up to Basil that we were ready. He pressed the control button with his beak and our tube turned in a perpendicular direction, luckily for me with the sock at the bottom. The last thing Basil saw before the tube dropped down into the darkness was three sets of terrified eyes.

We were shaken through the pipe system on our way down and I completely lost orientation. Left, down, right, down again, spinning but we eventually landed on some sort of foam in the post room with a soft thud. Basil was already waiting for us and released the flap by pressing the button. Beaks were very useful tools too I thought. Our tube gently rolled out into a tray and what Basil now saw was a tangled mess composed of several socks, two humans and a dog.

"That was fun again," said Ludwig, as he shook himself off.

I had managed to kick off the cap and untangle myself from Vanessa and Ludwig. Stiff, but very happy to get out of the tube unharmed, we all crawled out into the post room.

"I wouldn't go that far. I'm covered in dog hair, Ludwig," said Vanessa, more jokingly than seriously.

It didn't take us long to get the tube out on the tray, onto the floor and across to the pipe which would lead us to the outside of the building. The pipe was sealed with a plastic grate, but it was easily removed, and we were able to push the tube to the outside without any problems.

"Nearly there, everyone. This is now the difficult part. The tube needs to be moved across to our molehill. This is what we have to do. Ludwig — run across and wake up our shuttle driver. He needs to make the opening larger to get the bag in. Tell him we are on our way. Vanessa and I will roll the tube across the car park and, Basil, you will be our look-out man. Any questions? No! Good."

The tube was easy to roll despite the weight but made an awful loud noise on the tarmac. I was just hoping we could get it across before being spotted by one of the security guards. We were nearly there and pushed the tube up the kerb and across the grass towards our entrance with a last hard effort when a loud voice suddenly shattered the silence. "What's going on over there?"

I froze and looked to where the voice came from. A security guard was shining the beam of his torch in our direction. He must have heard the noise on the tarmac and was getting closer at a brisk pace.

"Quickly now, everyone!" I was panicking. "Get the cap off and help me get the sock out."

We frantically dragged the full and heavy sock out, pushed it up towards the top of the molehill and dropped it straight down on top of Ludwig who was already waiting at the bottom. We all jumped straight after, pushing the sock down the tunnel to move it out of sight.

"What's all this then?" The security guard picked up the tube, looked inside and then spotted our molehill. He had a thorough look around to check if anyone was there, then dropped on his knees to inspect the molehill. There was nothing to see when he shone the torch beam down the hole. But then he stuck his hand down the hole and rummaged around inside, nearly getting hold of the bag. Luckily, we had just moved far enough down the tunnel for his hand to reach. That was close.

***

After that close call, we were visibly flustered as we got back from our mission. It was early in the morning already and not really worth going to bed. I pretended to take the sock with the equipment directly to my workplace so that I could immediately start work on the devices. I had a lot to prepare before the football match and I was sure that nobody would object; plus, the others reported to the Logistics Collection Agency and confirmed that we had completed our task.

Work had not started yet, nevertheless I had a good look around the warehouse to make sure the coast was clear. I got myself a trolley, a plaster and a pen and pushed the sock to a remote place in the warehouse, far away from the office. Very high up along the racking system I found the perfect spot and moved two glass jars out of the way.

"It should be safe here," I said to myself and wrote something on the plaster. I stuck my head into the sock and attached the plaster to one of the objects, took out some items and put the two jars back on the shelf. One final check around, then I put the sock with the remaining items back on the trolley and down the ramps again into my office. I laid the contents on the floor next to my desk: several mini-cameras, two smart phones and a blue bag. My plan was now in place and my first card had been dealt. We probably had to go back though to get more equipment. This was only the start.

***

"Mr Dillon. What happened last night?"

"Well, Ma'am it was all very strange indeed. I was doing my rounds outside when I heard a noise in the car park and saw this tube rolling across the car park. Almost like someone was pushing it. I ran across immediately but couldn't find it at first. So, I had a good look around and then found it open right next to a very large molehill," replied Mr Dillon, holding the said tube.

"A drink, Mr Dillon?"

"Don't mind if I do. Thank you, Mrs Kingston."

"You fool. I am not asking you if you want a drink now! I want to know if you were drinking last night?"

"Drinking last night? No ma'am. I never drink on duty."

"Mr Dillon. You have had years of exemplary service, for which we are grateful, but this story is hard to believe," said Jemima Kingston. "So, how do you suppose the tube got there? All on its own?"

"That's the funny thing, ma'am. It appears that it had been moved outside through an air vent in the wall from the post room. The strangest thing about it is that it's a tube from Mr Jackson's office."

"But Mr Jackson disappeared two weeks ago without any trace. How the Devil could it have come from his office? How strange. Look, Mr Dillon. I don't think explaining this story to anyone else would do your career any good. Why not just leave it to me and not mention a word about it again?"

"Errm, I suppose so, Mrs Kingston."

"There's a good chap. Thank you, Mr Dillon. You are dismissed."

Cromwell's head was poking out of the top of Mrs Kingston's handbag, ears at full extension and eyes wide open. Something important had just happened, of that he was sure. But what?

"Now, now Cromwell. Don't be alarmed. Let Mummy look after the real world," she said stroking Cromwell's head.

Mrs Kingston took the tube from the desk, placed it in her draw, sat back in her chair and started mulling over all of the strange events of the last few weeks. Firstly, Cromwell appeared and then

Mr Jackson disappeared. Then she heard strange voices coming from her handbag. And now last night. Something suspicious was going on and she was going to get to the bottom of it. But first, better ask her closest friend about it. She took her mobile out of her bag and dialled.

"Felicity dear. How are you? I need to talk to you about something. How about a cup of tea this afternoon?"

***

Chapter Twelve
Special Ops

The pub was densely packed to breaking point with every seat taken, often by more than one creature. In every standing area everybody was shoulder to shoulder, even the tables were now temporarily converted into viewing areas. But there was one thing which obviously differentiated the spectators today and that was colour. One half of the pub was wearing the blue and white scarves of Lower Molehampton whilst the other side wore the red and white ones of Upper Molehampton. It was the first round of the Moles' World Cup and my idea of using smart phones as viewing screens proved immensely popular. Nobody had ever arranged anything like this before and the excitement and anticipation for this event was so high that even the moles, who would normally make a clear distinction between their lives and the lives of the others, were in large attendance and for the first time let their aura over power slip and join in with the masses. The temptation of watching the cup live was too much and today everyone was equal, just as they preached. This was a big day indeed.

A large smart phone took up most of one wall and acted as a big screen for everyone to watch. And above the surface I had several mini-cameras planted in different molehills to broadcast the famous game from different angles live down here. I sat at the back of the pub with a device I had constructed to change between the different cameras, and as kick-off was fast approaching it was time to turn on my system. The din in the pub was growing with the opposing sets of fans singing their songs and hurling light-hearted abuse at each other. The beer was flowing, scarves were flying — we were all set for a wonderful afternoon of action. With a pang of nervousness, I switched on my system. The screen flickered and suddenly the pub became eerily silent. Then the screen turned white and the crowd sighed quietly but turned into an even larger sigh as the screen flashed again and turned black. My nerves were frayed. I was very experienced with such equipment, but I hadn't had any time to test my set up. Then, after a series of flickers on the screen, accompanied by the ups and downs of the excited crowd, the football pitch suddenly burst into the pub with an almighty cheer. But the smartphones did not only transmit the pictures but also the noise from the pitch, so we had a unique live experience.

Upper Molehampton's ground was a normal village football pitch with no stand or any sitting possibilities, just a white railing set back about two metres from the edge of the pitch. There were the standard goals at either end and two small shelters on one side of the pitch for the trainers and medical staff. This particular football pitch was not in the best of condition, with many patches of flattened mud scattered around the playing surface. The white lines to mark the playing areas had been newly painted this morning and of course there were also hundreds of molehills decorating the two-metre strip of grass around the pitch. But this was no ordinary day because today was the long-awaited football match between Upper Molehampton and Lower Molehampton. The rivalry was intense. Both teams had been playing in different leagues for years with Upper playing two leagues higher at the moment. The two teams had not played against each other for years and all requests for friendly games had always been spurned. However, this year they were drawn against each other in the cup — the ultimate cup tie in the region and the scene was perfect to ignite old rivalries. This was my world of course, which is much larger than that of the moles. For them it was the World Cup.

The match had already drawn considerable support with a few hundred away supporters with their blue and white scarves already in attendance. Football was not a game associated with the people from Upper Molehampton who preferred the game of rugby.

However, with a wealthy owner, Upper always managed, by hook or by crook, to be the better side and play higher up the leagues. Today, the home supporters brought with them a luxury looking tent, adorned with red and white scarves, which they placed on the opposite side of the pitch from the away supporters. The scene was set for the epic showdown. AFC Upper Molehampton versus FC Lower Molehampton!

***

"Hopefully you will all be well-behaved today, Mr Cross," said Sergeant Dawson, seriously.

"I am sure the match will pass without incident, Sergeant. I am not so bothered about any trouble but just look at the state of this pitch. Where have all of these molehills come from? I have never seen so many in one place and so suddenly. They weren't here yesterday. Every single piece of grass around the pitch has been destroyed by these hills but strangely enough nothing on the pitch itself."

"Moles don't like noise, Mr Cross. They are blind and like their peace and quiet. Everybody knows that. But I heard that the noise made by the stamping of feet during training usually stops them from digging directly under the pitch," said Sergeant Dawson.

A roar of laughter far down below filled the Tunnellers' Arms as Sergeant Dawson blurted out his comment. If only he knew he was being televised in a pub under the ground and what the moles were really capable of. Well, one day he certainly would!

The big screen caught the Sergeant walking straight towards where the camera was positioned. We saw the underside of his boot as he raised his foot and thumbed down on our viewing point. "Damn moles!" The screen went blank, followed by a huge sigh of disappointment from both sets of supporters. Of course, I had known before that there naturally was a high risk of someone trampling on a camera, so I even had tunnelling teams on standby to quickly dig new viewing hills and replace the cameras to ensure an uninterrupted live transmission of this event. After just a short

215

break one of the back-up cameras took over from a different angle and a sigh of relief went through the pub.

"Sorry, everyone," I shouted from the back. "I'm afraid this will be unavoidable with all of the people trampling around up there."

"Don't worry, Connor," shouted Mr Tinker. "You've done a wonderful job. This is the most fun we've had for ages."

Personally, I thought that the quality of the transmission was not so great, but as this was the first time of experiencing live-viewing down here nobody was complaining.

***

"Oh Jemima. Jemima dear," shouted a woman from the other side of a tent.

"Felicity, come and join us," shouted Jemima back.

"I didn't expect to see you today, Felicity. You hate this sort of event. You told me on the phone you wouldn't come."

"I do hate this sort of event my, dear Jemima darling. But as you may remember, I am the mayoress, and it is my duty to attend such ghastly events. Just look at that common rabble on the other side of the pitch. I get shivers up my spine just thinking about this."

"It's not that bad, Jemima," said Felicity, passing a red and white scarf across. "Here's a scarf for you to support our team."

"No thank you, dear. Must keep up appearances," said Jemima and wrapped Cromwell up in the scarf instead.

"What in God's name are these idiots doing now?" Cromwell asked himself. He poked his head out of Jemima Kingston's handbag and saw her standing in a tent with plastic windows looking out to some sort of field. On the other side of the field he saw people standing amongst hundreds of molehills. Everybody was wearing either a blue and white or a red and white scarf, like the people in the tent and the one Jemima had just looped around his neck. What a strange sight he thought!

***

216

The game itself was a pulsating affair with the ball flying up and down the pitch at an extremely fast rate. There was not much skill involved on either side, but lots of running, jostling and sweating. The crowd in the Tunnellers' Arms were enthralled with the encounter and the excitement knew no bounds. The tackles were flying in, players were pushing and shoving each other, trainers were yelling across the pitch and the spectators followed every piece of action with great enthusiasm.

"Come on, ref. That was never a foul."

"Oooooh, nearly in."

"Penalty, ref. Come on!"

"You must score from there. Unbelievable. My grandmother could have scored that."

The noise of the crowd moved up and down with the speed of the game and the shouting went on for some time until eventually there was a loud cheer from the blue and white scarves. Lower had scored.

"Yes. Come on you blues! Let's give the reds a good thrashing."

The game remained, deservedly, one-nil to Lower for the rest of the game as the clock slowly ticked towards ninety minutes. As the referee indicted an extra two minutes of injury time, Lower were well in control, keeping sensible possession in their own half.

"Not going to score now are you, Upper" someone shouted out.

"Run out of time, haven't you? And luck!"

One of the Lower players decided to pass the ball back to his goalkeeper, trying to waste a little bit of the valuable time remaining. The opposing team were far away and didn't even pose a threat when the ball rolled along the grass at a slow pace and approached the relaxed keeper who stooped down to pick it up. Then out of nowhere, a small divot of earth popped up in front of him. The ball jumped up and rolled right over his foot towards the goal. The surprised keeper, not the most agile of sportsman I hasten to add, twisted around and lunged for the ball. But it was too late. Goal for Upper!

"Yeeeeessssss!"

There was a huge roar from the red side of the pub followed by howling and boos from the other.

"Cheats!"

"Who put that molehill there? We agreed there was a ban on digging during the game!"

It was the last action of the match and the final whistle was blown leaving the score one-one and finally balanced for the next leg. The AFC Upper Molehampton players celebrated deliriously whilst the FC Lower Molehampton players just looked bewildered. A very lucky draw indeed.

***

Vanessa sat in the back of the pub and smiled smugly as animals of both supporters came up and begrudgingly handed her money.

"You didn't bet, did you, Vanessa?" I was suspicious. Vanessa was part of the digging team. Was there foul play involved in that goal?

She just looked at me, smiled and just carried on collecting money.

Mr Tinker approached her too and handed over his money. "I can't believe how lucky you are, young lady. Placing a bet for one-one and getting exactly that result in such circumstances. Scandalous is all I will say." He was knitting his brows and sounded more angry than disappointed.

"Oh, don't begrudge my win, Mr Tinker. All won fairly and squarely I would like to add," said Vanessa, with a smirk and I had good cause to doubt that.

"Fairly?" I asked. "Somehow, I have a funny feeling that was arranged," I said sarcastically. "The funny thing about this is that you happen to work with the tunnellers. You arranged it, didn't you?"

"What me? Connor! Shame on you for even suggesting such a thing?" Her grin was cheeky when she packed up her money, stood up and walked over to the bar. Of course, this was foul play. What else?

***

The Lower Molehampton fans were still standing on their side of the pitch finishing their beers and pies and heatedly discussing the final moments of the game. They all felt they were robbed and, in my opinion at least, were right to think so. Some of them started frantically stamping on the molehills to vent their frustration at the obviously guilty party in the unexpected outcome of the game.

The Upper Molehampton fans stood complacently in their tent celebrating their lucky draw with canapés and wine. Meanwhile, their mayoress stood proudly in the corner collecting her winnings after correctly betting on the one-one result.

***

Colonel Pickle handed over his money to Colonel Bacon.

"There you go, Colonel. I hope you will enjoy your winnings," said Colonel Pickle.

"And fairly won I must say, Colonel Pickle," he said with a sly smile on his face.

"Hmmm. Fairly won? I am not so sure about that. I thought we gave clear instructions for no digging under the pitch during the game?" asked Colonel Pickle, sceptically.

"Yes. Those were the instructions I passed on. I have no idea how this could have happened. Quite shocking," replied Colonel Bacon trying to hide his sarcasm.

"Quite shocking indeed." Colonel Pickle's face was stern and motionless.

"So down to business, Colonel. How are Mr Jackson and his team getting on in the Logistics Collection Agency?" requested Colonel Pickle.

"Very well I have to say. They are very quick learners and proved to be successful in all of their scavenging missions so far. As you know, Mr Jackson was the one who came up with the idea of broadcasting the football match by using equipment from his former

219

job. He needed so much equipment that he had to go on a second mission to collect everything," said Colonel Bacon. "A truly wonderful idea and excellent motivation for our workers. I must say that Mr Jackson is a very talented and resourceful man."

"Just from this one act he has become very popular. I can see that Mr Jackson has considerable talents that we can harness. Once he has completed his real mission we might well keep him on as he may prove to be much more useful to us," said Colonel Pickle.

"I thought the idea was to deactivate him as soon as he has completed his mission," Colonel Bacon reacted with surprise.

"Yes. That was the idea, but you must agree he is quite a useful chap," replied Colonel Pickle. "But you are probably right. He should end up in a jar when all of this is over. He knows too much."

"Far too much. And what of his colleagues?"

"Get rid of them just as soon as the mission is complete. We will keep using Mr Jackson until he is of no further use to us anymore and then get rid of him. Just like we do with everyone else," said Colonel Pickle seriously.

"Yes. Just like everyone else," added Colonel Bacon.

"I think we should begin their Special Operations training immediately. What do you think, Colonel? Are you ready to send them out on their real mission?" asked Colonel Pickle.

"Yes. I have everything set up and I can introduce them to the Special Operations Department tomorrow. We will train them intensively and as soon as they are competent we will have them complete this important mission," said Colonel Bacon.

"Yes. The mission must be completed as soon as possible. It's imperative to get Professor Wingnut back as soon as possible and smoke out the moles who are responsible for the theft," said Colonel Pickle harshly. He looked around to make sure nobody was listening. "Trust nobody, Colonel Bacon. Nobody at all," whispered Colonel Pickle.

Colonel Bacon nodded in furious agreement.

***

"I still can't believe what happened yesterday, Vanessa. You had something to do with it and you are just not telling!" I was still angry for obvious reasons.

"Connor. Just what do you take me for? You're just a bad loser. Upper fairly drew the game. It's not my fault the Lower goalkeeper is such a duffer. Fancy not being able to pick up such a tame back pass."

"I still call it a stitch-up," I replied.

"Let's concentrate on what we have to do today. Look, there is Mr Tinker's store."

"Yes. Colonel Bacon told me to report here for our introduction in the Special Operations Department. Not sure what it has to do with Mr Tinker though," I said.

"Follow me." It was Cleopatra's gruff voice coming from behind us. She had of course been following us as usual and now brushed past with no further comment leading the way into Mr Tinker's store.

"Good morning, Connor." Mr Tinker welcomed us from behind his counter.

"Good morning, Mr Tinker."

"Good morning, Mr Tinker," said Vanessa brightly. "Have I got time to spend my winnings?"

"Ignore her, Mr Tinker. She's just teasing you," I said.

"We all know the game was rigged. A scandal for sport," replied Mr Tinker.

Cleopatra stood next to a heavy, red curtain at the back of the shop and growled.

"I think she means for you to follow her, Connor. I must admit I am surprised to see you here so soon after your arrival. You really must have shown some talent to be selected so quickly. Well done. Just like your father I would like to add," said Mr Tinker.

"My father?"

"Yes, Connor. Your father was also selected. Didn't anyone tell you. He was a pioneer of the early special ops missions before it developed into what it is today. He provided us a wonderful service and sourced many useful items. And he was one of the first to experiment with infiltration, more commonly today known as Morphing, I let you know."

Cleopatra growled again and simply said, "Now."

She pushed the curtain to one side, revealing a metal door, then pressed a buzzer and a few moments later the heavy door creaked open into a large open-plan office with moles working feverously at different desks.

"Come on over here and I'll let you know what's going on," Colonel Bacon boomed from the inside of the office. "Welcome to the Special Operations Department."

We walked through some desks and then followed the Colonel into a briefing room.

"Let's get going. The first thing I will say to you is that this department is ultra-secret. I hope you understand the meaning of that. I will also remind you that you are only here due to the special circumstances regarding the stolen memory of Professor Wingnut. Mr Jackson here supposedly knows where it is, roughly, and claims he can have it returned to safety. Once your mission is complete you will leave this department, and you may never say anything about this to anyone."

"What happens after the mission, Colonel Bacon?" asked Ludwig.

"You can apply for a job and see what happens, just like everyone else. Alternatively, you can elect to be reprogrammed and take a new life form. Of course, in that case you will leave your memory behind for us to administer. Isn't democracy wonderful?"

"When does the training begin, Colonel?" asked Vanessa.

"Right now. But first, let me explain how the Special Operations Department functions." Colonel Bacon started explaining and carried on with a stern voice. "The management might sometimes deem it necessary for special operations to be completed for the good and benefit of everyone down here. Sometimes it is a simple manual job, for example, the laying of tubes from the pub down to our bar. Yes. That is our responsibility too. But there is also work to keep us safe and sound. And these operations can of course be more dangerous and require thorough training," the Colonel pointed out.

"Do we go back as ourselves, Colonel?" Basil wanted to know.

"Good lord no. It is not possible once you have left your previous life to go back as that being. You have separated from your shell and that is the end. Just imagine if someone from your previous life saw you. Unthinkable. What we do is use your processor and memory together and implant them in another being. You can then take control of that being."

"So, are you saying I could go back as a cat?" asked Vanessa, curiously.

"Yes, exactly that. Once it has been decided what mission needs to be completed, we will train you to perform the functions of that particular being. For example, a cat. How to meow and purr, and all that. You know. And once that training has been completed, and we are sure you can actually pass as a cat, then we have you implanted until the mission is over."

"How are we implanted?"

"That is the tricky and dangerous part, Mr Jackson. For this to work, your processor and memory are turned into a special white fluid. This fluid is then transported by birds and needs to be accurately dropped onto the being you are to take over. The fluid only needs to make contact with the skin for the infiltration to work," described the Colonel.

"You mean we become bird poo?" exclaimed Basil with a look of shock in his face.

"Well, it you want to look at it that way." Colonel Bacon seemed amused.

"The whole thing seems a little farfetched, Colonel. What happens if the bird misses its target?"

Looking at me the Colonel said, "Then you are returned to us and we start the whole process again. But if you do exactly as you are told in the training then I am sure it will work. So, it is essential that you pay the upmost attention. We normally have a very high success rate I let you know."

"And how do we know the mission is over? I mean, how do we leave the being we have taken over?"

Still looking at me the Colonel replied, "Oh, that's easy, Mr Jackson. Just get to Mr Tinker's store and he will do the rest for you. In fact, we are directly below his store at the moment as you know. Don't worry. It will all become clear and you will be fully briefed and trained of course."

"When do we go on our real mission to find the Professor?"

"Not so fast and all in good time. First, Mr Jackson, you will go on a trial mission for two days only and as soon as that is over, and you have completed it successfully, we will then send you on your real mission. Normally we do not send trainees back so quick on a real mission but as times are different, and our needs are pressing, we will have to make an exception with you lot. A lot of planning will be required and I understand you want to be involved in it, Mr Jackson?"

"Yes, Colonel Bacon. That is correct," I replied.

"You must brief me on your mission before you go so that you are completely prepared and leave no stone unturned. We cannot risk anything happening to you. Are we clear?" said the Colonel, slyly.

"Yes, we are and of course I will keep you up to speed on everything we do. Absolutely everything," I promised. "And I will of course keep Colonel Pickle informed too."

Colonel Bacon looked at me nervously. "There's no need for that Mr Jackson. No need at all to trouble the busy Colonel with minor details. Leave me to worry about all of that," he replied.

"As you wish Colonel Bacon." I thought about what Colonel Bacon had just given away.

"Do you really know what you are doing?" whispered Vanessa in my ear.

"Trust me on this Vanessa. I do know exactly what I am doing," I whispered back confidently.

***

I was sitting on a box waiting for my trainer to come. My dog trainer. Yes, I was chosen for training as a dog, can you believe that? Vanessa was selected to be a cat. Basil a horse and Ludwig a human. We were split up and taken to our respective training rooms and that was where I was waiting when the door opened and in walked the most elegant dog I had ever seen.

"Hello, Connor. I am an Afghan Hound and my name is Duchess. Welcome to your training."

"Thank you, Duchess. A pleasure to meet you," I stammered back.

"What do you know about dogs, Connor?"

"I must admit I have never owned a dog, so I don't know much. Rather nothing to be frank."

"Owned? Did you say owned?" said Duchess. "Well this is the first key fact for you. You can't own a dog and what's more, as you humans suppose, you cannot actually own an animal at all. You might be its master as a human, but you may never own it. If you are going on an operation as a dog, you need to study their characteristics and act exactly like they do. You certainly don't want to be given away or arouse suspicion. So you must pay attention and follow my lead."

"Wouldn't it be easier to send a dog as a dog and then there is no need to do this training?" I asked.

"Of course, Connor and we sometimes do that. But you have to remember the mission is the most important factor. If it means you going as a dog to complete a mission, then that is what you have to do. I understand so much that you have to go on a mission to retrieve an important article. A top secret mission. Well, you are the one who has the information, but you can't just go walking in as another human, can you? And we know because we've already tried. The two policemen guarding your house didn't fall for it and sent them packing. Therefore, you need to go in as something else, something which cannot be suspected. Therefore, it is better to train for the unexpected and be prepared for all eventualities. This is why we are called Special Operations. The more life forms you are trained in, the more versatile you are as an operative. Today you will be trained as a dog and next week maybe as something else. Our most highly trained operatives can pass off easily as over ten different types of creature without raising any suspicion. Any questions?"

"Sounds plausible to me and I will of course do this. Dogs. What do I know about dogs? Well, generally they live in houses and bark when the doorbell rings. They cannot open cans and therefore have to wait to be given food. Also, they have to be taken for walks to go to the toilet. And, if they are not well-trained, they have to be kept on a lead. There we go. That's a good start I think. Oh yes, one more thing. They believe that doors open magically if they just stare at it long enough."

"Oh dear. There's a lot more to the life of a dog. Anything else you might know?"

"Oh yes, I forgot. They like to steal food and pretend it wasn't them."

"Well, Connor. I can see you have a lot to learn so let's start with the basics. How do dogs great each other?"

"I am not certain about that, but I am sure you are going to tell me!"

"Dogs greet another dog by sniffing their rear ends. That's also how they identify."

I felt disgusted just about the thought of it. "Lovely, I'll just pretend to be a very shy dog. Let's move on to the next topic."

Duchess looked at me sternly, "Oh no, Connor. You will have to practice it, or you are not going anywhere. We will try it out in a few minutes time along with some other basics."

"Oh no I'm not. I'm not sniffing your rear end. No offence, Duchess but no!"

"No offence taken. But you will have to do it if you want to go on a special mission. Think yourself lucky. If I were a cat, you would have to learn to stand on ridiculously narrow things, high above the ground. The thought even makes me shudder. And then there is the fur licking part and the puking it back out again. Now that is disgusting, Connor. Think yourself lucky."

I looked at Duchess and with a judder of my back, "I really don't think I'm going to enjoy this!"

"Don't worry, we can leave the sniffing to later. Let me explain some very basic facts. Firstly, how to approach another dog when you are greeting. You first move around in an arc, then approach the rear and sniff. Bark to show protection, for example when the doorbell rings or a stranger approaches. If you want to show happiness, then simply wag your tail. Dig or chew if you are bored. Stick your tail between your legs if you are frightened and show your teeth to express anger. Lying on your back will show that you feel secure and relaxed in your environment."

"What about if I am hungry or need to go to the toilet? I can't speak so I must be able to do something."

"Good question. Pace back and forth in front of where you eat to show hunger or in front of a door to show you want to go out. My advice is always to act as passively as possible and don't over act your role. You will be taking over the function of another dog and you will never be able to copy its behaviour. Best thing to do is be as quiet as possible, do the basics and learn from your environment so you can complete your mission."

"But I can't train here, Duchess. I am a human and not a dog."

"You are correct and that is your biggest challenge. But nobody said that special ops was easy. My advice is to learn as much as you can here, so you can implement it when you first go out. We will make it easy for you and choose a farm dog for your first training. They usually spend most of their time outside independently and have little contact with humans, unlike a dog in someone's house To replicate that behaviour requires a very advanced level, Connor. Come on, we can do some basics to get going. Go over there to the box and put on the false ears and tail so we can practice."

Although I felt really stupid, I did what Duchess asked me to do. I found the pair of headphones with cardboard dog ears fixed onto them and put them on. Then I slung the belt with a tail around my hips.

"Great, Connor. Almost there. Now down on all fours and let's practice."

I wasn't enthralled about the prospect of this but what choice did I have! I went down on all fours and approached Duchess head on but then moved to the right and past her in an arc fashion. With a cringed face, I approached her rear end and sniffed but then withdrew as quickly as I could.

"Too quick, Connor! You must linger and sniff more intensively. I'm sure you've seen dogs do it before. Let's go again," Duchess commanded very patiently.

With an air of defeat, I went back to my starting place and did exactly what Duchess asked of me.

"Well done, Connor! That's it. Not difficult is it?"

We then played through some different scenarios such as requesting food, indicating to go to the toilet, barking for protection and so on. By the end of the day I had learned the basic dog behaviour and was probably just able to pass off as a very passive farm dog, hoping I could avoid meeting any other dogs, so I would be spared the initial greeting ritual.

"What will I have to do on my trial mission," I asked.

"You will be given an easy mission because all you really have to do is to learn to take over the function of a dog and manage to pass off without raising suspicion. But first, you have to go to the Bird Dropping Department to find out how that works though. Your mission will be to land on any dog you can find and then take over for two days before returning."

"How do I return? The Colonel mentioned something about Mr Tinker."

"Yes, exactly that. You will have to make your way to Mr Tinker and he will then make the arrangements for your return. Don't worry, he knows what to do and has all the equipment. You will go on your mission today by the way," added Duchess. "Now off you go and good luck."

I left and headed off to the Bird Dropping Department to wait for the others to complete their training.

***

"Wow, that was great," said Ludwig. "Being a human sounds like so much fun. I can eat when I want, whenever I want, go to the toilet by myself. In fact, I can decide about everything. Fantastic. Much better than being a dog I think."

"Hmmmm, being a human is not all that it is cracked up to be," I said. "You have to go to work every day, cook your own food, do the cleaning by yourself and pay tax to the government, of course."

"Tax. What's that?"

"Best you don't busy yourself with that, Ludwig. Just enjoy yourself!"

"Well, I intend to make the most of it and do all of the things I couldn't do before. And you are going as a dog, Connor?"

"Yes, and I must admit I am not really looking forward to it."

"And neither am I," piped in a moody looking Vanessa.

"Not a surprise there," added Basil, sarcastically.

"I have to go as a cat and catch mice at night time. And learn how to fight. Imagine that!" said Vanessa.

"Actually, I find that hard to imagine," I said smiling at her.

"My name is Flight Sergeant Splat." A mole in a blue Air Force uniform shouted at us as he entered the room. "You all must pay special attention as this is the most complicated part of the mission. If you fail, you have to come back and try again and that, ladies and gentlemen, takes time and effort — something we haven't got a lot of. I need you to get it right the first time. Now follow me over here."

The Flight Sergeant led us to a wooden frame with four plastic bottles strung underneath. The bottles were hung upside down with their necks facing down, pointing through holes in a wooden platform for stability and held in position with garden twine. The bottle bases were cut open and the frame itself was suspended with rope from the ceiling so that the whole contraption swung freely above the floor.

"Do we have to get into these?" asked Basil.

"Yes, you do, but not in the form you are now. You will be turned into a thick, white fluid and then filled into the bottles. This way you can be dropped above your target by our bombing birds."

My face had already turned white, but from fear. "Will we be aware what is going on?"

"Yes. You will be fully aware of everything and communicate with the mice until the release point."

"Mice. Did you say mice?" asked Vanessa.

"Yes, the mice are the direction finders and stand on the platform next to the bottles. They take aim and then release you. All you have to do is stretch out your arms and legs and control the direction of your drop."

"You mean like parachuting," I asked.

"Correct. But without a parachute. The fluid is very thick, and you are inside it in a miniature form. When you stretch out your arms and legs, you will change the shape of the bomb and thus control your fall. Your job is to steer directly onto the target."

"How the hell can we practice that here?" asked Vanessa, with a questioning expression on her face.

"I was just coming to that. Come over here to my flip chart and I will teach you how to steer." The Flight Sergeant then showed us using pictures on the flip chart and explained how we could control our descent. It sounded easy in theory, but I was sure it would be much more difficult in practice.

"So, just to recap. Push out your arms and legs into a star shape and you will stretch the fluid and slow down your descent. Tilt to the right and you will fly to the right. The same applies to the left. Move your weight forward and you will dive and increase your speed. Got it?"

"I suppose so. When will we try it out?" I was not so convinced that we had enough training.

"Right now. Come this way please. Follow me to the Morphing machine."

We followed the Flight Sergeant out of the room and along a corridor to a solid wooden door with a sign above — MORPHING — where we found Mr Tinker waiting for us, standing next to a strange contraption with lots of different cables coming out of it.

"I hope you've all listened carefully," said Mr Tinker.

We all nodded and stared at him with big eyes.

"Please don't worry. This is completely safe and won't hurt. I promise. All you have to do is jump into this big canister and wait for the process to begin. It only takes a minute and you will be awake and aware of everything," he said.

"Exactly what process?" asked Vanessa looking puzzled.

"A miniaturising fluid will be poured in, the canister sealed and then shaken with you in it. You will then come out as a very thick fluid resembling bird poo. We've used this thousands of times and it works just fine. I will programme the machine so that your mixture will only work for two days, so you must return before that time is over. For other, more sophisticated operations, I can programme it for longer periods of time. Trust me — I've done this loads of times!"

"You are going to turn me into bird poo?" Vanessa was shocked. "This is getting worse as the days go by. What next?"

"Yep," replied Mr Tinker simply. "Right, who's first?"

I put my hand up, climbed up a ladder to the top of the canister and lowered myself inside. I looked up and saw a funnel, a lever and a mole grinning down at me. The canister was made of clear plastic, so I could see the nervous faces outside and they could quite easily see the fear on my face. Vanessa simply made the thumbs up sign to me, but I didn't return her gesture. Mr Tinker nodded to the mole above me who immediately pulled the lever to release a thick, white fluid which splatted right on top of me and filled up the entire canister. I could just about make out the shapes of the others through the thick fluid. It was a strange sensation, sitting in thick goo and still being able to breathe. My motions were naturally slower, but I regained all of my senses.

Mr Tinker and the mole put the lid on and screwed it shut.

"Stand back please," I could hear him say.

He pulled a lever on the wall and the canister was violently shaken in all directions for a few moments. The only sensation I had was being thrown around against the walls of the canister and as promised, it didn't hurt because I was cushioned by the thick fluid. He stopped the process and then signalled two other moles standing in the room. They pushed an empty jam jar next to the canister and got me out with a spoon. Whatever chemical reaction had taken place had turned me into a miniature white blob, about the tenth of the size of the others who were standing there just looking at me in disbelief. My body was completely cocooned in a semi-transparent, gooey material which really did resemble bird poo. To my surprise it was warm and actually quite comfortable. I pushed my hands out and pressed against the glass. I pushed harder with my arms, but the fluid didn't break. My movements were slow and because of the fluid my vision and hearing was not so good but enough to make out my surroundings. I had full function over my body, just like Mr Tinker had promised.

When Mr Tinker nodded again, the two moles removed the canister, put a clean one in its place, screwed a lid on my jar and pushed me to the wall.

"You are very small, Connor," shouted Vanessa, looking down at me. "Are you OK?"

"It's a strange sensation but I feel fine. Go ahead and do it," I shouted back.

The process was repeated three times and a few minutes later all four of us were in four separate glass jars, looking at each other in bewilderment and ready for our next adventure.

"Good luck to you all," shouted Mr Tinker. "See you back here in two days."

Chapter Thirteen
Morphing

"Come on. Get these jars up to Mr Tinker. Get a move on. We haven't got all day, you know!"

Four moles picked up a jar each, placed them on a small trolley, pushed them out of the room, along a tunnel and into another room with a small opening in the wall, just large enough to fit a jar. I was placed in the opening first, pushed to the end and now sat on top of a wooden board. It was very dark in the room and even though my vision was somewhat impaired because of the gooey mixture, I was able to make out day light coming down a long shaft directly above me. Then something was pressed on the wall and the next thing I knew was a rattling sound when the wooden board started shaking violently before it shot up the shaft as though someone was using a pulley system. The board banged against the sides of the wall as I was shot high up towards the surface until the pin prick of light became ever larger and my jar suddenly popped out into the light surroundings of another room. Yes, I was back on the surface again and the sight of daylight certainly made me feel cheerful. Well, as cheerful as you can imagine sitting in a jar disguised as bird poo. I sat on a wooden board directly next to a well-worn table with the light coming from a small window. Where was I?

"Aah. Another jar," said a somehow familiar voice.

A huge hand grasped around my jar, lifted me up and put me on the table. One of the fingers pressed a button and the wooden board went back down the shaft with a clatter and the squeaking of moving ropes. Very soon all four of us were sitting on the table looking at each other again through the gooey fluid. I now recognised the huge person wearing a brown knee-length workman's coat. Mr Tinker. But not the Mr Tinker from below- No, this was the Mr Tinker from above. Mr Tinker junior. The shaft connected both shops — unbelievable. Obviously, there was more to the Tinkers than meets the eye.

"Hello, Mr Jackson. Never expected to see you here again. You have been the talk of the village since your disappearance. Delighted you are safe and sound. Aaah, Miss Forsythe-Twyke. So, this is where you've been hiding all this time. Your mother has been very worried about you. And this must be Ludwig, Farmer Rye's missing dog. And you are?" Mr Tinker asked in the direction of Basil.

"My name is Basil and I am a duck from the River Angler."

"Sorry. Never heard of you but pleased to meet you nevertheless."

"What on earth is going on here, Mr Tinker?" I had to shout as the goo absorbed most of my voice and made it sound very dull.

"This is the arrival and departure area for special ops, Mr Jackson. My father and I have been running this along with our pigeons for years. It's a special profession in our family. We worked very closely with your father by the way, but you never would have known anything about this. He was an early pioneer of our operations you know."

"Yes, I have already been informed about that. And your pigeons will deliver us to our targets I presume?" I couldn't believe it. All these years this had been happening directly under my very nose and I never knew or suspected anything. My father. The Tinkers. The pigeons. How could that have happened?

"Quite right. My homing pigeons have been specially trained for these missions and that is exactly where you are going now."

"But where exactly are we going?" asked Vanessa. "We were just told we were going on a trial mission, but we know nothing specific."

"You are going to the equestrian centre in Upper Molehampton. Apart from horses of course, there are a few dogs and cats around, so you can all train and practice in your new roles and all keep together. We usually use the equestrian centre for the first training run because its close and simple."

"How do I know which horse I will be?" asked Basil.

"You can look through the bottle and choose a horse. Just tell the mouse on the platform and they will direct the pigeon. Once the positioning is complete you will be released and then it's up to you to accurately home in and land on any horse you want. This applies to everyone else by the way. My tip though is to land on something stationery for the first time. Landing on moving targets is a skill you need to develop," explained Mr Tinker. "Come on. Let's get you up in the air."

Mr Tinker carried us out of the room, walked to his homing pigeon shed and placed the jars on a table next to two wooden frames. Exactly like the ones we had seen in our training. He took plastic bottles from a shelf on the wall, made sure the caps were secured, turned them upside down and stuck the bottle necks through the holes in the platform, just as we had seen before. Then he secured all four bottles with garden twine, ensuring there was still enough play for the bottles to move. He used a wooden spoon to scoop my blob out and poured me through the opening on the base of the bottle. I slithered down the bottle until the goo came to a stop in the neck with my head facing down.

"Are you OK there, Mr Jackson?" asked Mr Tinker whilst repeating the process for Ludwig.

"It's not the most comfortable position I have ever been in, but I suppose it will do," I said looking across at an upside-down Ludwig in the bottle next to me.

"Won't take too long and then we'll have you up and away," he said and poured Vanessa and Basil into their bottles.

"We're ready," he commanded and four mice wearing brown flying caps and goggles scurried out of a hole in the wall, up a ramp to the top of the table and across to Mr Tinker. "Please drop them off at the equestrian centre. This is their first run out so please go easy. You know the routine."

The mice jumped onto the two wooden platforms, stood next to a bottle each and held on the twine. Mr Tinker then summoned a pigeon from the roost, tied a harness around its belly and attached the wooden frame Ludwig and I were on with solid string.

"Let's go."

Mr Tinker carried the pigeon through the door holding it high above his head. The platform hung below the bird and he made sure that the string couldn't tangle in its wings. As soon as he was outside, he released his gentle grip and the pigeon lifted off into the sky with a whoosh of its wings with the platform swinging erratically from left to right under its belly, while the mice held on tight to the twine.

Being upside down was not the most comfortable journey but afforded me a perfect view of our picturesque area. We flew low at first, over some buildings in Lower Molehampton before gaining height, leaving the village and ground far below us. Once we were at a cruising altitude the pigeon hovered gently in the sky and, apart from the sound of mild wind and the odd flutter of the pigeon's wings, we just floated on the thermals. The platform's erratic movement had stopped, and it was now moderately swinging. I turned my head and looked up at the pigeon's feathered belly and the white clouds hanging in the lovely blue sky. Below was the River Angler, the two villages, the castle ruin, the factory and I could even make out Farmer Rye's house with the old willow tree and Anglerton in the distance. It was a wonderful view considering my impaired eyesight in the gooey mixture. When we went over the campsite, I imagined I could even smell the fish-laden smoke rising from the chimney. This was exactly what I had imagined flying to be like — majestic and serene. I loved it and looked across to see how Ludwig was doing. He didn't return my gaze but had his frightened eyes fixed on the ground. He obviously wasn't enjoying the stunning view and experience. The mice had now let go of the twine for the first time and were looking at the ground through tiny observation holes in the platform. I heard the noise of beating wings as the second pigeon glided in and joined us high up in the clouds. Vanessa and Basil joyfully waved at me from their bottles swinging underneath their bird.

"The equestrian centre I believe," shouted the mouse next to me across to the other bird.

"Yes, correct," confirmed another mouse.

The two birds glanced at each other, appeared to nod and then smoothly glided off in the same direction. We were now above Lower Molehampton and started to descend smoothly. The sun had just come out from behind a cloud and was shining directly on the river, bathing it in a beautiful silver shimmer. We descended across the river, glided over the castle ruin and started our final approach towards the equestrian centre. The buildings of Upper Molehampton got closer as our target came into sight.

"Attention please!" shouted out the mouse next to me. It was difficult to hear as his voice was being taken by the wind. "We are nearly ready for our bombing mission. We will first fly over the target, so you can choose where you want us to drop you off. What are you looking for?"

"I would like a placid dog, preferably one which is not moving, or even better sleeping," I shouted back at the top of my voice.

The mouse instructed the bird who instantly dove sharply towards the centre, pulled up slightly again as we glided over a horse riding field, and then circled slowly to give me a clear view of the surroundings below. At lunchtime the equestrian centre was very quiet. Some horses were peacefully grazing in one of the fields, the jumps and the barn looked abandoned and there was no one outside between the farmhouse and the luxury cars parked in the car park.

I spotted a light brown dog outside the barn which was enjoying a sleep in the midday sun. "The barn. The barn," I shouted excitedly at the mouse. "Look, over there. There's a dog at the entrance of the barn and seems to be asleep. Can you see it?"

"Yes. Seen." The mouse again gave instructions to the pigeon who immediately decreased our altitude and hovered directly over the dozing dog, just a few metres above it.

"We're going to do a practice run first, to help me acquire my aim before we go back for a second run when I will release you," shouted the mouse to me.

We swung in a large circle, straightened up and then flew in a direct line right above the still unsuspicious dog. The mouse looked through its observation hole and concentrated on the dog. "Now!"

With a loud squirt the pigeon dropped its poo like a guided missile towards the dog and only just missed the target. The spat landed right next to the dog who didn't even budge but carried on enjoying its midday slumber in the sun completely oblivious to the events around it.

"OK. That's close enough. Let's do the final bombing run."

"Are you ready?" cried the mouse.

I gave the thumbs up to indicate I was ready and we then circled in for the final run. I braced myself and readied for the drop, trying to remember everything we had been taught. My eyes were now firmly fixed on the fast approaching dog below me. When the mouse shouted "release", the cap was pulled away and I felt myself first sliding and then shooting out of the open bottle. I was now in free fall and spinning uncontrollably towards the ground. The short drop was terrifying, and I frantically tried to recall how to put out my arms and legs to regain control. Then I remembered the star shape and to my amazement my gooey fluid held its form and slowed my fall. By dropping my weight to the left and right accordingly I was able to guide myself towards my target and passed the horses in the paddock right next to it. I dropped slowly until I was directly above the dog, balanced myself by keeping my arms out and gently fluttered down like a leaf. Landing directly on its furry back was the last thing I remembered from my first drop.

***

The light brown bulldog was lying on the ground right in front of a barn and next to a paddock, just dozing off in the warmth of the midday sun. The first bird dropping splatting on the ground close to her wasn't enough to wake her up but the second one hit the mark right on her back with a low thud. Her eyes shot open, she looked around in sharp motions to see what had disturbed her midday snooze and then jumped up, wildly looking around. She then did the strangest thing. She stood up on her rear legs, like an animal performing a trick in a circus, walked a few steps, dropped back down on all fours and ran into the barn and out of sight. Thankfully nobody witnessed the event and so the unusual performance of the dog went unnoticed.

***

This set of eyes peering directly at the horses in the paddock were certainly not my own. I stood up, subconsciously with only the rear two legs, like a human being would, until it fully dawned on me that I was now a dog. Connor Jackson in control of a dog to be more precise. What a strange sensation indeed. I had to concentrate very hard and commanded the dog, or me I should say, to get down again onto all fours, which thankfully worked immediately. I swung around and saw the open barn door with a pile of straw at the back. "Go to the barn and hide in the straw." I commanded myself again and ran. I needed to get my bearings and compose myself. And I needed to get used to being in control from the inside of a dog. I wasn't a human in the physical sense anymore, but I was obviously having the thoughts of a human. So, what I needed to do was to get full control of my thoughts in order to act as a dog. No training can prepare you for such a sensation, but I had to get used to this, and quickly!

"Oh my! This is going to be difficult," I said to myself. I looked around the barn from my position in the straw and reassured myself that I was alone. Away from prying eyes, I decided it would be best to start practicing some actions and the behaviour of a dog. This was easier said than done as they were two completely different things.

Dog behaviour, as instructed by Duchess, could only be put into practice with full body control, so this was my first priority. I concentrated very hard and encouraged myself to perform some basics like wagging my tail, pricking my ears up, walking on four legs and so on. I carried on doing this until I felt comfortable and could master these simple actions. And now time to practice the behaviour of greeting another dog. Approaching a pile of hay for instance, I pretended it was a dog. I repeated it over and over again until I was content, but one last try I thought. I tackled the pile of

239

hay in an arc, approached the rear, and was in the act of sniffing deeply when I suddenly heard a bark and a voice.

"And what are you doing, Rosie?"

A black and white border collie, or at least I thought that's what it was, was looking at me with certain suspicion. "It can talk. And I can understand it," I said to myself in amazement.

"Errm," I stammered back. "Just sniffing something," I said very unconfidently. "Finished now. Time to sleep again, very tired." It was the only thing I could spontaneously think of.

Thankfully the dog accepted my explanation, and then went straight for my rear end. I now had full control over the dog and its complete sense of smell — much more of course than humans. I did the same and we sniffed each other intensively. Too intensively for my liking. No, disgusting actually.

"You're different today, Rosie. Is something wrong?"

"So, my name is Rosie," I said to myself.

"Oh, so tired today and not feeling my normal self. I don't think I've had enough sleep," I replied extremely quickly. "Must go now. Bye." I ran off through the open barn door, leaving a confused looking border collie behind me.

"Not enough sleep," the border collie muttered to himself. "Damn lazy dog. All she does is sleep and now she's complaining of not having enough. Typical bulldogs!"

***

"Who are you hiding from?" purred a voice quietly.

I quickly looked around to see where the voice came from but couldn't see anyone.

"Looking for me?" the voice said again. "Up here!"

A brown and white cat was sitting high up on the barn's gutter.

"Is that you, Vanessa?"

"Fortunately for you, yes, it is. You don't look like you are doing a good job at being in disguise. Who are you running away from?"

"I've just had an encounter with another dog who became suspicious after smelling me. I thought I was doing a good job until then. How did you know it was me?"

"It really wasn't difficult to work out who you were, owing to your un-dog like behaviour. But to make you feel better I've also had my problems and also some fun. I ran into a horse and we spoke for a few minutes about the lovely weather."

"You can talk to other animals too? Stupid question because you are talking to me!"

"It seems we can all communicate with each other. Quite cool really. I then saw a dog and decided to meow a greeting, unfortunately I barked instead, and the dog ran off as quickly as it could in complete alarm. Not sure how that happened. I certainly need some more time to practice how to be a cat."

"Yes, that's what I have been doing since I've arrived. Practicing how to be a dog, I mean. I am quite satisfied with my progress despite my un-dog like behaviour. I will be happy when my actions are second nature, just like riding a bicycle you know. Then I won't have to concentrate so much on wagging my tail."

"Connor, have you seen any sign of Basil and Ludwig yet?"

"Not yet. But you shouldn't call me Connor. That would really give me away," I said.

"What is your dog name then, if I can't call you Connor?"

"The border collie called me Rosie, so I suppose that must be my name," I replied. "And your name?"

"I haven't got a clue. Oh, this is going to be fun. How the heck are we going to address each other?"

"Hang on. I can see you have a collar so come down here and I will have a look."

"But you're a dog. You can't read." Vanessa gracefully jumped down from the gutter onto a trailer and then down to the ground next to me, like she'd been a cat all her life.

"I rather hope I can still read. Now let's have a look."

She came next to me and I looked down but couldn't read it.

"Damn," I said.

"What is it?"

"I've got paws." I tried to move the collar into position. "This will be difficult."

"Let me do that for you," another voice said.

We both turned around and saw a man walking towards us in very unnatural movements, as though he was drunk and not in complete control of his body. He stopped next to the trailer.

"Ludwig. Is that you?" I asked.

"Yes! It's me, Ludwig. Hey, this is cool being a human. I can do whatever I want. Hands are just so practical, and I can see you are having problems. May I be of assistance?" Ludwig was proudly looking down at us. "Being so tall I can see much more, but having only two legs to balance on is a challenge."

"Well, I have paws now but cannot use them to turn over the collar. Even though I have four of them."

"Well I can," said Ludwig and jumped up in the air. Damn. I wanted to bend down but did something completely different. "OK concentrate," the man squinted his face in concentration and slowly bent down.

"Oh, this is very funny indeed," he said chuckling.

"Yeah, but can you read? I bet you still can't read, can you Ludwig?" said Vanessa teasingly. "Come on Ludwig, what is my name?"

Ludwig looked sternly at the collar, then his face turned into a smile. He opened his lips but then closed them again. Finally, he gave up. "Nope. Can't read those strange squiggles," he said.

"OK, but can you please turn the collar, so I can read it. And they are letters, not squiggles."

"Your name is Fussy. Perfect, a very fitting name for you. Fussy Vanessa! I am Rosie by the way and now a girl," I said in a silly voice as I broke into a giggle.

"And my name is Bill. Bill Farrow. Sophisticated, don't you think? And quite fitting." Ludwig stood upright and proud, but he seemed a little lost in his pants and shirt hanging over his belly.

"Well, now all we have to do is find Basil." Fussy jumped back up on a stack of straw. "It shouldn't be too difficult to find a horse on an equestrian centre, should it!" she said ironically.

"Not quite as easy as you may think," a voice said from a corner of the barn.

"Basil, is that you?" We all turned around but there was no horse.

"Where are you Basil?" we all blurted out at the same time.

"Over here."

"Where is over here? I can't see you." There was still no horse. Only a small hedgehog came crawling out from below one of the trailers which were parked in a tidy row next to the barn.

"Basil?"

"I missed," said Basil miserably.

"You missed! How the heck could you miss a horse? They're huge," asked Fussy with amazement.

"Well I was perfectly on course to land on a horse but suddenly a gust of wind blew me away. I lost control and landed on this unsuspecting hedgehog resting at the bottom of a bush — and now I'm a hedgehog. And please don't ask me my name. I don't believe hedgehogs need names. So, let's just stick to Basil, all right," he said.

"No, let's call you Prickly. Just like your mood and appearance Basil," said Fussy with a laugh.

"Very funny, Vanessa."

"Fussy."

"What's fussy?" asked Prickly.

"Me," the cat said.

"Well, we all know that. What's new?"

"No, silly. My name is Fussy."

"That makes sense I suppose. So, what's the plan?" asked Prickly.

"I think we should explore this place and try to get used to being someone else," said Fussy. "It is the reason we are here, isn't it? To prepare for our mission. Don't you agree, Rosie?"

"Yes, I do. But let's stick together. And Ludwig, I mean Bill, you can help. It will probably look more realistic if we stay close to you. And in case there is a problem then you can fix it. Right?"

"And me?" said Prickly, desperately. "I can't keep up with you, can I? And what should I even practice? Not moving and sleeping? I was trained as a horse. Not to the nocturnal life of a hedgehog!"

"I have an idea," said Bill. He stooped down, gingerly picked up the hedgehog and put him in his pocket. "There we go, Prickly. A free ride for you. Just stay still and sleep as much as you like."

"Very kind of you. At least it is dark in here, so I can stay awake! Anyhow, the last time you gave me a free ride I was in your mouth ready to be eaten," a muffled voice shouted from the pocket.

"Don't worry. Hedgehogs are far too prickly to be eaten!" said Bill with a sense of humour.

We spent most of the day walking around the centre practicing our new roles. Fussy kept her distance but stayed in range. She had proven her agility skills before and was in her element as a cat, jumping up on objects, climbing and balancing in risky positions. I stayed by Bill's side, just like a loyal dog would do, and used the time to sniff my way around the place. And Bill. He had his hands in absolutely everything. For him, it was his first experience of using hands and there was no looking back, whereas I felt rather frustrated because I had to rely on Bill for nearly everything.

By the end of the afternoon we had all successfully gained sufficient control of our bodies to at least visually pass off as our new role. Even Bill had started to walk around quite naturally and didn't look like someone walking on the moon with gravity boots. Only Prickly's time was certainly different than he had planned. He just sat in the darkness of Bill's pocket and listened to everything around him.

As the evening came closer we agreed it was time to split up and take on our roles independently of each other. Bill put Prickly under a trailer and covered him with a pile of leaves, presumably to sleep as he had been wide awake the whole time in his pocket. However, I didn't think there wouldn't be much time for him to relax as the nocturnal life of a hedgehog usually began in the approaching darkness.

"And me? What about me?"

Bill threw his hands in the air. "Fussy! Just do what cats do."

"Well, I also need something to eat and somewhere comfortable to sleep."

"Go into the fields and catch a mouse then. That's what cats do."

"A mouse? I'm not eating a mouse."

"Then you have to go hungry. Farm cats don't live a comfortable inside-life. They must fend for themselves. I used to live on a farm and know these things. There is no cat food I'm afraid."

"You can practice licking your fur and then vomiting it out," a sleepy voice said from the pile of leaves. "I've heard that is what cats do. Serves you right for eating poor, innocent ducks!"

"Really. I'm not doing any of those things. What an awful thought. I think I will just hide somewhere and go to sleep. What a torture that is being a cat. I will not eat mice or my own fur, and I'm not fighting. No. No. No." Fussy made a great show of her disappointment as she walked off in a big strop.

"Suit yourself then and remember to meet back here in the morning," said Bill as she left. He turned around and started walking towards the house. "Rosie. Heal," he shouted and off I bound to his side.

"Fine," Bill added as I wagged my tail in delight.

I noticed he was becoming noticeably agitated as we got closer to the house. "You look worried."

"I am worried. I am supposed to interact with other people now. You can just roll up in a basket and go to sleep and hopefully nobody will notice you. I cannot go unnoticed and to be perfectly honest am not sure what I have to do. Do I have to kiss my wife?"

"Maybe the best thing is that we both go into the house. I find my basket and you can come and ask me if you are uncertain. Just try and remember what you were taught."

I tried to comfort him as best as I could, but Bill had spent the day outside and hadn't even approached the farmhouse or any human being for that matter. Instead he had only focussed on how to use his hands and walk upright without tumbling. He hadn't even met his wife and had no idea what she even looked like. And certainly not her name. The crunch time for him was now fast approaching.

"Here goes." Bill anxiously opened the door.

I followed him into the farmhouse and immediately found a dog basket in the entrance, along with a water bowl and an empty food bowl. I sniffed the basket, got in and curled up on the soft blanket. For the moment I felt very contended with being a dog. "What are you going to do now, Bill?" I certainly had the easier role to play.

"I think I will go inside and wait for my dinner," he said. "And then I will drink some beers in front of a nice roaring fire. That's what my master usually does in the evenings. It looks very relaxing."

"I am starving too. Can you find me something to eat?" When it came to the essentials, Bill's newly found skills had their limit. He didn't know where to find my food, so I probably had to go hungry.

"Give me time to scout around. I have absolutely no idea what is in this place or where to find your food. Look, there's a water bowl next to your basket. You can at least get a drink and I'll try and come back soon."

"What if I need to go out to the loo?"

"Hold on. We've just been out all day. You had your chance for a poo. I can't think for you now, can I?"

"Then I might just bark in the night, so you can let me out."

"If you purposefully annoy me, I will tie you up in the barn right now and you can sleep with the other animals. Think about that. I'm sure the dog basket in the house is much more comfortable."

"Why don't you just let me sleep in front of the fire? I promise to be quiet."

"No," said Bill. "You belong in your basket. Look, I'm the human now so you have to do what I say. Not the other way around, right" he said trying to grin through his anxiousness.

"Whatever. But I'm really famished now, Bill. Go and find something for me, will you?"

"I would look rather silly if I asked my wife where the dog food is. As I've already said, give me some time to find my way around."

"I can smell food. Hmmmm, a delicious roast. Why can I not have that?"

"No, Connor, I mean Rosie. Dogs should not be given food like that. Farmer Rye always fed me from a can after he had finished his meal. For realism you will have to wait!" Bill turned around. "And please stop getting on my nerves. I need to get in control of my life now." He closed the door behind him. As I had nothing better to say I rolled up in my basket and dozed the time away. There was nothing else for me to do.

"Bill. Bill. Is that you? Where have you been all day?" I was startled by a loud woman's screech from somewhere in the house. "I haven't seen you since lunchtime. You do know how much work we have at the moment. And we have plans this evening. Where have you been all day?"

There was just silence in the house. No reply from Bill.

"Bill. Where are you? Answer me now," she screamed again at the top of her voice.

"Err, just doing things, darling. Nothing special."

"Things? Nothing special? It's our wedding anniversary today, remember? And the Forsythe-Twykes are coming for dinner soon. I hope you are ready. They'll be here in a few minutes."

I just sat there in my comfortable dog basket thinking that Bill's situation really couldn't be any worse, but I couldn't think of anything I could do right now to help him. With a rumbling stomach, I settled down again in my basket and tried to sleep but I was rudely woken up again by two things.

First, the doorbell rang, and then the woman started yelling again at the top of her voice. "Bill, why isn't your stupid dog barking?" Feet were trampling down the stairs and then the door to the hallway burst open to reveal a very angry looking woman. I started barking to announce the arrivals.

"That's a little late, isn't it," she said glaring at me on her way to open the door. "Mr and Mrs Forsythe-Twyke. So delighted to see you," she said in her high-pitched voice.

Bill came running into the hallway still wearing his grubby work clothes. The Forsythe-Twykes and Mrs Farrow just stared at him. Bill didn't miss an opportunity to do everything wrong he possibly could.

"Nice to meet you," Bill said to them. He really had forgotten most of what he had been taught.

"But you already know them, Bill," his wife squawked back.

Mrs Forsythe-Twyke extended her hand to shake Bill's but he didn't respond. Instead, he went around her in an arc and started looking at her behind. Oh dear. It was at this moment that I decided to intervene to save him. I jumped out of my basket and started barking as loudly as I could. I had to try at any rate to get the attention away from Bill and I obviously had the desired effect, at least for a short moment.

"Bill, get your dog under control!" cried out Mrs Farrow and quickly ushered her guests through the hallway and into the house. "Go and get changed into something suitable immediately and come back in a different frame of mind. What has gotten into you today?" She threw an angry look to Bill.

Bill shrugged his shoulders and obediently plodded upstairs.

***

Later in the evening, a visibly distressed Mrs Farrow escorted her guests to the door to bid them farewell. "I'm just so sorry about this evening. I have no idea what got into Bill."

Bill was just standing there in a knee-length flowery dress looking extremely flustered.

"Don't worry, dear. See you tomorrow then!" said Mrs Forsythe-Twyke, compassionately.

Mrs Farrow slammed the door, barged past Bill and ran up the stairs.

"Didn't go well then, Bill?" I said.

"You could say that. This whole evening was a mess. Everything just went downhill after I got changed as instructed. My wife, actually everybody, just looked at me the whole evening. What's wrong with a dress? It's much more comfortable than trousers but my wife had steam coming out her ears."

"Go on, Bill. I think there's more coming."

Bill looked down at the floor and started shuffling his feet. "I know we spoke about it in training, but I couldn't practice live. As a dog I don't have hands. And using these strange metals tools to eat with is damn overrated if you ask me."

"Cutlery, that's what we call it. So what did you do?" I asked but at that point somehow already knew what was coming. Ludwig was obviously not in control of his bodily functions and still had his dinner smeared over his face.

"I was so hungry. And really nervous. So I just stuck my head in my plate and ate just like I normally do. Mr Rye never complained, and it is much quicker. Really!"

"You did what?"

"I have never done this before. I just forgot!"

"What did your wife say?"

"She burst out crying and called me a disgusting animal."

"Doesn't sound good. Anyhow, Bill, I'm absolutely famished, and your dinner smelt so fantastic. A real torture for me. Can you get me something to eat now please?"

"Don't worry, I did something right and found you some food."

"Great. What have you got me?"

"No idea, Rosie. You know I can't read so you will have to do that for me."

He lowered a can and turned the label in my direction.

PAUNCH

"Paunch? I'm not eating paunch. How disgusting."

"Well bad news for you because that was the only can I could find and how should I know what is written on it. I just saw the picture of a dog on the can. I love it personally. For me it tastes fantastic. I'm still a dog at heart! But I must say my wife's roast chicken tasted better. Sorry."

"Shut up Bill. Just open the can and put it in the bowl. I will have to pretend it's something else."

Bill opened the can, took a spoon out of his pocket and put the mixture in my dog bowl. It smelled absolutely vile and I was really disgusted. But did I have a choice? So, I closed my eyes, concentrated not to smell it and just lapped it up as quickly as I could to get it over and done with. Yuk!

"Look, I think I should leave you to be Rosie. Time for bed now," said Bill.

"Sounds like a good idea. But don't do anything stupid in bed tonight," I said. "Try not to dig yourself deeper than you already are, will you!"

"I think I should just keep quiet and try not to be noticed. Maybe have that beer in front of the fire now." he said, mumbling to himself not expecting an answer. "Good night, Rosie."

"Good night, Bill." I just felt so sorry for the real Bill when he came back. He will be in so much trouble and would have absolutely no idea what he had done!

Chapter Fourteen
Learning

I stirred, and my eyes flickered as the first rays of light shone through the window in the door. I stretched out my legs and then I suddenly remembered I had four of them. "Yes, Connor, remember you are a dog now," I thought to myself. I tried to roll over to a more comfortable position in my basket when I realised I couldn't move. Something was in the way. Oh no! Bill was lying next to me, his head and legs hanging over the edges. The night couldn't have gone for him as planned.

"Wake up, Bill. Wake up! What are you doing here?" He was fast asleep. I nudged him gently. Still no reaction so I decided to try a dog-like waking up and licked through his face. He reacted immediately.

"Where am I? What's wrong?" he murmured groggily.

"You're sleeping in the damn dog basket," shouted his wife as she burst through the door to be confronted with yet another strange sight of her husband. "That's what's wrong?"

"Damn. How did this happen?"

"The beer maybe?" I whispered in his ear. "I bet you can't remember letting me out either!"

Ludwig had never drunk a beer larger than a thimble size and possibly had too much. He was so happy to have the freedom of being able to do everything for himself, but being a human suddenly was a lot for him to cope with in such a short time. He had let me out dutifully at some stage in the night and must have carried on drinking beer in front of the fireplace all by himself. And then, instead of going to bed with his wife, he went to sleep in a place he knew well and snuck into the dog basket.

"Must have been sleep walking my dear," he said looking up apologetically from the dog basket.

"Sleep walking? Bill, you are acting very strangely. It wouldn't surprise me if you had slept here all night," his wife said angrily. "Did you drink too much after your performance at dinner?"

***

Bill and Rosie were not the only ones to wake up next to each other. Fussy, wasn't happy with her current lot in life but decided to make the best of it sleeping in the leaves next to Prickly. At least the place was soft, dry and well-hidden from other cats. She didn't go out to catch any mice, didn't fight and didn't clean her fur either. Prickly was just bored as there was not much he could do. As a duck he was used to being very active and covering large distances either in the water or in the air. As a hedgehog his limitations were quite unwelcome. This life was far too so slow for him.

***

We all met at the trailer next to the barn early in the morning. It was another lovely late autumn day with only a few solitary white clouds decorating the otherwise clear blue sky. Thankfully Bill had changed into trousers after his wife chased him upstairs and then kicked him out of the house.

"So, how was your night, Connor, erm I mean, Rosie?" asked Prickly.

"Oh, not too bad. I couldn't control myself and really needed a pee. As I haven't got any hands and couldn't let myself out, I had no choice but to raise the alarm by barking," I said with a grin.

"You think you're clever, don't you?" Bill was looking a little perplexed after the latest events.

"Maybe. But later this evening we will be back, and you will be a dog again and then I will have the hands and you will have the paws," I said with a chuckle. "Bill. And I believe I heard your wife say that you are in the dog house and I think she meant it quite literally. You should keep a low profile today as you have raised enough suspicion already if I were you."

"What's that supposed to mean?" Fussy pricked her ears.

"Well, Bill wore a dress for dinner after greeting his guests' doggy-style. Then he ate dinner without using a knife and a fork. Then he drank too much and finally he slept in the dog basket with me. His wife is really not too impressed with her husband at the moment, you can imagine," I said with a grin.

"You did all of that in one evening, Bill. Respect!" chuckled Fussy.

"How was your night?" digressed Bill. "You look awful. Your fur is covered in leaves and you look, well, unkempt. And you probably haven't eaten either. Not very becoming of a Forsythe-Twyke."

"You are right on all counts. Just wait until we are back. You won't be amused when I show you the real me."

"And I'm bored and hungry. I trained to eat grass, just like a horse, not to live under leaves and do nothing. When am I going to eat? I've really got the short straw here, haven't I," lamented Prickly.

"Don't moan. How could you have not hit a horse? Tough luck, Prickly," said Fussy, moodily.

"Hedgehogs eat creepy crawlies," said Rosie. "I remember reading about it in a book."

"What are creepy crawlies?" asked Prickly with suspicion.

"Oh, caterpillars, worms, beetles. Things like that," explained Fussy.

"Bill. Get a shovel and dig in some earth. We have to find something for Prickly to eat," I asked. "It should be easy to find him some beetles or worms so we can continue what we came for."

"How long do we have to put up with this charade?" asked Fussy.

"Only for today. We have to return this evening," I said. "We really need to get going now and learn how to control our thoughts and behaviour, so we get enough practice for our mission."

"You mean practice sitting in a pocket or under a bush?" asked Prickly, with frustration.

"The main reason we are here is for us to learn how to authentically pass as another creature. Please concentrate on that Prickly. I am not quite sure how you can contribute to our mission right at this moment, but I am sure that we will find something important for you to do."

"I could get to enjoy this if only I could avoid my wife," said Bill, trying to look at the bright side.

"What's her name?" asked Fussy, already anticipating the answer.

"No idea, haven't asked her yet!" Bill didn't realise what he had just said. "Do we really have to go back?" he asked. "I'm sure I can master this, and we are already here. I just need more time to adjust."

"The Morphing process is only temporary," I said. "You know the moles have power over us at the moment. Trust me and I will get us out of this mess," I said. "But for now, yes, we have to go back tomorrow as instructed by Mr Tinker, whether we like it or not."

"Are you sure you have a plan, Rosie?" asked Bill.

"Yes, I do. If you don't want to end up on a fork you must trust me. My plan is not one hundred percent complete, but some blocks are already in place. Now, I need more information and think carefully of how to put my plan into action. And I am very sure we are being monitored, maybe even by both sides, so we must act naturally and do what we have been told so we don't arouse any suspicion. I want you to go out and practice in your new roles. This is an equestrian centre with rich and well-connected people. Let's find out who is here and what they are talking about. We might stumble on some useful information. We meet back here in two hours. Be inconspicuous. Be secret."

"And me? What should I do?" asked Prickly, somehow disheartened.

"You can sit in Bill's pocket again," I said. "No, even better. Bill, why don't you just put Prickly into something unsuspicious and place him near the people in the restaurant, so he can listen to their conversations without being seen. Prickly will be our secret bug!"

Fussy spent the next two hours being as much like a cat as she could. She balanced across the top of fences, explored the stables, hid under any object she could and prowled around the equestrian centre office. As cats are generally cuddly creatures and well accepted by humans, she had easy access everywhere and was stroked a lot as she purred around people's legs and feet in the restaurant.

I spent the first hour thoroughly exploring the equestrian centre, which I — believe it or not — had actually never visited in my life. I practised dog like activities and looked out for things which might be useful. When there was nothing else for me to do, I decided to lie on the floor at the bar and listen to what the Upper Molehampton's high society had to say.

Bill found a bag for Prickly and placed him under a table in the middle of the restaurant. Then he decided to listen to the onlookers in the riding hall, avoiding direct contact with people, especially with his wife. He still felt uneasy as a human and tried not to arouse more suspicion than he already had.

"Does this belong to anyone?" cried out Mrs Forsythe-Twyke, holding a red leather handbag above her head. Prickly had been sitting in the darkness for a while, blind to the world around him and just listening to the conversations. Now he was thrown around as the bag was swung from left to right.

"Oh my! That's my handbag. What's it doing over there?"

"I have no idea, Mrs Farrow. I just saw it under the table and wondered who it belonged to. At least the bag has found its owner".

"Thank you so much, Mrs Forsythe-Twyke. That's very kind of you. I bet my husband has been up to no good again. I still have no explanation for his behaviour and I'm so sorry for yesterday evening."

"He's probably had too much contact with that rabble from Lower Molehampton," said Mrs Forsythe-Twyke, looking around and making sure that everyone could hear her.

***

The trailer was secluded, parked in high grass between the barn and another building. It probably hadn't been moved in years and I doubted if the wheels still moved. Fussy was sitting in an old flower pot on the roof, letting the sun shine on her fur, purring away in delight. I sat and looked towards some horses as Bill sauntered very slowly towards us, seemingly without a care in the world.

"So, anything interesting to report?" I asked.

"Why, yes," said Fussy, stretching herself out of the flower pot.

"Stop. I have some bad news. I've lost Prickly!"

"Bill? You've lost Prickly?" I said with panic.

"I put him in a bag and left him in the restaurant, just like you said. But now the bag is gone."

"What does the bag look like?"

"Red and made of leather. Oh yes, it had some dangly things on it too, but I am not sure what purpose they have? I found it in the house and took it!"

"Damn," was all I could think of saying.

"It's one of your wife's handbags, Bill." Fussy was visibly bored with the conversation.

"A what?" Bill didn't have a clue and had never heard of a handbag before.

"A handbag, Bill. Women use them to carry there essentials around," explained Fussy. "And I know where it is."

"You know where it is?" I asked.

"Yes. Bill's wife took it into the office cursing Bill under her breath."

"Great," said Bill. "I will go and get it!"

"I am afraid it's not that easy. She locked it in a filing cabinet and put the key in her jacket. But she was still there working on her computer when I left a few minutes ago."

"Damn," I said again. "How on earth are we going to get the key back?"

"Bill, you caused this mess so it's your job to get us out. Any ideas?" said Fussy in a straight manner.

"Not yet. Let me think," said Bill, slowly.

"We haven't got time to think," I said. "We need to get the key back and quick."

"The good news is that I saw the jacket, but the bad news is that she's wearing it."

Mrs Farrow was still sitting at her desk doing some work on her computer. Fussy had managed to climb up a wooden pallet leaning against the wall just under a window and had peered into the room.

"How are you going to get the key out of it?"

"I have an idea," I said. "Listen to me."

***

On the third ring the woman picked up the receiver of an antiquated cord telephone and put it against her ear. "Farrow's Equestrian Centre. How may I help you?"

"Oh, Bill. It's you. And what do you want?"

Her facial expression changed to one of disappointment on hearing her husband's voice, but before she could answer, a cat screeched at the window and Mrs Farrow swivelled around in her chair one hundred and eighty degrees in the direction of the noise, the telephone cord wrapping around her body. She heard something burst through the door and spun around again twining herself even more in the cord. A wet and dirty dog sprang across the desk and put its dirty paws all over the sleeves of her jacket and was out of the office before she even realised what had happened.

"Bill. Are you still there?" she said shakily and pressed the receiver against her ear.

"Oh dear. Look at the state of your jacket. Let's get it off." said Bill as he entered the office. The whole incident only lasted seconds, but Mrs Farrow was so surprised that she didn't even question how he had arrived so fast. So, he spun the chair around to free his wife from the cord and helped her out of the jacket quickly before she had a chance to change her mind.

"That damn dog of yours," she shouted. "Look what it's done to my jacket."

257

"But why would, Rosie do such a strange thing darling? I just saw her run off just before I came in."

"I'll get your dog and dish out some discipline!" Mrs Farrow still had not regained her composure. She shoved Bill out of the way and stomped out of the office.

As soon as his wife had left the office Bill rummaged through the pockets, found the key and opened the cupboard. Just like Fussy had said, the handbag was sitting on the middle shelf with a scared looking Prickly sitting in it. Our little diversion had worked perfectly.

"I bet you're glad to see me for once," said Bill. "Let's get you out of here."

***

Bill was standing next to the trailer with a grin on his face as he waited for the others. He had thrown Prickly out of the window to make sure his wife did not discover him carrying her handbag when he left the office. He obviously enjoyed the last few minutes of action. Fussy came around the corner dragging the red leather bag with her mouth. Shouts and curses came out of the bag when she stopped right in front of Bill's feet. Then Rosie came bounding around the corner. She was panting heavily and sprayed the others in water as she shook herself off.

"Your wife is really mad, Bill. She followed me across the fields but couldn't keep up with me very long in her high heels. That must have looked rather funny. Right, Bill, don't just stand around. Get Prickly out. You've got the hands so use them."

"What the hell did you do with me?" shouted Prickly in Bills direction. "I couldn't trust you as a dog and I certainly can't trust you as a human, can I?"

"Sorry, Prickly. I only did what I was told. How could I know that someone would take this bag away from the hiding place?"

"And where exactly was your hiding place, Bill?" Fussy was curious.

"Under a table in the restaurant."

"Aaah. I see your tactics. Use the obvious place so nobody would think of it as a secret."

"OK, everyone. Let's stop it now. We've wasted some time with Prickly's disappearance but we should now see if anyone has come up with anything valuable from today. Fussy, what about you? Did you see or hear anything unusual?" I tried to get everyone back on our focus.

"I didn't really hear anything. But I saw Mrs Farrow enter her office with another woman. The woman gave Mrs Farrow an envelope, who then put it in the cabinet along with the handbag. It was strange because she didn't even look what was in it. Apart from that I have nothing else to report on. The other woman then left in a hurry."

"Well, you never know if that could be interesting." I said. "And what about Bill?"

"I also didn't hear anything unusual. But I saw something in the cabinet. There was a hole at the bottom of the cabinet. The one I got the handbag out of I mean. With a pipe coming out of the wall. Maybe not so special but it looked a little out of place and worth mentioning. What do you think?"

"Hmm. It certainly sounds a little strange." I said wondering if there was a connection to the tube systems of the government agency by the way Bill had described it. "And now you, Prickly."

"Well. I actually heard a lot but I can't say who said what as I was stuck in that bag."

"It doesn't matter. Go on, Prickly. What did you hear?"

"There were too many voices at the restaurant and I couldn't really hear anything. But it got juicy when someone found the handbag. I believe her name was Mrs Forsythe-Twyke."

"Stop. What name did you just say?" said Fussy.

"Forsythe-Twyke."

"That's my mother," said Fussy. "What happened then?"

"Well, I obviously couldn't see anything, but I heard the two women talking — Mrs Forsythe-Twyke and the other voice was Bill's wife. The bag was swinging back and forth, so the voices were a bit confusing at first. But then they walked into the office and put the bag down."

"And what did they talk about?" I asked.

"Mrs Forsythe-Twyke asked Mrs Farrow to increase the number of animals available to her meat processing plant. She said the quota system did not meet the demand and had to be increased. She was quite annoyed and made it very clear that they needed a lower allocation of turkeys this year and more ducks — apparently because ducks are more popular at Christmas these days. She also said that a message had to be sent to the minister immediately and explained that she demanded influence in return for her cooperation. Oh yes, she asked if she received the envelope.

"But what's mama got to do with all of this?" Fussy was shocked.

"Absolutely no idea," I replied.

Prickly looked up towards Fussy. "The next bit is about you. But it's not so nice, Fussy."

"What did she say?"

"Mrs Farrow asked if the police had any information on your disappearance. But your mother called the police incompetent, and, in any case, believes that you probably ran off with one of your strange friends. She said you were more interested in socialising than taking over the family business."

Fussy was visibly furious and somehow sad at the same time. "So that's what she thinks of me. I'll show her what a family business means if I have the chance that is. All she cares about is her dratted meat production line. For her meat is just a product which comes in a plastic bag. And she constantly drops the prices to make eating meat more attractive. But at the same time, she complains about not having enough animals for slaughter. Strangely enough, she never mentions where she gets them from."

"I'm sure your mother didn't mean it like that, Fussy. She must be so anxious now. You know that some people say strange things when they are upset," said Bill in an attempt to comfort her. "Incidentally, so far you sounded like meat is just a product to you too. But now you sound like you despise your mother for her business. Would you take over the company at some stage?"

"No. How could I. In principal I have nothing against eating meat, but I have something against it as the mass production industry it has become. I only once visited her Factory and saw the conveyor belts and slaughter areas. I think it is so inhumane what she is doing. Or better put, inanimal."

"Sorry, Fussy. It must be difficult for you right now, but we must carry on. Time is running out before we have to go back. Let's talk about it later." I looked down at Prickly. "Anything else?"

"Not sure, but she told Mrs Farrow that their plan was nearing completion, however, there were some unfortunate complications. She said that Cromwell was in the right place with Jemima Kingston."

I looked surprised. "Did you just say Jemima Kingston?"

"Yes. Why?"

"She's my boss! The plot thickens. What complications? Did she mention anything specific?"

"Yes. She mentioned your house. And that it was being watched so nobody could get in without giving away what side they are on. Then the conversation finished, and I ended up in the cupboard."

"Bill. Bill. Where are you?"

Before I could say anything else a loud shrieking voice echoed in our direction. I wasn't quite sure at that moment what to make of it, but I thought that everyone had done an amazing job and I was also certain, that these bits of information were connected to something I did not quite understand yet.

"Oh dear. It's my wife. What does she want now?"

"Probably her jacket and maybe even the key," Fussy figured. "Where's the key anyway, Bill?"

"Oh, it's here. In my pocket."

"You still have the key to the cabinet?" I asked.

"Yep. Sorry but I forgot to put it back in the jacket. I've done something wrong again, haven't I?"

"On the contrary, at last you have done something correct," I said jokingly, but the funny thing was that Bill wasn't even aware he had.

"Why?" asked Bill, looking puzzled.

"Because I now have a plan. But I need you to hide from your wife because I have an important job for you, Bill. Go to the house and find three jam jars, some plasters, a pen, some flour, a spoon and some water."

"Why on..." started Bill.

"Bill. Just do it," said Fussy. "In fact, I'll come with you to make sure you get the job done correctly."

***

Bill Farrow got on the ferry across the river Angler from Upper Molehampton to Lower Molehampton carrying a red leather handbag and a small plastic bag. He was accompanied by a cat and a dog.

"Good evening, Mr Farrow. Where are you off to if I may ask?" asked Mr Cross suspiciously, observing this strange sight.

"Good evening, Mr... erm. Oh, just to get some things from Mr Tinker and then back later."

"Is everything OK, Mr Farrow?" asked Mr Cross, wondering why Bill did not appear to be acting as he normally did. Not only that but he was also carrying a woman's handbag and had a cat following him. He also seemed to have forgotten his name? They had known each other for years! Why would Mr Farrow not remember his name?

"Yes, everything's OK. Thank you," said Bill, as he turned around trying to avoid any further contact.

When the ramp lowered with a clank and rattling of its chain after a short crossing, Mr Cross nodded his head towards Bill for them to leave the ferry.

"Strange," Mr Cross spoke aloud to himself as he watched Bill walk off slowly in the distance. "He's acting so strangely today. I hope there is nothing wrong with him. Maybe he has been drinking?"

***

"Open this door please, Bill," I indicated by standing in front of it. Bill closed the door behind us and turned on the light. He placed his wife's handbag and the plastic bag in the middle of the room.

As soon as we got off the ferry in Lower Molehampton we had walked straight to the football pitch and entered the building with the changing rooms. Due to the normally low crime rate in the village nobody ever thought about locking the door which now worked to our advantage.

"Right, everyone. Listen carefully," I said.

"Where are we?" complained Prickly from inside the handbag. "Can someone let me out please."

"Ouch," Bill winced as he griped inside the bag and put Prickly on a bench. "Damn prickly animals!"

"We are in the changing room of FC Lower Molehampton."

"Why are we here?" Bill wanted to know.

"Because this is where the main part of our mission will play out and we need to talk in complete secrecy before we go back. Now listen carefully. I originally thought there were only two parties involved in our mission; the moles and professor Wingnut's kidnappers, who could also be moles. However, with the information overheard by Prickly, it appears there is a third party. Fussy's mother and Bill's wife. How do they all fit in? I am not sure exactly, but it seems clear that they all want to get hold of the Professor and that the Professor is our key of getting out of this mess."

"Why is the Professor so important to them?"

"I will come to that in a minute, Bill. You will probably think I am mad but we will have to give them the professor, so we can maybe return as ourselves again. Don't worry, it's part of my plan."

"Then why don't you at last go ahead and tell us your plan?" asked Fussy, impatiently.

"Yes I will. But not all of it, just some parts. I know you wouldn't knowingly say anything and please understand that I do trust you all. However, if any of you are taken by whatever side and your memories interrogated, then you could reveal my plan and bring it to failure. All you need to know for the moment is that I intend to hand over the Professor as agreed with Colonel Bacon and Colonel Pickle. We will give them what they want and they will give us what we want."

"It all sounds very cloak and dagger to me."

"It is, Fussy. But now let me explain what you need to know, OK?" I then explained to my friends in great detail about my easy plan involving Mr Lawnsworthy and a key for his house. This was exactly the story I intended to present to Colonel Bacon and Colonel Pickle. We all needed to tell the same story.

"I will say one more thing — expect to improvise! And that is all you need to know and will know."

"It sounds quite simple. Too simple if you ask me," said Bill.

"Then you shouldn't muck it up this time, should you?" said Prickly, rather sarcastically.

"Bill? Please get the jars and other things you collected from your house." There was one more job to do before our mission was over and we had to go back to Mr Tinker's store.

"Here they are."

Bill took everything out of the plastic bag and listened carefully to my instructions. Under Fussy's and my direction he mixed the flour and some water from a sink in the changing room into a runny white paste and filled it into the three jars, then put a plaster on each of them. After a bit of practice his hands just managed to write 'Professor Wingnut' in fairly legible handwriting on all three plasters. It wasn't easy for Bill but he managed it with great concentration. Then we hid the jars in different places in the home team's changing room.

"OK, finished," I said. "Let's go to see Mr Tinker and go back below."

We walked the short distance to Mr Tinker's store and were allowed in after knocking on the rear door. We all winked at each other and smiled. I think we had all had enough action in the last two days.

"Good to see you back and perfectly on time." said Mr Tinker who was cheerfully smiling at us.

"How did it go for your first time?"

"Oh, quite good considering all things," said Bill, looking at the ground.

"But I see there are only three of you. Where is the fourth?" said Mr Tinker with alarm in his voice. "You haven't lost him, have you?"

"No, don't worry. Everything is OK, Mr Tinker. He's in here," said Bill holding up the handbag.

"That's strange. I was told to expect a horse!"

"Long story!"

"OK. In with you now and let's start the process of you going back. Please follow me to the reversal room. It's in the shed at the back. You just need to sit there until the effects of the Morphing wears off and then we will have you returned down below in a jiffy."

"What happens to the real Bill and the others?" Bill was interested to know.

"They will naturally be confused after you left their bodies and won't remember a thing. I will tell Bill that he came here to have his wife's handbag repaired, became dizzy and decided to have a short nap. It won't be easy, but I think I'll be able to convince him to carry the hedgehog back. The dog will follow naturally, and cats always find their way home. Don't you worry about them!"

Mr Tinker pushed the wall until it clicked and released a mechanism to slide the door to the side, revealing a hidden room with cabins of all sizes, some even large enough for horses. I remember a white vapour hissing up around my feet until it enveloped me completely and then nothing.

***

Mr Cross was visibly puzzled when a fast and confident walking Mr Farrow approached the ferry again two hours later. He was still carrying that red handbag and in the company of his dog. But this time the cat followed him mistrustfully at some distance.

"Good evening, Mr Cross. Lovely to see you. A fine evening isn't it!"

"Yes, good evening again, Mr Farrow. Lovely evening, I agree. Did you get everything you wanted from Mr Tinker?"

"Everything what?" replied Mr Farrow.

"Everything you wanted to buy. You told me when you crossed earlier that you wanted to get some things."

Mr Farrow looked at Mr Cross and shrugged his shoulders and frowned. "No idea what you are talking about. I just needed to get my wife's handbag repaired, that's all."

Mr Cross looked questionably at Mr Farrow as he left the ferry with his dog and the very unkempt cat.

***

"Darling. Darling. I'm home," shouted Bill from the hallway.

"And about time too, Bill Farrow," screeched his wife and came pounding down the stairs. One glaring look at Rosie was enough for the unfortunate dog to put her tail between her legs and quickly retreat outside.

"I've repaired your handbag, darling," said Bill lovingly.

"My handbag. How did you get it and why have it repaired?" She shouted as her anger built up again. "I hope you now have a very good explanation for yesterday, Bill. Wearing a dress, putting your head in your dinner on our wedding anniversary and then sleeping in the dog basket. Who knows what else you have been up to!"

Bill looked at his wife in total bewilderment. "I have no idea what you are talking about, darling," he said passing the open handbag back to his wife.

Mrs Farrow snatched it angrily from him and put her hand inside. With a loud scream, she dropped it on the floor and fainted in the protecting arms of her loving and confused husband.

Chapter Fifteen
Plotting

The click-clack noise was getting louder and closer as he approached the conference room. The door opened, and he entered. The President was wearing his normal pin-stripe suit, pink shirt and bowler hat and stood at the entrance of the room with great authority. He eyed each of the twenty-one ministers standing around the table next to their chairs. Then he slowly walked across to his chair at the head of the huge wooden table and sat down. He straightened his chair and looked at the ministers with his beady eyes. Looking down at his papers he quietly said, "You may now sit," and all of the ministers sat down in one synchronised movement, looking at the President in great anticipation.

"We have a lot to get through today, with one very important item on our agenda."

The President waved the orderly away, after he filled up his glass and took a sip from his water. His movements were slow, purposefully designed to build up pressure in the room. And it worked. The intense silence was broken by the loud snapping of a pencil and the President's, and all other eyes, immediately shot in the direction of the noise.

"Nervous are you, Mr Minister for Entertainment?" asked the President, looking intensely at him.

"Aaah, no, Mr President. I'm not, I'm not, not nervous at all," he stuttered back.

"Well, one of you should be nervous. One of you here is a traitor. One of you wants to overthrow me and I can tell you something — I will find you!"

"Now, Minister for Entertainment. Please proceed and give us your update."

"In conjunction with the political officers, I can confirm that we have a satisfied work force. We have been active in ensuring that they have everything they need to make their lives comfortable and of course that they remain loyal. Our work force must know how happy they are to be kept alive down here."

"Yes, yes now go on, Mr Minister. You always say the same things. Is there anything new?" demanded the President.

"There has been a strong increase of tunnelling and molehills in particular around Trout Lane, in the front and back garden of number four. And the man who lives there has drastically increased the use of gas to stop us. Of course, he doesn't know that we use the gas for our entertainment. A very good situation for us at the moment. Dig by day and laugh by night," he said laughing alone in an attempt at a joke. "By the way, is anyone here able to tell me why there is such intense activity at this particular spot?"

"You are the Minister for Entertainment, not Special Operations. Therefore, you don't need to know. Accept the fact and don't ask questions. Carry on with your report," the President said harshly.

"Yes, of course, Mr President. There is one more thing. The football match we recently televised was an enormous hit. Mr Jackson's idea went down extremely well with everybody. I have never seen so much excitement here before. The second leg of the cup game will also be televised in two days and I just hope we have the same response. It is certainly a mole, I mean morale booster in these difficult times." The Minister for Entertainment tried yet again to crack a joke to a silent room.

"You may sit, Mr Minster," said the President. "Minster for Allocations!" barked the President.

The Minister for Allocations stood up and read through his lengthy list of current allocations.

"And last but not least, a five percent increase in the Food Factory allocation. This is the third consecutive monthly increase and, in my view, unsustainable," finished the Minster. He nervously gazed down at his notes and tried to avoid looking at the President.

"It is not your business to comment on the reasons, Mr Minister, but to do!"

"Of course, Mr President. Sorry."

"But you might have a point. Please explain yourself?"

"Well, it's like this," carried on the Minister, still looking very nervous. "It is normal at this time of the year, I mean with Christmas coming up, that consumption of meat increases. We are normally able to increase the Food Factory demand for peak periods and balance it out later. However, the current increase, by far, exceeds the one of past years and over a longer period of time. We are down to only three percent in our surplus and processor store — this is a dangerously low figure. Leaves us with little flexibility in case of an emergency. The political officers press gang a large number of our work force into entering the Factory and we even turn around new arrivals immediately to keep up. This leads to fear and bad morale, which the Minister of Entertainment forgot to mention by the way. Well, the bottom line is that if this high demand of meat persists, we will have to cut allocations to other groups."

"A very comprehensive report, Mr Minister. I understand your concerns and suggest we have a private meeting before our next conference," added the President quietly.

"Minster for Political Correctness. Your report!"

The Minister for Political Correctness coughed to clear his voice. "Mr President, I cannot agree with my colleague. Morale isn't low. On the contrary. The Minister for Entertainment is perfectly correct as always — I briefed him myself only yesterday. Next point. The current tunnelling work has led to an increase of laughing gas which, as we all understand, leads to a good end to a hard day. The first leg of the football match was a real hit and morale is extremely high. The next game is in two days and I suggest we have another effort in recruiting people for the Food Factory in the build up to the match. Just the right timing if you ask me. And by the way, I much prefer the use 'recruiting' instead of 'press ganging'," he said, looking directly at the Minister of Allocations. "I intend to publish an amendment on our commonly used terminology next week."

"Mr Minister. Why is it necessary to recruit more for the Food Factory just before the match? Surely it would be good to keep morale at a high level?"

"Yes, Mr President. But morale is already high. And fear is equally important. Fear leads to loyalty. Do you not agree Ministers?" he said looking around the table and finally at the President himself.

All of the ministers nodded their heads in firm agreement.

"Then we have an agreement on that point then. Make sure it is very public, Mr Minister," the President said sternly.

"And now, Ministers. On to the next point. The report from the Minister for Security."

"Ministers. We have all been busy since our last meeting looking for the whereabouts of Professor Wingnut and the culprits who stole him. It is a most dangerous situation to be in," said the Minister for Security, turning his head slowly with a killing glance into the face of every minister.

"But what can you tell this conference, Mr Minister?" ordered the President.

"Mr President, as you are already aware, we know of the location of the Professor, but we have no access to the house at the moment. Just to keep the rest of you up to date — most of you are unaware that the Professor is currently sitting somewhere in the house at number three Trout Lane. The very house belonging to Mr Jackson. Now you know why there is a lot of tunnelling activity," said the Minister and then went on to explain about the failed recovery attempt and the arrival of Mr Jackson.

"Do you mean to say that the Professor's jar is up there and Mr Jackson, the only person who knows its exact whereabouts is down here," shouted out the Minster for Environment.

"Yes, Mr fellow Minister. That is unfortunately correct."

"What are you doing about it?" demanded the angry minster.

"We have fast-tracked Mr Jackson and his friends, so they can return and retrieve the Professor as quickly as possible. They have successfully completed scavenging tasks and had basic training in special operations. They are now ready to go back and complete this important mission. We are certain that by the end of the second leg of the football match the Professor will be back safe and sound with us. Once we have him the traitorous mole will be exposed and publicly punished."

"But surely you must know by now who the traitor is, or even traitors are Mr Minister?" probed the Minster for Environment. "So much time has already passed since the Professor was stolen."

"Maybe it's you! Just admit it, so we don't have to spend further effort looking for the mole," retorted the Minister for Security angrily.

"Me? Don't be preposterous. I'm the most loyal here. The mole is someone else in this room!"

The Minister of Security looked around the table and addressed his colleagues again. "As ministers we all have special authority and privileges. What's more, we all have access to the Memory Warehouse and the power to secretly send our operatives through the Morphing programme on special ops. And because of this secrecy, the initiator is unknown to the rest of us. It's true, it could be any one of us. So please, dear colleagues, don't be offended by the Minister for Environment. But," looking intensively around the great oval table again, "whoever stole the Professor has been extremely clever and covered their tracks so far. You will make a mistake though and I will be there waiting for you."

When the Minster for Health, followed by the Minister for Sport, then the Minister for the Environment and finally the Minister for Tunnelling and Molehills had reported on their activities, the President called an end to the conference and ordered everyone to reconvene after the next football match. The ministers shuffled out of the room, passed the President, who stood guard at the door to look each and every one of them directly in the eyes before they silently left the room. Then he went back inside the room where Colonel Pickle was waiting for him.

"Colonel," he said. "I have absolutely no idea who the mole is. One of them intends to oust me and take control of our world. We cannot let that happen."

"No, Mr President. I fully agree. We cannot let that happen, but I also have no idea or suspicion. However, whoever is behind this coup is very sly and an expert at covering their tracks. Our mole is a mole with a wealth of experience and a wide network of contacts."

"How confident are you that your plan will work, Colonel?"

"I am one hundred percent confident, Mr President. Our mission to retrieve the Professor has been planned out accurately. And our team is prepared. Nothing will go wrong!"

"Go through the plan with me again, Colonel."

"It's quite simple, Mr President. Mr Jackson will infiltrate Mr Lawnsworthy, his former neighbour, who apparently has a spare key. He and his colleagues will then enter the house through the front door, using Mr Lawnsworthy as cover. This way, Mr Jackson can simply walk out the door with the jar."

"That sounds too easy. There are police guarding the house and the other side is also watching. What about them?"

"Mr President. Sometimes easy plans are the best ones. The police won't see Mr Lawnsworthy go into the house. His colleagues will distract them and the other animals at the same time. Trust me."

"And how have you planned to get the Professor back down here?"

"Mr Lawnsworthy will walk directly to Mr Tinker's store, well-guarded by our side, and then Mr Jackson will come back down below along with the jar. It will be so quick that the other side will not have time to react. The distraction is well thought through and all eyes will be somewhere else."

"But, Colonel, the other side could well have knowledge of our plan and be there waiting for us."

"That I have covered, Mr President. I will personally lead our force and we will create a shield so thick around Mr Lawnsworthy that they won't even stand a chance to react or change the course of the situation."

"It sounds as though you have thought of everything, Colonel. At least I can trust you. I hope," he said with a sigh escaping his lips. "But have you also thought about Mr Jackson? What will you do if you are tricked by him. We will have to dispense of him once he has finished his mission and he may well be aware of that too. Shame that is, really. I've heard the man has a lot of useful abilities."

"I have thought of that as well, Mr President. I will have his female colleague, the Forsythe-Twyke girl, taken as security for the safe return of the Professor and the memory stick Mr Jackson mentioned during his debriefing. Cleopatra will be briefed and on hand ready to assist should it be necessary. The plan is safe and sound as far as I'm concerned, Mr President."

"Oh yes, the memory stick. I am glad you thought of that too. That could hopefully contain important information about the sneaky, traitorous moles. Well done, Colonel Pickle, and good luck with your mission!"

***

"Colonel Bacon," a voice came from behind the wooden door.

"Yes, Minister. I have come as requested."

"The hour is coming for our last chance of success. The odds are against us I believe but in surprise we can be victorious. What is your plan?"

Colonel Bacon then laid out his plan in detail to the unknown minster.

"And how do you intend to foil their plan, Colonel Bacon?"

"I have managed to turn and recruit a lot of the work force and now built up a substantial army. It wasn't too difficult because the fear surrounding the Food Factory allocation and the oppressive regime are causing more discontent than imagined. We cannot risk the workers having a revolution and leaving them in control, can we? We need to show strength and lead the way."

"Yes, that is exactly why we are doing this. This old fashioned political system can't carry on and we are the new ones to take this forward. Our new political system will mean reward through successful work and punishment through bad work. Much more motivating than this old-fashioned political ideology that we are all equal. We can see it is not working. Freedom for our workers is what we need. A free market economy run by demand for goods and services."

"Like the meat industry, you mean?"

"Yes, exactly that, Colonel. Now please go on."

"I intend to let their plan run as they intend and Mr Lawnsworthy can go into the house and bring out the jar. It is pointless risking ourselves as we don't know where the jar is anyway. But as soon as he is out in the open, I have arranged for a bombing raid on Mr Lawnsworthy and all involved parties arranged by Colonel Pickle. A raid so massive that all of them should be hit and the advantage will tilt in our favour."

"What if Mr Lawnsworthy is not hit, Colonel?"

"Not a problem. I have thought of that. We will have so many on our side that the jar will come into our possession nonetheless."

"Excellent, Colonel. I knew I could trust you with our cause. One last question though. How do you intend to deliver the jar to our leader, Mr Cromwell?"

"Cleopatra will be briefed and be there to facilitate the handover. She will also be the one to make the grab for the jar. May I suggest that you make contact with Mr Cromwell and ask him to be in the vicinity of Trout Lane when the time comes so Professor Wingnut can at last be handed over."

"Yes, I will do so, Colonel Bacon."

***

"Did you hear that, Felicity?" said Jemima Kingston.

"Hear what, darling Jemima?" replied Felicity Forsythe-Twyke.

"I just heard a voice again."

"My voice, darling. I was just speaking to you."

"No. A deep voice. A man's voice. In fact, two voices."

"But we are alone, Jemima darling. How could you have possibly heard men's voices? Oh, hold on. Don't tell me you are

274

hearing voices again coming from your handbag perhaps?" said Felicity, with a great tone of sarcasm.

"Look. I know it sounds strange but yes, exactly that. Men's voices coming from my handbag!"

Felicity looked strictly at Jemima. "Is work causing you bother at the moment, dear? Maybe you should see a doctor or take some time off. You have obviously got too much stress."

"I swear I heard someone say Trout Lane before the football match. And then something about Cleopatra handing over Professor Wingwhatever," explained Jemima, with a puzzled look on her face looking down at the dog who had just poked his head out of her bag.

"Aw, so cute, isn't he," said Felicity, patting Cromwell on his head with a sly smirk.

***

"Cleopatra. I have another mission for you," said Colonel Pickle.

"Whatever you command, Colonel. What should I do?"

The Colonel then went on to explain his plan with Mr Lawnsworthy.

"And you want me to kidnap the young lady if things go wrong?" confirmed Cleopatra.

"Yes. That is what I need you to do. I will give the order if necessary."

***

"Cleopatra. I have another mission for you," said Colonel Bacon.

"Whatever you order, Colonel. What should I do?"

The Colonel then went on to explain his plan with Mr Lawnsworthy.

"And you want me to grab the jar when your plan swings into action?" confirmed Cleopatra.

"Yes. That is what I need you to do. I will give the order if necessary."

***

The moles were carrying the blue and white colours of FC Lower Molehampton and stood in a perfectly straight line in front of the Colonel.

"I expect the other side will be doing the same, but we must be quicker. I need you to dig tunnels underneath the whole of the pitch with access chutes stopping just below the surface. We cannot give away our position, so don't build any hills. But we need to have our teams sitting in advantageous positions right underneath the pitch. You know — just in case Lower needs any additional support during the game. Those cheats from AFC Upper Molehampton stole our win in the last minute of the first leg. We will not play with kid's gloves this time," explained the Colonel clearly.

"But, Colonel Pickle, we will all miss the game," pointed out a disappointed mole.

"Yes, you are correct. But sometimes in life sacrifices must be made. Now off you go. You haven't got much time."

***

The moles were carrying the red and white colours of AFC Upper Molehampton and stood in a perfectly straight line in front of the Colonel.

"I must first congratulate you for your actions in the first-leg. Your timely molehill certainly worked to our advantage, but I suspect that FC Lower Molehampton will now be planning counteractive measures. Therefore, your mission is to build as many tunnels as possible under the pitch, so we are well-prepared for any eventuality," barked out the Colonel.

"But, Colonel Bacon, we will miss the second leg," pointed out a disappointed mole.

"Yes, you are quite correct," said the Colonel harshly. "Now get going and do your work."

276

Chapter Sixteen
The Mission

The Angler Inn in Lower Molehampton was a rustic pub just like any one you would expect to see in the countryside: fireplace, leather chairs, wooden beams and a well-worn carpet. As the name may well suggest, the pub was adorned with items to do with fish and angling. Nets were hung on the wall, fishing rods suspended from the ceiling and pictures of proud anglers presenting their best catch were hung on every spare space. There was no space for a television and, to be perfectly honest not really needed, as most of the frequenters spent most of their time discussing the fish that got away, or comparing the size of the ones which didn't, over a good pint of locally brewed ale.

But sometimes there were more important things than fishing because today was the eagerly awaited second round of the County Cup. The radio in The Angler Inn crackled and burst into life

"Welcome to Radio Molehampton bringing you live the first round, second leg of the County Cup. Yes, today is FC Lower Molehampton versus AFC Upper Molehampton and we hope our listeners are treated to an action-packed match. This match is evenly poised at one — one following the strange last-minute equalizer by AFC Upper Molehampton in the first leg. The pitch is in good condition, the sun is shining, there is no wind and the fans are out in force. There can't be many people left at home in Upper or Lower Molehampton. Sit back in your chairs and enjoy our live commentary."

The atmosphere inside the pub in Lower Molehampton was subdued though, as today most of the regulars were actually at the match itself to see it live.

But the pub below the ground was a completely different kettle of fish. The atmosphere in the Tunnelers' Arms was electric with every vantage point taken in front of the big luxury screen, with mice even sitting in lampshades to get a good view. And today they could listen to the live broadcasting from the radio, which Connor had managed to install. The left side of the pub belonged to the blue and white supporters of FC Lower Molehampton and the right to the red and white colours of AFC Upper Molehampton. Both sets of fans were building themselves up into a frenzy with songs sung and insults hurled. Fortunately, the sound level was so intense that nobody even noticed when the radio commentator announced the County Cup!

The TV flickered a few times and then the pitch surrounded by rival sets of supporters appeared on the screen with a burst of colour. The picture quality was much better today. Also, this time Connor had arranged for the cameras to be placed in trees and on top of the changing rooms rather than in the molehills to be trampled on. Hopefully there would be no interruptions in this game.

The fish and chip shop with its mobile trailer was doing a roaring trade in pies, beers and of course fish and chips, right in front of the changing room. This side of the pitch belonged to the home fans of FC Lower Molehampton and most of the village must have been there including the Khans, Mr Rye, Mrs Cross and the Singh family, adding to the already loud atmosphere of the raucous home fans.

There wasn't much noise coming from the luxury marquee tents on the other side of the pitch, apart from the faint chink of glasses and the haughty laughter of people enjoying expensive champagne and delicious canapés.

***

The four of us sat nervously inside Mr Tinker's store, the one below the ground, and readied ourselves for the mission. I beckoned them to come closer and put a finger against my mouth.

"Hush now and listen," I whispered so quietly that the others could only just hear me. "Remember!" I said, "we might have to improvise?"

"Well, here is the first change to the plan," I continued after the others had nodded their consent with serious faces. "As soon as we are up in the air, and not before, you have to instruct your birds to fly to the football pitch. Nobody must know about our change and even our birds must think we are flying to my house until the very last moment," I explained earnestly. "Surprise will be our main advantage and further instructions will follow in the air."

***

"Damn. Blast. Bloody damn moles," muttered Mr Lawnsworthy to himself.

He was dressed in his normal attire of blue garden overalls and wellington boots and jumping up and down in a rage between the hundreds of freshly dug molehills which surrounded him. In the past few weeks Mr Lawnsworthy's, up until now beautifully kept garden, had been cultivated by a large number of molehills but in the last two days the activity had drastically increased.

"Why me? My pride and joy destroyed. Just look at the other gardens here, nearly unaffected by these damn moles. Why me?" He asked himself and was nearly in tears, despairingly looking around him. He walked towards a small patch of remaining grass and just before he could place his feet on his beloved lawn… yes, you guessed it right, a molehill sprouted up from nowhere. "Stop!" he shouted.

Mr Lawnsworthy careered around his garden. Quite fast, considering his age. He grabbed his garden spade from the shed and started smashing the molehills with a wild laugh and great glee, building himself up into a howling fury. He hopped and bounced around and smashed them down one by one with a dangerous glint in his squinted eyes. "There, that should teach you to mess with me!" he shouted and turned around to survey the success of his work.

But, one by one, the molehills popped up again until eventually Mr Lawnsworthy sank down on his knees and leant against his spade. Normally, anyone in earshot would have been concerned by his long and loud groan. But not today. There was nobody in Trout Lane to make sure he was alright. Everyone had gone to see the County Cup, which Mr Lawnsworthy didn't care much for. He was far too busy tending his garden to worry about a silly football match!

He was still on his knees when he saw shadows moving around on the ground very close to him. "What's that?" He looked up and saw a large flock of birds circling directly above his garden.

Splat. Splat. Splat.

The first bird droppings began to fall ominously close and all-around Mr Lawnsworthy.

"And now this!" he said to himself.

The first range of droppings had found their target.

***

"Bombs away," bellowed the mouse and looked below to follow the white droppings fall in the direction of a man in blue overalls standing alone in a garden. "Range finders successful," he shouted, looking up at the pigeon. "Let's circle at this altitude and drop our real loads."

The pigeon nodded and continued to circle above the man standing in the garden with the rest of the bombing flock. Each pigeon was laden with a platform and two upside-down bottles.

***

We had just been through the Morphing process at Mr Tinker's place, ready for take-off and with apprehension as our mission got ever closer. Mr Tinker held the two birds above his head, pushed them up gently and with one big flap of their powerful wings, they went towards the blue sky with us hanging upside down in our bottles in the wooden platforms swinging below them.

"Good luck on your mission, whatever it may be."

"Trout Lane I understand?" shouted out the mouse next to my bottle.

"Yes, yes please," I replied.

***

"And there's the whistle and they're off," screamed the commentator in excitement down the radio. "It's Upper Molehampton with the ball first and going straight on the attack. Number nine is sprinting down the right wing with the ball, he cuts inside and drives straight towards the penalty area. Oh dear. Oh dear indeed. We don't want to see this. Lower's number four cut him down in a rather vicious challenge. The Upper player is rolling across the ground; about ten times so far. Very melodramatic. And the players are pushing each other around. This is an exciting start to the game but we really don't want to see this. And now, what is the referee doing? My, after only thirty seconds Lower's number four has a yellow card. I have a feeling this will be a feisty affair."

The atmosphere in the pub below the ground had already reached fever pitch as both sides were now openly arguing with each other. The barkeeper shouted out for order but couldn't be heard above the din. This was going to be an exciting afternoon.

"Number nine is up again and stepping up to take the free kick. He appears to have made a miraculous recovery after looking mortally wounded in the challenge," said the commentator. "Oh no. He's booted the ball woefully high above the goal. Nothing to trouble the Lower keeper though, which is a good thing. Just remember the equalizer at the end of the first leg! He is not that skilful between the sticks. And now a long goal kick and it's Lower on the attack. Tackle, long ball and Upper are running in the other direction. They will soon run out of energy at this pace."

***

281

The two pigeons flew slowly over Lower Molehampton towards Trout Lane, accompanied by two flocks of pigeons, one on the left and one on the right. My plan was working just as I had predicted.

"Now listen to me," I shouted to the mouse. "You will do exactly as I say. I want you and the other pigeon to fly directly through both flocks of birds, down through the houses, up again, back through the flocks and then at maximum speed away from the melee towards the football pitch."

"But I thought…" started the mouse.

"Yes, you thought. But there has been a change of plan. Do as I say!"

To my great relief both pigeons instantly turned to the right and did exactly as I instructed. The effect was immediate. Both flocks broke ranks in the confusion and in an effort to identify the two rogue birds all ended up flying in one big mass. The man in the blue overalls looked in awe at the sight above him. In the confused dog fight the two rogue birds managed to burst out of sight, flying low between two houses. The two flocks of birds had now merged into one and continued flying erratic circles above Mr Lawnsworthy's property at Trout Lane.

"And now to the football pitch. Keep flying low between the houses and gain height just before we reach the pitch. We won't have time for any ranging shots, so I want you to just drop us in a low-level mission directly over the pitch. The spot at the centre is your aiming mark," I said, commanding the mouse who passed the instructions to the pigeon.

"But that's too risky! What if you miss your target?"

"Leave that to me but thank you for your concern," I replied. "Yes, releasing at a low level with little time to control our falls is risky but there are plenty of targets down there."

***

"We've been tricked. After those birds down there between the houses!" shouted Colonel Pickle at the mouse from the inside of his bottle. He had decided to take personal charge of the mission, not knowing who he could entrust with the command. There was now no room for error and the two rogue birds had to be caught.

"Follow me!" he screamed back towards the melee of birds hoping that his flock would recognise him and be able to disengage from the confusion.

***

"Abort, everyone, abort!" shouted Colonel Bacon from his bottle. Like Colonel Pickle, Colonel Bacon had also decided to take personal charge. "Follow the flock of birds breaking away," he ordered.

***

"And it's in. Upper have scored and taken the lead. It's FC Lower Molehampton nil, AFC Upper Molehampton one. Scored by number nine, James Plitherington-Squire. He wheels around to celebrate in front of the tents but I can't see much of a reaction coming from the away fans. Too busy chatting and eating I think. If the scores stay the same, Upper are through to the next round. We are twenty minutes through the first half and Upper are in front. Plenty of time for Lower to come back in, what I must say is, a quite evenly contested match so far."

***

"Get ready everyone," I shouted. "Spread yourself as quick as you can on release and aim for any moving person on the pitch. It doesn't matter who you land on. Any odd person will do. I will run off the pitch so just follow me."

The wooden platforms and bottles were swinging strongly below them as the two birds approached the pitch in a steep dive, levelled out and continued directly towards the centre spot.

"Release us when you are ready," I shouted to the mouse, who nodded and peered through his aiming hole until the centre spot came in to view.

"Release," shouted the mouse and all four mice simultaneously released their loads. The white blobs slithered through the necks of the bottles, fell towards the ground and didn't take long to find their targets. The two pigeons soared towards the sky. Their mission was over.

***

"The ball is back on the centre spot and the players are getting ready for Lower to kick-off again. The referee is in position and puts the whistle to his mouth. Wait. Now he stopped and looks up at the sky. In fact, everybody is now looking up at the sky. What is going on up there?" asked the commentator as two pigeons flew in low and hard towards the centre spot when suddenly a white bird dropping splat directly on the referee's forehead. For a few seconds he stood motionless, but then started running off the pitch.

"What's this now? I can't believe it. A bird has just dropped its load directly on the referee's forehead. How very unfortunate for him. And now? This is most extraordinary. He is running off the pitch and wait, there's more. He is being followed by Upper's goalkeeper and number nine, the goal scorer. And now Mr Mason, Lower's trainer, is also darting off. The four of them are running down the street as fast as their legs can carry them. I have never commented on such a strange set of affairs before in all my time as a sports reporter. This is most odd!"

The Tunnellers' Arms far below the ground fell into silence.

***

Cromwell waited impatiently at the entrance of Trout Lane. He had managed to get away earlier whilst Mrs Forsythe-Twyke conveniently distracted Mrs Kingston. He didn't want anything to go wrong today and had arrived in plenty of time to witness the increase in birds, the arrival of the two pigeons flanked by two flocks of birds and the confusing melee above him.

284

Now he was mesmerised by four people and a dog running down Salmon Road towards him. The first person was wearing black shorts, a black T-shirt and had a whistle in his mouth. The second a green shirt and big gloves. The third a red T-shirt and white shorts. Their football boots made a strange clattering noise with the studs hammering on the surface whilst the fourth person was wearing a suit and pulling behind him on a leash a rather large dog. The five ran straight past him and down Trout Lane, heading towards number three.

"I thought I had seen it all," said Cromwell, with his mouth open and his tongue out. "Until now!"

***

Mr Lawnsworthy was shaking his head in disbelief when he inspected the remnants of his front garden. He had just come out when he heard an unfamiliar clattering sound. He turned around and was met with a rather odd scene. A group of three men dressed in football clothing and Mr Mason, Lower Molehampton's trainer, dragging his dog behind him, were running along Trout Lane in his direction. He was too flabbergasted to say anything when they went straight past him, without even recognising his presence, through his open front door and into his house. A few seconds later they exited his house again. But instead of a whistle the referee was this time holding a key in his hand.

"What. What the dickens..." started to say Mr Lawnsworthy, but the men just ran directly towards number three's front door. Today Connor Jackson's house was unprotected as the two policemen from Anglerton, normally guarding the house since his disappearance, were needed at the football match. The referee unlocked the door, they all went in and slammed the door with a loud bang.

Mr Lawnsworthy was joined by a very small dog and they both stared at number three, with their mouths open.

***

"Well, we still haven't kicked off since Upper scored. The referee is still missing along with the two Upper players and Lower's trainer. Hang on, there appears to be a fourth official coming out of the changing rooms. Yep, he has just put on a black shirt and is running out onto the pitch. No, I am mistaken, it is not a he, but a she. A female referee. She is now speaking to both captains and putting the whistle to her mouth. It seems the match is back on ladies and gentlemen. Upper are two men down, but only one goal up and now at a severe disadvantage. Even the Upper fans are out from their tents now and watching the mind-boggling scenes."

The Lower fans on the pitch and in the pub below the ground roared their team on. Upper did not have a goalkeeper on the pitch and was also missing their key striker. Lower could smell blood.

***

The pigeons came in low and fast with their wooden platforms swinging wildly below them.

"Look. Over there," shouted Colonel Pickle from his bottle, "I can see them. They are running away from the football pitch. After them! Dive towards that group at the closest half of the pitch," he ordered to the mouse.

As the game had not yet kicked off, all Upper players were in their own half in a huddle discussing what had just happened. The Upper supporters also gathered on the touchline to find out what was going on and had not yet returned to their champagne tents. Just at this moment everyone noticed a loud flapping noise from two big flocks of pigeons flying towards the football field at great speed.

"Release!" The first bombs dropped towards the pitch and the remainder of the bombing squadron aimed, successfully it must be said, at the Upper players in red and spectators alike.

***

The second wave of pigeons swooped in directly behind the first pigeon squadron.

286

"Look. Some of the red players have been hit. And some of the spectators too. Where are they running off too?" shouted Colonel Bacon from his bottle." He frantically spun around in his bottle and saw a group of four men and a dog running down the street away from the pitch with a group of other men following them, some of them in red T-shirts.

"There they are. Over there, running away from the pitch. The others are already after them. Aim for the blue players," he ordered the mouse. "I will go for the blue number eleven," he shouted on being released from his bottle.

***

"Unbelievable?" screamed out the commentator. "There are birds pooing directly over the pitch and some of the spectators have been hit. And some of the players as well. They are trying to wipe the white mess of their shirts. How disgusting. And there are more birds approaching. I really cannot explain these strange events. It looks like a bombing mission if you ask me. More of the players are now leaving the field of play followed by some spectators. And now what?"

The new referee hadn't even had chance to start the match again after Upper's goal. She stood there with the whistle stuck in her unmoving mouth, her eyes wide open. The players on each side of the field were waiting with extremely confused looks on their faces. The referee didn't really have much of a choice. After pondering for just a moment she blew her whistle for the seven Lower and five Upper players left on the pitch to play. The Lower players kicked off and went straight into the attack.

The pub below the ground was silent. As were the spectators at the football pitch and in the pub above the ground.

***

"After them," shouted Colonel Pickle. "After the referee!"

He had landed on the number three player of Upper Molehampton and was now taking the lead, followed by four Upper Molehampton players and several Upper supporters. They all ran after the referee, the goalkeeper, the number nine player and the man with the dog as fast as they could.

***

If Mr Lawnsworthy and Cromwell thought they had seen the last of the strange events today, they were sorely mistaken. They witnessed yet another group of people running down Trout Lane directed towards them. Football players in red and supporters with red scarves. The group clattered directly past them towards Mr Jackson's house and stopped outside. The number three player gathered the group in a huddle, apparently giving out instructions. But when the front door of number three Trout Lane didn't budge, they just stood there waiting.

With some more noise coming their way, Mr Lawnsworthy and Cromwell again turned around to another group of people running their way and the scene almost repeated itself. Only this time the people were in blue. They also ran straight to house number three and gathered outside on the pathway opposite to the group in red, with the number eleven player barking out his instructions.

***

"Wow, Connor, that worked well," said the goalkeeper looking at nobody in particular. They were all sitting on the sofas in Connor's living room. "By the way, which one are you, Connor? I'm Ludwig."

The referee answered, "Here I am!"

"We really confused them, didn't we?" said the trainer. "And I'm Vanessa by the way."

"We sure did. Everything worked exactly to plan. We caused maximum confusion, gained some time and we now conveniently have the two groups outside. The only thing we don't know is which

288

one of them are the memory thieves. But then again, it's not my problem anymore."

"And now?" asked the striker. "They are all waiting outside, as expected. The only difference to the original plan you laid out to them was that strange detour via the football pitch. If your aim was to confuse everyone, it sure was successful. Even I don't have a clue what is going on. But now they know we are here and can just force themselves in, find the jar and then it's over, can't they?"

"Aaah, Basil. But you've missed the trick in my plan. Of course, they know we are in here but the point is that the eyes of the whole village must be on Trout Lane by now, not on the football match. Everything is completely public, restricting their actions, and they have no idea what we will do next!"

"OK, Connor," said Basil, but didn't sound entirely convinced.

"And what is that?" I exclaimed looking at a dog next to the couch."

"It's a dog, Connor."

"I can see that but what's it doing here? We should only be four."

"When I infiltrated the trainer, I realised I had a lead in my hand and ended up pulling the dog after me. It must be the trainer's dog," said Vanessa, patting the dog on its head.

"Let's just hope it hasn't been infiltrated too, for our sakes. But no time to contemplate that now. Time for phase two to swing into action." I stood up, went to the phone and dialled a number.

"Is this the local news channel? Great. There is an international incident going on at number three Trout Lane, Lower Molehampton. I suggest you get over here right now with a camera crew."

I then made another call. "Detective Inspector Samantha James?" I asked. "There is something strange going on at number three Trout Lane. I can't get a hold of Sergeant Dawson. Could you come by as fast as you can please?"

"Right everyone. I just need to go and get some things and I'll be right back," I said, leaving the room with everyone looking at me in stunned silence.

***

This was the first time I had been in my house since the day of my kidnapping. It was actually quite a strange feeling returning to my house when I was supposedly dead. Well, not quite dead and if my plan worked, then most certainly not and I would return again soon. I went into the kitchen, took a glass jar from a cabinet, some flour from my larder, a pen and plaster from a drawer. I then mixed some of the flour with water, sealed the lid and wrote Professor Wingnut on the plaster. Upstairs I found four wide brimmed hats. They were in fact from my father and I had never got rid of them. I returned with the hats and four cloth bags for the others who were still sitting in my living room.

"So, this is what we are going to do now," I said with a grin.

"I can now see why you never explained your plan to us in detail, Connor. We never would have understood it!" puffed Basil.

***

"What now?" groaned Mr Lawnsworthy.

He and Cromwell were still standing in the street staring at number three when the white van from the Angler County News screeched into Trout Lane and pulled up outside number three. A team of three jumped out and set up their cameras and bright lights. Then a police car with sirens blaring skidded into Trout Lane and stopped right next to the van with squealing brakes.

***

"Wear these hats to protect yourselves from any bombs that will undoubtedly come in our direction. We cannot risk being infiltrated. And put something in your bags. Anything to make it look like you are carrying something," I explained and put my bag on the table with a thud.

"Is that what I think it is, Connor?" asked Vanessa.

"Yes, this is the famous Professor. I collected him from my room just now and am ready to hand him over. Just not the way they expect."

I sat down in my favourite chair, turned on my television and tuned in to the local channel.

***

"This is Angler County News reporting from number three Trout Lane in Lower Molehampton. The scene where the resident, Mr Jackson, has not been seen after an apparent robbery and kidnapping a few weeks ago. The latest twist in the tale came in the middle of the cup game in Lower Molehampton only this afternoon. In fact, the much-delayed match has started again. Our sources report that for yet unknown reasons the referee, Upper's goalkeeper, Upper's number nine and Lower's trainer left the pitch and are now hiding in Mr Jackson's house. Also, some players and supporters from both teams apparently gave chase and are now gathered outside. The police are asking questions but are receive nothing more than blank faces and the shrugging of shoulders. Let's see if we can get an interview with Detective Inspector Samantha James."

***

"Your name please, sir?" asked the policeman.

"Lawnsworthy. Gerald Lawnsworthy."

"And you live in this house?"

"Yes I do."

"Can you tell me what happed this afternoon, Mr Lawnsworthy?"

"Well, it actually all started with a massive attack of molehills in my garden. Front and back. And some birds flying over landing their droppings strangely close to me. And on me. Look at the state of my overalls. Almost as though they were aiming for me. And then..."

"Yes, Mr Lawnsworthy. That is very interesting but not really relevant for what is happening in number three right at this moment, is it? Please tell me what you witnessed!"

"Oh yes."

291

Mr Lawnsworthy then went on to explain about the referee and three other men who ran into his house, then the two groups of players and supporters who descended on Trout Lane.

"Did the referee say anything to you?"

"No, nothing. He went straight into my house and came out with the key to Mr Jackson's house."

"You have the key to Mr Jackson's house?"

"Yes. He gave it to me years ago. In case there was ever an emergency. I put it on a hook next to my door and showed him where it was. But he has never used it in all these years."

"How could the referee know where to find the key? Don't you think that's odd?"

"Well yes. I, hmm. I never thought of that. He was rather quick come to mention it. So, he must have known which key it was too. Funny thing that."

"Do you know Mr Simpson, the referee?"

"No. I have never met him or heard of him in my life."

"Strange isn't it, Mr Lawnsworthy?" said the policeman with a high amount of suspicion.

"I suppose so," replied Mr Lawnsworthy. "Oh yes, and there was also a very small dog standing with me. It was here a few minutes ago," he said looking around. "Gone now I suppose."

***

A large Doberman Pinscher peered at the scene in Trout Lane from the side of a house.

"Confusion. Perfect," muttered the dog to herself.

***

"Connor?" said Basil. "How long are we going to wait here?"

"Oh, a while longer, Basil. We want to cause maximum confusion and really make sure that neither side capture us when we walk out with the Professor's jar. We need him ourselves," I replied.

I went across to the radio and turned it on.

"I really can't see Upper turning this around in the second half. It's half time now and the score is Lower Molehampton two, Upper one. Lower most certainly have the upper hand following the decimation of the teams and Upper is still without a goalkeeper."

I smirked and turned off the radio, went to the phone again and dialled a number.

"Is that Mr Kennedy?" I asked. "Is your brother at home with you? That's good. I have a hot tip for you. There are lots of valuable things at the changing rooms at the Lower Molehampton football pitch. Wait until they are unattended after half time is over and then see what you can find."

"Connor. What are you up to?" asked Vanessa, looking perplexed.

"Just wait. You'll see," I said with a cheeky grin.

"Five minutes everyone and we're leaving," I said seriously. "Any final questions?"

***

When the door to number three opened widely, the television crew reacted immediately and shone the beam of their bright light towards it and braced themselves for action, anticipating someone coming out. Nothing happened at first but then the goalkeeper and Upper's number nine burst out at the same time. The strange scene was caught on camera and noted by the bemused police. The goalkeeper was now wearing a large floppy hat and carried a bag in his gloved hands as he went past the blue group. The number nine player also wore a floppy hat and carried a bag but ran towards a red group. They both carried on down Trout Lane in a zig-zag pattern through the front gardens. The groups were both dazed and needed a few moments to react before the blue group decided to chase the goalkeeper while the red group sprinted after the number nine player.

Then two more people came out of number three Trout Lane: the referee and the trainer, Mr Mason.

"Stop. I've got it!" shouted the referee, loudly.

Both groups screeched to a sudden halt and turned around.

"Over here. It's me," shouted the referee from the front garden of the house. "I've got it."

"No. I've got it," shouted Mr Mason standing next to the referee.

The referee, Mr Mason and the dog started running down the street leaving Trout Lane, past the two groups who were now motionless and had given up the chase on the first two. The goalkeeper and the number nine player, who were now not being pursued any more, ran the most direct route towards the football pitch, whereas the referee and Mr Mason split up and took two different and very indirect routes.

The film crew followed whoever they could in their van, trying to film the confusing scene directly from the open door. The policemen split up and gave chase on foot with their whistles blowing.

***

The goalkeeper and the number nine player arrived at the changing rooms first and went into the home room. They put their bags on the floor in the centre of the room and waited.

***

"Listeners. You won't believe what I am now seeing," said the commentator with bemusement, speaking now in very short sentences to offer immediate commentary.

"The referee is running back towards the football pitch, followed by a group of the missing players and supporters. It looks like they are chasing him. And there's more. Mr Mason and his dog are also coming back to the pitch from a different direction. He is also being pursued by the other group of missing players and supporters. This is highly odd. Wait. They are both heading towards the changing rooms and have now entered the building. Their

294

pursuers are hot on their heels and only a few hundred metres behind."

***

A panting referee and Mr Mason burst through the door of the changing room where the goalkeeper and the number nine player were already waiting for them. They also placed their bags on the floor.

"Took your time, Connor!" said the goalkeeper, with a laugh.

"OK, let's do it," I said still panting.

They closed the door to the changing room, opened the window and climbed out, leaving Mr Mason's dog inside to guard the bags. Then they closed the window from the outside.

"And now to Mr Tinker's store. We will have to hurry as time is of the essence now."

"Connor. What about the Professor?" shouted the goalkeeper, towards the already running referee.

"Oh, don't worry about him. They can all fight over him," I said turning my head as I ran away from the building.

***

"The game is now of second importance to the strange events going on in the changing rooms," shouted the commentator from the radio.

"The two groups of players and supporters have just arrived at the entrance to the changing rooms and are now all pushing and shoving to get through the door. And what's this? The referee, Mr Mason and the two players are running away from the back of the building. Oh, by the way, the score is now three to one for Lower Molehampton. If you are still interested that is."

***

The scene in the changing room was one of utter chaos as the two groups of players and supporters all squeezed into the room at the same. About twenty people were now crammed in, grappling over the bags which were sitting on the floor, fighting to retrieve the stolen memory.

"Here it is. I've got it," shouted one of the supporters in blue.

"No, I've got it," shouted one of the supporters in red.

"Hang on, this bag only contains a stone," shouted one person.

"Yeah, this one too," added another person.

"I've got the jar," cried out somebody else.

"And there's another jar under the bench."

"And I've got one too from the first aid cabinet."

"And I've got one from the laundry bag."

The group of jostling players and supporters had ripped the place to pieces after they had realised that there was more than one jar but now fell into a silence with four of them holding memory jars.

"What's that written on them?" shouted out somebody.

"Professor Wingnut," a player in red shouted, followed by loud shouts and more scrumming as everybody tried to get the jar from him.

"But my jar also has Professor Wingnut on it!"

"Mine too!"

"And mine also."

The room fell into silence again.

***

"Hello, Mr Tinker," I said, now panting heavily as we burst through his door. "Back below please."

"OK, over there please. You know the process."

We went into the shed and prepared ourselves for the reverse Morphing process, to let the referee, Mr Mason and the two football players return to their lives and us back below. The gooey mixture had only been prepared for a few hours, just enough time for us to conduct the mission.

"Are you sure your plan is going to work?" asked Vanessa.

"Yes, of course."

"But we have left the professor behind and I thought we needed him to get back out. We have no bargaining chips, Connor. We will be down here forever," blurted out Vanessa very alarmed.

"Look, don't worry. I have everything under control. If my plan works, and it is running well at the moment, then we will be back on the surface in a jiffy. Trust me please," I said reassuringly.

"OK, Connor, but I don't feel good about this," whispered Vanessa back.

Mr Tinker junior led us to the cabins to start the procedure and before we knew it we were heading back down below in our glass jars. At the bottom Mr Tinker senior completed the reversal process.

"Thank you, Mr Tinker," I said looking rather smug. "You have been most helpful. I expect you will have a busy day from now on in."

"Busy? It is complete madness. I have never sent so many to the surface in such a short space of time. And so much secrecy today. I have no idea what is going on. I don't even have time to watch the football match," explained a rather flustered Mr Tinker.

"Follow me everyone. We have things to collect and get out of here," I whispered to my friends."

"Where are we going, Connor?" asked Ludwig.

"You'll see. Now come on," I said opening the door to the store.

"Oh, Mr Tinker. Just in case anyone wants to know where we are, please tell them we were exhausted and have gone to our rooms to rest," I said with a wink.

Mr Tinker nodded and smiled back.

I led my friends towards the nearest station to take a shuttle to the memory warehouse. We walked as fast as we could without raising any suspicion and were now standing in front of the round metal entry door. I ushered them in and walked towards some trolleys at the beginning of the racking system. Vanessa, Basil and Ludwig stopped and looked around in awe. What greeted their eyes was a huge cavern stretching as far as the eye could see, with aisle upon aisle and row upon row of shelves. The whole racking system was jam packed with glass jars.

"My goodness," exclaimed Vanessa. "What an amazing sight. And these are all memories — how scary. I am beginning to understand why we have so many molehills on the surface."

"What's going to happen now will surprise you even more than this sight. We are going to go into the racking system and retrieve a memory."

"Believe me, Connor, nothing can surprise me anymore. And whose memory are we going to get?"

"Oh, only the Professor's," I said turning around to fetch a trolley.

"What did you just say?" called out Basil.

"You heard correctly."

"But we left the professor's jar in the changing room!" exclaimed Basil.

"We left a jar with his name on. Yes. In fact, four jars with his name. But the real one is down here in the warehouse and has been for ages. Look, I don't have time to explain things fully now but I will when we get to the surface. I needed to play for time and get back below to plan our escape. Everything on the surface today was just a distraction and it worked. All of the key players in the 'Professor Wingnut game' are on the surface, the warehouse workers are watching football, we are here on our own and more importantly so is the professor. But I believe they will soon realise they have been tricked. So, we haven't got long to complete our escape."

I took them down an aisle, up a ramp in the deserted warehouse and followed a walkway deep into the racking system. At a chalk mark on one of the uprights I turned right and then left at another chalk mark. We were now high up and deep within the racking system and surrounded by thousands of jars all stacked up on the shelves.

"Wow, this place is amazing," said Vanessa, blowing out as she looked around. "Is this where all of the memories are stored?"

"Yes, and it is exactly where we will end up if we cannot get out. This place is the end game after the transition period down here, unless of course you are lucky enough to find employment. And I can guarantee you that, after today, we will not find employment."

"But there must be hundreds of thousands of memories here," added Vanessa, amazed.

"More than that I think. Here we are," I said and stopped at another chalk mark on the racking system. "Help me would you? We have to move a few jars out of the way."

Vanessa and I removed some jars from the shelf and put them on the walkway. I then looked into the hole, stretched out my arm, pulled out one more jar and held it with great care in my hands.

"Here we go. May I present to you the famous Professor Wingnut," Vanessa, Ludwig and Basil were looking at me and at the jar in disbelief.

Vanessa put the other jars back in the hole so nobody could see the empty space behind.

"So this is what has been causing all of the excitement," said Ludwig.

"Yes, this is the reason why I am down here. All because of this damn jar."

"Wait!" exclaimed Vanessa. "It hasn't got Professor Wingnut's name on it. It says John Smith."

"I know. I changed the name and decided to put a name on it which is so common that nobody apart from me could find it. Don't fret, it is the real one."

"And now what, Connor?" asked Basil.

"Now we have to hurry over to the pub and speak to the landlord. He has something we need."

"Stop being so mysterious, Connor," Vanessa sounded impatient. "Just tell us what we are doing!"

"I am not entirely sure. The Professor just told me to collect the envelope from the landlord that he left there. The contents will tell us how to get out of here. That is all I know I'm afraid."

"And that is your plan?" asked Vanessa.

"Yes, that's it! I know it's not much but the Professor assured me everything we need is there."

"You spoke to the Professor?" stammered Ludwig.

"Yes I did. Look, no time now. We must go. I am sure the others will be on their way back down and most certainly very furious. They will have great urgency to find us, so we must stay one step ahead. Ludwig, can you remember the equipment you got me from the store? Let's go to my office and collect it!"

"Yes. Why?"

"Because we are going to need the overalls, shovels and buckets right now," I said.

I then walked very briskly back the way we came, pushing the glass jar on a trolley ahead of me.

"Shopping Street station please!"

The shuttle we arrived in was still waiting as we walked out of the warehouse. It ignited into life and lurched away from the station as the lights of another shuttle were approaching from the rear.

Chapter Seventeen
The Return

The players and supporters in the tight changing room just stood looking at each other in silence, waiting for someone to make the first move. Nobody spoke and nobody moved.

"Grab them!" shouted somebody with authority suddenly.

"Get the other two jars," shouted the voice again and the crowd started brawling over the jars.

An Upper Molehampton player was on the floor frantically trying to defend his jar from two Lower Molehampton players, who were on top of him, scratching and clawing for the jar. A Lower Molehampton player was pinned against the wall with two Upper Molehampton players trying to prize the jar out of his hands. The jars swapped sides a few times and no team seemed to gain an advantage. Then one of the spectators, who was defending a glass, got pushed towards the door and spilled outside onto the ground. She got up and sped away, followed by both Upper and Lower players and spectators. The rest followed and the fighting continued outside in the open.

***

"This is Radio Molehampton bringing you live commentary from the first round, second leg of the County Cup. Yes, today is FC Lower Molehampton versus AFC Upper Molehampton. For those of you who have just joined us, we have to report on the strange events of today's game. The referee and some players from both teams ran off the pitch in the first half for no obvious reason and after a short break the match continued with a replacement referee, but short of players. We are now in the seventieth minute and the score is FC Lower Molehampton four, AFC Upper Molehampton one. Upper had taken an early lead but, following the disappearance of their goalkeeper and star striker, they have now fallen three goals behind. There isn't really a way back for them, so it can only be an exercise in damage limitation, even though the missing players have returned, but ran straight into the changing rooms followed by some spectators and haven't come out since. But wait. I can see somebody coming out. Yes, it's a Lower Molehampton supporter. She was trying to run away but has just been rugby tackled by an Upper supporter and goes tumbling. Now something which looks like a jar is rolling on the ground and somebody from Upper grabs it. No wait. His legs got kicked away by a Lower player. The jar is on the floor again and now Lower have it back. Everybody appears to be out of the changing rooms and fighting on the grass. Apparently over the glass jar. Oh yes, I can see it. But it seems that some more people have glass jars and that's what they are all fighting about. Why in the name of God are they all fighting over some ordinary glass jars? I have no idea. And by the way, Lower Molehampton has just scored their fifth goal. Ladies and gentlemen, it is now five goals to one. The match itself has turned into a side show."

***

"Colonel," shouted one of the Lower supporters. "Where are you, Colonel?"

"Over here."

The two voices who shouted back were standing next to each other and stopped fighting instantly.

"I'm Colonel Pickle," shouted one of the voices, an Upper Molehampton player. "And who are you may I ask?" he said looking at the other voice, a player from Lower Molehampton.

"I am Colonel Bacon," yelled the player back. "Come on Lower, let's get those glass jars."

302

The fighting continued but the Upper diet of canapés and champagne was obviously much better than pies and beer because the players and supporters of Lower Molehampton started to tire much sooner. Eventually Upper ran out winners and were in possession of all four glass jars. They surrounded the worn out blue team who were now all sitting on the floor in dejection.

"Keep hold of the traitor Colonel Bacon," shouted Colonel Pickle. "I will deal with him later."

Colonel Pickle instructed the four glass jar bearers to follow him and they ran off away from the pitch towards Mr Tinker's store.

***

The Kennedy brothers were hiding behind a tree observing the strange events at the changing rooms, and as soon as everybody had gone, quickly left their lair. Even though they found the room completely destroyed, there were things of value to be found. Smartphones, wallets, watches — you name it, it was all there and they stuffed everything into bags and smiled at each other.

"It's Christmas today," said one of the brothers. They couldn't believe their luck.

***

Meanwhile, back below the ground!

A man, a woman, a duck and a dog, all dressed in blue overalls, were pushing a trolley with a large bucket. The bucket was the type used for earth excavation in tunnelling operations and contained four shovels. The four of them were obviously a tunnelling crew but the only strange thing about them was their location. They were walking down the road with all of the shops, disco and pub, which was not the usual place for tunnelling crews to be hanging out. Normally they would have stood out but not today as the shopping street was deserted. They were all also wearing their tunnelling helmets which obscured their faces — but why would they be wearing them here? They approached the pub and went inside, pushing their trolley in front of them.

***

"The landlord please," I said to the dog working behind the bar, yelling at the top of my voice to be heard above the din.

"The landlord?" asked the dog back.

"Yes, the landlord!"

"One minute."

The dog disappeared though a door and returned just a moment later accompanied by a man who I instantly recognised. He was the father of the current inn keeper in Lower Molehampton.

"Yes?" he asked curtly.

"You must be Mr Pullmann, the landlord?"

"Yes. And who's asking."

"My name is Connor Jackson and I would like to talk to you privately."

"Can't you see that there is a football game on and we are a bit busy."

"Professor Wingnut instructed me to see you!" I whispered in his ear.

"Come on, come this way, and your friends too," said Mr Pullmann with his eyes wide open. He looked around to make sure nobody heard. He was obviously scared. "Quick with you now."

We pushed our trolley through the hatch and went into Mr Pullmann's back room. He closed the door and locked it. The bar was full to breaking point with everybody engrossed with the unusual events at today's football game. Normally a tunnelling crew with a trolley would have attracted everybody's attention, but not today. No. Nobody battered an eye lid as we entered the pub and we went into the back room of the bar completely unnoticed.

"What do you want from me?" said Mr Pullmann, with fear in his voice.

"Professor Wingnut told me he left an envelope with you and we had to collect it," I explained.

304

"Yes, that's true. I was wondering when somebody would come and get it. Where is the Professor now? I haven't seen him for ages."

Connor pointed to the large bucket. "He's inside."

"Well then, let the poor man out then," said Mr Pullmann, angrily.

"I think you should take a look for yourself," I said pointing to the bucket.

Mr Pullmann pulled the shovels apart and saw the jar. "Oh dear. When did this happen?"

"I'm not sure," I replied. "But probably quite soon after he gave you the envelope. He knew what was about to happen and wanted to ensure he left a plan in place. Look Mr Pullmann, we don't have much time and we are being hunted. Can you give me the envelope please?"

Mr Pullmann stretched up to the ceiling and removed a wooden panel. The envelope fell out and into his hands. "Here you go. I have no idea what is in it. The Professor just told me to give it to whoever asked for it."

I took the envelope and opened it. There was a sheet of paper and all it contained was a number written on it: 0458457889.

"What does it mean?" I asked.

"I have no idea. I have just seen it for the first time and the Professor didn't want to tell me about it. For my protection," he said.

"But surely he would have given the envelope's location away during interrogation?" asked Vanessa. "It doesn't make any sense to me."

"Usually yes, Vanessa, but his memory was stolen by the thieves presumably to find out exactly that. I am sure the Professor knew it was a matter of time and was trying to delay things. Or he had another plan and we are part of it," I said.

"Are you the thieves?" asked Mr Pullmann, suspiciously.

"Not exactly. Well maybe yes. I prefer to call us the keepers for the moment," I replied. "We are just trying to do the right thing and get out of here."

"So, what is the number, Connor? What could it mean?" asked Vanessa.

"Sorry, I have no idea."

"And now?" she carried on fearfully.

"Ease up, Vanessa. I know you want to get out of here. Just like me. Let's all think about what it could be. I'm as much in the dark as you are."

"A room number?" asked Ludwig.

"No," replied Mr Pullmann. "Room numbers down here don't look like that."

"A tunnel number?" asked Basil.

"Also no," Mr Pullmann answered.

"What about a molehill location," I suggested.

No," said Vanessa. "They look completely different," drawing on her experience from the observation molehills.

"I know," she said. "It looks more like a telephone number."

"You could well be correct, Vanessa. Let's call and find out, however, I don't have a phone. There's one in my office but it's too dangerous to go back. Also, I can only call numbers below the ground."

"I've got one," exclaimed Mr Pullmann.

"You've got a phone?" asked Vanessa, with surprise.

"And why not? I also have my contacts. What's more, my telephone can call out."

"How come you can call out?"

"Take a look around you. Do you really think I can organise all of this by just steeling things from above the ground? No. I need contacts. I'm a well-connected man I let you know."

"OK, let's make the call then," I said excitedly.

Mr Pullmann pulled a chair out of the way and took a blanket off a large object on the floor to reveal a rather large phone. Of course, the phone was a real size phone on the surface so twice our size. It was one of the old phones with a dial on the front.

"I haven't seen one of these for years. Did you find this in a museum?" I was amused.

Mr Pullmann just smiled at me.

The holes were rather large to me down here, so I had to put two of my fingers in the zero hole to dial the numbers. After I had dialled the last number the phone rang about six times until somebody picked up and answered.

"Eternity Projects. How can I help you?"

I paused, then nervously said, "Who am I speaking with?"

"As I said, this is Eternity Projects. My name is not important. I presume you want to come to the surface?" the mystery voice asked.

"Yes," I said nervously back.

"Go to molehill DG4563 and await further instructions."

"I need to write that down."

"No! Don't write anything down. Just remember DG4563," the mystery voice repeated and put the phone down.

"And?" said Vanessa, impatiently.

"I spoke to a man's voice from a company called Eternity Projects and he told me to go to molehill DG4563. You are the molehill expert Vanessa. Over to you!"

"OK. I need a map."

***

Colonel Pickle and a team of four men, all carefully holding a glass jar each, were standing in Mr Tinker's back room far below the ground.

"Have you seen any suspicious activity today Mr Tinker?" demanded the Colonel.

"Suspicious activity? Why yes. Today has been the busiest day I have ever experienced. I really can't understand why so many of you should be going on special operations when the football match is on. Even I am missing it. Unless of course you were all going to watch the match live," replied Mr Tinker.

"Has a group of four just come through? A man, a woman, a dog and a duck?" pressed the Colonel.

"Yes, sure. It really wasn't that long ago."

"Did they have a glass jar with them?" asked the Colonel quickly.

"No. Nothing."

"Are you sure, Mr Tinker?"

307

"A glass jar is rather large and I wouldn't have missed it. Believe me they had nothing with them."

"Did they say where they were going?"

"Yes, Colonel Pickle. They said something about returning to their rooms to rest."

"Mr Tinker. Call the police and on my order, they are to be hunted down, arrested and held for questioning."

"Yes, of course, Colonel. Whatever you say. Right away."

The Colonel turned around to the four men. "So, if Mr Jackson does not have the jar, he really must have left it for us as planned. The question now is which of these jars is the real Professor Wingnut? Let's go to the memory debriefing room and find out. Follow me men. We will deal with Mr Jackson and his team later. If his plan is to hide down here for as long as he can, it won't work."

Colonel Pickle and his four men left the store and Mr Tinker immediately called the police.

***

Cromwell was in a real state. He had run furiously after one of the groups following the goalkeeper then changed direction to follow the referee. It was all to no avail as he saw them all squeeze into the changing room and start fighting over the jars. He stayed around to witness the arrest of Colonel Bacon and his followers by the special ops and then decided it was probably best to make his way back to Mrs Kingston's handbag. He hadn't planned on going back at all and his plot was now in tatters. No professor, no coup and no power. It was only a matter of time before he was caught.

Cromwell trudged around the edge of the football pitch and back to the tent where the Upper supporters were still eating their canapés and drinking champagne, blissfully unaware of the score. He saw Mrs Kingston, found her bag under the table where she was sitting and climbed inside. It appeared she hadn't even noticed he had gone missing.

Cromwell decided it would be a good idea to call the Minster to inform him about what had happened. At least to warn him off. Cromwell unlocked the phone and dialled the number.

***

"Did you hear that, Felicity?"

"Not again. What did you hear now, Jemima? I really am getting worried about you."

"I heard voices coming from my bag again."

"Yes. I am sure," said Felicity, sarcastically. "And what did your voices say this time?"

"I am not one hundred percent sure, but I am certain I heard someone say that the Professor was in the hands of the government. Most strange."

"The government has the professor?" repeated Felicity back nervously.

"Yes, I am sure. Why have you gone so white, Felicity? Are you OK?"

***

Cleopatra had witnessed all of the events including the arrest of Colonel Bacon by the special ops and the return of Colonel Pickle with the jars. She made her way back to Trout Lane and went into the garden of number two. She quickly looked around to make sure nobody was looking and went into the greenhouse in the garden.

***

When Colonel Pickle's shuttle screeched to a halt at the warehouse station, he saw the dust of a departing shuttle in front of them.

"To the interrogation room, men," shouted the Colonel and marched briskly from the platform followed by four moles carrying their jars.

Inside the memory interrogation room the Colonel ordered one of the moles to put the jar on the table and align it with the device above it. He then pulled a switch and the room became pitch black followed by a blue light which shone from the device down towards the jar. The Colonel waited patiently for a person to appear in the jar but nothing happened.

"Damn. Wrong jar. Next!" he shouted. And again, and again.

It did not take long until it became obvious that all four jars did not contain a memory but were just plain, white goo, and a rather livid Colonel Pickle burst out of the interrogation room. "Nothing. Nothing. All of the jars are fake. Back to the shuttle everyone. We must find Mr Jackson and arrest him immediately. And who the hell has the Professor? This must be the work of Mr Jackson."

***

Colonel Bacon sat alone in a police interrogation room. He knew the game was up and was awaiting his fate. The door opened and Colonel Pickle came in.

"I never would have thought it. My colleague Colonel Bacon is a traitor. What the hell were you thinking of?"

"Don't sound so smug. You and your lot have had control down here long enough. Maybe our plan didn't work this time but it will next time. Your days are numbered believe me and also that of a planned economy. The way ahead is revolution and a free market economy."

"Oh, come now. You surely don't believe all that codswallop. There was a free market economy a long time ago, only to be replaced by a fair system where we are all the same — all equal. Nobody needs to worry about anything. The government can dictate everything."

"You can't convince me, Colonel Pickle. Now let's get this over with. What do you want?"

"You know what we want. Names. Give me names. Who are the conspirators? And most importantly, who is the traitor mole of a minister?"

"I am not giving you the name of the minister. And even if you tortured me, or read my memory, you will not find out the name of the minister for one very simple reason. I don't know who he is. The minster was a middle man between me and our true leader and our meetings were always in secret. I never saw him, just heard his voice."

"And your leader? You may as well tell me because I will find out when I read your memory."

"You are correct. His name is Cromwell. And you don't need to go and find him because he has already left us and is in a very safe place," said Colonel Bacon with a smirk. "He is being looked after very well by someone on the surface. A living person so you can do nothing about it and can't get to him."

"We'll see about that," said Colonel Pickle, sternly. "Guard!" he shouted.

"Yes sir," the guard sharply said entering the room.

"Take Colonel Bacon to the Food Factory and get rid of him. He will be much more use on a plate than down here. I will interrogate his memory later and I'm sure I will find out more names."

"And what about the others we arrested, Colonel?" asked the guard.

"Have their memories extracted then send them to the Food Factory too. Feed the lot to the humans. We'll soon see what they think of supply and demand in their free market economy."

***

Lower Molehampton was all but deserted, apart from outside Mr Tinker's store. A group of football players, the referee, Mr Mason and some supporters had just left the store looking rather confused.

"What are you doing here?" one of the supporters said to Upper Molehampton's number nine?"

"I have no idea. The last thing I can remember was scoring a goal and then bird poo landed on my head."

"Yeah, the same happened to me," said the confused looking referee.

311

"Hadn't we ought to go back and see what is happening? We've got a game to play," said Mr Mason. "And where's my dog?"

***

"And I thought nothing else could happen today, but I am so wrong," said the radio commentator. "From my vantage point I can see the group of missing players, supporters, Mr Mason and the referee running back towards the pitch. And here they are. The new referee has stopped the game and is now going across to speak to the referee who ran away. Upper's goalkeeper and the number nine are back too. Is the referee going to allow them back on? It certainly appears so. A decision has been made, yes, for sure. The first referee is back on and he is beckoning the players to come back on the pitch. It's eleven against eleven again. The score is FC Lower Molehampton six, AFC Upper Molehampton one. There's twenty minutes left and Upper have everything to do if they want to get to the next round.

***

The police were in their rooms listening intently to the radio, closely following the events at the football pitch and slow to react when they got the order. They were not too keen at all to go out and search for Mr Jackson and his team. In fact, it was the kind Mr Jackson who had arranged for radio coverage in their office. The first place they went to, their rooms, drew a blank. It was a large place, down here, to search and so they decided to split up and check their workplaces as they had no other information to go on. Where else should they go? One police team went to the memory warehouse, one to the tunnelling operations room, one to the store and one team to the food logistics in the hope of finding them. Nothing. And there was nobody to ask as everybody was watching the game.

***

The police on the surface weren't much quicker in reacting to all of the commotion and eventually mustered up some motivation and ran towards the changing rooms. Of course, the fighting had finished and all of the players and supporters had already dispersed. But it wasn't all bad news for the police as they caught the thieves in the act. Yes, the famous Kennedy brothers were caught with the loot in their hands and the police reports the following day were full of praise for their own good work.

***

A huge cheer erupted in the pub. This time from the Upper Molehampton supporters. They hadn't had much to cheer about for quite a while, but their team was now complete again and fighting to get back into the game. Upper had just scored a goal and again from their talisman number nine, all the while the tunnelling crew, still unnoticed, walked towards the door to leave.

Vanessa turned to us. "We have no choice but to go to my workplace at the Tunnelling Operations Centre and get a map. I know it's risky but it's the only place I know where we can find one."

"I agree. It will be risky and they are surely out there searching for us by now. But we have one advantage on our side and that is everybody down here is distracted by the game. There's only fifteen minutes left of the game and that is not enough time to go to your workplace, work out where we have to go and then actually get there. Time is not on our side," I said. "We must hurry and get out of here before the game is over and normality returns."

"Then we should get going," replied Vanessa, turning around to leave.

"I never thought I would hear myself saying this, but I really hope Upper Molehampton miraculously score four more goals and draw the game. Thirty minutes of extra time would help us greatly."

***

313

Another roar erupted from the pub and the screams of "Come on Upper" could be heard as Vanessa pushed the trolley in front of her through the thong of supporters out of the pub. We followed Vanessa along the shopping street to the station and jumped on a shuttle to the Tunnelling Operations Centre. The journey seemed to take an age because we were all nervous and scared but in reality, it only took a few minutes. When we arrived, the station was deserted, like most places today. No voices, no noises and nobody to be seen, and three more goals to score.

***

Nobody saw Cleopatra lurking in the shadows, watching their every move. It seemed as though she knew their moves in advance and was already waiting for them. She pricked her ears up and sniffed the air, smelling their frightened scent. She fleshed her teeth and waited, her beady eyes firmly fixed on the four friends as they walked towards Vanessa's place of work at a spanking pace.

"Best you don't come into the office. I know where the maps are so I only need a few moments," said Vanessa. "See you in a jiffy."

The others were nervously waiting in the dark tunnel for Vanessa to come back when they heard the whooshing and rattling sound of another shuttle approaching in the distance.

"Come on, Vanessa," Ludwig whispered to himself. "This waiting is making me crazy."

But today, time wasn't on their side regardless of how many more goals Upper Molehampton could score in the football game in the hope of sending the match into extra time. A group of policemen suddenly appeared in the tunnel and immediately spotted Connor, Ludwig and Basil. For them at least the game was up.

"There they are. Grab them," shouted the front mole policeman.

There was nowhere to run and within seconds they were surrounded and pushed against the wall.

"Got it," said Vanessa, coming out of the operations centre with a smile.

314

"And her too," ordered a mole sergeant. "We've got the lot. Inform Colonel Pickle immediately!"

"That won't be necessary," came a deep voice from the darkness.

"Who said that?" asked the sergeant.

Cleopatra emerged from the darkness, slowly with her teeth shining like daggers in the night. "I said that," came the gnarling reply.

"We are under orders from Colonel Pickle to arrest these criminals and take them back for interrogation."

"I know. And I am also under orders from Colonel Pickle to escort you all to a secret location along with Professor Wingnut," said Cleopatra, sternly.

"And where is Professor Wingnut?"

"I think you will find him in the bucket, Sergeant. But we don't have time to waste now so do as I say. I will take the lady and the rest of you will escort the others with the bucket. Now follow me."

Cleopatra grabbed Vanessa with her vice like jaws and sharp teeth, picking her up like a rag doll and bound off towards the station with a terrified Vanessa hanging in her mouth like a broken stick, still clutching the map in her hands. Connor wanted to move towards her but was forcefully pulled back by a policeman.

"Don't even think of it," said the policeman. "Now all of you, follow the dog!"

Two shuttles were waiting at the station. Cleopatra went straight to the front one and threw Vanessa in. "Sit there and don't move!" she said with a deep and dangerous growl.

"The rest of you squeeze into the other shuttle and follow us," Cleopatra ordered the driver.

Then she sped off into the tunnel with Vanessa cowering in her seat and the other shuttle following in a long and hair-raising journey through the dark. There were sharp lefts and sharp rights, abrupt descents and harsh climbs. There wasn't much space in the shuttle as we were all packed in like sardines, but still room enough for us to be thrown around and jolted violently.

"I don't know where we are, but we are definitely going up," I whispered to Ludwig.

"I know. Strange journey. It's certainly not the way we came here. I am completely disorientated," whispered back Ludwig. "I think this is game over for us. Jars and the Food Factory."

***

"And what a dramatic finish this is listeners. Upper Molehampton have managed to get back into this game and only need one more goal to draw and send it into extra time. We are in injury time now and Upper are attacking like mad with Lower defending for their lives. And what's that on the pitch? A molehill has just popped up. And another. Oh my goodness, they are popping up everywhere. But Upper's number nine has the ball and is dribbling around the molehills with great skill. Other players are tripping over though. And now it's only a defender stopping number nine from being clear through on goal. This is an exciting climax listeners. The referee is looking at his watch. Surely, he must blow the end of the game soon. The defender is going in for the tackle to stop number nine but, no, it can't be true. He fell over a molehill that has just burst through directly in front of him. Now, number nine is lining up his shot. He only has the goalkeeper to beat. Shoots. And it's in. Unbelievable. What a finish. The referee has whistled for full time and it's over. Upper have come back from five goals behind to draw the game. A thrilling six goal draw listeners and you must stay tuned for another exciting thirty minutes of football."

***

The shuttles both came to a customary dusty landing in the tunnel. There were no signs and no lights. It was pitch black. But then the sound of a button being pressed was followed by a dull light emitting from a weak light bulb hanging from a cable shoddily attached to the roof of the tunnel.

"We are here!" exclaimed Cleopatra.

316

"But here's nothing," commented the sergeant.

Cleopatra went across to the wall ignoring the comment and brushed away some earth with her paws, revealing a small wooden door.

"This is our new interrogation cell," said Cleopatra with a snarl. "Dark, damp and small. We will have them talking in no time. Damn criminals! Now get them in and guard the door. Everyone but the girl. She's mine. My bargaining chip and for me to ransom," she ordered the sergeant.

"Where is this place?" demanded the sergeant. "I'm completely lost."

"You don't need to know our location. And you had better never mention this place to anyone or you will end up on a plate like they soon will," she said menacingly, putting fear into the policeman's eyes.

Cleopatra then turned towards the first shuttle driver. "Leave now and bring Colonel Pickle back here. Tell him I have the girl as instructed and will take her to a safe place to enjoy. I'm hungry!"

Vanessa was still cowering on the floor directly next to Cleopatra, shaking in fear, when she was picked up again and thrown into the shuttle speeding off into the darkness once more.

***

"Colonel Pickle," shouted out the driver.

"Yes, over here. What is it?"

"They've been found along with the professor. Cleopatra has the girl and the rest are locked up in a very safe place. They won't be able to escape from this place," said the driver.

"And where is this safe place?"

"Cleopatra instructed me to collect you and take you there."

"Cleopatra cannot order me around. I'm the Colonel. Not Cleopatra. However, she does have the four criminals and at last we have the professor back, so I suppose I will make an exception."

***

"Are you OK?" asked Cleopatra looking at Vanessa with a surprisingly kind face.

"What did you just ask me?"

"I asked if you were OK."

"And why would you be interested in my well-being when you want to rip me to pieces?"

"Oh no. That was all a show."

"A show? Grabbing me with your teeth doesn't feel like a show. Anyway, a show for who?"

"For the police. I needed them to believe that I was following the Colonel's orders to make him come here too. It's all part of my plan, and your plan too of course."

"My plan and your plan? I didn't know we had a mutual plan!"

"No you don't, and neither does Mr Jackson, but he will soon. I need you to trust me and do as I say, which I can understand is hard for you at the moment. Please believe me — I am on your side."

"On my side? I can't quite work that one out but then again, nothing surprises me anymore after today's events. Well, I don't see I have much of a choice, do I?" announced Vanessa.

"No. Not really. We have to collect something and I need your help," explained Cleopatra, as their shuttle screeched to a halt in a non-descript station. "Follow me now. It's not far."

They left the station and walked along a very dimly lit tunnel. It was a place not often visited and must have been well away from the hustle and bustle of the rest of the mole world. After they had turned left into a much smaller tunnel they stopped at some wooden boards covered in dirt and pulled them out of the way revealing yet another tunnel. It was also quite dark but freshly dug and Vanessa followed Cleopatra to the end of the tunnel just being able to see her.

"Here we are," Cleopatra whispered in a secretive way. She started digging furiously in the ground spitting out earth all over Vanessa and in no time had dug out a small brown bottle.

"What's this?"

"This, young lady, is your way out of here."

"My way out?"

"Yes, and I need you because I can't open the bottle myself. Open the bottle please, take the tablets out and put them in your pocket. All of the tablets but one."

Vanessa was excited and puzzled at the same time but did what Cleopatra asked. "And now?"

"And now we will go back to the others and hopefully Colonel Pickle will be waiting for us."

"Colonel Pickle? Surely, he is the last person we want on our heels. He wants to arrest us!"

"He does but I have a different plan for him."

***

Colonel Pickle arrived at the station and shook himself off. He was dusty and dishevelled after the bumpy ride to this remote location he had never been to. And very impatient.

"Cleopatra," he called out.

"Sir, Colonel Pickle. Down here," came a voice from down the tunnel.

Colonel Pickle followed the voice and found a police sergeant and three policemen.

"Where is Cleopatra?" demanded the Colonel.

"She will be here shortly. She left with the young girl clamped between her teeth to collect something. She said something about a bargaining chip and that you would know why she had the girl. Is that correct?"

"Yes, that's correct. I ordered her to take care of the girl in case we got tricked. And the criminals? Where are they?" asked the Colonel.

The sergeant nodded in the direction of the wooden door. "In there Colonel."

"But I was asked to come and see Cleopatra. She should be here."

"I am," a voice said from behind them as Cleopatra walked around the corner with a terrified looking Vanessa in front of her.

"Where have you been, Cleopatra?" asked the Colonel irritably.

"Just had to get something which will interest you."

Cleopatra looked at the sergeant. "You may leave now. We will handle this."

"But we will need them," said the Colonel firmly.

"No. We don't need them Colonel. What we need is secrecy and the less they know the better it is. Especially for them!" said Cleopatra menacingly and flashed her teeth at the policemen.

"Well, if you say so. You are normally right in such matters," Colonel Pickle gave in.

"We saw nothing and we don't know anything," spat out one of the policemen in fear before they all hastened back down the tunnel and out of sight of Cleopatra and the Colonel.

Cleopatra waited until the shuttle had left the station. "Let's go in and see the criminals, shall we?"

The dull light from the corridor shining through the open door was enough to expose Connor, Ludwig and Basil sitting on a dirty and damp floor. They shielded their eyes from the light now bursting into their dark room. Well, it wasn't really a room — it was more of a hole in the wall made of bare mud. Cleopatra and the Colonel stood in the doorway.

"And now we have everybody and most importantly the Professor. The President will be happy. Colonel Bacon has been unearthed as the mole and it won't be long until I find out the location of the ringleader, Cromwell and his accomplice on the surface. He hasn't been acting alone but has received help and the only question is from who. And now you lot. We will take the professor for interrogation to make sure it is really him. This time you will all be locked in here and will stay here until I am ready for you. Cleopatra will stand guard."

"No," Cleopatra firmly stated.

"What did you just say?" retorted the Colonel angrily.

"I said no. This is not what we are going to do. Vanessa. Take out the tablets from your pocket and give one to each of your friends. Keep one yourself. Then put the bottle on the floor in front of you."

The Colonel moved to intervene but a snarl from Cleopatra was enough to stop him in his tracks. Vanessa dealt out the tablets with Connor, Ludwig and Basil looking on in amazement.

"Now hold on here. I'm the Colonel and I give the orders around here."

"Maybe you do, but you are not part of our plan. However, we do need you, that is the reason you are here."

"Can someone please tell me what is going on?" I asked.

"Yes, Mr Jackson. These are the only remaining tablets from Professor Wingnut's Eternity Project. No other tablets exist and no more can be made. The only person who knows how to make them is the Professor here. This is the reason why everybody wants to get hold of him."

"And what exactly are these tablets for?" I asked.

"These are Professor Wingnut's eternity tablets. With only one tablet you can return to your former life. Not only that but you can also move from above the ground to below the ground in the same form. This was the secret project the professor was working on. But his technology is so dangerous, it really can't fall into the wrong hands. And when I say the wrong hands I mean Colonel Bacon's gang who tried to steal it. And also the President. The professor was working on other secret projects as well and his knowledge must be kept secret and hidden."

"Can't you just destroy his memory," I asked.

"No, it is impossible for memories to be destroyed. As you already know moles have been given the task of administering the memories but in the last few years they have become too powerful and started, amongst other things, special operation missions. Having the professor's knowledge would give them unrivalled power and that we cannot allow."

"This is going too far," said the Colonel. "Cleopatra, you are a member of Special Operations and you trialled the first eternity tablet. Where is your loyalty now?"

"Yes I did and I am grateful for the chance you gave me. This is why I asked you here — to give you a chance like you did with me. I trialled the tablet and have been going into both worlds as myself over the last few weeks and I can say the tablet worked just fine with no side effects. But we have a problem."

"And what is that?" asked the Colonel.

"Seven tablets were produced and thankfully there weren't any ingredients left to produce any more. One tablet was stolen though, which prompted the Professor into taking urgent action. He suspected the remaining tablets would end up with the wrong people. That's why he gave me one and the remaining five in this bottle were removed from the laboratory. Knowing he would soon be put in a jar, he hid them in a secret place. He also knew that his memory would be dangerous for anyone who interrogated him as it would lead them directly to the bottle. It was really just a matter who would interrogate him first. So the Professor entrusted me to deploy delaying tactics to ensure that his memory and the bottle ended up with the right people. It was me who hid the bottle in the secret place which an interrogator could not have discovered. For this to happen they would have had to decommission me and interrogate my memory. The question was who would be first to get to the Professor's memory? Colonel Bacon or you? But then we had the theft and the unexpected arrival of Mr Jackson. The mole who stole the tablet is on the surface and has orchestrated everything from there. He is up to no good and he is most certainly not acting alone."

"Cromwell?" asked the Colonel.

"Yes. Cromwell. He arranged to have the professor stolen and taken to the surface and I am sure he couldn't have managed this without help from somebody above."

"And who could this be? I assume it is a human?" asked the Colonel.

"Unfortunately, I have never been able to work out who is conspiring with Cromwell, but it must be somebody well-connected. I can only agree with you that it must be a human. I've been working for both sides in an effort to find out who is on what side and who can be trusted, and to make sure that nobody got hold of the professor. When Mr Jackson came on the scene, I knew exactly what had to be done."

"And what's that?" demanded the Colonel.

"That Mr Jackson will be the keeper of the Professor and his memory. As it cannot be destroyed it must go somewhere and I have decided this is the best option. This is our plan and I know the Professor would agree with me."

"What did you just say?" I asked.

"Yes, you Mr Jackson. You will return to the surface with your friends and you will keep the Professor in a safe place. You, and your friends, are being entrusted with the safekeeping of the jar so nobody can use the technology."

"But how will you stop Colonel Pickle, the President, Cromwell or his accomplices sending Special Operation teams to go and steal it back?" I asked. "This will never end and we will be permanently hunted all of our lives."

"I can't guarantee that for sure but what is certain is that Professor Wingnut can't stay down here to be interrogated or fall into the wrong hands. This dangerous technology must remain locked in the glass and away from harm, never to be used by the wrong people. Also, the tablets must be used so there are no more left and then there is no trace," explained Cleopatra.

"I understand that. But there is one more tablet in the jar," I said.

"Yes. And that is for Colonel Pickle. That is why he is here."

"For me?" asked the Colonel, now unsure of his own authority.

"Yes, for you. There is only one tablet remaining and I am giving it to you. I could destroy it but I believe you could put it to better use. Only those of us in this room now know about the tablets and the Professor. All you have to do is keep the tablet for yourself and experience eternity if you so wish. Give it away and you won't. So I think that is a good deal to buy your silence. I am sure you will come up with a good story to present to the President. The Eternity Project and the Professor's technology ends here in this room with us."

"That is treason, Cleopatra," said the Colonel.

"No, it's a good offer. Eternity or not Colonel. Either you are in on this and can have an eternity tablet or I will destroy it in front of your eyes. What's it to be?"

Without waiting for the Colonel to answer, Cleopatra looked at Vanessa and me. "Get up and scrape the earth away from the wall over there and remove the wooden board. You will find a very narrow tunnel, only large enough for you to crawl through. Now, take your tablets!"

"Eternity," replied the Colonel resolutely.

"Then Colonel, take it and I wish you luck!"

After the Colonel had left with the bottle, and without uttering another word as he headed back down the tunnel to the station, Cleopatra made sure we would also be on our way.

"OK, have you all taken your tablets?" asked Cleopatra.

"Yes, but I can't feel any effects," remarked Basil anxiously. "Are you sure they work?"

"Me neither," added Ludwig.

"No you won't straight away. You need to get to the other side first. There you will find a switch. Press it and just sit down. It will take about thirty minutes to expand back to your original size. Please be patient and wait until the process is fully over."

"How will we know when it is over?" asked Vanessa.

"When you have regained your full size and functions. Oh, and you humans might also find you have an additional function," said Cleopatra, winking at us. "Now off you go. I've got a few loose ends to tie up out down here so don't wait for me."

"What loose ends?"

"Oh, Colonel Bacon and his friends. They have been assigned to the Food Factory and I want to make sure it happens. With them gone all traces of this story will disappear."

"But what about their memories?" I asked.

"Yes, their memories! They have to be stored down here, I am afraid there is no other way but I will make sure they are so well hidden that nobody can ever find them."

With that I turned around, stooped down into the narrow tunnel and crawled inside with my friends right behind me. We had had many scary experiences in the last few weeks, but this was the most harrowing; not knowing where we were or if we had been tricked and would be locked in here. The tunnel was pitch black and I couldn't even see the hands in front of my face. I had to feel my way with my hands, and even though the darkness was disorientating I knew we were going up and quite steep as well. And just as I was about to start panicking, my head hit a hard object. I felt around to find out if the tunnel went in a different direction. But it didn't. It was blocked by something hard and heavy, so I carefully started pushing and revealed a sharp stab of daylight. I squinted as I pushed my way through to the surface, desperate to escape the claustrophobic tunnel.

Vanessa was the last one to come out of the tunnel after Ludwig and Basil and we were now standing in a greenhouse. We could just make out a house and a garden through the milky windows.

"Where is the switch?"

"Here it is," said Vanessa, pointing to a switch on a metal upright.

"Better pull it then," I said quickly.

A white gas was ejected from a hose on the ceiling and in no time the greenhouse was filled with a smoky vapour. We put the flower pot back over the hole, the hard object I encountered on our way out, and sat down to wait for the gas to do its business.

"Connor."

"Yes, Vanessa." I said, coughing a little.

"Was all of this part of your plan?"

"Most of it. But certainly not being captured and the last part with the Colonel and Cleopatra. I really had no idea she was on our side the whole time."

"I think we are now safe, so you have time to tell us everything you know," said Basil.

I then went on to explain in detail about the events in my garden all those weeks ago and how I came into possession of a jar, containing a white fluid and the name 'Professor Wingnut' written on a plaster. I told them about the kidnapping and the van and then the next thing I knew I was being set free from a box and told I was in transition. And the rest you know. Well, most of it anyhow."

"And you kept the jar in your house not knowing what it was?" asked Ludwig.

"Yes, exactly. I had no idea what it was. How could I? But nevertheless the jar intrigued me so much that I decided to take it to work. And when mysterious things started happening my gut feeling told me it had something to do with the jar. Naturally I didn't tell anyone it was in my office and I kept that a secret down here too. I didn't have a plan at the beginning but I kind of thought it was best if only I knew the real location and everybody else thought it was in another. So, when I was kidnapped the jar was in my office, but everybody thought it was in my house the whole time, including you. If I had been put in a jar as well, they would have found out about the real location. To make sure that wouldn't happen I made them believe that I didn't know where the jar was but that I was also the only person who could get it back, with your help of course. I played for time."

"So, we got it back from your work place but we never knew we were doing it?" asked Vanessa.

"Exactly. Can you remember the sock in the tube when we left my office? Well, the jar was in there along with some sophisticated listening equipment. When Basil and I got the equipment, I took a blue bag with me and put the jar in without Basil noticing and then covered it with other stuff. I then took the jar to the memory warehouse in a place nobody would find it."

"So the Professor was back below the ground the whole time and only you knew. Wasn't that dangerous?" asked Vanessa.

"Yes. And no. It was the last place they would think of looking for him. They had no idea he wasn't in my house and that was exactly what I wanted them to believe. I needed time to collect information and come up with a plan."

"But how did you get all of the information?" asked Basil.

"That was actually not too difficult. I renamed the Professor's jar with another name and interrogated him. Remember that was my job down there and was kind of my job up here too. But I didn't record the information he gave me — that would have been far too dangerous. The Professor told me all about his secret programme and how it was imperative that the moles didn't get hold of his technology. He knew they would then have power too dangerous for their own good. He worked on the Eternity Project with two colleagues; Mrs Hullington and Mr Cromwell. Mrs Hullington knew too much and was deactivated by Mr Cromwell, who was, or is, a political officer. Obviously a very dubious one. His plan was to steal the Professor along with his technology. So he had the Professor deactivated and took one of the tablets. Apparently, he is not a scientific person and needs the Professor's knowledge to fulfil his plan."

"But there's something I don't understand," quizzed Vanessa. "Why didn't the Professor take one of his own tablets and escape?"

"I asked exactly that question when I interrogated his memory. He did contemplate it but then knew he would be hunted the whole of his life, so he decided to wait for the inevitable decommissioning. He really didn't want to be involved in this anymore. His intelligence and knowledge were being abused and he wanted an end to it all."

"That I can understand," replied Vanessa.

"So how did you find out who was on what side?" asked Ludwig.

"I listened to them!" I said.

"And how did you do that?" asked Ludwig.

"Easy. When we went to my office to get the equipment to televise the football game, I also collected eavesdropping equipment which I have been happily using ever since. I sat in my room in the evenings and also took it to work and listened to the people I distrusted. It wasn't too difficult and nobody suspected the equipment I had wasn't for the football game. I knew that Cromwell was the lynchpin in all of this but never found out who his two accomplices were. There's a mystery minister down there and there must be a person on the surface helping him."

"But, Connor, why did you go through with the whole mission today? Going to your house, all of the glass jars, the football game and so on. You knew that it was not in your house?" asked Ludwig. "I really don't understand what it was all for."

"That's the clever bit, Ludwig," I explained. "After speaking to the Professor I knew we needed to get to the pub unnoticed to find the information to escape. So I worked out that if I could confuse them enough and distract them that would give us exactly that chance. Also, by coming up with a plan to get the equipment from my work place gave me the chance to get the professor back down here. It kind of didn't work perfectly but it was the only way I could think of. The football game was the perfect cover for this escape plan and probably our only chance of getting our lives back."

"Did you know about Cleopatra's role and the tablets?" asked Basil.

"The tablets no, but I was a little suspicious of Cleopatra's role. The Professor told me when I interrogated him to go to the pub and find out where we had to go next to escape. I think Cleopatra was the security mechanism in the whole plan. If somebody else would have gotten to the pub, then Cleopatra could easily have stalled them and kept the location of the tablets a secret. Cleopatra would then have escaped to the surface and only she would have known the location. However, Cleopatra played both sides against each other."

"So we were used?" asked Basil.

"Kind of. Cleopatra obviously wanted to make sure that the Professor's memory ended up with somebody she could trust and that the tablets were taken care of. I was her solution and by default all of you too. Thankfully there was luck on our side, namely Cleopatra and the extra time in the football match of course."

"Talking about that. I wonder what the score is?" said Vanessa.

***

"Listeners, this is the tensest and most thrilling finish I can remember in my time as a football commentator. The match finished six goals to six and there is no other way to decide this cup tie than a penalty shootout. We are now right at the end of it and both teams have scored three and missed one with only one penalty remaining each. Upper Molehampton's number nine is stepping up to take the penalty. He is placing the ball on the penalty spot and walking back for a long run up. Will he convert it? And he's off. No, he's missed it. A molehill suddenly sprouted up right behind the ball as he was running up to take it. Unbelievable scenes and another strange incident. The ball hit the molehill, flew high above the goal and landed in a field behind. Now number eight is stepping up to take Lower's last penalty and also elects to have a long run up. And he starts his run. If he scores this one, then Lower are in the next round. A molehill pops up and he swerves out of the way. Then he jumps over another molehill and kicks the ball and… it's in! It's over. Lower Molehampton are in the next round.

***

"Just look at you, Vanessa. You are growing and growing and, oh my, you are much bigger than me," exclaimed Basil.

"You're right. The tablets and whatever this gas is must be working. I'm growing back into my original size again. Cool. And you too, Connor."

"Thank goodness this is working because I was actually wondering if this was just some kind of sick joke. But then again, it worked for Cleopatra. She has been going up and down changing her size all the time."

"Oh look, Basil, you are so small," said Ludwig, with a laugh. "Do you want to play?"

"Very funny and the answer is no. Ducks don't play with dogs."

Suddenly, the gas abruptly stopped being emitted from the pipes and after a while we were able to make out the garden and the house again through the opaque windows.

"And now?" asked Basil.

"No idea," I said. "I suppose we should now leave."

"But where are we?" asked a puzzled looking Vanessa.

"Again, no idea. Maybe we should not attract too much attention and all leave one by one. Basil you go first, then Vanessa, then Ludwig and I will go last."

"So, is this the end of our adventure? Are we real again? Are we alive?" asked Vanessa, completely taken aback about this new situation.

"It appears so. But is this the end? Somehow, I don't think so and I am sure we will all meet up again. You never know, as the

329

keeper of the Professor's memory I might just need to come back and ask for your assistance. For you and I, Vanessa, that shouldn't be a problem as we can see each other in our villages."

"Oh you think so. You're from Lower!" she said sarcastically but with a smile.

"But you have to get fish and chips from somewhere. I can't recall Upper selling such things," I added jokingly.

"And you, Ludwig? I will come and visit Farmer Rye and see you there but I'm not sure if we can still talk to each other once we leave this greenhouse — I've never seen a talking dog before. Well not before all of this happened I have to add," I added smiling at him.

"A talking dog. Now let me tell you something, Connor. You may believe that dogs cannot talk and maybe that is because you don't understand our language but let me tell you that we can understand all animal languages, including yours," said Ludwig, wagging his tail in obvious delight.

"And you, Basil? It might be a little more difficult to tell you apart from other ducks," I asked.

"Well, like Ludwig, I can understand all languages and I can certainly differentiate between ducks. It appears we can do more than land on a plate for you to eat. Or for you to play with," said Basil, looking at Ludwig. "You can find me in the roots under the old willow tree. Ludwig can find me if you can't talk to animals. We certainly understand you."

"What do you intend to do with the professor's jar?" asked Ludwig.

"Oh, no need to worry about that. I've already got a very safe place for that."

"So, who's the memory thief now?" asked Vanessa, with a smile.

"I prefer the word keeper," I said winking at Vanessa. "And I can now answer another question."

"What's that?" asked Ludwig.

"Look, we can all talk to each other even though we have returned to our normal selves. Look, Vanessa, you and I can talk to animals. This must be the additional function Cleopatra mentioned."

"Welcome to our world," said Basil.

"OK, off you go now, Basil. I'll open the door and make sure it's safe."

Chapter Eighteen
Normality

The young boy was cycling around outside a house experimenting with different skids on the grit driveway. He cycled as fast as he could down the driveway and suddenly braked hard as he reacted to a rather large, low flying bird with a green head shooting out from his garden and directly towards him. The front wheel locked and the rear lifted from the ground. He pressed against the handlebars to keep himself from going over the top and the bicycle under control. The bird flew low from the back garden and gained height as soon as it spotted the boy. It just managed to climb enough to miss his head and then circled above the garden it had come from. The young boy threw his bicycle to the ground and stared up towards the bird.

"Wow, that was close," he said, smiling mischievously. Then he pulled out a catapult from the side pocket of his trousers, picked up a stone from the driveway, turned towards the bird and took aim.

"And just what do you think you are doing," shouted a young woman.

The boy jumped in fright, let go of the sling by accident and dropped the catapult on the floor. The stone flew off in a completely different direction than its intended target. But it did find a target as the sound of breaking glass could be heard somewhere in the street.

The young woman came out of the garden from where the bird had just come from and walked up the driveway. "Don't let me catch you doing that again," she said sternly, looking at him and walking off up the road.

"And why were you in my garden," cried out the boy after her.

She didn't reply.

The boy scratched his head and stooped down to pick up his catapult. To his amazement a large brown dog beat him to it before he could reach it. The dog came bounding out of the garden, up the driveway, picked up the catapult and ran off down the street.

"What is going on today?" said the boy aloud to himself.

"Who on hell did that," shouted a man coming out of his house.

"Oooops, I'm in trouble now!"

"Yes, you are," said a voice behind him.

The boy spun around and saw a man walking towards him from the garden and up the driveway.

"Yes, Earl. You are most certainly in trouble with Mr Lawnsworthy."

"Mr Jackson. What are you doing here and why are you coming out of my garden? People were saying that something had happened to you and that you were missing."

"Long story, Earl. I might tell it to you one day," I said and walked off towards the angrily approaching Mr Lawnsworthy.

"Hello there, Mr Lawnsworthy. Nice to see you again. I don't suppose I could have my key, could I? Seemed to have misplaced mine," I asked cheerfully.

"Your key. I am sorry I don't have it any more!" he said at his wits end!

"Why not? What happened to it?"

"Ask the referee!" he answered curtly.

"The referee. What do you mean?" I asked, already knowing the answer.

"Or maybe ask Sergeant Dawson. He's on his way here now," he said looking angrily at young Earl.

"Oh look, Mr Jackson. Your front door is open," said Earl, excitedly pointing at my door. "It must have remained open after all of the funny goings on this afternoon."

I smiled and walked off in the direction of my house.

***

I was sitting in my bedroom, my favourite place by the way, taking in the beautiful view of the valley and certainly enjoying sitting here. I was back on the surface and amazingly alive again. The late autumn sun accompanied by cold air threw a warm golden light over the two villages with a light haze floating over the river. I looked past the ferry crossing the river and saw Farmer Rye's old stone farmhouse and the old willow tree hanging over the river. I then adjusted my gaze right below me to Trout Lane. All of the front gardens were littered with the remains of old molehills, apart from Mr Lawnsworthy's garden. In fact, he was now proudly standing in his driveway, with a look of victory on his face, inspecting his nice new green lawn. He had a company remove the destroyed lawn from his front garden, concreted it over and then had artificial grass laid. He would not suffer from molehills here ever again. On the other side of the street Earl was playing with his bicycle. And of course I could see the greenhouse in his garden, which had strangely appeared shortly before all of these strange events began some time ago.

It had been a hectic time after returning and quite difficult explaining all of the strange events involved around my disappearance. I was helped along by a letter in a blank envelope I found in my post box. The letter itself was from the government and looked very official and genuine. It explained to whoever wanted to know that I was seconded on a government mission and that if anyone had any questions they should call the number written in the letter head. Nothing could surprise me anymore.

Sergeant Dawson came calling on me just as soon as he learnt I was back and we went to the station together, where he had the intention of questioning me very intensively, but I thought it best to just hand over the letter right at the beginning of the questioning. He read the letter intently and looked at me suspiciously. It was clear that he didn't believe a thing and decided to call the number. I had no idea what he was told, or who the voice was, but he looked ever so serious and nodded profusely during the course of the call. After putting the phone down he closed my file, told me he had no further questions and that I was free to go. There were obviously powers above me working in my favour but I had no idea who they were. It seemed Eternity Projects and Cleopatra had a long reach.

Just as soon as I arrived home, the doorbell rang and my boss, Jemima Kingston, was standing there looking rather agitated. She didn't seem overly pleased to see me, so without further ado I handed her my letter as I wasn't willing to enter into a conversation with her. She looked at me with the same suspicion Sergeant Dawson had done before and reached for her mobile phone. A dog's head briefly appeared over the edge of her handbag and I had the feeling it gave me a rather angry gaze before it disappeared back into the safety of the bag.

Mrs Kingston called the number and again I had no idea with whom she spoke. All I know is that she also looked ever so serious, nodded and then angrily stuffed her phone back in her bag and told me she expected me back at work on Monday morning. She turned her back on me and walked off down my driveway in a huff.

The events surrounding the football match had now passed into history, probably into local folklore too, and the village had returned to normality. I was sure the strange events at the football pitch would dominate all conversations in both Lower and Upper Molehampton for years to come. For me, well I was just happy to be back home, but I did have a certain amount of sorting out to do as my house was still a mess following the events of the kidnapping.

Prior to my adventure, I believed only in our physical state, here one moment and then gone the next, leaving no trace of our existence apart from dust and bones and the memories of others we leave behind. All those memories and all of our stories and life experiences lost, disappearing with us along with our physical presence. And, to be honest that would be such a shame, were it to be true of course.

I sat there contemplating about life and how, contrary to my former beliefs, it never really ends. Our memories are not gone like a puff of smoke, as most think, but are stored for eternity well below the ground under the administration of the moles. That I now knew. And the moles?

Well, the moles have an important role in the running of the world, or at least the Molehamptons. They are not just blind creatures digging tunnels and making molehills to annoy everyone. Quite the contrary. The moles store and administer all the memories that would otherwise be lost, and to make space, they bring the excavated earth to the surface. What a simple explanation this is for all of the molehills we see everywhere. Yes, and I have just experienced something most unbelievable which proves that life never really ends. Our stories and experiences are open books, which are never finished.

Like this story is not over, as stories never are. There was still one final job to be done.

But enough of me. What about my friends? I am sure they also have their stories to tell too!

***

The elegant duck with the green head and a bright yellow beak was enjoying the early morning sun on the river. It was a cold morning and winter was fast approaching but this did not deter the duck from enjoying its natural habitat. It swam out from the roots of the old willow tree and set course for the middle of the river and just stayed there for some time as though taking in the lovely surroundings after a long absence. The duck dipped its head into the water to feed, then flapped its wings to lift away from the surface, flew majestically just above the surface of the river towards the ferry, which was crossing the river. There was only one car on the ferry and a young woman next to it looking towards the old willow tree.

Farmer Rye was a happy man and so was his dog, Ludwig, who was frantically wagging its tail and jumping up to Mr Rye at every opportunity. Ludwig had just returned from out of the blue after disappearing some time ago but thankfully he was in good condition and had been well fed by somebody. If only Farmer Rye could speak to the dog and find out where he had been over the last few weeks. If only! The dog sat on the driveway to the farmhouse obviously enjoying the early morning sun, looking towards the old willow tree next to the river. He could see the duck majestically flying above the surface of the river towards the ferry with a young woman standing next to a car.

Vanessa's reappearance caused obvious glee in the Forsythe-Twyke household. Her disappearance was not so difficult to explain as her parents were too busy with their business to worry about where she had been. A simple story of a few weeks in the seclusion of a Buddhist temple in Nepal was enough to deflect any further interest or questioning and, according to her family, would have been typical of her behaviour. She really needed some fish and chips but, not wanting to miss the last ferry, decided to cross the river early in the morning. She was standing next to her car, taking in the crisp air and enjoying the view of the river. She could clearly see the roof of Farmer Rye's farmhouse, the old willow tree bending over the river and a duck flying just above the surface of the river in her direction.

***

"What about the Professor, Colonel Pickle?" asked the President. They were again alone in the conference room.

"The professor is back down here and safe and sound in a new high security memory storage area. No need to worry, Mr President. Everything is in order and back to what it should be," said the Colonel, lying to the President.

"I didn't expect anything else from you Colonel. You are a good and loyal man. What about the memory thieves? What can you tell me about them?"

"The real culprit was Colonel Bacon. He double crossed us and arranged for the Professor to be stolen in the first place. But we captured him along with his fellow conspirators. All of them have been decommissioned and sent to the Food Factory. We don't need to worry about them again. Our mole amongst moles has been unearthed."

"And what about Mr Jackson and his friends? He tried to double cross you too," said the President.

"Oh that. That was part of our plan to uncover the conspirators," said the Colonel, lying again.

"Yes, very good, Colonel. But what about Mr Jackson and his friends? They know too much."

"I have had them all decommissioned like we discussed. In fact, everyone involved in the events of the Professor's theft have been rounded up and decommissioned," said the Colonel, still lying. "Only you and I know the true events and names. All of the memories are together with the Professor in the high security storage and only I know the location. Don't worry Mr President, there are no loose ends. Even the policemen who captured Mr Jackson have been decommissioned."

"And the Eternity Project?" asked the President.

"The project was officially closed with the decommissioning of the Professor. The secret remains in his jar." This time the Colonel wasn't lying but even he didn't know the whole truth.

"And you are sure you are the only person who knows of its whereabouts?" demanded the President. "We will soon need the memory again to find out everything the Professor knows."

"Quite sure, Mr President. The secret is safe with me."

"And Cleopatra? What of her?"

"Also decommissioned," said the Colonel, feeling the pill bottle in his pocket. The President didn't know about the pills as even Cromwell kept that secret from him. Apparently, there was a lot the President was not told.

***

The phone rang in an office. "Mrs Farrow speaking."

"Clementine, darling. Felicity Forsythe-Twyke here. We must meet as soon as possible. We need another plan."

"Since when have you called me Clementine?"

***

The phone rang in a handbag.

"Mrs Kingston speaking."

"Jemima dear. Felicity. We must meet as soon as possible. You have something I would like to borrow."

***

The first thing I did after clearing up my house was to have a safe installed in my bedroom wall. It was made of steel and concreted into the wall with a very loud alarm to deter any would be intruders. Professor Wingnut was now safe and sound resting in his jar in this very dark and secure place. The key was in an even safer place.

Cleopatra was also enjoying the early morning sun as she lay fully alert on the pathway leading to number three Trout Lane, guarding the house as though her life depended on it. She snarled and growled at every moving object. Around her neck was a think black leather collar with a small wooden barrel hanging below her snout. The barrel contained a key and nobody was going to get that in a hurry.

And what about the final job? Surely you must have asked yourself about that. Well, this job in question was the memory stick which contained the conversations I recorded and you might remember that I buried it in Mr Lawnsworthy's garden on the night of my kidnapping. After that the last known place was in the front pocket of Mr Lawnsworthy's garden overalls, which was observed by Vanessa when she was on her observing duties. The overalls were kept in his garden shed. This was a job for Cleopatra! I needed to have the memory stick back.

And with regard to molehills, I certainly had a different opinion about them now and of course I still had some in my garden. Who didn't? Most people would flatten them but no, not me, not anymore. I would leave small items next to them at night time and look in delight the next day to see they were gone. I even left all of my single socks for them. I mean, what else could I do with single socks?

And of course. How could I forget the Kennedy brothers? Well, the hapless thieves were still in police custody for the duration of the investigation. Sadly, for them, they were at the scene of the kidnapping and at the changing rooms at the end of the football match. The police were even able to trace a call made to them from number three during all of the tumult at the football game. There was just too much circumstantial evidence against them and they wouldn't be pestering the world of Lower Molehampton, Upper Molehampton and Anglerton for a while at least.

***

Mr Lawnsworthy had successfully completed his front garden and decided it was time to sort out his back garden, which was covered with hundreds of brown patches. He had flattened the molehills a few days ago and thankfully no new ones had appeared. The moles must have gone away to pester someone else he thought, and about time too. Anyway, they had probably been scared off by all the commotion of the last days. He went into his shed to get some grass seed, a rake and his beloved garden overalls. He found them in a heap on the floor along with a broken wooden hook. He picked them up and to his amazement saw that there was a gaping hole right at the front where his pocket should have been. He inspected the hole and came to the conclusion that an animal must have been in his shed and used some of the material to make a nest. Mr Lawnsworthy stood there scratching his head and wondering if anything else could happen to him.

"Damn mice," he said aloud.

***

Cleopatra held the tattered and frayed blue cloth front pocket in her snout and waited patiently in front of my house. It wasn't difficult for her to knock up the wooden latch to Mr Lawnsworthy's shed and go inside. What was more difficult was getting the memory stick out of the front pocket of his garden overalls — not the easiest of tasks

340

for a dog! The easiest option was simply ripping the pocket out with her teeth and that is exactly what she did, leaving the damaged overalls in a heap on the floor. I now had the memory stick so I could listen to the conversations I recorded all those weeks ago and then try to locate the numbers and monitor any calls should they become active again. Having information of course is better than not having it. You never know when it will come in useful.

However, there were parts of the adventure still open and questions remained unanswered. What about the greenhouse in Earl's garden, the company called Eternity Properties, the letter, the mystery minister and Cromwell? And what would Colonel Pickle do? And of course who was the mystery person helping Cromwell on the surface. It surely couldn't be my boss, Mrs Kingston? Or could it? I must admit it was ever so easy for her to get an answer about my disappearance. I will have to investigate all of this further and get to the bottom of these questions flying around in my mind. I knew I wasn't entirely safe as keeper of the Professor's memory, but at least I had the dependable Cleopatra as my first line of defence, and a very effective one too. The second line of defence was me and my listening equipment.

I sat in my bedroom with my headphones on, listening intently. A phone rang.

Epilogue

The room was dark and damp with a lone table occupying the centre, a smartphone lying right in the centre of it. It vibrated and rang four times. The noise was deafening in this small and silent place. The mole fingers stabbed at the phone to take the incoming call.

"Yes."

"Minister. Cromwell here. I have a plan!"

THE END
(Maybe)